Crescendo

cre
sce
ndo

joanna howat

First published in 2024 by
Flying Dog Press

Copyright © Joanna Howat

No part of this publication may be reproduced, distributed, or transmitted in any form or by any means, including photocopying, recording, or other electronic or mechanical methods, without the prior written permission of the publisher, except in the case of brief quotations embodied in critical reviews and certain other noncommercial uses permitted by copyright law.

ISBN (paperback): 978-1-3999-8983-1

Book designed and typeset by InsideStudio26.com

Printed in the United Kingdom.

For Graham, Archie and Clemmie

All thoughts, all passions, all delights,
Whatever stirs this mortal frame,
All are but ministers of Love,
And feed his sacred flame.

Samuel Taylor Coleridge

one

New Year's Eve found Jamie Fenton standing outside a cottage in a small North Yorkshire town, sniffing the air. 1992 was promising to be the big one, his own personal *annus mirabilis*, the year that would justify the spectacular underperformance of the previous twenty-one. As he strode beneath a colourless sky through Zoe's front gate and out onto the street, a robin landed on the bonnet of his car. The bird cocked its head at him and they contemplated each other for a moment until, with a cavalier flick of tail-feather, it deposited a viscous white splat on the Fiesta's turquoise paintwork and flew away.

Jamie laughed to himself and reached into the back pocket of his jeans for the ironed handkerchief that he knew would be there, wiping the bonnet without so much as a muttered swear-word. The fact that he had woken up in Zoe's bed more than compensated for having bird muck all over a clean hankie. She had allowed him to stay the night. It wasn't lost on Jamie that this concession on her part had considerably bolstered his optimism regarding the coming year.

His strategy with Zoe, to supplement what he saw as his low-to-moderate attractiveness by making her laugh enough to want him around as a serious - what, *boyfriend? prospect?* - seemed to be working. And there were other ways in which he was becoming a grown-up. OK, so he still lived with his parents and neither cooked nor laundered for himself, but that was by no means the only measure of adulthood. He had managed the whole of the previous evening in the pub without drinking to excess. That was a first.

Student days behind him, he was now officially a young professional. Work was, well, work and best not dwelled upon for too long. Nobody except Zoe really enjoyed their job; that his was bearable was testament to his own tolerance and maturity. Furthermore, his powers of persuasion had gone beyond earning him a night in Zoe's lumpy but nonetheless inviting double bed. Not only had she agreed to throw a party that evening, she was also about to come to lunch with his family, even though she didn't 'do parents'.

Zoe was still in the house deciding what to wear. Jamie had been burdened by no such decision. Having forgotten a change of clothes in a flurry of sleepover excitement, he was still in yesterday's shirt and beer-stained Levis. A swirl of icy wind served as a reminder that he'd left his coat in the pub. He leaned against the flank of the car, jangling his keys, but when Zoe emerged, clutching her pager and a large red potted plant, she was dressed for work.

'I have to go up to Leyburn,' she said. 'One of their vets is ill.'

'Now? I thought you booked the day off?'

Zoe had set the plant down on the garden wall but kept hold of the pager and was staring at it.

'I agreed to be on call today so I could definitely have the evening. I didn't think they'd need me.'

Jamie was about to say that he had promised his mother, which was true, but decided against it. Zoe already thought he was too dependent on his parents, which was probably also true. Instead he put out an arm to pull her towards him. Catching the scent of Timotei on her hair, he wished that they could forget about Leyburn *and* lunch and go back to bed. Now, he would have to turn up without her when this was supposed to be the start of a long and meaningful relationship between Zoe and his family. Only seconds ago he had been convinced that nothing could put a dampener on the day.

'Not to worry,' he said. 'The party will be more fun, anyway.'

'I'll make it up to you later. I promise.'

'You'd better.'

Zoe extricated herself and scooped up the pot plant.

'It's a poinsettia,' she said, handing it to Jamie. 'Apparently they bring mirth and celebration.' She moved around Jamie's Fiesta to her own mud-lashed pickup and flashed him a grin. 'Will you give them my apologies?'

'I'll try, but they'll be too busy being mirthful and celebratory.'

Zoe climbed into the truck and chugged away. His mother would hate the poinsettia. She thought anything brightly-coloured was vulgar. Jamie put it into the footwell of his car, got into the driver's seat, pressed 'play' on the tape deck and set off. The first chords of Beethoven's *Pathétique* sonata fought their way through the car's inadequate speakers. Between gear changes, the fingers of his left hand drummed on his thigh in accompaniment. As he headed out of town towards the village where he lived with his mother and father, Jamie promised himself that he would find time during the afternoon to play that very piece. Beethoven would be the perfect antidote to the thwarting of his plans, but until he could get to the piano, he was on his own.

In just a few minutes he was coming up the hill past the petrol station which was also the village shop. The road bisected the neatly-clipped village green: King's Head on the left; cricket pitch and church on the right. The two visible faces of the clock on the church tower declared that he was late. Jamie turned right and there was The Hall; three storeys of Georgian sandstone, presiding over the cricket square and dwarfing the cottages which clustered around the green.

On the forecourt was a removal van. Risking his father's wrath for churning up the gravel, Jamie braked sharply outside the porticoed entrance. Inside, four overalled men were grappling with a large, blanket-wrapped object. As he grabbed the poinsettia and slid out of the car, a spaniel burst through the doorway, causing one of the men to swear and another to stumble, buckling under the weight of the awkward-shaped load. Juno hurled herself at Jamie, all four paws off the ground, trying to lick his face as he gently batted her away, his attention fixed on the activity beyond.

Esther Fenton hovered in the hallway, waving her arms and dodging her head from side to side so as to be seen from behind the removal men.

'Hello, darling,' she called. 'Where's Zoe? Is she coming separately?'

'What's going on? They can't take the piano away.'

Juno rushed back into the house. Jamie waited, the grand piano's bulk blocking his mother from sight. The men gave a final heave and it was through the door and being manhandled down the steps. A fifth man dropped one of its disembodied legs as he tripped on the threshold.

'CAREFUL!' bellowed Jamie's father from inside the house. 'It's not bloody firewood!'

'Could someone tell me,' said Jamie as both of his parents hove into view, 'what on earth is happening?'

Bernard Fenton pointed cryptically upwards.

'You may well ask, son. You may well ask.'

'What's that supposed to mean?' said Jamie. 'Where's it going?'

'You - '

'Bernie, please.' His mother had hold of his father's arm and was rubbing it. Jamie opened his mouth but his mother angled her neck in such a way that he knew he was being shushed. 'It was an accident. Come inside, darling. You still haven't told me why Zoe isn't here.'

Jamie offered the potted plant. 'She sent you this.'

His mother eyed the poinsettia with suspicion. 'That was thoughtful of her. Why don't you leave it on the step just there?'

As Jamie followed his mother and father into the drawing room, he tried to view their surroundings as Zoe might have seen them, had she been there. The room was bigger than the ground floor of her house and was dominated by an enormous Christmas tree in one corner. The tree was perfectly conical, dripping with glass baubles and ablaze with fairy lights. Beneath the stone mantelpiece, which was garlanded with foliage from Jamie's mother's wild garden, a log fire crackled and spat sparks of willow onto the hearth. Zoe would have said it was like being in a Victorian Christmas card.

And it *was* the perfect festive scene, or would have been were his eyes not drawn to a sizeable hole in the ceiling where a chunk of plaster had fallen away, exposing the wooden boarding behind. The hole was exactly above the spot where the piano normally stood. Looking somewhat lost, the duet stool was still in situ, piled up with sheet music. If the ceiling were anything to go by, he didn't want to think about what damage might have been inflicted on the piano.

'What happened? Why didn't you call me?' Jamie said to his mother. 'I gave you Zoe's number.'

'Mrs Cole was going to,' said Esther, 'but I asked her not to. I didn't want to disturb your evening. And really, it was just a case of calling the repair company. Well, and the plumber. We were lucky they could come so quickly.'

'Luck? Is that what you call it?' Bernie looked as though he was about to say something further but stopped as Jamie's sister, Caz, in a shapeless velvet dress with a matching rust-coloured Alice band, got up from her seat on the fender and came towards him.

'Nice work,' she whispered into his ear as she kissed him on one cheek before planting a second kiss on the other.

Her husband, Steve, his jaws working committedly on chewing gum, was also on his feet. 'Good one,' he said, shaking Jamie's hand.

'What? What are you talking about?'

No-one answered. Caz and Steve's daughters, Ruby and Pearl, whom Jamie thought were about seven and five, were ushered over by his mother. They had been born during

Jamie's teens, when Caz was younger than he was now. Pearl attached herself to Caz, clinging around her waist, her head buried in the folds of her mother's dress. Ruby stood looking at Jamie expectantly.

'Hi, Rubes.' Jamie made a little bobbing movement; he'd been about to squat down to Ruby's eye-level but then changed his mind, resulting in what must have looked like a rather awkward dance move. 'Will *you* tell me what's going on?'

'You haven't brought Zoe.'

'Ruby!' said Caz. 'That's not polite.'

Pearl looked up with interest.

'She couldn't make it,' said Jamie, too distracted by the removal of the piano to attempt any further explanation. 'She says she's sorry.'

'What does *that* mean? *What* couldn't she make?' said Pearl in a strident voice, her arms still wrapped around her mother. Still at a loss, Jamie went to stand by the fire and was immediately too hot.

Bernie was at the drinks trolley, pouring sherry. Standing, like Jamie, at six foot three, the crystal glass in his hand looked tiny and in danger of being crushed at any moment. Unlike Jamie, Bernie was not one of those people who slouched in apology for their height. He stood tall, wearing his dark navy suit well; his sandy curls, which were starting to lighten and recede, rested gently on his collar.

'It means,' he said, 'leave Uncle Jamie alone. He's up to his armpits in trouble as it is.'

'Oh, come on, that's enough. What have I done?' Jamie looked again at the hole in the ceiling and then at the space where the piano had been. There was a dark patch on the rug that was clearly wet. Above the drawing room was the big family bathroom with its ancient plumbing. The previous day, wanting to be at his most fragrant for Zoe, he had decided to run himself a bath. After a good ten minutes, with the bath still only a fraction full, he aborted the idea and went for a shower instead. In his haste he must have forgotten to turn off the taps. He sank onto the fender.

'Good God,' said his father. '*Fi*nally the penny drops.'

'I don't believe it,' said Jamie, weakly.

'Neither did we. Have you any idea - ?

'*Bernie!* Not now.'

'And look at the state of you. Couldn't you have shaved, at least?'

Bernie held out a glass of sherry to Caz while still looking at Jamie, who put a hand to his chin as he stared upwards. The plaster left around the hole in the ceiling was inches thick, probably original. Heavy, too, no doubt. He imagined water cascading down through the floor onto the piano's precious spruce-and-ebony casing. As usual, the lid had been propped open, leaving the hammerheads horribly exposed. That piano, with its scrollwork music stand and lyre-shaped pedal box, was a work of art. What he had done was nothing short of sacrilege.

'How bad is it?' he croaked.

'Never mind,' Esther soothed.

Bernie's attention switched to Caz, who was shaking her head at the glass of sherry.

'Sorry, sweetheart. I always forget. I'll get you something soft in a minute.'

He retracted the drink and gave it to his wife, then lit a Café Crème.

'Dad,' said Caz, 'the children.'

'Oh, nonsense,' said their father. 'A bit of smoke never did you two any harm.'

Caz sighed but said nothing more. Esther, arranged on the sofa in languid fashion, her long legs crossed at the ankles, sat up, studied her glass for a moment, then drank its contents in one.

'Mmm,' she said, and held it out for another. Bernie left his station at the drinks trolley to pour, muttering something about responsibility.

'It's in hand, darling,' Esther said to Jamie. 'It'll be back before you know it. Let's not spoil the day. The good news is that nothing else was broken.'

'Just a priceless grand piano, you mean?' said Bernie. 'Got off lightly, didn't we?'

'Mummy, my dress is itchy,' announced Ruby. She rolled her shoulders alternately and scrunched up her nose. 'Why couldn't I wear leggings? Uncle Jamie's got his jeans on. It's not fair.'

'Mine feels horrible too,' said Pearl. 'It's all sticky.'

'That's because you spilled juice on it,' said Caz. 'And you're wearing them because it's New Year's Eve and we want to look nice for Granny and Grandpa.'

'But Uncle Jamie's not smart,' Ruby persisted.

'From the mouths of babes...' said Jamie's father.

'Any chance of a lager, Bernie?' said Steve. 'No, wait, I'll go. Caz, babe, I'll get you some water. Jamie?'

'Beer please, mate, if you're offering,' said Jamie. Something fizzy and alcoholic might rid him of the nauseous feeling he'd had since realising that he was responsible for the desecration of the piano. His brother-in-law's muscular form disappeared into the hall and out towards the cold-room where Bernie kept the things he didn't drink. After a few minutes he came back with two cans, trailed by Mrs Cole, provider of everything from family roasts to pressed handkerchiefs, patting her hair.

'Lunch is ready,' she said. 'I hope you're all hungry.'

The dining room was across the hall and would have had views over the village green had the panelled wooden shutters not been closed. The only light came from two silver candelabra on the table and a dim chandelier. The room smelled overwhelmingly of beeswax polish. Hunting pictures were hung on the walls; in the gloom they could have been the same scene, reproduced half a dozen times. A grandfather clock, whose display was stuck at five-to-twelve, emitted syncopated ticks which irritated everyone in the family except Bernie. Jamie had never liked this room; as a child it had been out of bounds, the place where his parents entertained people his father wanted to impress. It was not somewhere he associated with relaxation, even without his current desire to slink up to his bedroom, away from any further reminders that his pretensions to maturity had taken a severe if not fatal blow.

'Grandpa,' said Pearl, 'why's it so dark in here?'

Bernie raised an eyebrow. 'We don't want the whole village watching us eat lunch, do we?'

They arranged themselves around the table. Caz put cushions on the low-slung antique chairs for the girls and spread napkins across their laps. Esther hastily removed a place that had been set for Zoe. Bernie distributed wine and took his seat at the head of the table in one of the carvers.

'So, Jamie,' he said, 'I had nine holes with Archer yesterday. He seems quite pleased with you. That's a great opportunity you've got there. You wouldn't have landed anything like that in London.'

'Oh, darling,' said Esther to Bernie, 'he would have found something in the end, I'm sure. But then,' she added with a coy glance at Jamie, 'you wouldn't have met Zoe if you hadn't come back to Yorkshire.'

'Mum, please!'

'You still haven't said why she isn't here. I was so looking forward to meeting her.'

'Me too,' said Ruby.

'And me,' said Pearl.

'I think we all were,' said Caz, laughing.

'She had to work,' said Jamie. 'She was on call.'

'Veterinary science,' said Bernie, swirling his wine, 'that's a proper degree. Not like geography. I should have insisted you did something more useful.'

'You did,' said Jamie. 'I wanted to study music, remember?'

'That's just a hobby,' said Bernie. 'Estate agency is a career. You'll be wanting to get your foot on the property ladder soon. You can flood your own bathroom, then.'

'Take no notice of your father,' said Esther. 'There's no rush. Although I'm sure Zoe's very good at what she does. She did a great job with Juno's ear.'

'Yes,' said Jamie, 'and that bite on her hand has healed quite nicely.'

'Oh,' said his mother. 'I'd forgotten about that. Poor Zoe.'

The conversation paused as Mrs Cole set the beef in front of Jamie's father. Bernie was up again, sharpening a knife against a steel in flamboyant manner.

'I can't believe you left that tap running,' he said as he began to carve.

'I know,' said Jamie. 'I'm sorry.'

'It's all right, Uncle Jamie,' said Pearl to his right, patting his arm. 'It was an old piano. Granny can get a new one.'

'No, sweetheart,' said Bernie. 'Granny can't. It's a Pleyel. They cost a fortune.'

'You said it wasn't worth anything,' said Ruby.

'I said it was priceless,' said Bernie. 'That means it's very valuable. It was Granny's twenty-first birthday present from your great-grandparents.'

'Don't distress the child,' said Esther. 'The piano will mend. Now, let's concentrate on lunch. It looks as though Mrs Cole has excelled herself.'

After pudding, Caz got up to help clear the dishes. Steve was telling Esther how well his electrical company was doing despite the Current Economic Climate.

'Yeah.' He clasped his hands together in front of him and flexed his shoulders. 'I've just bought a fifth van.' He took a swig of lager, which Mrs Cole had decanted from its can into a glass when he wasn't looking. 'All this stuff about a recession is overblown if you ask me.'

'I'm not sure - ' Jamie began.

'Hard work,' said Bernie. 'That's what gets rewards.'

Jamie threw his napkin down onto the table with more force than was necessary. 'Yes, Dad,' he said under his breath, 'you've made your point.'

He slumped in his chair, sipping wine, fingers twitching. Rather than being able to slope off for half an hour to play the Beethoven, he was now obliged to hang around while his father belittled him. And he had only himself to blame.

By the time Caz came back to the dining room, their mother and father, at opposite ends of the table, were midway through a loud discussion about a New Year's Day shoot that Bernie was reluctant to attend. Steve stared into his empty glass as though willing it to be refilled, oblivious to Ruby and Pearl who were prodding each other with increasing violence.

'It'll be full of old codgers,' Bernie was saying. 'And the forecast's bloody awful.'

'It's not *that* bad,' said Esther. 'The lunch will be good. And they keep a decent cellar.'

Pearl knocked over a glass of water. Caz reached over her and began to swab the spreading pool with a napkin.

'Are you seriously still doing that?' she said. 'Blasting living creatures out of the sky?' She stopped and froze, bent over the table, as though surprised by what she had said.

'What do you mean?' Bernie said.

'It doesn't matter,' said Caz.

'No, tell me. I'm interested.'

'Let's just leave it.'

'Have you ever stopped to consider,' said Bernie, putting down his glass, 'how much shooting contributes to the rural economy? Apart from the gamekeepers, who rear the birds and feed them all year, maintain the drives and butts and keep predators away, there are the beaters, the picker-uppers, not to mention all the income for the pubs, the hotels and catering staff. None of them would have jobs if we stopped the shoots. Have you thought about that?'

'It's just my opinion,' Caz said in a low voice. 'It doesn't seem right to me to kill things for sport. Never has.'

Jamie looked around the table. Steve was still staring into his glass. The girls took the opportunity to slip down and creep out of the room. Esther was lounging in her chair. Caz returned to her place and sat down, taking a sip from her water.

'You haven't gone all bleeding-heart liberal on me have you, Caroline?' said Bernie.

'No, I - '

'Next thing you'll be eating lentils and reading the *Guardian*.'

'Bernie, enough now,' said Esther.

'You'd think we'd brought her up to know better.'

'Better than what?' Jamie heard himself say. 'Better than to think for ourselves or question any of the pearls of wisdom you hand down to us?' Caz frowned at him, but his father had been needling him all day. It was time to fight back. 'Look at her!' he said. 'She doesn't want to cause an argument; she wants to keep the peace. But guess what? *I* don't care. Everything I do is wrong anyway, so what does it matter?'

'I don't think you're in any position to take the moral high ground,' said Bernie. 'A boy who can't even run himself a bath without causing thousands of pounds' worth of damage?' He shook his head and laughed to himself.

'I'm sick of this,' said Jamie. 'I've already apologised. Mum, please thank Mrs Cole for me. And Dad, you might be Mr Bertie Big Bollocks round here, but that doesn't mean you have to act like such an arsehole.' He stood up from the table, marched out of the house and sped off with as much dignity that a turquoise Fiesta could afford him.

two

Too frustrated to head straight back to Zoe's, Jamie drove for a while in the opposite direction, where the roads were hillier and bendier. In the fading light of late afternoon, he chucked the Fiesta through a series of sharp turns with Beethoven's sonatas up loud, doing his best to avoid the potholes. His father had a presence that discouraged insubordination. He exuded authority and confidence, neither of which he had managed to pass on to his children. In fact, Jamie couldn't remember ever openly disagreeing with Bernie before. It was the sort of thing Caz used to do in her more rebellious days, before she had the girls. But Bernie's behaviour towards Caz at lunch was nothing short of bullying, and no-one else would have said anything about it.

What Jamie couldn't work out, as the road straightened and narrowed, squeezing between the tall, weedy hedgerows, was why he had chosen this particular occasion to rise to his father's bait. Was it because of his earlier conviction that he was about to assert some long-overdue independence from his parents, or had he just lost his temper? Both might have been true, but it was also connected to the piano, of course.

He was angry, no, *seething* over his own stupidity. Not only had he deprived himself (and his mother) of the Pleyel, he had gifted his father a huge metaphorical stick with which to beat him. That Bernie had not passed up the opportunity was predictable, but he had seemed almost pleased to have concrete evidence that his son was a loser. Thank goodness Zoe hadn't been at lunch. And thank goodness he could spend the rest of the day at her house where he would be neither disapproved of nor judged.

The lights were on inside Zoe's cottage which was good news, because Jamie hadn't yet progressed to key-bearing status. He found her in the sitting room, hanging fairy lights around the sash window. Her work clothes gave off an equine tang which he found unexpectedly alluring.

'You're back in good time,' she said.

'I just called my father an arsehole,' said Jamie.

'You did not.'

Her lips were pressed together in the manner of someone trying to keep a straight face. She turned away and her shoulders started to shake. 'Sorry,' she managed, but she bent over and put her hands on her knees.

'Are you laughing?'

When she faced him again, the sides of her mouth were twitching. 'You can't… call your father… an arsehole… He's your father!'

Jamie watched her struggling to contain herself, wondering how this could be funny until it occurred to him how absurd he himself must have looked, self-righteously storming out of his parents' house into his ludicrous company car. Zoe's laughter was infectious; she had a habit of being amused by the most unlikely things. He began to laugh too.

'I called him Bertie Big Bollocks as well.'

'Oh, Jamie,' she said. 'You're brilliant.'

'He deserved it.'

'Do you think…' she said, snorting, '..you brought them… mirth and celebration?'

'I doubt it,' said Jamie, remembering the red plant that was still outside the house. 'But he can shove it. I'm fed up with him always finding fault with me.'

Zoe sat on the sofa and began to untangle another string of lights.

'And did you do anything?' she said. 'For him to find fault with?'

Jamie flopped down next to her. There was a hole in his jeans just below the biggest beer stain. In his rush to leave he had again forgotten a change of clothes and would need to wear the same things for the party. And now he would have to tell her about the piano and it was going to make him look a total idiot.

'I had an accident. With some bath taps.'

'How can you have an accident with bath taps? Did you sit on them?'

'As in I might have forgotten to turn them off. For quite a long time. Enough to flood the bathroom and the drawing room ceiling and for the plaster to stave in the piano.'

'No. Oh, no. You love that piano.' Zoe had stopped laughing.

'Only as much as my mother does.'

She poked her little finger through the hole in his jeans and wiggled it around.

'So, in the circumstances, how come *you* called *your dad* an arsehole? I'm struggling a bit with that one.'

'Because he was picking on Caz when she dared to say something about shooting.'

'Now I'm getting the picture.' Zoe removed her finger and kissed him. 'Sounds entirely justified.' She stood up and backed out of the sitting room. 'Noble. Gallant.' When she reached the stairs she stopped at the bottom. 'Right. I'm racing you to the bedroom and you're giving me a head start.'

three

The kitchen in Zoe's cottage was a hot press of people: her friends, mainly; horsey types, young farmers, work colleagues. Dance music thudded out of the stereo. Everyone was shouting and smoking. Bowls full of cigarette butts littered every surface; the mouth of a plastic swing bin vomited empty beer cans and wine bottles onto the floor.

Jamie had been flitting between conversations all evening and now found himself in the company of a group of guys who were downing pints in one. It was like being back in the union bar at university, just with different beer. When it came to his turn, he upended the can over his open mouth and tipped the contents straight down. The others looked at him with respect. After three or four rounds he wiped his mouth and looked across at Zoe, who was by the cooker with some girl-friends.

Zoe put up her face to Jamie for a kiss as he arrived beside her. She was wearing pink lipstick and black eyeliner and was drunker than he had ever seen her. The make-up, which she rarely used, made her look different; a more worldly version of herself. She was moving her head and shoulders although she wasn't in time with the music and no-one else in her group was dancing.

'You defended your sister,' she said. 'I really, really, really like that.'

'Thanks.' Jamie bent to kiss her again but because she was moving, his face collided with her neck and some of her wine sloshed onto the floor. Her friends eyed him as though he was an unwelcome intrusion into their conversation. He gave up and went back to the drinking game.

It had been Jamie's idea to give all of their guests a glow-stick when they arrived and at five to midnight he went around the house turning off the lights. The result was a sea of bouncing neon which left trails in the darkness like the remnants of psychedelic sparklers on bonfire night. In the sitting room, where the TV was on, people were shouting a countdown.

'..SEVEN, SIX, FIVE, FOUR, THREE, TWO, ONE…'

..and then Big Ben was chiming. All around Jamie there was kissing. Couples were latched onto each other with ostentatious affection; those less attached grabbed the nearest person for a brief slobber before moving on. Jamie fended off a determined-looking girl who was lunging towards him and cast around for Zoe.

She wasn't in the sitting room, so he waded back into the kitchen but she wasn't there, either. As he turned towards the stairs he saw her coming down, concentrating on each step, clinging onto the handrail.

'Where were you?' he said. 'You missed New Year.'

'I was in the loo.'

'But you weren't here for the bongs.'

He sounded like a petulant child but he couldn't help himself; after the debacle that was lunch he needed to get his plans back on track and that had included them seeing in the new year together.

'I know. I didn't realise what time it was. Whatamuppet.' She stood looking at him with her head on one side, smiling. 'Happy New Year,' she said. 'It's 1993, sorry, 1992. Now come here and kiss me, you big gorgeous lump.'

The music was cranked up even further and Jamie was dancing with one of Zoe's friends from the surgery whose name he couldn't remember. He had last seen Zoe doing shots in the sitting room but there were so many people in the house that it was easier to dance with the person in front of him than to try and find her. The lights were still off and he had drunk enough to imagine that he was on the dance-floor of a city-centre club rather than a smallish kitchen in a northern market town. Both Jamie and his partner had piled glow-sticks around their necks and arms. They were flinging themselves about like a pair of demented strobe lights when he felt a tap on his shoulder and wheeled around, catching a man full in the face with his flailing arm.

'Sorry, mate,' he shouted.

'Telephone.' The man made the universal sign with one of his hands and held the other to his cheek, stretching his jaw. 'Sounds important.'

Jamie staggered across to the phone by the back door and picked up the receiver from the worktop.

'Hello?'

Even with a finger in one ear, he couldn't hear a thing. He unhooked the phone from the wall and yanked open the door, stretching the cord to the maximum and pulling its plastic loops taut.

'Oh, Jamie, thank goodness.' The voice was high-pitched and breathless, so unfamiliar that it took a moment to work out that it was Ruth Cole. 'Jamie? Are you there?'

'Yes, I'm here. Is everything all right?'

'No. No, love, it's not.'

Someone closed the back door. All of the noise from inside the house became muffled. But then, when he spoke, his own voice sounded muffled too and he was suddenly very cold.

'What's happened?' He strained into the phone, pressing it against his head so hard that it hurt.

'You need to come home. Now. There's a fire. I can't... I can't find your mum and dad.'

four

Jamie plunged back into the kitchen and up the stairs, leaving the phone in the garden. At the doorway to Zoe's bedroom he felt for the light switch, vaguely registering the protests of a couple who were underneath a pile of coats on the bed. He snatched up his keys from the bedside table and grabbed the first jacket that came to hand. Then, he clattered downstairs, trying to think back to the afternoon and whether his parents had mentioned going out for the evening. There had been the discussion about the shoot which triggered the argument, but that was all. The way his father had been getting stuck into the red, it was hard to believe that he was planning to go anywhere. Jamie pushed through the tiny hallway and was out of the front door before he realised that he hadn't seen Zoe to tell her where he was going.

Breathing hard, he threw himself into the car and was about to turn on the ignition when he remembered that he must be way, way over the limit. For a moment he sat, his hand on the car key, trying to work out whether there was any other way of getting to his parents' house. Everyone at the party was at least as drunk as he was. It was only a couple of miles; he could run, but that would take four times as long and who knew what could have happened in that time. He found a tube of Extra Strong Mints in the cubby hole near the gearbox and ate three. Menthol burned around his teeth and gums, forcing him to open his mouth for some normal air as he tried to imagine what he might find when he got to The Hall. He kept thinking *inferno*; wasn't that the word that was always used to describe a big fire? Something in Ruth's voice had told him that it *was* a big fire, that a disaster was unfolding while he dithered. His mind wasn't lucid enough to process what that could mean. What if he just drove for a long time, in the other direction, and slept in the car until tomorrow when everything would be clearer and calmer? But he had heard the helpless panic in Ruth's voice, could feel the beginnings of it in himself, and knew that he had no choice. He started the engine.

There were no other cars on the high street. The clock on the dashboard told him that it was just after three. He wound down the window, wanting the cold air to pinch at his face and clear his brain but it only made his eyes water. As the car left town he kept his foot hovering over the accelerator, staying at forty. Blue lights appeared in the rear-view mirror. For a split-second he was convinced that the police knew that he was drink-driving and were coming to arrest him. As he slowed down, he had a sense that the bones in his legs were disintegrating. Two fire engines flashed past. He set off again, legs still shaking, wiping his eyes and forcibly concentrating on the dark road. He allowed himself to accelerate to sixty.

The village green was lit up like a fairground. Police cars formed a semi-circle in front of the house. Just ahead of them was the glow from a pair of ambulances. His father's precious gravel driveway was crowded with fire engines, casting out their alkaline rays. Searchlights had been set up and were trained on the outer walls. There was no visible evidence of fire. Jamie abandoned the car on the cricket pitch and got out. The smell of smoke caught the back of his throat. He raced to the low wall at the edge of the forecourt and vaulted it. Thinking that the fire must be at the back of the house, he ran behind the fire engines towards a door in the wall which led to the rose garden. As he pulled it open, two fire-fighters blocked his path. One of them stepped forward through the doorway onto the gravel.

'You have to let me through,' said Jamie. 'My parents are inside.'

'What's your name, son?'

'James Fenton. I need to get in. Let me through!' He could hear the tenor of his voice rising.

'It's too dangerous,' said the man.

'It's my house. You can't stop me.' He tried to see past the fire-fighters but there was only darkness.

'You're not going in. It's too hot.'

The second man drew level with the first to form a barrier to the doorway. Both were at least as tall as he was.

'My parents… are they still inside?'

They looked at him without expression.

'What if they're in the garden? They might be concussed, or, or, or overcome with smoke or something. Please.'

The two men glanced at each other.

'Your mum and dad aren't out here. We've looked. I'm sorry.'

Jamie took a step back and charged at them. Despite his bulk he barely knocked them off guard. They caught him by the arms and held him, waiting for him to stop struggling. When they released their grip he stood leaning forward, hands on his knees, his insides churning with beer and menthol and terror. A cold sweat was soaking the back of his neck and running down into his collar. He straightened. When he got out of the car the air had felt wintry, but now an intense heat was radiating from the house. There was an unmistakable smell, not just of smoke, but of burning. Primary colours were bouncing off the firefighters' helmets and he wondered whether he might be hallucinating before he realised that there were still several glow-sticks hanging around his neck. He ripped them off and flung them to the ground.

'It was your housekeeper who raised the alarm. Over there.'

The man pointed to where Ruth Cole and Willie, his parents' gardener, were pressed together behind the police cordon which stretched across the green and behind the church.

'Go and talk to her.' His tone softened. 'You need to get away from here. No more heroics.'

Jamie looked up at the house. Shutters still masked the ground-floor windows but behind the glazed front door, where the stairs began, the hallway was bright with flickering colour. Someone had kicked over the poinsettia which was still on the front step. On the first floor, where the main bedrooms were, the windows glowed faintly orange. The second floor was still dark. He craned his neck to see the side of the house where his parents slept.

'MOVE!'

Through the open window of a fire engine, the driver was gesturing at him. Jamie climbed back over the wall onto the cricket pitch. The two fire-fighters followed and they all watched as the vehicle moved up to the doorway to the rose garden. Three men jumped out and began bashing at the brick with sledgehammers.

'Hey!' Jamie shouted. 'They can't do that! Tell them to stop!'

'They need to get the appliance in there. It's the only way we can get to that part of the house.'

The old wall gave easily under the impact of the hammers. Behind it, Esther's beloved roses waited to be bulldozed and trampled.

A breeze was gathering strength, bringing a skein of smoke which briefly obscured the lights from the fire engines. As Jamie turned away, tasting ash on his tongue, he heard glass shattering. He whipped around. One of the first-floor windows had exploded.

In front of a row of cottages on the left of the green, the elderly gardener stood with his arm around Ruth Cole. Her face was turned into his shoulder. Jamie jogged towards them, away from the two fire-fighters. His mouth was so dry from the smoke that he could barely swallow and was sucking in great, heaving breaths. He ducked under the tape. Willie gave Ruth a gentle squeeze and her head jerked up.

'My poor boy.' She moved away from Willie and held out her arms to him. 'Come here. My poor boy.'

Jamie found that he was bent over, sobbing into her hair. In his childhood he had been comforted countless times by Ruth Cole. Now, her frame felt frail; no longer solid and reassuring. No-one had said so, but it was obvious that his parents were inside the house.

Caz ran towards them from her car, her slippers skating in the mud. 'Where are they?' She stopped and grasped at the cordon to steady herself.

Jamie let go of Ruth, who took Caz's mittened hand in her own bare one.

'I woke up smelling smoke.' Ruth's voice was hoarse. 'It wasn't in the cottage so I went out into the yard and... I saw it coming out of one of the upstairs windows. I called the fire brigade and then I came over here to get Willie.'

'We went back to the courtyard,' said Willie, 'and we shouted and shouted for your mum and dad. I tried to get in through the kitchen but it was too hot; I couldn't even touch the door handle.' Tears had exposed little tracks of clean skin down the old man's blackened face.

'They were fine when I left them,' said Ruth, her voice starting to crack. She pulled a hankie from the pocket of her dressing gown and dabbed her eyes.

Caz, who had been holding Ruth's other hand, chafing it gently, burst out, 'You mean they're in there?'

'There was nothing we could do,' said Ruth. 'We couldn't get inside.'

'The fire brigade are here now,' said Caz. 'They'll get them out.'

No-one spoke. They stared at the house. Ruth cleared her throat.

'Pet lamb,' she said, 'they're not coming out.'

'The heat's too intense,' said Jamie. 'The firemen can't get in, either.'

Ruth was right; his parents were not only inside, they were trapped. There was no way they could get out. Until now he'd held a kernel of hope that they would appear, coughing and dishevelled, thankful to be alive.

'Ohh.'

Caz pulled away from Ruth, her hand over her mouth. She sank to the ground with her legs folded underneath her.

'Come on up, love,' said Ruth. 'The grass is soaking.'

But Caz shook her head as if she were unable to move. Jamie hauled her to her feet. It was an effort; she was a dead weight. His jaw ached from clenching his teeth. Caz collapsed into him and he braced himself against her. They stood, mute, hypnotised by the rampaging fire. Watching was grotesque but it was impossible to look away.

By now the top floor was silhouetted against the sky, lit from behind by flames. The roof was no longer there. A gusty wind chased burnt flakes through the air. Every now and then there was the low, crumbling sound of falling masonry. More windows blew out. Police were marshalling a small crowd that had assembled, shepherding people back from the cordon with outstretched arms. Jamie recognised them as neighbours from the cottages around the green. Outside the King's Head, more people were standing in little groups, cradling glasses and smoking, the hum of their conversations audible whenever the wind changed direction and fanned the roar of the fire away.

Another layer of internal wall collapsed with a crump, leaving the second-floor façade exposed. There was a collective gasp. The back section, those neglected rooms where Jamie and Caz had dressed up, fought and played hide-and-seek, had gone.

'Juno,' said Caz suddenly. 'Where's the dog?'

'Oh, God.' Jamie tried to dispel a picture of Juno's

trusting face but that only made the image sharper. It was unbearable; he wanted to kick something or scream.

Ruth closed her eyes and seemed to shrink into her dressing gown.

'She had a quick wee and came back in before I left,' she said.

'The poor thing,' said Caz, her hand over her mouth again. She began to cry, shuddering in the puffa jacket that she was wearing over her pyjamas.

'I've brought brandy.' The pub landlord had wandered over, carrying a tray. 'Thought you could do with a drop of the hard stuff. Take the edge off, maybe.'

'Thank you,' said Ruth. 'That's kind of you.'

Jamie reached out for a glass and took a sip. The brandy was harsh, with no sweetness or depth, but he drank it anyway, wanting to feel its slow, coursing burn.

'Caroline?' The landlord held out the tray to her.

'No. Thank you.' Caz was shaking her head, backing away into Willie's garden wall.

'Might steady the nerves, pet.' Ruth picked up a glass.

'Don't if you don't want to,' said Jamie.

Caz hesitated for another couple of seconds, then took the brandy, gulped it down and put the glass back onto the tray. It made her cough.

'Eight years.' She was taking deep breaths, her shoulders rising and falling under the bulky coat. 'Just like that.'

'It was only the one,' said Ruth. 'Don't be too hard on yourself.'

Something exploded. It was the loudest thing that Jamie had ever heard; it made the ground shake and he was deafened for several seconds. He realised that he had dropped the brandy glass. Above and behind the house was a huge ball of white light. Fire-fighters crouched on the forecourt, using their engines as cover. Jamie swallowed in an effort to release the pressure in his ears.

'What was that?' Caz whispered.

'I don't know. The electrics? The boiler?'

Near the cricket boundary, a camera bulb flashed from where a group of reporters had gathered. There was a shout from the house. Fire-fighters scurried away from the forecourt like a scattered nest of mice and hurled themselves over the wall onto the cricket pitch. With an enormous crack, the top section of the front façade collapsed, throwing rubble out onto where the fire-fighters had been standing. Bricks and plaster rained onto the fire engines. With a muffled rumble, the first floor folded in on itself. Flames blew sideways into the night. High up on cherry-pickers on both sides of the house, more fire-fighters pumped water into the void behind the walls. Tiny flecks of black floated through the air like a dark snowstorm.

Jamie hadn't noticed the approach of a man who was now standing in front of them. Gripping a wide-brimmed cap to his chest, the county's chief fire officer offered them his condolences.

'Thank you.' The words, which Jamie intended to sound noble and contained, were a pitch too high. He knew what he was supposed to do; his father had been saying it for years: *Step up, be responsible.* But the situation was too overwhelming. He wished he were still at the party; that there had been no phone call. That he could run away. Then he saw Caz's pale face, her huge eyes trained on the fire officer, taking in the confirmation of what they already knew.

'Do you know how it started?' Maybe the question could buy enough time for him to somehow stem his unravelling, to get a grip. A mess of memories spooled before him: garden cricket, birthday cakes, piano duets. He listened to the answer without interest. It hardly mattered; the outcome was still the same.

'It's too early to say. I've never seen a fire rip through a big house so rapidly. There'll need to be an investigation.'

'Would… would it have been quick?' Caz's voice was a murmur.

'Again, I can't…' The officer paused. Jamie clenched his teeth again, willing the man to lie, if lying were required. Ruth grabbed Caz's hand. 'It's likely they were overcome by smoke before the fire took hold,' he said.

'Thank you,' Jamie managed to repeat. 'And please, thank your team for everything they're doing.'

The officer replaced his cap and set off across the cricket pitch. It was starting to get light. Flames licked at the sky above where the upper floors of the house had been. In the distance, the Cleveland Hills were coalescing into shape. It was the same view that Jamie had enjoyed from his bedroom window for most of his life, now available to the whole village for the first time in over two hundred years. On the gravel in front of the house, he could still see the flashes of neon from the glow-sticks. The poinsettia was now buried under fallen masonry. Afterwards, he would swear that he had heard the church bells ringing.

five

Caz turned off the ignition but stayed in the driver's seat. Through the windscreen, the mock-Georgian windows and sharp modern bricks of her house were indisputable, but she had no recollection of driving home. If asked, she would have said that she was still on the village green.

The steering wheel was dripping with what could only be unnoticed tears. She tugged a tissue from her sleeve and held it to her face, trying to pin down any details that she could remember. There was the sky, flushed with the orange of a new day; no, a new year, just as the flames were beginning to recede. That was when the people from the village, the reporters, and God knew who else, started to drift away, back to places untouched by fire. Those people would resume their lives in a way that she and Jamie could not. Before that, there was her little brother talking to the chief fire officer, trying to be brave for them all but looking like a small boy again. She should have done something to comfort him but she was too fixated on the fire, awesome in the most literal sense, its violence and cruelty absolute.

As she watched the flames she had imagined them as paint on canvas; their beauty and brutality at complete odds with one another.

Back further, and there was her arrival at The Hall, panicking but confident that her parents would have escaped before the fire took hold. Rescuing people from burning buildings was what fire-fighters did. It was unthinkable that no-one would be able to save them.

By now, Chestnut Drive was completely light. But it was New Year's Day: curtains were still closed, cars sat on driveways, hangovers were being slept off. At the house across the road, a tabby cat mewled on the doorstep to be let in.

Caz's feet were cold and wet in her bedroom slippers but still she didn't move. Once she was inside, the consequences of the fire would no longer be her own; she would have to share them with Steve and her daughters. Ruby and Pearl would be distraught, bewildered, demanding. What was going to equip her to deal with this? Was it possible to grieve and give sympathy at the same time? She was going to need energy that she did not possess.

More immediately, she had no idea what she would say to them. Perhaps Steve would have already sown the seeds in their minds that something was wrong. Unlikely. They had never had to deal with anything of this magnitude. He would be just as much at sea as she was.

As if summoned by her thoughts, Steve appeared at the passenger window in the shorts and t-shirt he wore for bed. Caz leaned over to unlock the door and he climbed in, closing it gently so as not to make a noise.

'Jesus, Caz, it stinks of smoke in here. It can't be good for you, breathing that in.' He wound down his window.

Cleaner, colder air wafted in. Until then Caz hadn't noticed the rancid atmosphere inside the car.

'Are the girls OK?'

'Still asleep.'

'So they don't know there was a fire.'

'Not yet.'

'Oh, Lord.'

Steve waved at a neighbour walking his giant poodle along the pavement and then shuffled to face her. Caz leaned her head against the steering wheel. It was too much effort to form any words.

'Babe,' he said, 'is everything all right? I mean… not all right, but you know, not too much damage? You look knackered.'

She had assumed that Steve would deduce, given that she had been out all night, that something terrible must have happened. To her mind it was obvious; but to Steve, ever the optimist, perhaps it wasn't.

'Your parents. Are they OK? How bad was it?'

Caz peeled her face away from the wheel. Steve now looked concerned in a way that he hadn't when he got into the car.

'Nobody could get to them. They were trapped. They're dead, Steve. They're dead. The house is gone. My parents are dead and I couldn't do anything to help them.' She could feel the words accelerating as she uttered them, spilling from her mouth with no direction from her brain. Steve was staring at her, one hand gripping the dashboard, the other, inexplicably, the handbrake.

'That can't be right,' he said. 'Did anyone look outside? Maybe they got away.'

'No.' Did Steve not realise that there had been dozens

of fire-fighters there, checking every possible scenario? 'They were definitely inside. There's no doubt.'

'Shit. Oh, shit, Caz.'

'How are we going to tell the girls? What should we say?'

'Do they know how it started?'

'Steve! What does it matter? We need to think about Ruby and Pearl. They'll be up soon.'

'Yeah. Sorry. You're right.' He clicked the handbrake on and off several times.

This wasn't happening; she had stepped outside reality. The two of them sitting there, her crying onto the steering wheel, Steve fiddling with the car, was just something she was imagining. She closed her eyes and inhaled the silence, but when she opened them again nothing had changed. Steve took his hand off the brake and massaged his jaw.

'Listen,' he said. 'Do we really need to upset them right now? Why don't we leave it a couple of days until things settle down?'

'We can't. They have to know.'

'Think about it for a minute. What good will it do?'

Maybe it wasn't so unreasonable. They could go into the house and pretend that everything was normal, sit at the table and eat lunch. Hell, she could let them off sprouts. The eating of vegetables, which had been a top priority only yesterday, was now risibly unimportant. Afterwards, they could watch a video. If she could keep it together, perhaps they didn't need to be told just yet. It would give her chance to process what had happened, rationalise it in some way.

'Do you think we could? Wouldn't it be wrong?'

'There aren't any rules, babe. From where I'm sitting I can't see any harm in it.'

'I don't know.' She dried her eyes again and stuffed the tissue back up her sleeve.

'Caz.' Steve put a hand on her knee. 'It'll be all right. *You'll* be all right. You've still got me and I'm not going anywhere. Come on, let's go inside. You must be freezing.' He opened the car door again and she followed him along the path and into the quiet house.

Caz stood under the shower for a long time, watching the foam slide off her skin, letting the shampoo cleanse the smoke from her hair. How easy it was. She could put on fresh clothes and no-one would be able to tell that she had been anywhere near a fire. Which she hadn't, really. She had observed the police cordon without question. Jamie, she was told, tried to get to the house but was forced back, whereas she had done nothing but stand there and watch. There was a time when she would have fought like crazy to get inside. In the short teenage years before she became a mother, she'd had no regard for her own safety. On the contrary, she had actively tried to sabotage it. As if to remind herself, she lifted her left arm and twisted it to reveal the whiteness of her inner wrist. They were, of course, still there: the little scars that criss-crossed the pale skin, glossy under the glare of the shower light.

Ruby and Pearl had never seen these scars. Even in summer, Caz would wear long-sleeved tops with the cuffs pulled right down to her hands. Steve knew, naturally. When he asked her, early in their relationship, what they were, she told him that they were a stupid thing she did, once, and he left it at that. They never talked about them again. There was no need; they were from a time before Steve, before Ruby and Pearl, before she had to be present and functioning and stable. It was, she supposed, reassuring for everyone, her parents and Jamie included, that she had healed, matured and settled. There was no way she would have risked going near that fire, no way she would have risked leaving her children without a mother.

But there was a weight that came that. She didn't resent it, but she felt it nonetheless; the leaden responsibility of motherhood. It never left you, even for a moment.

As she stepped out of the shower, Caz wondered whether Jamie was still at The Hall. Only then did she remember leaving him on the village green, briefly envying him his freedom. He could have stayed there for as long as he needed, whereas she had felt the pull of her family, drawing her home. Jamie would have the space to grieve for their parents in his own way while she would have to be strong for Ruby and Pearl. They would look to her for reassurance that their world hadn't ended, that their family life would carry on much as before. But first, she and Steve would have to hurt them with the most horrific news. Caz pictured how their faces would change, crumpling in shock and pain. The thought made her chest ache.

She dried herself and she sat on the bed, hugging her arms to her sides. Her job was to protect her children, not to make them wretched. They were too young to take on something so awful. Bernie and Esther were supposed to watch Ruby and Pearl grow up, witness them go through school, their first jobs, their weddings. She had never imagined a point when her parents wouldn't be there. Their presence: immutable, dependable, often judgmental and sporadically disapproving, was something she had, foolishly it now seemed, relied upon as the bedrock for everything.

Steve called up from the kitchen, asking if she wanted tea. One of the girls passed the bedroom door on the way to the bathroom. Caz put on some clothes, brushed her hair and went downstairs.

She got through the morning by listening to a pop station on the radio while roasting a chicken. Steve sat at the kitchen table, polishing his golf clubs. Ruby and Pearl wandered in and out, clutching their Barbies and pestering for drinks and snacks, their obliviousness testament either to their parents' acting skills or their own childish self-absorption. Whichever it was, their soon-to-be-ruined naïveté was crushing.

By one o'clock the table had been cleared and laid. As Caz poured orange squash into four glasses, the jug felt too heavy to grip. She was deadeningly, carkingly tired. The plate of food in front of her looked unmanageable even though her portion was smaller than Pearl's. The smell of the gravy made her stomach churn. She didn't even have the energy to pick up her knife and fork and instead sat staring at the wall while everyone else tucked in.

Their kitchen table was a world away from the formality of her parents' dining room but the very act of sitting down to a meal was an inevitable reminder. She had a sense she often had when something bad happened, of lost innocence. How unaware they had all been that everything was about to change; how she wished it were possible to go back in time and reclaim that antediluvian ignorance. The stupid disagreement at lunch had been her fault; if she hadn't taken issue with her father then Jamie wouldn't have felt the need to step in and defend her. It wasn't even something she was in the habit of doing any more; why had she picked that moment, when her parents were just hours from being taken away from them? Despite her mother's attempts to jolly things up again after Jamie's departure, the mood had been spoiled and they had left shortly afterwards. And even then, as they drove home, she thought the worst thing to happen was that they'd had a family row. How little they knew.

'Aren't you hungry, Mummy?' Pearl had stopped eating and was looking at her, knife and fork in hand, her matted-haired Barbie face-down on the table next to her place mat.

'Not really, sweetie.'

'Mummy thinks she might have a bug.' Steve skewered a roast potato.

Ruby had stopped eating too and was surveying her critically.

'Are you going to be sick?'

Caz glanced at Steve, who was still chewing, clearly expecting her to take his explanation and run with it. But she couldn't lie to them. Not giving the whole truth was one thing, but actively telling lies was another. She wouldn't do it. It wouldn't be fair; none of it was. Bernie and Esther were dead, she had lost her parents, Ruby and Pearl had lost their grandparents. Keeping it from them wasn't going to make it any better.

'Actually,' she said. 'It's not that. I've got some bad news and we're all going to have to be very brave.'

Ruby's initial response was borderline hysterical. She screamed and screamed, thrashing around with her arms, her lunch abandoned. At one point she threw herself to the floor. Caz and Steve looked cluelessly at each other across the table until Caz got down onto the carpet and held Ruby until she collapsed against her, whimpering, exhausted by the force of her reaction.

Pearl sobbed quietly, disappearing upstairs in search of a stuffed dog that her grandmother had given her. Steve went to the video shop and they spent the afternoon watching Disney films, the four of them wedged together on the sofa. Later, Caz would not remember any of the titles; her focus was on Ruby and Pearl the entire time, looking for signs of distress. Both girls were subdued but calm. Caz sensed that the physical proximity to her and Steve must have been soothing.

That night the girls went to bed at the usual time, Caz ensconced on the bottom stair, ready to spring up and tend to them, prepared to take them into their own bed if needed, but there was no sound.

six

Jamie found Zoe alone in her kitchen, still in her party dress, collecting up debris from the evening. The windows and back door were open but the smell of ash and nicotine lingered. His eyes were strained and smarting from smoke and lack of sleep; his clothes reeked of the fire. For a terrible second it struck him that he might be wearing the dust of his parents' remains. He wanted to tear off the contaminated clothes right then and there, in Zoe's chilly kitchen, but he couldn't; he no longer had any others.

When she saw him in the doorway, Zoe put down an armful of bottles and cans.

'Where've you been? I was worried about you.' She took a step nearer. 'Why are your clothes so dirty?'

Jamie stared at her, blinking.

'Oh my God, Jamie. What's happened?' Her face was pale, scrubbed of the make-up. 'Someone said you took a call. I found the phone outside.'

He ran a hand through his gritty hair.

'There was a fire,' he said. 'At my parents' house.'

'A *fire*? Are they OK?'

She reached out to him but he needed to sit down. They had cleared the kitchen of furniture for the party and there were no chairs. Jamie leaned back against the wall and slid down it until he was sitting on the grimy floor. He rested his forehead on his knees, then tipped his head back and rubbed his face, not wanting to give the answer.

'Jamie?' Zoe was kneeling in front of him, one hand on his arm, peering into his face. Normal breathing was impossible. He pursed his lips and drew in air through his mouth several times, noisily, like a boxer before a fight. His throat still burned from the smoke.

'They're dead.'

He turned away to avoid seeing her reaction. Her shock would be further confirmation that it was real. The words sounded overly dramatic, as though he were making a fuss and Zoe would tell him that he was being ridiculous. She clasped his face to her chest and he put a hand down on the sticky lino as she rocked him, stroking his hair.

'Can you tell me what happened?'

It was hard to remember the order of things. His mind was racing through a warp-speed slideshow of the night. But it was all jumbled in with the childhood memories that had overwhelmed him while he was watching the flames and couldn't be rearranged into any kind of logical sequence.

'I don't know,' he said. 'I don't know...'

Zoe got up and came back with a glass of water. He began to gulp at it but his throat was too dry and it was difficult to swallow. Sitting next to him against the wall, Zoe rubbed his back until he stopped coughing.

'It was too late,' he said. 'Too hot to get them out.'

'I'm so sorry,' said Zoe.

'The house is destroyed. There's nothing left.'

Zoe put her arm through his and looked up at him. A cold wind chased through the kitchen.

'Even the dog,' he said. 'Juno died too.'

'Oh, Jamie.'

She leaned her head against his arm and they sat there for a few moments. Then Jamie jerked upright, pressing his hands to his face.

'The last thing I said to him. We were laughing about it. I'd forgotten until now. How could I…?

'You didn't mean it. He - they - would have known that.'

'I did when I said it. He'd been getting at me all afternoon and then he started on Caz. But I didn't, Zo, I really didn't.'

'I know. Don't think about that now. It was just words.'

Jamie let Zoe draw him towards her again. What he wanted more than anything was to go home. He could wait in his bedroom until his mother came up with tea and the world would spin normally again. But there was no Hall and no mother. There was just this girl, who was moderately into him, and her little house that was not his home.

'What are you going to do?' said Zoe.

'I need to find out where they are.'

'Of course. It must be awful, not knowing.'

It was. Worse than awful. Tomorrow he would go back and he would keep going back until his parents were found, but for now he needed respite from the scrutiny of the neighbours, the fire-fighters, Ruth, Caz. He had seen them looking at his reactions, trying to work out what he was thinking and even taking their cues from him. Jamie didn't want to be responsible for anyone's cues. He had never liked to be the centre of attention.

'Please don't,' he said when he noticed that Zoe was watching him.

'I only want to know that you're OK.'

'Can we not talk for a bit?'

She gave him a little upside-down smile and picked up the phone. 'I'm going to find you a change of clothes.'

Jamie wandered into the garden, opening his mouth wide to take in the uncontaminated air. His lungs were tight with toxins. The day was drizzly and dismal. A robin landed on the fence and he wondered whether it was the same one from the day before, the car splatterer. They looked at each other for a few seconds before it disappeared into the next door garden. Not much would have changed for that robin in twenty-four hours. But things *could* change in the shortest amount of time. It was like falling through a trap door. He could have let his father's needling wash over him, let Caz fight her own battle, smoothed things out and stayed on at his parents' house after lunch. He could have missed the party; he probably would have sat up with his father drinking claret and he could have checked the house before going up to bed. But really, the last part of that was fantasy. He had never done such a thing in his life. More likely, he would have perished along with everyone else.

Something gold and shiny caught his eye from one of the bushes. He bent to retrieve an empty bottle of Asti Spumante and took it inside.

Zoe had gone back to the cans and bottles. Jamie stooped to pick up a few more from the kitchen floor and took them to the sink.

'It's OK,' she said. 'I'll do it. Why don't you go and lie down? You must be exhausted.'

'I'd rather be doing something,' said Jamie.

She stretched to kiss his cheek. 'Andrew from work is bringing some clothes. He won't be long.'

Silently they set about tidying the house. Zoe emptied beer cans and Jamie flattened them. They screwed up their faces at the ones that had been used as ashtrays and which clogged the plughole with soggy brown cigarette ends. Zoe loaded the bottles into separate black sacks for recycling. Jamie hoovered the sitting room while she mopped the kitchen floor. They wiped down surfaces, changed the bed linen and put all of the towels in the washing machine. When they had finished, they counted the wine stains on the carpet and the cigarette burns on the sofa. There were twenty-nine.

'That's why you have a party before you've bought anything nice,' Zoe said.

Someone knocked at the door. Jamie stayed out of the way while she accepted a couple of stuffed carrier bags.

'Here,' she said to Jamie when her colleague had gone. 'Have a shower. It might help.'

Upstairs, Jamie stripped off the filthy clothes. The jacket, which he had appropriated when he left the party, was pocked with burn marks. The jeans were black from smoke. He kicked them across the bathroom; nothing would induce him to wear those things ever again.

Stepping into Zoe's narrow bath, he crouched beneath the shower which had barely enough force to get him wet. In frustration he lathered soap and scrubbed at himself, wanting to feel some friction on his numb skin. The pressureless water dripped and trickled and left him cold. He towelled himself dry, unable to warm up, and pulled out a sweatshirt and some joggers from one of the bags. Zoe tapped on the bathroom door and came in.

'There are two police officers downstairs,' she said. 'I asked them to come back another time but they said it wouldn't take long.'

The officers, one male, one female, wanted to know when Jamie had arrived at The Hall and how long he had stayed. They asked about lunch, and whether anything unusual had happened, and about Bernie and Esther's bedtime routines. To build up a picture, they said. It was all irrelevant. Within twenty minutes the officers had left to visit Caz.

Zoe went out for a Chinese takeaway and they set upon it like Labradors. They fell onto the sofa, ignoring its crusty new holes, and switched on the television. The local news was on; behind the presenter in the studio was a photograph of a burning house.

'Shit,' said Zoe, lunging for the remote control. 'Should I turn it off?'

But Jamie was hardly registering what was being said. He saw the reporter standing on the village green, what was left of The Hall smouldering in the background. He heard 'prominent Yorkshire businessman and charity supporter' and then, there was a shot of his father, standing next to Mrs Thatcher. The reporter assured them that an investigation had begun into the cause of the blaze.

'What about Mum?' he said. 'It wasn't just him.'

'Maybe they don't have her on film.'

Jamie thought of his mother, always content for Bernie to take the limelight, happiest at home in the garden with Juno. In death, as in life, his father was the star.

He was still awake, lying on his side facing the wall, when Zoe came to bed. The cup of tea she'd brought him earlier stood untouched on the bedside table. She spooned in behind him and kissed his shoulder. He took her warm hand and pulled it across his stomach.

'Are you all right?' she said. 'Can I get you anything?'

'Zo?'

'Hmm?' She nuzzled his neck.

'I'm homeless.'

'I know.' Zoe pulled gently away and he felt her plumping up the pillows. When he turned she was leaning back against the headboard in a faded George Michael t-shirt, her face shadowed by the anglepoise lamp on her other side. He shimmied up beside her and she took hold of one of his hands in both of hers.

'This is going to be a dreadful time for you and Caz. Do you think she might need you; that you ought to be together?'

Jamie thought for a moment of Caz and Steve and their brand-new house, of their life which he knew so little about, of his nieces whose birthdays he couldn't remember. He thought of Caz, mumsy and vulnerable. It would be intolerable to have to live with her grief as well as his own, to have to talk to her about what had happened and agonise over how it could have been prevented. That was absolutely not what we wanted.

'No,' he said. 'Caz has got Steve. And the girls. She doesn't need me hanging around.'

Jamie stared across the room at the dressing table mirror with blue and red rosettes pinned around its frame.

'Can I stay here?'

'..Of course you can.' The delay was so small that he could have imagined it. Long after Zoe turned off the lamp he lay, sleepless in borrowed boxer shorts, ashamed not to be thinking about the death of his parents but about that missed beat.

seven

Sleet drove towards them from the direction of the house, powered by the determined easterly wind, stinging their eyes. Two fire-fighters stood on a hydraulic platform suspended over the western end of the wreckage, hosing water into the only part of the building that was still smouldering. At the other end of the forecourt, a flatbed truck stacked with scaffolding was being unloaded, piece by careful piece, into the house.

It was inconceivable that they could have had lunch in there two days earlier; that it had been someone's home, *his* home. All that survived were part of the façade and the outer walls, now windowless, and inside, the three chimney stacks, left, right and centre. Nothing in between. In the gaps where the front windows had been, you could see right through and out of the other side. And his father had insisted on keeping the shutters closed for privacy.

The sleet was turning to snow. Zoe turned her wet face towards him, out of the wind.

'Holy shit.'

She clamped herself around his waist. Jamie inched an arm over her shoulder, his movement impeded by the borrowed clothes. Andrew, Zoe's colleague, whom Jamie remembered meeting at the party, was a chunk shorter and probably a stone lighter than he was. The coat, at least, was a good, thick one. It had the practice's logo across the back. Even outdoors it smelled of sheep and wearing it made him feel like somebody else.

At ground level, the fire-fighters were starting to sift through the ash and rubble. In places it was knee-high. They were wading through the effects of thirty years of marriage, condensed into charcoal and cinders. Jamie willed them to tread carefully. Somewhere amongst it all were his mother and father.

'Do you think they'll ever find them?' he said over the top of Zoe's head, shielding his eyes, still watching even though they were too far away to see what was going on.

'I don't know,' said Zoe. 'It's just hideous.' The hood of her coat had blown off and her hair was gathering tiny white crystals. She put a hand to his face. 'You're freezing. Maybe we should go home. There's nothing we can do here.'

'Why don't you go and sit in the car?' he said, brushing snow from her head. 'I'll be there in a minute.'

Zoe took off her scarf and wound it around Jamie's neck. It was a long, loose-knitted thing, cumbersome but warm. She tucked it into the top of his jacket and went back to her pickup.

The entire property was still cordoned off. Ruth Cole had been told to leave her cottage while the building was made safe and had gone to stay with a friend. Caz wasn't around, either. When Jamie phoned, Steve told him she was in bed.

Jamie wandered around the edge of the churchyard and across the cricket pitch. A couple of people waved to him. Others looked away as he approached. Fair enough; he wouldn't have known what to do in this situation, either. When he reached the blue-and-white police tape he stopped. What was left of the exterior walls were being buttressed from the inside. Already he couldn't remember what was supposed to be where. Just in front of him, a man in a fluorescent jacket studied drawings on a clipboard and gave directions as to where the scaffolding should go. The building looked like a shrivelled house of cards.

A fireman approached him from the rose garden. Its ruined borders, flattened by tyre tracks, were fully exposed to the village now that the wall had been demolished. Jamie wondered whether he had seen this man before; it was hard to tell people apart under a helmet and safety gear.

'We found this, sir. At the back, where the French doors were.'

The man held out an open palm. In it lay a disc of blackened metal, slightly twisted but otherwise intact, tiny against the heatproof gauntlet. The lettering was still legible: *Juno* and, underneath, the Fentons' phone number. Jamie turned away until he was confident of being able to speak.

'She must have got out of the bedroom somehow. Did you find the rest of her?'

'Just that.'

'What about my parents?'

'We haven't been able to reach that part of the house yet. We're working to stabilise what's left of the structure.' The man closed his hand around the name-tag. 'I'd go home, Mr Fenton, if I were you. We'll let you know if there are any developments.'

Jamie returned to Zoe's pickup and they went back to her cottage, but the rest of the day was impossible. They were unused to being cooped up together and neither of them could settle. Zoe kept asking Jamie if he was OK, or whether he needed drinks or food. Jamie stood by the window, looking out into the street, waiting for the phone call that he was both anticipating and dreading; the one that told him that his parents had been found. Like a couple of caged tigers, Jamie and Zoe slunk around each other in an elaborate pattern of interaction and avoidance. There was nothing they wanted to talk about. Until this, they didn't do serious stuff: they had sex and went to the pub; they had a laugh. He didn't know what Zoe would think of him now that he wasn't fun anymore. It was hard to know how they were going to *be* with each other. At least in the evening there was the TV.

Zoe went back to work the following morning. Jamie spent the day, and the two after that, huddled on the village green in Andrew's coat as if he had been sponsored by the West of Yore veterinary practice to stand there. Neighbours began to approach him shyly, bringing mugs of tea or soup; once, even a meat pie. They wanted to know that he was all right, he realised, not that he was *not*, and so he said little, accepted their kindnesses with gratitude, and waited for them to move away.

Half-way through the fifth day, there was an increase in activity. Police cars, which had been coming and going, arrived and stayed. Two black vans drove into the courtyard. The ground was covered with snow and Jamie could no longer feel his feet after hours of standing and watching. As he began to walk up and down, stamping to regain some circulation, he noticed a group of reporters, in the same place as before, near the church. They were setting up their equipment. He was about to stride across, to demand to know what was happening, when another police car drew up alongside him and Caz stepped out, wearing a big fur hat with ear flaps which obscured most of her face.

'They said I needed to be here.' She took hold of his arm.

'Why? What's happening?'

'I don't know. They wouldn't say.'

The female officer who had accompanied her said nothing but stepped to one side, looking away from them as they stared into the pitiless wind towards the house. She said something into her radio and then nodded slowly at the reply.

'What is it?' said Jamie. 'Tell us, please. We've got a right to know.'

'They've found human remains,' she said.

'Oh, God,' said Caz.

Remains. Not *bodies.*

'They'll be bringing them out shortly.'

'Out where?' said Caz. 'Can we see them?' She turned to Jamie. She must have been wearing mascara because there was black running from her eyes. 'Will they need to be identified?'

'That might not be a good idea,' said Jamie.

'The identification process will be complicated.'

'But where are they taking them?' said Caz.

'We've informed the coroner. There'll be a post-mortem and then an inquest.'

'How come they knew before we did?' Jamie gestured over his shoulder at the reporters.

The officer looked at the ground. 'I don't know,' she said. 'Someone must have tipped them off. It happens, I'm afraid. But we've got the vans round to the side so they won't see anything.'

There must have been other questions he should ask, but Jamie couldn't think what they might be. None of the details mattered. Nothing could be salvaged from any of it. For some reason he thought of one particularly argumentative dinner, years before, when Caz had suggested that their father loved to play lord of the manor in his big house. Bernie's reply was that the only way he would ever leave was in a coffin.

Someone put cups of coffee into their hands and they murmured thanks without noticing who had brought them. They stood, clutching the cups long after the coffee had gone, frozen in position, still scanning the house. And then, without warning, the two vans, one after the other, came out from under the archway to the courtyard.

'Oh, Lord,' said Caz. 'They're in there. I can't bear it.' She pulled the hat down further over her face.

'At least we know where they are,' said Jamie. But there was no relief. There was only the knowledge that he had no more reason to stand on the green every day and that this part of the story, which still left room for uncertainty, however small, was over. It had all taken place against the backdrop of a new year, now a miserable, yawning void that would somehow have to be filled.

The vans crept along the drive, onto the road and away. Flashes went off as they passed the group of waiting reporters and then, once they had gone, the lenses panned around towards where Jamie and Caz were standing. He swung them both away from the cameras so that their faces couldn't be seen.

'Mr Fenton?' It was the police officer, the radio still in

her hand. 'My boss is asking whether you might consider saying a few words to the press.'

'Oh,' said Jamie. 'No. No, I couldn't.'

'It doesn't have to be much, maybe just thanking the emergency services, that sort of thing.'

'Why? Can't they give us some privacy?'

'I understand.' Her thumb worried at the little aerial on the radio, pinging it back and forth. 'So many people knew your father round here, that's all. Maybe you and your sister could discuss it.' She moved away to the other side of the police car.

'I think you should,' said Caz.

'Why me?' said Jamie. 'You're the eldest.'

'I'd be no good. I can't stop crying. Listen, before you decide, you need to see these.' She unzipped her handbag and pulled out a sheaf of cards bound by an elastic band. 'There are loads more at home. They're addressed to both of us.'

Jamie took the bundle and eased the elastic band away. They were sympathy cards, the usual kind, with flowers and swirly gold lettering. The cards were mostly from people he didn't know; each one with a handwritten tribute inside. Some even had little anecdotes about his father. After he sold his factory, Bernie had been on the board of so many charity committees that Jamie lost count. Despite this, he had never considered that people might hold his father in genuine affection. Bernie was a showman and he was rich, but he was also a grammar school boy from humble beginnings, a grafter who had made his money. At one point he had even considered going into politics. To Bernie, a microphone was an opportunity. His voice was made for public speaking; sonorous but with a retained hint of local accent, just enough for people to know that he was one of theirs. It was nonsensical, but Jamie wished that his father were there to make the statement for him. Bernie would have known exactly what to say.

He opened the final card in the pile, written in uneven capitals by a farmer whose name he recognised, who lived up the dale, alone except for his livestock and a couple of sheepdogs. Jamie had been there, once, with his father, and stood in the man's muddy yard in his school loafers while they chatted. At the time, Bernie was fighting to save the local auction mart. The campaign succeeded. The man would have had to drive for half an hour to buy that sympathy card.

Caz was watching him, waiting for a reaction. Across the green, lights and cameras were already in place. The police officer stepped out from behind the car. Jamie gave her what could barely be described as a nod, which sent her scuttling over to the reporters.

'God, Caz, what the hell am I going to say?'

She looked at him blankly. It was clear that she would offer no help. Before he could order his thoughts, the police officer was back.

'They're ready for you,' she said.

They dawdled, Jamie restricted by his borrowed trousers, Caz clinging to his arm. The police officer trailed behind them. Someone positioned them at the lych-gate, hemmed in by broadcast equipment and a handful of journalists. The day was dropping to dusk; there were only a couple of lights but they were so bright that he couldn't see anything in front of him. A microphone on the end of a long pole was lowered near to his face and a disembodied voice told him he could begin.

'Hang on,' said the police officer, holding up a hand. 'Have you got a tissue?' she said to Caz. 'You might want to…' She tapped below one eye with a forefinger.

'Oh.' Caz scrabbled in her pocket. 'Thank you.'

Jamie waited while she wiped her eyes clean. They stepped forward together.

'Um,' he said. 'My sister Caroline and I, um…' He looked at Caz, his mind empty. She gripped his arm harder. He had no words.

'Take your time, Jamie,' said someone from behind the lights and cameras.

He stared into the glare, waiting for the words to come. Nobody moved or spoke. He breathed in and out several times.

'I just want to, um…' His face was paralysed by the cold. Even if he could conjure up something to say, he didn't think his jaws would work. But there was still nothing. All he could call to mind were the things he couldn't say: how unfair it was, how their lives had been devastated, and how he wished everyone would bugger off and leave them alone. He turned from the lights, mumbling an apology, leaving Caz stranded in the pool of brightness as he stumbled away.

'Can *you* give us anything, Caroline?' he heard someone say, but then she was beside him again and together they picked up their pace. By the time they reached the police car they were almost running.

Jamie didn't watch the local news that night. Zoe told him that it was fine; that the footage had showed him unable to speak, clearly grieving. It was dignified, she said. Caz called, wanting to talk about the fire, but he wasn't in the mood and he cut her short, which made him feel guilty.

After supper he and Zoe went to the pub but he had no conversation and the beer tasted stale and sour.

Later, he lay in bed, thinking of the hill farmer, whose name he could not now remember. He wondered what the man would have thought about his inability to say even a few words in tribute to his parents and those who had tried to save them. The answer was obvious: that he was a miserable imitation of his father.

eight

On the same evening, Caz watched the coverage from the sofa in her sitting room. The report showed the departure of the two black vans, followed by her own appearance alongside Jamie in front of the cameras. Poor Jamie. He wore the same confounded expression as he had when he was speaking to the chief fire officer. Standing there with him, his inarticulacy hadn't seemed strange; the blinding presence of the cameras would have made it hard for even the most seasoned public speaker to think rationally. On screen, though, those lights weren't obvious. To anyone watching, Jamie was just a young man, way out of his depth, unable to form a sentence. Caz hoped that others would find it as endearing as she did.

Yet she had, again, done nothing to help him. She had ducked out and left him floundering, unable to find anything meaningful to say. It wasn't even a conscious decision; she simply could not have spoken to those cameras. Jamie probably felt the same way but she hadn't considered that at the time. Instead she had fished out those sympathy cards, which she had been meaning to show him, hoping they might be a comfort, and used them as a means of coercion. The cards were now on display all around her, crowded onto every surface in the room along with the dozens of others which Jamie hadn't seen.

Upstairs, Steve was supervising the girls' bed time. When she turned off the television she could hear the squeals from one of the raucous games he liked to play with them after their bath. It normally infuriated her that he would rev them up just when they were supposed to be winding down but tonight their exuberance was cheering, their resilience something to be marvelled at. She was the grown up, yet she couldn't manage ten minutes of normality. At the end of her vigil at the foot of the stairs on New Year's Day she had been awake for forty-eight straight hours. Her sleep pattern was ruined. She cried constantly. The ability to put on a brave face was gone. And that was before the discovery of her parents' remains.

Ruby and Pearl were keeping their distance, unsure what to make of this new, collapsed version of their mother. If they were too young to appreciate the enormity of what had happened, it was probably just as well.

Caz got up, intending to wash up the tea-things. When she reached the kitchen table she paused, her attention caught by a bottle of beer which Steve had opened before going upstairs. It was nearly full. Steve often drank beer at home. Usually she was blind to it; he bought the bottles himself and kept them in the garage, always clearing them away afterwards so that she didn't have to touch them. She didn't even like beer, but they didn't take any chances. Now, the sight of the bottle reminded her of the brandy that she'd drunk on New Year's Eve. Both were part of a forbidden world. In accepting, she had broken a promise she made to herself when she was pregnant with Ruby; never to drink again. She could taste it now; the pleasant shock as the brandy hit her tongue, the smarting as it trickled down her throat.

It wasn't such a big deal. The circumstances were extreme. She was an adult quite capable of taking a drink, just one, in eight years, without reawakening that roaring, grasping need that she had managed to conquer. There was no reason to give it any more thought. She walked to the sink, ran a bowl of water and put the dishes into it. Then she turned around and went back to the table.

The glass bottle was cold and dripping with condensation. When she picked it up it left a ring on the table. The label, *Budweiser*, was red, white and blue; harmless-looking. She sniffed the neck of the bottle. The beer smelled yeasty and slightly sweaty. Whatever she wanted, it wasn't this. She put down the bottle and left the room.

The stairs vibrated beneath Caz as she climbed them, which could only mean one thing. In the girls' room, Steve stood between the two single beds, his face resigned. Ruby, in spotty pyjamas, was jumping from one bed to the other, her hair flying behind her. With the stuffed dog wedged under her arm, Pearl grabbed at Ruby every time she came near, trying to topple her onto the mattress. Pearl's plump little-girl feet poked out from under her old-fashioned nightdress (another gift from Esther); her hair clung to her face where it was sticky with exertion. The room, dark except for a revolving nightlight, was redolent of a disco; almost as noisy but with bunny rabbit wallpaper.

'Come on, monkeys, stop that now,' said Steve, 'or we'll all be in trouble with Mummy.'

He wrestled Ruby onto the mattress. Pearl shrieked and dived on top of them and Steve made a great play of pinning them both down for a goodnight kiss. He picked up Pearl and she chortled as he launched her onto her bed.

'Me, me!' Ruby scampered onto Pearl's bed to be tossed back to her own.

'OK, OK, no more. You've done me in.' Steve gave Caz a sheepish smile whilst holding Ruby down with one hand and Pearl with the other.

'But Daddy…'

'Night night, you two. See you in the morning.'

Ruby flopped onto her pillow theatrically as Steve backed out of the room. Pearl sat still. For a moment it seemed that peace was restored. Caz pulled *The Lion, the Witch and the Wardrobe* from the bookshelf. She had given it to Ruby as a Christmas present and had been meaning to start reading it aloud to both girls. But as she turned back to them, Pearl threw her pillow at Ruby, who jumped up and began beating Pearl around the head with it.

'Ruby! Stop that. You'll hurt her.'

'No, Mummy,' said Pearl between blows. 'I like it!'

'Look.' She held up the book. 'I thought we could read this.'

'Sorry,' said Ruby, seriously. 'We're too lively for a story.' Pearl wriggled off her bed and rolled herself up in Ruby's duvet until none of her was visible. Ruby sat on where Caz thought Pearl's head would be, still swinging the pillow.

'Stop! You'll suffocate her.'

Caz hauled Ruby off and grabbed the corner of the duvet, pulling on it until Pearl rolled loose. Their boisterousness was exhausting. She needed to get them into bed before she became either too cross or too tired to deal with them properly. Already she could feel desperation nagging at her edges and it took a superhuman effort not to abandon any semblance of authority.

'Right,' she said. 'Story or sleep.'

'But we're not tired,' said Pearl.

'At all,' said Ruby.

Caz straightened their beds and replaced their pillows, fluffing them up.

'It's school tomorrow, remember? I want to make sure you're all right about going back.'

Instantly deflated, the girls crawled into bed.

'Will everyone know what happened?' said Ruby.

'Probably.' Caz sat down on Ruby's mattress. 'I'm sure they'll be nice about it.'

'I'm not going to cry at school.'

'Me neither,' said Pearl.

'You don't have to be brave all the time. It's fine to cry if you feel sad.'

'Are *you* sad, Mummy?' said Pearl.

Caz couldn't answer. The tears, the bloody tears, were always there, waiting for the tiniest encouragement. Like now. She stood up and made a pretence of adjusting the curtains before sitting down on the gloomiest part of Pearl's bed.

'I'm fine,' she said. 'You don't need to worry. My job is to look after you and it's your job to let me.'

'And is it Daddy's job to look after you?' said Ruby.

'Exactly,' said Caz. 'Now: *Once there were four children whose names were Peter, Susan, Edmund and Lucy...*'

—

In the kitchen, Steve was at the table, drinking his beer. Caz opened the fridge, not sure what she was looking for, and closed it again. The washing-up was still in the sink.

'I'm worried about the girls,' she said. 'They seem to think they shouldn't cry.'

'It's good that they're taking in their stride,' said Steve. 'They're doing really well.'

'Yeah, but…'

'They know we're here if they need us. We'll keep an eye on them.' He took a swig. 'Are you OK?' he said. 'Now that… you know… they've been found.'

The bottle was almost empty but there was now a second one, unopened, on the table. Caz sat down opposite him. If she closed her eyes she would probably have fallen asleep there, on the hard pine chair, which was weird when she couldn't sleep in bed at night.

'I'm so tired. We've been waiting days for this and now I don't know whether it helps or not.'

'How about a cuppa?' He jumped up and switched on the kettle.

'No thanks.'

Steve clicked the kettle off again.

'Do you want me to run you a bath with the nice bubbles?'

'That's sweet of you, but no.'

'Or, or, I could nip round to Blockbusters and get you one of those romcoms?'

'No, Steve, really, I don't need anything.'

All of these were things she liked, but none of them were what she wanted just then. Steve was still standing by the kettle, looking at a loss.

'There must be something I can do.'

'I just keep going over and over it, seeing those horrid black vans coming out of The Hall. Then to see it on telly as well… What about their dignity? Why doesn't anyone care about that?'

'It's just what they do. Reporters. Try not to let it get to you.' He abandoned the kettle and shucked open the second beer with a bottle opener.

'I keep asking myself why, Steve. It said in the paper that it was likely a dropped cigar, or whatever it was that Dad smoked, that started the fire. How could he have been so stupid? Why wasn't he more careful?'

'It was an accident, babe.' Steve came to stand behind her and put a hand on her shoulder.

She leaned her face against his arm. 'But I miss them. One minute they were here, larger than life and the next… I can't take it in. Every time I try to concentrate on something else, I just keep going back to them being trapped in there, knowing the fire was coming but not being able to get out. I can't sleep for thinking about it, picturing their faces, imagining how they must have felt.'

The tears were flowing again; she couldn't help it. Steve hated it when she cried; he would probably prefer it if she threw things. He crouched down in front of her, his face agonised.

'Please, Caz. Try not to get upset. It'll only make it worse, torturing yourself like this.'

'I just can't make sense of it.'

She buried her face in his shoulder and sobbed into the neck of his sweatshirt. As he put his arms around her she felt the familiar dips and curves of his muscles. It was as if he were holding her up, even though she was the one on the chair. That was what she wanted; to be held tightly, almost smothered, so that she could forget to think. But just as she started to feel calmer, Steve pulled away.

'You'll be OK,' he said. 'Just give it some time. The girls need you, Caz. We all do. You'll get there.'

After Steve had taken his beer into the sitting room to watch the football, Caz went into the hall and dialled Zoe's number. Zoe was kind, asking how everyone was, but it was Jamie that she wanted to talk to.

'Sis.'

'J. I needed to speak to you. I don't know what to do with myself. It's real, now that they've found them. You're the only one who can understand.'

'Yeah. It's been a horrible day.'

Caz waited for Jamie to say more, hoping that he would articulate back to her what she was thinking, but he didn't.

'Don't you keep running through it all in your head? What they might have been doing that night, what time they went to bed, whether they knew what was going to happen to them once they realised the house was on fire?'

'The fire guy thought they would have been overcome with smoke first, remember?'

'Yes, but what if they weren't? How would he know? What if they *suffered*, J?'

Jamie didn't speak for a few seconds.

'I'm trying not to think about that. Maybe you should too. It won't help.'

'But I *can't*. We both need to deal with it. We can't pretend it didn't happen.'

'That's not what I'm saying, but we have to keep going, don't we? We can't just crumble. Everything's shit. Of course I know that, but I'm trying to keep busy. I think it helps. Zoe and I are going to the pub shortly. Maybe you should… not the pub, obviously, but I don't know, something. What about Ruby and Pearl? They must need plenty of attention at the moment.'

'Oh,' said Caz. 'You're going out. I'd better let you go.'

'No, no,' said Jamie. 'I didn't mean it like that. Just that it's probably not best to dwell on things too much.'

'It's OK,' said Caz. 'We'll speak again soon. Bye, Jamie.'

She hung up the phone. On the other side of the wall, the football commentator was shouting about a missed penalty. There was no point in trying to talk to Steve any further while there was sport on TV. She crept up the stairs so as not to disturb the girls and went to bed, knowing that she wouldn't sleep.

nine

Zoe was sitting in a high-backed leather chair, flipping through *The Field*, as Jamie emerged from the men's fitting room in his socks (or rather Andrew's), tags dangling from the two pieces of a navy suit. He pulled at the collar of the jacket where the plastic security device dug into his neck.

'What do you think?'

'Great.'

'You're not looking.'

She lowered the magazine into her lap. Jamie waited for a more considered opinion. He raised his arms and turned in a slow circle, as his mother used to instruct him to do when they were buying clothes. A twirl, she called it. An enthusiastic shopper, she was always a rich seam of suggestions as to what might go with what. He had never heard Zoe mention shopping or tell him that she had anything new to wear. She gave a little shrug.

'Yeah. Good.'

Grateful though he was to Zoe's colleague, he'd had enough of borrowed clothes. With a return to work imminent, he needed a new wardrobe. The suit was the first thing he'd tried on but by the time he turned back to the fitting room, Zoe had already picked up the magazine again, bouncing her foot against the leg of the chair. She reminded him of one of those men you would see hanging around shop doorways on Saturday afternoons, smoking and checking their watches because the football was about to start and their girlfriend was still in Topshop trying on jeans.

But this was not Saturday afternoon; it was Tuesday morning and it was Zoe's day off. She had agreed to come readily enough, but he suspected that she would rather be out hacking.

From her seat outside the fitting room, a chambray shirt produced a flicker of approval. But when he held up two ties, one over each shoulder, and asked which she preferred, she crossed one leg over the other and said, 'You choose.'

At the till, Jamie handed over his Access card and signed the slip.

'Would it be OK if I kept these on?' he said to the cashier, indicating the uppermost of three shoeboxes on the counter.

'Are you serious?' said Zoe. 'I used to do that when I was about seven.'

Jamie unlaced the borrowed shoes and dropped them into a carrier bag. 'I'm desperate. I feel like one of those ladies in ancient China with the bound feet.'

'Drama queen,' said Zoe. 'Those great hooves would take some binding. Come on, let's get a coffee.'

Jamie nudged a wooden tray along the metal counter of the café, which was in the basement of the department store and had a subterranean, airless atmosphere. The queue shuffled forward ahead of him. Behind the counter, percolators slurped and hissed; teacups rattled in saucers. Zoe had claimed a table by the wall. He held up a plate with a cheese scone on it and she gave him a thumbs-up.

At the table, he shimmied into a chair that was fixed to the floor. Zoe plopped a sugar cube into her coffee and stirred.

'I didn't know you were such a shopper.' She scraped butter onto her scone from a tiny plastic pot.

'I didn't know you weren't.'

'Clothes aren't really my thing. I prefer what's underneath.' A smile flickered at the edges of her mouth and Jamie felt something jolt inside him.

'We can't all walk around stark-bollock naked,' he said.

'Not in Harrogate.'

Jamie picked up his coffee cup which was scalding, presumably fresh from an industrial dishwasher.

'It feels good having new things. Like a fresh start. This might sound daft but today I'm just a regular guy with a regular life, out with his… girlfriend, buying clothes.' He stumbled over the word *girlfriend*, unsure if he was supposed to use it.

'A lot of clothes,' Zoe corrected him.

'Yeah, but like someone who doesn't have much to worry about. I felt… normal.'

'Normal?' she said, but she was smiling. 'When you're doing *that?*'

'What? Oh.' He followed her gaze to his fingers, which were performing arpeggios on the table. 'Just practising. I didn't realise.' With no piano to play, this was the next best thing. He'd been doing it a lot.

'Have the repair people been in touch?'

'They called me yesterday. They'd heard about the fire and weren't sure what to do. I'll need to go and see it before they can start work.'

The very mention of the Pleyel seemed to send his hands into overdrive, scooting madly up and down in what he recognised as the scale of E flat minor, melodic. The table was only long enough for two octaves.

'Would it be pathetic if I asked you to come with me?'

'Of course not,' said Zoe. 'I know how I'd feel if anything happened to Minty. I always think of that piano as your equivalent of a horse, if you know what I mean.' Jamie did. 'We can go later if you like. I guess the sooner they can get cracking, the better.'

Forcing his fingers to be still, Jamie took a bite of scone while he decided how to frame what he wanted to say next. He needed her to take him seriously.

'It must be hard having me moping around your house.'

She gave her head a little shake while she chewed. 'I've tried to imagine how you must be feeling.' Her parents were very much alive and ran a riding school near Knaresborough. 'But I can't even begin to. It's too devastating. You haven't said much, although in a way that's made things easier. I suppose I'm more of a do-er.'

'Me too,' said Jamie. 'Even now I wish it would all go away, so that I wouldn't have to deal with it any more. Isn't that awful?'

'No. You've been very brave. Strong.'

'Hardly. I'm just trying not to talk about it all the time.'

Zoe finished her scone and set the knife on her plate, fiddling with it until it was exactly straight.

'And does that help?'

'Who knows?'

'I wish there was more I could do.' She gave his leg a squeeze under the table and lowered her voice. 'I *could* try and take your mind off it.'

He covered her hand with his.

'Steady on,' he said. 'We're in Hooper's café.'

'Not *here*, you idiot,' she said. 'When we get home.' Her fingers worked up his thigh. 'But only if you want to. It might be too soon.'

'Sounds good to me,' said Jamie.

They bolted from the café and ran to the car park. Zoe kept her hand on his leg for the whole journey home. When she unlocked the front door, he threw the shopping bags onto the sofa, then drew her towards him in the tiny hallway. She put her arms around him and he kissed her, his hands at the small of her back, pulling her closer. He was already working on the clasp of her bra when the phone rang.

'One second,' she whispered.

She slithered out of his grasp and went to the kitchen. Jamie's hands fell to his sides. He heard her making what sounded like an arrangement and then she was back, doing up the buttons of her coat.

'Argh, I hate my job sometimes.' She looked at the ceiling and let out a big sigh. 'Mrs Thorneycroft's mare's gone into early labour. There's no-one else free to go up there.'

'But you're not free,' said Jamie.

She tugged on the waistband of his jeans and kissed his cheek. 'I'm the newest-qualified. I have to. I don't know how long it will take.'

He waited for the front door to close then flung himself onto the pile of carrier bags, groaning into the empty room.

—

Later that afternoon, Jamie found himself on an industrial estate just off the A1, following a man called Colin through the showroom of Robinson's Piano Sales and Repairs. After three hours, Zoe still wasn't back. He'd decided that the grown-up response would be to face the piano's prognosis alone.

'The good news,' Colin was saying over his shoulder, 'is that the keys were untouched. The fall-board, their cover, is a little worse for wear, but that's about it.'

'And the rest?'

Colin pushed open a fire door. 'I think you'd better see for yourself.'

What used to be the Pleyel was in the middle of the room. Its legs had been reattached and were the same lustrous black as ever. The keys, as promised, were unaltered and gleamed invitingly. However, it took Jamie several seconds to notice either of these things because somebody had taken a wrecking ball to the main body of the piano. The lid was broken in half. Beneath the ebony veneer, the spruce casework had crumbled like stale cake. At least half of the strings were broken; likewise the hammers and dampers. What was going on beneath was anyone's guess.

'Bloody hell… sorry. I… I wasn't sure what to expect.'

Colin steered Jamie to a chair. A teenager with a cowlick and the first sproutings of a moustache came in with a cup of tea.

'We thought you might need this,' said Colin. 'It must be quite a shock.'

Jamie looked at the man's face for the first time. His expression was pained. It seemed that the three of them;

Jamie, Colin and the Pleyel were united in agony. 'I must admit I've found it hard and it's not my piano. Terrible to see, terrible. Such a beautiful instrument.' Colin shook his head and gave the fall-board a respectful pat. 'But,' he said, brightening, 'it can be fixed.'

'Good as new?' said Jamie, faintly.

'Absolutely.' The man paused. 'It's going to run into thousands, though, I'm afraid. The parts are extremely specialised. The work will be painstaking and slow. The man-hours alone - '

'I don't care,' said Jamie. He forced himself to look again at the piano. Its annihilated state summed up the last couple of months. But he had a job, a credit card, and little in the way of other expenses. This was at least one thing that could be salvaged, something that was within his gift to put right. He stood up. 'When can you get started?'

ten

Saturday morning and Jamie was awakened by the absence of Zoe beside him. It was still dark. He could hear her putting on her riding gear in the spare room and his first instinct was to call for her to come back to bed, but he knew better than to come between Zoe and her horse. Instead, he lay there, identifying the various sounds: the loo flushing, the cold tap on at full blast for her teeth, the creak of the stairs. Then, the whistle of the kettle and the chink of a mug before, lastly, the front door being pulled shut behind her.

In the four days since the shopping trip, Zoe had worked long hours and her offer of a distraction had not been repeated. While Jamie very much wanted to feel as physically close to Zoe as he had before the fire, there was a suspicion, which ran along in tandem, that doing anything fun was either disloyal or disrespectful to his parents, or both. Grieving people weren't supposed to have a good time. It was probably fortunate that he was about to return to work; after all, there was nothing enjoyable about *that.*

Back in the office for eight hours a day he would at least be occupied, which would be an improvement. As yet there wasn't even a funeral to organise. He and Caz had been told that it couldn't take place until the inquest had opened and the coroner had given permission. For weeks now he had been alone at Zoe's with nothing to do except watch TV.

Whenever they spoke on the phone, Caz, as predicted, only wanted to talk about the fire, to speculate over how it might have started and what exactly might have happened. To Jamie that was no help. Worse, not wanting to discuss it made him feel guilty. Uncharitably he told himself that Caz still had her house, her husband, her children. There was no need for her to keep going over the details of the fire when she had a multitude of other things to keep her busy. He stopped calling her.

What he really wanted was to play Rachmaninov, or Mozart, or, most of all, Beethoven. He knew the pieces in which he could lose himself. He'd never gone this long without a piano; even at university there was an old upright Waddington with a few duff keys and a missing pedal. Frustratingly, Colin from Robinson's had refused to be drawn on how long the repair might take. The feeling of immersion that he could get from the piano would be better therapy than anything else other than, perhaps, sex with Zoe. Plus, it would be guilt-free. His mother, a pianist herself, had been Jamie's encourager-in-chief. If music could have helped him, his mother would have been all for it.

Zoe had never played the piano. He imagined she'd been too consumed by horses when she was growing up to think about music lessons. While he was progressing through the grades, she would have been competing in gymkhanas and accumulating the myriad rosettes now stuck to her bedroom mirror. She was baffled by the way his fingers convulsed when he worked through piano pieces in his imagination. If he could play for her, she might understand, or maybe even begin to share, his passion. But that was impossible and anyway, Zoe spent what little free time she had with her horse.

By the time Jamie was up and dressed, *Grandstand* had already started but there was still ages before the rugby. Jamie sat eating cereal, watching the women's bobsleigh, ruminating on how any sport could become interesting if you stared at it for long enough. Take the winter Olympics, for example. He had seen most of the events at some point during his time off work and now considered himself somewhat of an authority on ice-dancing, curling and even the luge.

The coverage switched away from the Alps and back to the studio. France were about take on England at the Parc des Princes. It promised to be an exciting match, full of needle. *Le Crunch*, the newspapers called it. A year earlier, he and his father had been at Twickenham for the corresponding tie. They had driven to London in Bernie's Mercedes and picnicked with his father's friends in the car park. England had beaten France and they had gone home jubilant. Jamie snapped off the television, scooped up his car keys and left the house.

The stables were on top of a hill just outside the town. Zoe was leading her horse into the yard when he arrived. It was bone-freezingly cold; the concrete floor steamed where manure mingled with straw. Zoe stopped when she saw him and rocked back on her heels in mock amazement.

'Crikey,' she said. 'What are you doing here?'

'I came to see you, of course,' he said. 'Pub?'

'Look at me.' She indicated her muddy jodhpurs. 'I can't go like this. I'm filthy. And I need to get Minty rugged up.'

Jamie took a step forward. The horse raised its chestnut head. Their eyes were at more or less the same height.

'So this is Minty.' He stretched out an open hand and the horse grazed it with a velvety nose.

'The other man in my life.' Zoe was watching Jamie's face as Minty snuffled at his palm and he willed himself to appear as though he petted horses all the time and was perfectly relaxed in their company.

'I thought you didn't like the gee-gees.' She hooked an arm under Minty's neck and fondled his cheek. It was a familiar gesture; Zoe frequently stroked Jamie's face in the same way. He wondered if it was reasonable to be jealous of a horse.

'I never said that,' said Jamie. 'I just don't know much about them.'

'Maybe this is your chance to learn. How about a quick trot before I put him to bed for the day?'

Jamie glanced over Minty's glossy, bulky torso and the relative spindliness of the horse's legs.

'I'm too heavy,' he said. 'I don't want to break the poor bugger's back.'

'He's a seventeen-hand hunter,' said Zoe, patting Minty's neck. 'He'll be fine.'

'But I've never been on a horse before.'

This wasn't strictly true. As children, Caz and Jamie had been given riding lessons until a nasty fall left Caz with a broken collarbone and their mother decided it was too dangerous a hobby. That was when he began to learn the piano. He had horses to thank for that.

'Don't be a wuss,' Zoe said now. 'Come on.'

He followed her to a stone mounting-block where she asked him to hold the horse steady while she lengthened the stirrups. Keeping him still was more difficult than it looked; Minty persisted in looking behind him at what Zoe was doing and there was unexpected strength in his neck. When she had finished, they swapped places and Jamie climbed the steps, projecting what he hoped was confidence. He could hardly expect her to embrace his obsession with music if he wasn't willing to show an interest in hers for riding. And now that she had challenged him, he wanted to surprise her, to prove that he was capable of more than messing up television statements, buying clothes and playing an imaginary piano.

'That's it,' she said, 'left foot in the stirrup and... Excellent, you're on. We'll go into the manège. It's warmer in there.' She showed him how to hold the reins and led the way into the indoor arena. The game would have kicked off in Paris by now. Zoe let go of Minty's head collar and he began to walk around the edge of the sandschool.

'Good,' Zoe called. 'Sit up straight, that's it, heels down, keep the reins short. Trot on, Minty.'

The horse picked up speed. Jamie held on, unbalanced and uncomfortable. He would cling on. He would not fall off.

'Try to rise and dip as he moves. Keep your knees bent. Knees *bent*!'

Gurning with concentration, Jamie began to mirror the horse's movements, up and down, up and down. Instead of being jarred whenever Minty's front hooves hit the sand, he found that he could move in time with him, absorbing the shock. They trotted once, then twice around the arena. The cold air was exhilarating; he could smell the horse's grassy breath.

'Keep going,' called Zoe. 'You're a natural!'

Then, as if to prove the opposite, Minty switched into a different gear. The rising and falling stopped working; the horse was travelling too quickly for Jamie to keep up and he was bobbing around uncontrollably in the saddle.

'He's gone into canter,' said Zoe. 'Pull on the reins. Slowly, don't jerk him. And stop leaning back.'

But everything had gone wrong. His legs were fully extended forward in the stirrups, his body at forty-five degrees to the horse's back, his arms straight out in front of him. All sense of balance was gone. He pulled once on the reins, bringing his hands up to his ears.

The effect was like applying the handbrake to a moving car. Jamie was pitched forward into the back of the horse's neck, his face buried in the coarseness of his mane, hanging on but slipping off to the side. Minty was still moving, slowly, but tossing his head as if Jamie were an oversized parasite that he needed to shake off. Jamie was too out of breath to speak. Zoe was sprinting across the arena. By the time she reached him, his right foot was dangling inches from the floor and Minty was looking back at him out of one malevolent eye. The horse stopped and gave a loud, wet snort. Zoe grasped the reins and took hold of Jamie around the waist. He slid to the ground and they collapsed into each other while he caught his breath, feeling her shoulders shaking with laughter.

'Christ,' said Jamie, panting. 'That thing's evil.'

'Minty, you are a bad boy,' said Zoe, still laughing.

'That was terrifying.'

'Oh, come on, John Wayne. He was just having a bit of fun.'

'Yeah,' said Jamie. 'At my expense.'

'He likes you,' said Zoe. 'He would have had you off more quickly if he didn't. I'm proud of you.'

As she looked him in the eye, Jamie thought he saw a flicker of admiration. He stood up straight. He hadn't fallen off, which must mean that the horse hadn't won.

'Really?' he said.

'Really. But that's probably enough for one day.'

Zoe led Minty away and Jamie staggered after her, slowly enough to avoid the lusty kick which the horse threw back in his direction. When they reached the stable he leaned over the lower part of the door as Zoe set about the untacking process. He had no idea that there were so many bits of kit to remove. Eventually, she laid a rug over Minty's back and secured it.

The door to the adjoining stable had been left open. There was no horse inside and the floor was carpeted with fresh straw. No-one else was around.

The trot around the manège had awoken something in him that was nothing to do with equestrianism, an urge he hadn't properly felt since before the fire. After their shopping trip he had shown willing, unsure what would happen. In the end, he wasn't allowed to find out. Now, he waited while Zoe said an elaborate goodbye to the horse, tiptoeing up to whisper into the animal's ear and resting her face against his mane. When she came out Jamie took her hand, walking backwards to the next-door stable.

'Are you mad?' said Zoe, but she let herself be drawn inside. Jamie put his hands up inside her riding jacket and under the layers of clothing, finding the warmth of her skin. She shuddered slightly and pulled his face towards hers so that their mouths collided and Jamie tasted polo mints and coffee. He edged his hands higher, disappointed to discover that she was wearing a sports bra, the elastic of which sat impregnably around her ribcage. Straw rustled at his feet. It would be scratchy but there was something about the idea of collapsing onto it together that outweighed practicalities. He gave up on the sports bra for the moment and was about to remove his coat to spread it on the ground when his imagination leapt in a most unwelcome direction. His fingers pressed into Zoe's back at the thought of what a lit match could do to this straw, how quickly it would erupt into fire. And then, ineluctably, he was back on the village green, unable to tear his eyes from the blaze. He could even hear the beating of the flames.

'What is it?'

He was no longer kissing Zoe. She grasped his cheeks between her cold hands and peered into his face.

'Are you all right?' she said. 'Tell me what's wrong.'

'I'm sorry.' Jamie averted his eyes from her. 'I don't know what's the matter with me.'

He extracted his hands from under her jacket. She tugged down her jumper, tucking her polo shirt back into her jodhpurs.

'It's OK, it's OK.' Zoe hugged him, rubbing his back. 'We probably need to give it a bit longer.' Jamie began to speak but she shushed him with a finger. 'It would have been a massive cliché, anyway.'

He was too chilled to smile. Memory had overpowered his most basic instinct and now he couldn't imagine where his need had come from, or how it could be recreated. He knew that the effects of the fire would last, long after it had been extinguished. But he had to be able to function at this most basic level. And why, when what he needed was to be completely consumed by something, had he allowed guilt, or disloyalty, or whatever it was, to override that need? On a physical level it made no sense; he fancied Zoe rotten. But it was weeks since they'd had sex. He hadn't felt like it and she hadn't pushed it. In letting his mind wander he had managed to turn opportunity into failure. It couldn't be allowed to happen. There had to be some parts of his life where the fire couldn't intrude. Jamie wrapped his arms around Zoe and nuzzled into her hair; deflated, but with new purpose.

'Come on,' she said. 'Let's go home. And then let's go out and get pissed.'

When they got back, Jamie switched on the television. He sat through the English football scores and then the Scottish ones, waiting for the rugby result. England had beaten France in convincing but brutal style. He stretched out on the sofa and settled into the highlights, absently assessing the prospects of a Grand Slam. From upstairs he heard the lacklustre whirring of the shower followed by the roar of Zoe's hairdryer. The street-lamp flicked on outside the window. A sudden gust of wind whistled through the letterbox, making its metal flap rattle.

'Are we fit?'

Zoe, dressed for the pub in her good jeans and a shirt which was unbuttoned just enough not to be indecent, had come downstairs and was perched on the arm of the sofa.

'You are.'

Jamie inhaled her scent, the one that smelled of ripe figs that she saved for Saturday nights. Away from the stables and buoyed by the rugby, he was surprised by how quickly he had recovered. Zoe had understood. She hadn't blamed him or made him feel inadequate and she'd willingly followed him into the stable in the first place. Maybe things weren't so bad. He reached out with the thought of pulling her on top of him.

'No, you don't, sunshine. We're going to the pub.'

Jamie let his hand drop.

'Is this my punishment? For earlier?'

'Of course not. Why would you think that? There's a gang from work going to the Bay Horse. I said we'd be there.' She got up and ducked into the cupboard under the stairs for her jacket. When she came back she stood over him, looking at a big patch of mud on his jeans which must have come from the stables. 'Shall I wait while you get changed?'

Jamie didn't move. Zoe put the jacket down and checked her watch.

'Maybe it won't matter if we're a bit late.' She held out a hand, but Jamie couldn't let go of the thought that he had blown his chance and that she was now only humouring him. Or worse, pitying him.

'It's OK,' he said. 'It's fine.'

Zoe looked at him as though she were trying to decide how to placate a difficult child.

'Come to the pub,' she said. 'It'll be fun.'

'I don't want to. It's freezing out there and I'm too comfy.' He wondered at his wheedling tone. From her face, he saw that Zoe had heard it too.

'Hey.' She gave him a gentle prod in the stomach. 'You're too young to be an old fogey.'

'You go,' said Jamie. 'I'm not in the mood.'

Zoe straightened and cocked her head to one side.

'Are you sure?'

'Go.' He flapped his hand at her.

She bent to kiss him and then looped her bag across her body. Jamie watched the swing of her pony tail as she opened the door and went out, his twitching fingers repeating an unidentified trill on the cushion beside him.

eleven

Archer's estate agency had a wide, shallow shop-front overlooking Ripon's market square. For reasons that were historic and not entirely clear, it was a mark of seniority to occupy a desk at the back of the office. Jamie's desk was the full goldfish, right next to the window and within feet of a pedestrian crossing on the other side of the glass. He had been back at work for three weeks.

The tiny city centre was quiet, battered by weeks of rain and months of recession. At a greengrocer's stall in the sparse, bedraggled market, an elderly woman in a headscarf selected a single banana and dropped it into a shopper trolley. By the cut-price biscuit stall, a younger woman stopped to adjust the PVC cover on her baby's stroller. Behind it all, an eighty-foot stone obelisk pointed to the pewter sky and at the far end of the square, overshadowing the shops, were the towers of the cathedral which lent the city a kudos it could not otherwise have claimed. Without it, of course, Ripon wouldn't be a city at all.

As the clock struck eleven, a lone car crawled past the office window. They had been open since nine and so far there hadn't been a single customer.

Jamie felt the sting of an elastic band hitting his cheek at close range. He swivelled his chair away from the window. Across the desk, Chris gave a fist pump.

'Yesss!'

'Child.'

'You were staring into space. I'm saving you a bollocking from Archer.'

'Yeah, right.'

Of the three graduate trainees, Chris had been at the firm for longer and clearly believed himself superior to the other two. This was less obvious to Jamie. Chris ate a cheese and onion pasty for lunch every day and wore a tie with a tyrannosaurus pattern which he insisted was a brilliant ice-breaker with clients.

'Sold anything yet?' he said.

'Nope,' said Jamie. 'You?'

'Got a couple of things in the pipeline.' He curled the tip of the dinosaur tie, rolled it up to his collar and let it fall again. This was what he did when he was making things up. 'Can't tell you or I'd have to kill you.'

'That's such bullshit,' said Charlotte. She had a mass of curly dark blonde hair which looked like a struggle to control, but her clothes were tailored and not locally-bought. It was rumoured that her father owned a chain of BMW dealerships on Tyneside. Certainly, she treated her company Fiesta with ill-disguised disdain. 'I hate to break it to you, but you're not James Bond. You're a trainee estate agent in Ripon.'

'*Senior* trainee estate agent.'

'Whatever. And you haven't asked *me* whether *I've* sold anything.'

Chris laughed through his nose. 'You've only been here a month.'

'So what?' Charlotte adjusted a hooped earring with a manicured finger and stood up. 'I've got two little words for you: Whitegates Grove.'

Chris blanched. 'You can't have.'

'You'd better believe it.' She swung her handbag over her shoulder. 'I'm off there now, in fact. See you later, suckers.'

Jamie and Chris watched in silence as Charlotte marched through the office towards the back door.

'Do you believe her?' Chris whispered. Whitegates Grove was a development of large new houses on the edge of the city. Although they had been finished for over a year, all of them were still on the market. Getting a sale there was the Archer's equivalent to the holy grail.

'Who knows?' said Jamie. 'I guess we'll find out. In other news, I'm taking Mr and Mrs Sidgwick out on some viewings this afternoon.'

'I wouldn't bother,' said Chris, recovering his bravado. 'They're T-Ws. Time-wasters. They'll never buy anything in a million years. They just fancy a ride in Jamie's taxi.'

At lunchtime, Jamie stopped at reception for a new biro and noticed that the local newspaper had been crammed onto a shelf under the desk. In its normal position, on the coffee table in the waiting area, was an old copy of *Woman's Own*. As he reached down to pull out the *Yorkshire Courier*, Maggie, the office manager, put a restraining hand on his arm.

'Leave it, love' she said. 'There's stuff in there about your mum and dad.'

But he couldn't stop himself. Back at his desk, he read the double-page spread, inspired by the news that the inquest had been formally opened and adjourned. There was a picture of his parents at a black-tie dinner and a photo of the house with the white fireball behind it. The article ruminated over how much The Hall was worth and went on to celebrate Bernie as a local hero who, having been born on a council estate, had managed to make a fortune manufacturing ball-bearings and had married the daughter of a baronet. In a funny way it was comforting. Reading about his parents almost made them come alive again, or at least affirmed that they had been there in the first place.

However, the announcement about the inquest had also given the reporter an excuse to speculate all over again about how the fire had started. Even the grisliest details were repeated, the worst of which were that it had only been possible to identify Bernie by his teeth and Esther by her jewellery.

Nobody in the office except Charlotte had mentioned the fire since his return. On his first day back, she had told him how sorry she was and from then on made a point of being kinder to him than she was to Chris. Whether this was because she was genuinely sympathetic, or because she simply disliked Chris, Jamie couldn't tell. Maggie on reception adopted a maternal, rather pitying way of looking at him. The senior agents, who never spoke to him anyway, continued to ignore him from their rarefied position at the back of the office. Chris maintained the childish banter which Jamie suspected was his only means of communication.

—

Mr and Mrs Sidgwick arrived ten minutes early and made a great fuss of taking off their coats and hats while Jamie showed them information about the houses they had asked to view. Chris made rude gestures behind their backs. Then, Jamie waited as they put their coats and hats on again and led them out to the car park.

Bernie used to say that Jamie's boss was 'happy clappy.' All of the company cars were, at Archer's insistence, turquoise with a white fish symbol on the back. Jamie helped Mrs Sidgwick into the back seat of his own Fiesta. Her husband settled in beside her and they set off for their first viewing. It was, to be fair to Chris, exactly like driving them in a taxi.

'*Easy to maintain living space with excellent transport links,*' read Mr Sidgwick. 'That sounds ideal.'

Jamie pulled a face, keeping out of sight of the rear-view mirror. He'd been told to write the particulars using a set of stock phrases. The house was minuscule and backed onto the A1.

'Do you know what,' he said, 'I'm not sure that one's for you. Why don't we skip straight to number two?'

'Well, if you're sure,' said Mrs Sidgwick. 'What does this one say? Ah yes, *In need of updating and with no onward chain.* Well, John's quite handy, aren't you dear? And of course we're cash buyers.'

This house was little better. The owner had recently died in it and Jamie doubted that anyone had touched the interior since the 1960s.

'There's quite a bit of work to do,' he said.

'No problem,' said Mr Sidgwick. 'I like a project.'

They stopped outside the house, a semi on a small post-war estate with a neat garden and a newly-painted front door.

'Very nice,' said Mrs Sidgwick.'

'Yes,' said Jamie. 'It presents well externally.' He'd done the weeding and the painting himself the previous weekend, while Zoe was competing in the Wensleydale horse trials.

He juddered the front door open into a dark, thinnish hallway which gave onto an even darker set of rooms. Jamie couldn't imagine anyone wanting to live in such a depressing space. They all squashed into the kitchen and Mrs Sidgwick gave the wooden units a dubious eye. Some of them had curtains rather than doors. Mr Sidgwick tried to open a few drawers, all of which stuck on their runners.

'It would need a new kitchen,' said Jamie, 'but as you'll see, that's reflected in the price.' He poked his head through the serving hatch into the dining room. Rising damp had formed a tidemark of brown on the wallpaper which was peeling away like a succession of lolling tongues.

'It's all right, son,' said Mr Sidgwick. 'We've seen enough. Time to go.'

Back in the car, Jamie handed them the third set of details.

'This looks promising,' said Mrs Sidgwick. 'It's *unexpectedly re-available.*'

'Yes,' said Jamie, 'it was under offer until yesterday.'

The house was just around the corner on the same estate.

'A cul-de-sac,' said Mr Sidgwick. 'Lovely.'

'Lovely,' echoed Mrs Sidgwick. 'I've always liked the idea of a cul-de-sac. What does it mean, John?'

'No idea,' said her husband, cheerfully. 'Ask Jamie. He's the expert.'

'Um... it's French for dead end, I think,' said Jamie, aware that the definition didn't sound overly appealing. 'Why don't you take the keys? I'll stay here, out of your way.'

'You will not,' said Mrs Sidgwick. 'We need you to show us around.'

They all got out of the car.

A clipped privet hedge formed the border between the property and the pavement. Behind it, the driveway was well-maintained and lined with snowdrops. The front door and windows had been recently replaced. Inside, the dining room and kitchen had been knocked together to make a large, open-plan space.

'An island!' said Mrs Sidgwick. 'Imagine.'

'Yes, Pat.' Mr Sidgwick was opening cupboards. 'Look! There's a dishwasher.'

Jamie waited in the doorway until they were ready to go upstairs, where the main attraction was an ensuite.

'Our own bathroom,' said Mrs Sidgwick. 'How fancy!'

'Well,' said Jamie, 'there are only two of you, so technically any bathroom would be your own.'

'Yes, but an en*suite*,' said Mr Sidgwick.

His wife beamed at Jamie. 'It's perfect, dear,' she said.

On the way back to the office, the Sidgwicks went through the particulars again, exclaiming over the house's various features (*Coal-gas fire! Economy seven heating! Power shower!*). Alone in the front, Jamie was trying to decide what to do. It boiled down to either being decent, or doing his job. He squeezed the car through the narrow gates at the back of the office and into a parking space.

'We love it,' said Mrs Sidgwick. 'Don't we, John?'

'We love it.'

Jamie took up his copy of the details and pretended to study it.

'It's a bit over your budget,' he tried.

'What's a couple of thousand,' said Mr Sidgwick, 'when you've found your dream home?'

'We'd like to make an offer,' said his wife.

'Look.' Jamie twisted to face them. 'I shouldn't be saying this, but there's a problem with the house.'

'What problem?' Mr Sidgwick frowned. They both leaned forward, straining at their seatbelts.

'Actually, there are several. The reason the last sale fell through was the survey. The house needs a new roof, but worse than that, there's subsidence. The foundations aren't stable. I'm sorry, but I couldn't let you go ahead without telling you.'

'Oh.' Mrs Sidgwick looked crestfallen. 'What a shame.'

'Shame your company's prepared to sell a house that's falling down, more like,' said Mr Sidgwick. 'They always say estate agents are cowboys. I thought you lot were different.'

The three of them sat in silence, collectively misting up the windows. Jamie performed a contrary motion scale on the dashboard.

'I'm sorry,' he said again. 'I know how much you liked it.'

'What's important,' said Mrs Sidgwick, 'is that you were honest. We'll not let on. We don't want to get you into trouble.'

'That's right.' Mr Sidgwick clapped him twice on the shoulder. 'Let us know if anything decent comes up, won't you?'

'Of course,' said Jamie. Neither of the Sidgwicks moved. Jamie unclipped his seatbelt and reached to open his door but Mr Sidgwick clapped him on the shoulder again, this time leaving his hand there.

'We heard about your parents,' he said.

'Yes,' said Mrs Sidgwick. 'We should have mentioned it earlier, but we didn't know what to say.'

'Oh - ' said Jamie.

'You seem like a nice boy,' Mrs Sidgwick continued. 'We've got a son about your age. He's a guitarist in a band. They're touring round Europe. We've no idea when we'll next see him.'

'I like music too,' said Jamie, 'but I play the piano.'

'I knew it!' Mrs Sidgwick clapped her hands. 'I saw your fingers just now. Jake does that as well. It must give you a lot of comfort after all that's happened.'

'I wish,' said Jamie, 'but the piano's away being repaired. I'm missing it dreadfully.'

'That's bad luck,' said Mr Sidgwick. 'Let's hope they get it mended for you soon.'

Back in the office, Chris was waiting for him.

'Well?'

'No joy.'

'Told you.' He leaned back in his chair. 'Time wasters.'

'I thought they were quite keen. I'm going to make sure I find them something.'

'Archer won't agree. But it's your funeral.' Chris glanced at the open newspaper on Jamie's desk. 'Oh,' he said. 'Er... sorry.'

Charlotte picked up an elastic band and flicked it at his face.

twelve

It was nearly eight when Zoe came home from the surgery. Jamie was on the sofa drinking beer, watching more winter Olympics. He had muted the television in favour of Radio Three, which was broadcasting *Don Giovanni* live from the Royal Opera House. In his lap lay a polystyrene tray, empty except for a wooden fork and the smeared green remains of mushy peas. There was a blizzard on the screen; not because of the weather in France but because the aerial on the roof had been damaged by a recent storm.

'Can you believe this guy?' He gestured towards the television with his beer can. 'He passed a gallstone last week and he's just won a gold medal.'

'In what event?' Zoe strode to the window and snapped the curtains shut. 'Passing gallstones?'

'No-ooo,' said Jamie. 'Speed skating. He's Norwegian. What a legend.' But Zoe had gone into the kitchen and was clattering things around. He put down his beer and followed.

When Jamie came in he hadn't noticed the state of the kitchen but now, watching Zoe banging cupboard doors, he could see that it was a tip. The breakfast things were still in the sink. A dirty knife languished in the butter, which had been left out all day and was specked with crumbs. On the worktop, used teabags sagged in a pool of brown liquid which was seeping into the newspaper wrapping from his fish and chips. The mess was entirely his own.

Zoe, in marigolds, scooped the teabags into the bin. She squirted washing-up liquid into the sink and began to chisel dried Weetabix from a cereal bowl with the back of a spoon.

'I was going to do that,' he said.

'Obviously.'

'I *was*. I had a busy day. We went for a pint after work.'

'I thought you said the office was dead.' She turned to look at him, the gloves dripping soapy water onto the floor.

'Not *dead* exactly. Anyway, it got a bit late so I stopped for a takeaway. I only sat down for half an hour to eat it and watch some TV and then you were back. Let me do it now.'

He reached for the dishcloth but she batted him away.

'Jamie.' Zoe set the bowl on the drainer and peeled off the rubber gloves. 'We lost a cow and her calf today. I've worked a twelve-hour shift and I'm tired. I don't want to come home to this.'

'That sounds awful. I'm sorry. Go and sit down. You must be hungry.'

Zoe pulled the plug out of the sink and stood with her hands braced against it. Jamie opened a cupboard stacked with tins.

'I could do you something on toast.'

She laughed in a sad way and shook her head.

'Let me get you a glass of wine, at least, while I think what to make for you.'

'No, Jamie. Like I said, I'm tired. I'm going to bed.'

As he heard her footsteps on the stairs and the opera's first act drew to a close, he was still scouring the shelves, tempted to treat himself to a dessert of baked beans.

thirteen

There must have been a fault with the answering machine. The phone had been ringing for ages. If it came to a battle of wills between Caz, sitting at the bottom of the stairs, and the telephone, she wasn't going to lose. There was no-one she wanted to speak to except Jamie and he would never call her from work. In fact, he wasn't calling her at all. She understood, up to a point. He had a job and he needed to be together enough to do it properly. Perhaps he was frightened that if they spoke about their feelings, something uncontrollable would be unstoppered and irrevocably unleashed. Maybe he was worried that her grief was infectious and he didn't want to risk catching it. Whatever he thought, he wasn't going to share it with her.

Knowing Jamie as she did, she couldn't believe that he wasn't dwelling on the fire at all. His life had been turned on its head; even more, arguably, than hers had. Since he left university he'd been living with their parents; as far as she knew he was incapable of fending for himself. His physical reliance on them, she'd always thought, was a useful metaphor for his less visible emotional dependence.

Married with a baby at nineteen, Caz was used to living as a grown-up. Yes, she counted on her parents being around, but she had her own life. Jamie didn't. OK, so he had a girlfriend, but it didn't seem particularly serious. He was probably only staying with Zoe because he had nowhere else to go. It was awful to think that he might be forcing himself to act normally whilst at the same time inwardly disintegrating because he had no-one to talk to.

As children he had always been the steadier one. Not an angel, but never a shouter or an arguer or a havoc causer like she was. But this was major stuff. His refusal to talk about the fire couldn't be good for him. While the phone rang on, she entertained the idea that he might be confiding in Zoe, which was all very well, but they had only been together for five minutes and how could she possibly understand what they were going through? Steve wasn't doing a very good job of it and they had been a couple for seven years.

Whoever was calling, they weren't giving up. At last, Steve's voice cut in, explaining that no-one could come to the phone just now. They shouldn't say that they weren't at home, he had maintained when he was recording the message, in case burglars were on the line. Caz hadn't pointed out that if anyone did want to break into the house, they would be unlikely to announce themselves first.

'Caroline?' said the machine. 'It's me, Ruth. Calling at ten past ten on Tuesday. Are you there, pet lamb? I'm just after a little chat, see how you are. Come on, love, if you're in... Aw, maybe you're out. I don't know what you're doing with yourself at the moment. You're never at home.

Anyway, give me a ring when you get this. And look after yourself. Bye, pet, bye-bye, now.'

The more she ignored Ruth's calls, the more frequent they were becoming. Caz knew she would be concerned. Ruth had been part of hers and Jamie's entire lives: as a nanny, when they were younger, and latterly as their parents' housekeeper. There wasn't much that Ruth didn't know about their family. If ever their mother wasn't around, Ruth Cole would be there as back-up, qualified to hand out both discipline and reassurance according to their parents' rules. She was a kind of half-mother; someone in whom to confide, always giving it to them straight, but without any of the complications of a parent-child relationship. In fact, Ruth's advice was often more practical than Esther's. Which was why it was strange that Caz didn't want to confide in her now.

She was stumbling through the days, crashing, tumbling from one to the next. When she went to bed she couldn't remember what she had done during the hours when the girls were at school and Steve was at work. Somehow she was making sure that Ruby and Pearl got up, had breakfast and got to school on time. With monumental effort she cooked their tea and asked about their days. She managed this without any real engagement. Sometimes she had the sense that they were all under water. Voices seemed muffled and distorted; movements were vague and purposeless. At other times she felt detached from what was going on, as though it didn't matter what she did or said because she wasn't really in the room and life was carrying on without her.

What would help, what she was desperate for, was to talk to Steve or Jamie about the fire. If she could enlist either of them to go through the detail of it, the timings, the likely order of things before the fire started, she might be able to rationalise it in some way. She wanted a sounding board for how her father might have come to drop his… cigarillo, that was the word, where her mother might have been at the time, why no-one noticed. Neither of them were careless people. The most logical explanation was that Bernie had drunk too much claret and fallen asleep with the thing smouldering in his hand. Why, in heaven's name, hadn't Ruth Cole been around to keep things right, as she had been doing for their entire married lives?

That was horribly unfair. Ruth couldn't be held responsible for what happened after she had said goodnight to her parents and gone to bed. It was also not the reason that Caz didn't want to talk to her. That was simple: Ruth was not her mother.

Later that day, Caz found herself in the freezer section of the Co-op. It wasn't familiar territory; she never bought anything frozen other than peas and ice-cream. Sometimes one of the girls would go to a friend's house and come back asking why they never had Findus Crispy Pancakes, or those Turkey Twizzler things, at home. The answer was that she cooked everything from scratch (as taught by Ruth Cole, funnily enough) and was secretly judgemental about anyone who bought convenience food. The battles had been fought at their own dinner table years ago and now she was proud to say that both Ruby and Pearl were reasonably enthusiastic eaters of whatever vegetable she put in front of them.

She drew the shopping list from her pocket and studied it. There were the ingredients for lasagne, shepherd's pie and a mild chicken curry. She pictured herself at the stove, stirring béchamel sauce, imagining the effort involved. You could buy jars of that stuff, ready-made. Maybe it wouldn't matter, just for a while, until she got her mojo back.

On closer inspection, the giant freezers contained pre-packaged versions of virtually every meal she had ever cooked and plenty that she hadn't. With the surreptitiousness of a shoplifter she slid pizzas, packets of fish-fingers and potato croquettes into her trolley, followed by a smorgasbord of ready meals that would last the coming week.

She carried on along the aisle, anticipating the relief from the daily drudge in the kitchen. But if she couldn't be bothered to cook for Ruby and Pearl, what kind of mother would that make her? This food had dubious nutritional value. If she saw one of the other mothers from school at the checkout she would die of shame; not because they didn't buy these things themselves but because she was known for her obsession with healthy eating. She had probably been a bit superior about it. Most of them had jobs; whatever worked for them was their business. But she didn't have that excuse. What did she have to do all day that would preclude her from feeding her children from every major food group?

She unloaded everything from the trolley into the nearest section of the freezer, piling the cardboard cartons on top of the Viennettas and Arctic Rolls. But as soon as she started to move away, in her mind she was at home again, at the cooker, making béchamel. The imaginary sauce was stubborn with floury lumps which refused to dissolve no matter how hard she stirred. In the freezer, the discarded ready-made lasagne, peeked out from beneath some rejected garlic bread. Caz checked over her shoulder, put it all back into the trolley and moved on.

To get to the tills involved passing through the alcohol aisle. When the girls were very small she used to avoid this by double-backing along crisps and confectionery, running the gauntlet of their pestering for treats. More recently she had grown confident that this route no longer posed any threat and could be negotiated without fear. She would point her trolley forwards and aim for the checkout without registering what was populating the shelves. Today, she made the turn and was a third of the way down the aisle when she saw that she had chosen a spicy pepperoni pizza rather than a margherita. No-one apart from Steve would eat that. Leaving the trolley where it was, she took the offending article back to the freezer to swap it. When she returned, she noticed that she was at the Australian part of the white wine section.

She had never really drunk wine. Vodka, tequila, cider, yes, in spades, but not wine. Her parents used to drink lots of it, but she thought that was French, not Australian. She picked up a bottle at random and scrutinised the label. Chardonnay, thirteen per cent proof. Vodka was three times that. Perhaps this was what she needed: not spirits, but wine; mildly alcoholic, nothing that was going to do any serious damage. Just a bit of a boost. Judging by the number of bottles on the shelves, people must drink wine all the time and be perfectly fine. It probably wasn't even strong enough to be addictive. She put the bottle into the trolley and reached for another. After that, she got through the checkout as quickly as she could before anyone recognised her; not because of the wine but because of the convenience food.

—

There was just time to nip home before Ruby and Pearl needed to be collected from school. The answering machine was flashing again. Caz unpacked the shopping bags, putting the food in the freezer. When she stood the two bottles of wine on the worktop, it struck her that Steve might not think that buying them had been a good idea. She stashed one at the back of a drawer, underneath the tea-towels, and the other in the cupboard behind the laundry detergent; places where Steve would never look. Satisfied, she went into the hallway and pressed 'play'.

'Caroline, love? It's me again. You haven't called me back. Apart from anything else it's not polite. But never mind about that. Are you all right? It makes me nervous when you go quiet like this. It's been a lot for you I know, but you have to be there for those little girls of yours. Are you managing? Grief is a terrible thing but you have to get out of bed in the morning and put your best face on. A little bit of make-up doesn't hurt. Maybe just some rouge or some lippy. Anyway… you know you can always talk to me, don't you? Yes, well, that's all I wanted to say. Call me back, won't you? Ta-ta pet.'

So it wasn't just Jamie. Ruth thought she should be carrying on as normal, too, like it was the easiest thing in the world. Her mother would have understood. To Esther, the only answer when anything bad happened was to go to bed with a couple of valium. No point fighting these things, she would have said. Standing over the answering machine, Caz leaned her head against the wall. She stayed there for a few moments and then pressed 'delete'.

fourteen

It was early March, exactly sixty-seven days since the fire and even though the inquest had been opened there was still no word about a funeral. On the positive side, the repairs to the piano were well under way although this meant that Jamie was already fretting, not only about the bill but also about where the piano would be housed.

When the phone rang, Zoe was in the shower and Jamie was shaving. He raced downstairs, wiping at his face, and grabbed the receiver off the wall in the kitchen, imagining a veterinary emergency of some kind. It was Ruth Cole.

'Jamie, love, I wanted to catch you before you went to work. I'm worried about Caroline. Have you spoken to her?'

There were no radiators in the kitchen and Jamie was wearing only a towel. He tucked the handset under his chin and chafed his arms.

'Not really.'

'*Not really?* Either you have or you haven't.'

'OK then, no,' Jamie admitted. 'Have you?'

'No, pet, and that's my point.' Ruth sighed down the line. 'It's not like her. She's ignoring my calls.'

'Maybe she's busy.'

'Fiddlesticks. Something's not right. Will *you* try talking to her?'

Jamie thought of Caz, drifting around at home. He wondered whether Steve was a good listener and decided that he would rather be playing golf. If Caz wanted to talk about the fire, he doubted that Steve would be willing to join her in a detailed analysis. He wasn't that sort of guy. But Jamie wasn't that sort of guy, either. Ruth would be a much better bet. And Caz had friends, surely?

'I've got to go,' he said. 'I'll be late for work.'

'You will talk to her, won't you? She's had an awful shock. You both have. You need each other. Promise me.'

Jamie patted the shaving foam on his chin. Most of it had dissolved and he would have to start again.

'All right.' He hoped he had kept the lack of conviction from his voice.

As he replaced the receiver, Zoe came into the kitchen, her damp hair tied back in a ponytail.

'Bloody Ruth,' said Jamie. 'She's pestering me about Caz.'

'Pestering how?'

'She wants me to check on her. I bet she's been reading the horoscopes in the newspaper again.'

'Or maybe she just cares about you both.'

'She's not our mother.'

'I know.' The softness of her jumper brushed against his skin as she reached across him for the kettle switch. 'I'm sure she's only trying to look out for you.'

'Well, I wish she wouldn't. It's not helping.'

He had woken early, just as Zoe rolled out of bed and into the bathroom. On the mattress was a depression where her body had been, as if it were waiting for her return. Jamie shuffled over to her side of the bed, which was like crossing into another country where the air was fresher and sweeter. He inhaled the scent of her and slithered out from under the duvet, thinking about what they might do when she was finished in the shower.

In the bathroom, he lingered over his shave. The steamed-up mirror slowed his progress but he was distracted in any case by the shower curtain, which stuck to various parts of Zoe's body as she washed herself. And now here she was, in jeans and a jumper, making tea. He should have let the phone ring out.

'I know that look,' she said, as if reading his mind. 'I'll be out of here in five minutes. There's a lamb I need to look at in Horsehouse at nine.'

'As I said. Ruth, she's not helping.'

He didn't want to think of Caz when what was really bothering him, apart from his worries over the Pleyel, was that he hadn't even tried to have sex with Zoe since his catastrophic attempt at the stables. In their first month together, he would be turned on by the most random things; the birthmark on her ear, the fact that she would stop people in the street to pat their dogs, the way she sneezed, which convulsed her whole body and made a sound like a percussion cymbal. He kept all of this from her, of course, lest she should think him strange. Seeing her behind the shower curtain had rekindled that primeval urge, the thing he had always taken for granted but which had now become ephemerally precious. But who knew whether it would have led anywhere? The same thing could easily have happened again.

'In case you'd forgotten,' Zoe was saying, 'you've got work too. And make sure you tidy the kitchen before you go.'

She kissed him brusquely on the cheek and Jamie went back upstairs. He finished his shave and dressed in leisurely fashion. It was only when he had finished breakfast that he realised the time.

Before Jamie had hung up his coat, Jacob Archer called him into the office.

'You're late.'

Jamie shut the door.

'I know. I'm sorry. I was - '

'Don't make excuses,' said Archer. 'It's a sign of weakness.'

His voice was deep and rich with a hint of Welsh accent. It had the kind of range that reminded Jamie of his prep school headmaster and had the same ability to sound kindly and menacing in equal measures.

'Sit down, son. How are you doing?'

'I'm OK,' said Jamie. 'Thank you for asking.'

'I've been praying every night for your poor mother and father.' Archer's voice dropped to a whisper.

Unsure what to do with this piece of information, Jamie mumbled more thanks. Archer pulled a tissue from a man-size box, which sat on his desk next to a Newton's cradle, and pressed it to his eyes.

'Are you all right, Mr Archer?'

'Just a second,' he said, coughing. 'Frog in my throat.'

Jamie's gaze strayed to a guitar with a brightly-coloured shoulder strap, propped against the desk. It was well known that Archer liked a sing-song whenever there was an office party. *Kumbaya* was said to be a particular favourite. Happily, this was something that Jamie had yet to witness.

'Your father...' Archer cleared his throat again. 'Your father would have been proud of you. Staying at home moping never did anyone any good. You were right to get back on the horse.' Jamie tried not to grimace at the analogy. 'You know, I only took you on as a favour to Bernie. But I'm impressed with your attitude.'

'Thank you.' Jamie preferred to ignore the reminder of how he got the job.

'Good lad. Ludicrous about the funeral, though.' Archer said this as though it were a personal affront. 'You need to get them home to Jesus.'

'Yes, Mr Archer. We're hoping maybe by next month...'

'Anyway,' said Archer, as if someone had flicked a switch in his brain, 'I hear you took the Sidgwicks out yesterday.'

'Yes, but there was nothing suitable.'

'I'm not surprised,' said Archer. 'They're not serious buyers.'

'Actually,' said Jamie, 'they seemed pretty interested...' He tailed off, remembering that he had sabotaged a potential sale, but Archer was waving his observation away.

'No, son. We need to concentrate on the people who matter. The property market is on its knees. It's this recession. You know that, don't you?'

'Um, yes.'

'I'm going to give you a chance to show me what you're made of. There's a lady in reception, a Mrs Roe. I want you to butter her up. Sell her a house. She's got the money. She just needs persuading to part with it. Can you do that?'

'Yes, Mr Archer.' It seemed important to sound confident.

'Good. Let me know how you get on.'

Archer put on his glasses, picked up some papers and began to read. Guessing that the interview was over, Jamie headed for reception, picturing, even before he was through the door, a middle-aged lady in a tweed suit who would be demanding but scrupulously polite. Someone, in fact, like his mother.

The first thing he saw, sitting on the sofa, was a Great Dane. Next to the dog, and a good head smaller, was a woman. She was holding a compact mirror and applying scarlet lipstick in a manner that made him want to look away.

'Mrs Roe?'

The woman flipped the compact shut and unhurriedly stowed it in her handbag, a quilted affair with lots of gold chains. She glared up at him. Mrs Roe was probably not much younger than Esther had been. Her white-blonde hair was set in rigid curls and she had a mole above her lip. It would be too good if her first name turned out to be Marilyn.

'I'm Jamie. And who's this?' He approached the sofa with outstretched fingers.

'It's all right, Norman,' said Mrs Roe in a sugary voice. 'Mummy's here.'

The dog sniffed Jamie's hand and began to lick it, coating every inch of skin with Great Dane saliva. Jamie, immobilised by the dog's malodorous breath, was loath to retract his hand for fear of offending Norman and thereby Mrs Roe.

'Mr Archer tells me you're looking for a property.'

'A *property*?' She rolled her eyes as she mimicked him. The syrupy tone had vanished. 'Do you mean a house?'

'Yes,' said Jamie. 'A house. Do you have anything in mind?'

'A new one. It's for my son. He wants an ensuite bathroom and an open-plan kitchen.'

'Let me see what we have.'

As he rummaged through the filing cabinet, Mrs Roe fed meaty treats to Norman, the smell of which thoroughly outgunned the lavender pot-pourri on the coffee table. Hidden behind the reception desk, Maggie fanned the air and held her nose. Jamie pulled out details for a handful of houses, all of which Mrs Roe rejected for being either too small or too scruffy.

'Haven't got much, have you?' She stood up and paced around, peering at the enlarged photographs of long-sold houses on the walls. Norman stayed on the sofa, drooling into its leatherette cushions. Jamie thought for a moment. This woman was not the Sidgwicks and he'd been specifically instructed to sell her something. He could take her to the house he had refused to let them buy. It had both an ensuite bathroom *and* an open plan kitchen. He picked up the particulars, just as Mrs Roe leaned over the desk and plucked a piece of paper from the printer.

'This looks all right,' she said. 'Let's go.'

'Oh,' said Maggie. 'That one's only just come on the market. The owners want twenty-four hours' notice for viewings.'

'I don't care, said Mrs Roe. 'I want to see it. You,' she jabbed a finger at Jamie, 'sort it out. I'll wait.'

She returned to the sofa, where she took the dog's enormous head in her arms and covered his halitotic snout with kisses.

Thirty minutes later, Jamie was outside a new-build semi on a burgeoning estate, ringing the doorbell. It was answered by a woman with a harassed expression struggling to restrain a snarling Jack Russell. The dog had the ferocity of a much bigger animal and was clearly desperate to get to Norman. On the journey to the house, with Norman bestriding the back seat of the Fiesta in imperious flatulence, Mrs Roe had slapped down Jamie's suggestion that her dog might prefer to stay in the car during the viewing.

'Mrs Edwards? I'm Jamie from Archer's. Thank you for being so accommodating.'

'She wants to sell it, doesn't she?' Mrs Roe pushed past him over the threshold. The smaller dog yapped manically as Norman strolled into the hallway with a proprietorial air. Jamie gave the owner an apologetic smile and they trailed inside after Mrs Roe, who took a brief look around the ground floor and then marched up the stairs, presumably to inspect the all-important ensuite bathroom. In the garden, Jamie waited while Norman sniffed every shrub and cocked his leg across most of the lawn. The Jack Russell had been shut in the kitchen and was hurling itself at the glass outer door in deranged fashion.

'What about the garage?' shouted Mrs Roe from an upstairs window.

Jamie looked beyond Mrs Edwards to her terrier, mesmerised by the commitment with which it launched itself at the door, hitting the glass half-way up before sliding to the floor and beginning the process again, over and over.

'I'm afraid there isn't one,' called Mrs Edwards. 'But we do have off-street parking.'

'I made it clear,' said Mrs Roe. 'I want a garage.'

Jamie was about to point out that she had done no such thing, but she was already disappearing back into the house. Mrs Edwards dashed ahead of Jamie to wrestle the Jack Russell into her arms. The little dog looked as if it were about to combust. Jamie murmured his thanks and followed Mrs Roe, who was by now back downstairs, and the Great Dane out to the car where she fed Norman more of his noxious treats.

'Well,' she said, angling down the visor in the passenger seat. 'Some people have no idea how to train a dog.'

She pulled the lipstick from her handbag and loured at the mirror as she applied another layer. Jamie took the corners slowly, not wanting to be responsible for any mishaps.

'Put your foot down,' she said. 'I haven't got all day.'

When he got back to the office, only Charlotte was at the trainees' desk.

'Chris went on a viewing,' she said. 'Allegedly. I can't think who'd want to buy a house from that plonker.'

'He's not so bad,' said Jamie, loosening his tie.

'I bet he doesn't call you sweetheart.' She mimed flicking an elastic band towards Chris's empty workstation. 'Was that your client earlier? The woman with the massive dog?'

'Unfortunately,' said Jamie. 'Archer's given her to me as some kind of test.'

'I've got one of those, too. Mine's a bald, middle-aged lech who tries to pat my bum and thinks I don't notice. Makes me want to barf.' Charlotte put two fingers up to her open mouth.

Jamie's extension rang.

'Mr Fenton? This is Colin from Robinson's Piano Sales and Repairs. I'm afraid we've had a bit of a setback. It turns out our tools aren't specialised enough for your instrument. We're going to have to send it over to the Pleyel workshop in Paris.'

'But you said - '

'I know. It's just that we've never had one of these before. We can't afford to take any risks.' The reverence in the man's voice made it impossible for Jamie to protest, even though he was inwardly screaming no.

'It'll probably be a couple of months,' Colin continued, 'and the transport costs will add significantly to the bill, not to mention the repairs themselves.'

'Whatever,' said Jamie. In just a few seconds, the piano's return had been catapulted so far into the distance that he couldn't imagine the point at which he would need to hand over any money. On his trainee estate agent's salary, the price of the repair, however many thousands it would be, was just an incomputable number. He needed to check the limit on his credit card. Perhaps they would let him pay in instalments.

'On the plus side,' Colin said, 'it gives you a bit longer to, er, budget. And to make arrangements. We weren't sure whether you would have anywhere… anywhere to store it.'

fifteen

It was raining so hard on the way home that even on what Jamie's mother used to call demented setting, the windscreen wipers were struggling to cope. The glow of street-lamps fuzzed through the blurred windows of the car as it slushed through the high street in second gear. It was Friday night. There was no way the television was going to work in such weather. Crawling along in the wake of a bus, Jamie considered his chances of persuading Zoe to go out for a curry. The rain wouldn't put her off, but when he'd called at lunchtime she'd been about to perform emergency surgery on an aged dog belonging to a friend. She had sounded anxious. He hoped, for the dog's sake and hers, that it had been a success.

Jamie dived out of the car and into the house. It was chilly and unwelcoming; Zoe was strict about the heating not coming on before six. What he really wanted was a beer, but an audit of the fridge told him that they'd run out and he didn't feel like going out again just yet. Instead, he ran himself a bath with a liberal squirt of Zoe's pine-scented bubbles. Wary of leaving it unattended, he waited until it was full before fetching the portable stereo from the kitchen with his tape of Beethoven sonatas inside. Having been in the Fiesta on New Year's Eve, it was the only cassette he still owned and he'd been listening to it on repeat ever since.

On the shelf above the bath were a candle and a box of matches. Zoe liked to lie in the dark with just the candle for light. For ambience, she said. Perhaps if *he* created some ambience she might like to join him. The bath was rather narrow but that would make things more cosy. It would be the ideal start to the weekend.

Jamie pressed 'play' and the Allegro movement of Sonata Number One in F Minor burst through the speakers. Then, he picked up the matchbox and poked it open with one finger. He hadn't lit a match since before the fire, but there was plenty of water around should anything go wrong. Nothing in the bathroom was obviously flammable. The matches, with their bright purple tips, looked innocuous enough. Jamie held his breath and struck one, holding it to the wick of the candle until it flickered into life. Then, he blew out the match and ran it under the tap before dropping it into the sink. Everything was fine. Nothing bad had happened. He turned off the bathroom light and lowered himself into the water, playing along with the sonata on the edges of the bath.

Another two months to wait, but the Pleyel *would* be restored. Rather than having to play on his leg, or his desk, or the sides of a bath, for goodness' sake, he could have the real thing. It would take days, weeks, even, to play all of the pieces he had been missing. It would be glorious.

He could almost feel the cool, smooth ivory of the keys. He imagined the music now emanating from Zoe's stereo coming from his own fingers, filling the space. But which space would it fill? Zoe's house was out of the question; none of the rooms were anywhere near big enough. There were no other options. Just as he began to tense in frustration, the Prestissimo movement, with its extreme tempo and dynamics, moved on to the part that Jamie had been waiting for, the beautiful, lyrical section that was the polar opposite of everything that had gone before; a peaceful oasis in the roiling landscape of its surroundings. He sank further into the water and allowed himself to be soothed.

Downstairs, the front door banged. There was a brief pause before footsteps clumped up the bare wooden stairs.

'Enjoying yourself in there?'

In the open doorway, Zoe's outline cast a shadow in the weak flutter of candlelight. From the bath it was impossible to see her face. Jamie removed his feet from the taps and pushed himself up to sitting.

'It's been delayed,' he said. 'The piano. Can you believe it?'

The music stopped mid-bar, even though neither of them was anywhere near the stereo.

'That's a shame. You must be really disappointed.'

This wasn't the vibe that Jamie had been aiming for. 'No, it's fine. Listen, do you fancy getting in with me? There's plenty of room.'

To illustrate he pulled up his knees, leaving the tap-end free. The light, a naked bulb suspended from the ceiling, pinged into life as Zoe tugged on the cord by the door. Most of the bubbles had gone, leaving Jamie rather exposed.

He swished at the remaining froth in an attempt to cover himself.

The water had started to cool. In two strides Zoe was standing over him, still in her coat, not displaying any inclination to climb in.

'I asked you to tidy the kitchen.'

'How did the operation go? Is Bandit OK?'

'The kitchen. You said you'd tidy it.' Her mouth was a thin, cross line.

'Don't worry. I'll do it later. Why don't we go out? It's Friday night.'

'I don't want to go out. The mess will still be there when we get back.'

Jamie had never seen Zoe angry before. Normally, he could circumvent any potential friction by making her smile but now that he thought about it, his ability in that department had disappeared in recent months, too. This was turning into a conversation where being in the bath was a distinct disadvantage. He sprang up. Water clung to the hair on his body and slooshed over the side. As he stepped out, more dripped onto the floor.

'Jamie!' Zoe recoiled as though a wet dog were shaking itself in front of her. It was clear that she wasn't going to hand him his towel and he had to stoop to retrieve it from the pool of water on the floor.

'What's the matter?' He wrapped the sodden towel around himself and tucked it in around the waist.

'Isn't it obvious?'

'I didn't think you'd be so uptight about a few plates. I said I'd do them.'

She moved towards the loo. With a sigh she lowered the seat with her thumb and forefinger in the manner of someone handling toxic waste. As she sat, the anger seemed to seep out of her, leaving her looking dejected. She gripped her coat across her chest.

'It's not just the washing-up.'

'What, then?' He frowned, unable to think of another transgression he might have committed.

'This is my house,' she said. 'Even though I had to borrow from my parents and I'm mortgaged up to my neck. Christ knows it's no palace, but it's still mine.'

'I know that,' said Jamie cautiously, now standing in a puddle of cold water. On the windowsill the candle's flame trembled ineffectively, overwhelmed by the harshness of the overhead light. Zoe leaned back against the cistern, closed her eyes, then sat upright and opened them again.

'I'm really sorry,' she began, 'but we can't be together at the moment.'

Jamie opened his mouth to speak but she held up a hand for him to wait.

'You've been through the most enormous trauma, bigger than anyone should have to deal with. You're still grieving. You might not know it, but you are, and what we have isn't strong enough to withstand it. We don't know each other well enough, we haven't been together long enough. It's too much for both of us.'

'No,' said Jamie. 'That's not right. It's not - '

'We need to put things on hold. Just for now. You can stay here if you'd like to, as a friend. We could even make some ground rules so we both know where we stand. I want to help you, I really do, but not living as we have been.' Her eyes, when she raised them to look at him, were large and sad. Jamie took a step towards her but she stood up.

'I'll go and make up the spare bed.'

She walked past him and began unloading linen from the airing cupboard.

'Zoe, please. We haven't even talked about this. You can't just spring it on me. I'm not even dressed.'

With sheets and blankets laid across her forearms, she paused and turned.

'You're right.' She went into the spare room, put the linen on the bed and sat down next to it. 'I'll wait here until you're decent.'

She didn't even want to be in the same room as him while he dressed. Had she just banned nakedness between them? Jamie put on the clothes he'd intended to wear for the evening, after Zoe had shared a bath with him. What a stupid idea that had been. He wondered whether she had been planning to break up with him, or whether his untidiness had pushed her over the edge. What signs had he missed? She could even have made her decision before the fire and been waiting until she thought an acceptable period of time had elapsed. If that were the case, she had been in an impossible position, as, unknowingly, had he. Maybe she had merely been tolerating him all along, out of kindness. He remembered that tiny hiatus on New Year's Day, after he had asked if he could move in, and realised that he should have known then that this would happen. It was only a matter of when.

Without thinking, Jamie pressed the eject button on the stereo. The tape had been chewed up and hung out of the machine like spilled intestines. When Jamie tried to pull it loose, it stretched taut and snapped.

Zoe was standing by the window in the spare room.

'Just tell me,' said Jamie in a quiet voice, 'was any of this,' he gestured with his arms, hoping that she would know that he meant their relationship, not the tiny bedroom, 'real?'

'Of *course* it was. How could you think it wasn't?'

'Because you're breaking up with me without any warning whatsoever. I thought we just needed to get through this and then we could get back on track, you know, start to enjoy ourselves again.'

'It's not that easy, Jamie. You must know that.'

He wasn't sure if he *did* know. While he had managed, mainly, to blot out the image of the fire itself, that didn't stop him missing his parents, thinking of all the things that they could never do again together, wondering how in God's name they could just be *gone*. But that was where the passage of time was supposed to come in. It had been less than three months. He thought he was doing pretty well. He was twenty-two. It was miserable being miserable. All he wanted was to live normally again and he was trying his hardest.

'I don't know what to say, Zo. This isn't what I want. You've been amazing and I want you to believe me when I say that things can be better. Really soon.'

'They will be, I'm sure they will. But right now I think you should spend some time with your sister. You can do that and still stay here. She's the only one who really knows what it's like. You'll be able to help each other come to terms with everything. You say you don't want to talk to her, but that could be just what you need. That's not me trying to fob you off, it's what I think will be best for you. She can help you in ways that I can't, just because she's known you all your life. We only met four months ago.'

'Why does everyone think I should run to Caz when it's the last thing I want?

'It's not running. Don't you want to help her, too?'

'She doesn't need me. She's got Steve.'

Zoe rumpled her eyebrows in a question. She went to the bed and began to hook the corners of a fitted sheet over the mattress.

'Look at it this way,' she said. 'If you and I are going to have a proper relationship, do we really want it to have started now, in the middle of all of this? The most horrific thing has happened. It's more important for you to grieve, Jamie. Go through the process and you'll come out on the other side. I'll help you in any way I can, but you have to acknowledge it. After that, maybe we can start again.'

'Really?'

'Yes, really.'

Zoe smoothed the sheet and picked up a pillow case. She had made up her mind and he couldn't blame her, even though he violently disagreed. He couldn't hide at Zoe's anymore. Caz would make him confront what had happened, but he wouldn't let her force him; he would do it in his own time. And then, if Zoe was right, there was a chance that they could be together. He didn't like it, but he would have to go along with it. There was no choice.

'Stop,' he said.

She paused with a pillow halfway inside its case.

'I won't stay. Not like this. Let me phone Caz.'

sixteen

When Jamie called, Caz was trying to decide whether it was better that another week was over, or worse that there was a weekend looming that would need to be navigated. She was on the sofa again, stretched out with her legs up, watching a chat show without taking in who any of the guests were, or what they were saying. This was her nightly recovery period post-bedtime, when Ruby and Pearl were hyper even by their standards, no doubt made worse by all the additives that she was feeding them. Above her, coming from their bedroom, she could hear giggling and the odd thud. It was sufficiently noisy to make her anxious that they weren't sleeping, but not quite enough to warrant an intervention.

The role of housewife and mother, she had concluded, comprised largely of jobs that no-one else was willing to do. Food was the most obvious example: she hadn't the energy to cook properly anymore and nobody was complaining. The only person who could have taken issue with it was Steve, and he had been silent on the subject. In fact, he was as enthusiastic about some of her frozen specials as the girls were.

Until recently she had kept the house spotless; she'd even trained everyone to remove their shoes when they came in and leave them in a basket by the front door. But now, whenever she felt that she ought to do one of the mindless chores that she used to perform quite happily, like ironing or dusting, some unknown force would suck all of the impetus away and leave her wafting, ineffectually, around the house. Meanwhile, the dust was, quite literally, gathering. The ironing wasn't too bad, but that was only because she wasn't doing any laundry.

If she thought about it, she had an incredible amount of power. Whether they ate decent food, or whether they lived in a clean or dirty house, with clean or dirty clothes, was entirely in her gift. But was it really power, if no-one else wanted it? Power on its own was useless; it required momentum to drive it forward. And there was nothing powerful about neglect, or idleness, or indifference.

On a certain level, she was there for Ruby and Pearl. At the ages they were, their emotions weren't so complex that she couldn't manage them on autopilot. She found herself nodding and smiling, encouraging and sympathising, but in a glazed-over, disconnected way. Apart from the crying, neither of the girls appeared to have noticed any change in her behaviour. But how long would it be before Ruby started to look at her askance, or one of them would wake up and wonder what had happened to their pristine home, their freshly-laundered clothes, the homemade cakes after school?

Such was the state of affairs when the phone rang and Steve called from the kitchen, asking if she could answer it because he needed to look in the garage for his five-iron.

'Who was it?' Steve was standing in the doorway, swinging his golf club dangerously close to the rubber plant on the hall table.

'It was Jamie. He wants to come and stay. Something's happened with Zoe.'

'Yeah?'

'I told him it was fine. That's OK, isn't it?'

Steve rested the club against the wall and smiled. 'If that's what you want, it's good enough for me.'

Half an hour later, Jamie arrived in his funny turquoise car, lugging a rucksack over the doorstep. Steve showed him to the box room and she could hear him opening drawers and cupboards, putting things away. When he came downstairs, he bypassed Caz and went straight to the kitchen, where Steve gave him a beer. She followed, wanting to ask if he was all right, but Steve had already engaged him in a conversation about work and Jamie was telling a story about a nice elderly couple and a battle-axe who was impossible to please.

'Some people.' Steve was shaking his head. 'You should have seen the bloke whose house I rewired last week. He was nice as pie until I gave him my bill.'

'I know, mate,' said Jamie. 'Shocking.'

Caz listened, puzzled. Jamie wasn't presenting like someone who had lost his parents and split up with his girlfriend. He was smiling and laughing with Steve as though he had just popped in for a quick drink and a chat. Unlike her, he didn't look dishevelled, or tired, or miserable. She rubbed her thumb over the scars on her wrist, a recent habit which was causing them to throb again. It wasn't an unwelcome sensation; it seemed apt that something on the outside of her body should mirror what was on the inside.

'Jamie,' she said, interrupting the conversation, 'why have you broken up with Zoe?'

Steve took a tub of ice-cream out of the freezer and waved the scoop at Jamie.

'Yes, please. Any sprinkles?'

'Jamie,' Caz repeated.

'Chill out, Sis,' said Jamie. 'It's just temporary. Nothing to tell. I'll be back there in no time. Don't worry.'

'That's not why I'm asking,' said Caz. 'I thought you might be upset.'

Jamie took a bowl of ice-cream from Steve and began to attack it.

'Jesus, no,' he said between mouthfuls. 'But thanks for having me. I can't wait to see the girls tomorrow. It'll be great to get to know them better.'

When Caz got up the next morning, Steve had already left for golf. In the kitchen, Jamie was administering cereal. His very presence seemed to have doubled the noise factor; there was more energy in the room than she could cope with and she had to force herself not to turn around and go straight back to bed.

'Uncle Jamie!' Pearl squealed as he filled a bowl almost to the brim with Rice Krispies. 'That's way too much.'

'Is it? Sorry. That's what I'd have. I thought you'd want the same.'

'But I'm only five,' said Pearl.

'So you are. My mistake. What about you, Rubes? You're at least twenty-three. You must be able to handle a big bowlful.'

Ruby giggled. 'I'm seven. It's too much for me, too.'

'This is impressive,' said Caz. Jamie was fully dressed while she was still in pyjamas. He looked the opposite of her: awake, lively and engaged.

'Well, I might have been a bit... remiss on the domestic front when I was at Zoe's. I've decided to up my game.'

'Are you staying here forever?' said Pearl.

'Just for a while, until I get sick of you.'

'That's rude,' Pearl said.

'We'll get sick of you first,' said Ruby.

Caz waited until they had finished breakfast and sent them upstairs. After nearly ten sleepless hours in bed she was still exhausted; she needed caffeine but they had run out of coffee. It struck her that she had been wearing the same pyjamas for over a week; they were grubby and smelled ripe. Her hair felt greasy. She hauled herself to the sink and began to clear up.

'How are you, Jamie, really?'

'I'm fine. I told you.'

'You can't be. *I'm* not and I haven't just had a break-up.'

'You do look a bit under the weather.'

'I can't stop crying. I can't be bothered to do anything. I'm only just keeping it together, I miss them so much.' Caz looked at the clock on the wall, blinking to make out the time through the unwanted tears. 'Flip. It's tap in ten minutes. I need to get dressed. The girls need their shoes. They probably haven't put the right kit on.' The thought of sprinting upstairs, organising Ruby and Pearl and making herself presentable made her head hurt.

'Relax. I can go. Just tell me where it is and what to do and I'll take them.'

'No, no, it's OK. It's my job - '

'Caz, let me. I can manage. Go and have a rest or something. Presumably I can drop them off and pick them up later? They won't want me hanging around.'

She gave him instructions and then collapsed onto the sofa. This wasn't the right way round. They had taken Jamie in because he had nowhere to go, but he was acting as though nothing was wrong, whereas she couldn't even manage taking her daughters to a dancing class. As the elder sister - by four years - she should be taking charge. With herculean effort she propelled herself upstairs and into the shower, leaving Jamie to shepherd Ruby and Pearl to their tap lesson.

She had just finished dressing when she saw a dirty pickup truck pull up outside the house. Seconds later, the doorbell rang. What struck Caz first when she opened the door was that the young woman in front of her was wearing riding clothes; you didn't see those very often on their street. The second thing she noticed was her lustrous brown hair, tied up in a ponytail. Her own hair was still wet and lifeless; her hairdryer had packed up and she hadn't taken the trouble to replace it.

'Are you Caz?' the woman said. 'Sorry to disturb. I'm looking for Jamie. I wasn't sure which was the right house. I'm Zoe.'

It occurred to Caz that she should be angry with this person. She had, after all, just dumped her little brother at the worst imaginable time. Or she assumed that was what had happened. Jamie didn't seem upset, she had no idea what the circumstances had been, and Zoe's face looked more concerned than callous.

'Is he all right?' Zoe was saying. 'I wasn't sure I'd be welcome.'

'He seems OK. Why don't you come in? He'll be back shortly.'

Caz led Zoe into the kitchen. Her natural impulse was to be friendly but that carried with it the risk of being disloyal. Zoe had gone to the sink and was looking out of the kitchen window.

'Nice garden,' she said, even though the view was mainly of a swing and seesaw combo. 'Your daffodils are almost out.'

'Yes. Thanks.'

'This is a bit awkward,' Zoe said. 'I'm sorry. I didn't come to make things uncomfortable.'

'No offence,' said Caz, 'but why did you?'

Zoe produced a boxed cassette from her pocket and put it on the table. It was one of Jamie's beloved piano tapes: Chopin's Nocturnes.

'I found this. None of the others survived apart from the Beethoven and that broke yesterday so I thought he might want it. Especially now the piano's going to take longer.'

'Is it?'

'So he said yesterday.'

That's it, Caz thought. He must be upset not to have mentioned the Pleyel. She wondered where Jamie was thinking of storing it. He must know that they couldn't possibly have it at home. It wouldn't even fit through the door.

'I know the timing's awful,' Zoe said, 'and I feel dreadful about it. I'm hoping he'll talk to you. We hardly knew each other before the fire, not really. I thought it would be a good thing for him to be with his sister. You must both miss your parents massively and I just can't imagine what that's like. Oh, no, have I upset you? I'm so sorry. I didn't mean to do that. Oh, no...'

It was happening again; the uninvited tears whenever anyone said something sympathetic. They were relentless; not just a little welling-up that could be contained by a bit of blinking and a quick dab with a tissue but rivulets of them, coursing their inevitable channel down her face and dripping onto the nearest surface. Caz ripped off a piece of kitchen roll but before she could do anything with it, Zoe had crossed the room and was hugging her with a surprisingly strong grip.

'Shh,' she said. 'Take it easy.'

Caz relaxed into her, letting herself be held. Zoe seemed in no hurry to pull away, swaddling Caz in her horsey smell, leaving her no room to do anything apart from cry. It was curious; this was the most comforted she'd felt since the fire and yet Zoe was a total stranger. They were still standing in this way when Jamie wandered into the kitchen.

'Oh,' he said. 'Everything all right here?'

'Fine,' said Zoe, releasing Caz. 'I came to see you but ended up putting my big foot in it.'

'No, no,' Caz protested. 'It's me. I can't help it. It wasn't anything you did.'

Jamie looked from Caz to Zoe, and then at the cassette on the table.

'Oh, wow. I thought these were all gone.'

'We listened to it once in my car. You must have left it in there. I found it this morning.'

Caz, slightly recovered, wondered if she ought to leave, but Jamie's large frame was taking up most of the doorway and neither of them was looking at her; their attention was focused entirely on each other.

'You didn't have to go,' said Zoe.

'I did, really. Just tell me: was it anything to do with the stables?'

'No! Absolutely not.'

'The stables? What happened at the stables?' said Caz, sensing that this might be her only opportunity to find out what had gone wrong between them.

'Nothing,' said Jamie and Zoe, almost at the same time. Jamie moved to the table and picked up the cassette. He took it out of its box and studied the label. Zoe checked her watch.

'Listen,' she said, 'I'd better be going. Minty's not going to ride himself. Take care, Jamie. You too, Caz.'

For the rest of the weekend, Jamie mainly kept out of Caz's way. He seemed happy to play with the children; in fact he was just as boisterous as they were. On Sunday afternoon she tried to join in with a game of Frustration but within minutes her attention had wandered and everyone complained that she wasn't keeping up.

And then, on Monday, Jamie came home from work with some news. The coroner's office had granted leave to hold a funeral for their parents and authorised the papers that would be needed for probate.

seventeen

A week later, Jamie and Caz left Chestnut Drive on foot. It was a raw, early spring day; the ubiquitous north-easterly that had been buffeting the town all winter had still not abated. Carried on the wind was a late blast of snow which was too wet to settle but cold enough to have numbed their faces by the time they reached the high street, where the offices of Walker and Steadman, their parents' solicitors, resided above Barclays Bank.

'This doesn't feel right,' Caz said as they walked up the stairs. 'We haven't even had the funeral.' It was all in reverse. Without having said a proper goodbye to their parents, they had been invited to learn how they were to benefit from their deaths. She didn't care about the money and she couldn't believe that Jamie did, either. Perhaps it would be nice for the girls to have a little something for when they wanted to buy a car, or needed a deposit for a house, but otherwise there was nothing they needed. All she wanted was the thing she couldn't have. No amount of money could help with that.

Caz's memory of Geoffrey Walker's office was drawn from her only previous visit, yet it was clearer in her mind than most of the things that had happened only last week. She had been about sixteen and for some reason had witnessed the finalising of the sale of Bernie's ball-bearings factory. Then, the office had been like something out of Dickens; crepuscular, wood panelling, leather. In the intervening years, someone had given the place a facelift.

There was no polished wood in sight; only dusky pink walls and corporate grey carpet. Even the solicitor's desk was a rectangular lump of filing-cabinet metal. Walker himself, an anachronism in his three-piece suit, sat hunched in a glaring pool of up-and-down lighting.

'Ignore all this,' he said, gesturing at the decor. 'Nothing to do with me. Interior designers, can you believe?' He shook his head sadly. 'At a *solicitors.*'

Jamie murmured something sympathetic which Caz couldn't make out. Walker didn't respond but reached for a cut-glass decanter, incongruous on the post-industrial desk.

'Whisky?'

They both declined.

'I don't want to pre-empt anything, but you might be glad of it.'

Caz and Jamie looked at each other. Surely this was just a formality. There wasn't supposed to be anything controversial. Walker poured himself a couple of fingers and stared into his glass. With a defeated sigh, he opened a cardboard file that rested on the desk in front of him.

'I'm not sure how best to say this.'

The room felt suddenly cold. Caz wished they hadn't come. Whatever Walker was about to say, she didn't want to hear it. He took a slug of the whisky and pressed his lips together.

'As you know,' he began, 'your father became a Lloyd's Name after he sold the factory.'

'I remember something about it,' said Jamie, 'but I was too young to understand what it was.'

'He was so proud,' said Caz. 'It was like he'd finally been accepted into the old boys' club.' She remembered being determined to show her father how unimpressed she was, how pathetic she found his social-climbing. At that age she already hated her parents for sending her to boarding school when she thought they should be abolished and was mortified with shame by pretty much everything Bernie stood for. It was the residue of those feelings that had resurfaced on New Year's Eve in a calamitous case of bad timing.

On the other side of the desk, Walker was watching her, waiting for her to refocus on the conversation.

'Sorry,' she said. 'Carry on.'

'Yes,' said Walker. 'Well. What he wouldn't have told you was that late last year, his syndicate was obliterated by a long-tailed asbestosis claim, running to tens of millions.'

'A what?' Caz said.

'Can we have that in English?' said Jamie.

'There are risks with these things,' said Walker, 'and the group of underwriters your father joined was highly exposed. Maybe they should have seen it coming. All the signs were there, apparently, not that I would know. It was all to do with sickness claims against big businesses in the United States, claims that the syndicate assumed would never be made.'

Caz was trying to concentrate. She heard all of the words but couldn't process what they meant. Jamie was frowning, the fingers of his right hand working furiously on his thigh.

'Hang on,' he said. 'They were betting against employees suing the companies that made them ill?'

'Basically. It's complicated.'

'Jesus.'

'Oh, Lord,' said Caz. 'That's dreadful.'

'Your father was horrified when he found out. For what it's worth, he had no idea what he was putting his money into. Someone convinced him that it was a dead cert and he didn't ask any questions.'

'So the claimants were properly compensated?' said Jamie.

'Yes. But your father's personal fortune was wiped out.'

'Completely?' Jamie, gripping the plastic arms of his chair, swivelled to face Caz. 'Surely he didn't put *everything* into this...' He cast around the room as though he expected to find the right word written on one of the walls. '..this... *thing*.'

'I'm afraid so.'

'What about Mum?' said Caz. 'She had means of her own.' This would be the silver lining. Their father might have made money, but their mother had inherited plenty, too.

Walker was shaking his head again. 'She did. It all went in there. I'm sorry.'

'How did we not know about this?' said Jamie. 'Why didn't anyone warn us?'

Caz tried to recall anything that might have suggested that their parents were broke. Lunch on New Year's Eve had been the same as usual; rib of beef, good claret. No sign of scrimping. Bernie must have been covering. He could have been in denial, or working like crazy behind the scenes to make some money back. But their mother… Esther regarded money in the same way she saw bodily functions; grubby, but necessary. Never to be discussed. Even so, if she had been aware that Bernie had effectively gambled everything away, she would have shown some sign of being angry with him. On that last day, Esther had treated Bernie with her normal brand of patient affection. No, Caz was positive that she couldn't have known.

'The small piece of good news,' Walker was saying, 'is that there are some funds to cover funeral costs. And the building and contents will be covered by insurance, after the inquest. Bernie normally left this sort of thing to me. I'd be happy to carry on dealing with it if that helps.'

Caz glanced at Jamie. He had that small-boy look again. She couldn't imagine either of them tackling the paperwork involved in the insurance claims for The Hall.

'And then there's the Pleyel,' said Walker. 'I understand it was taken away for repair just before the fire. Because the damage happened separately, the insurers will settle on that straightaway. Incidentally, your mother requested that the piano be left to you, Jamie.'

Caz grabbed Jamie's hand and squeezed it. 'That's something,' she said. 'It wouldn't be any use to me. But what about Mrs Cole? And Willie?'

'Our housekeeper and gardener,' said Jamie. 'They've been with us for years.'

'I know.' Geoffrey Walker spread his hands on the table. 'Hopefully they'll understand. It's a most regrettable set of circumstances.'

When they emerged from Walker's office, the snow had stopped and the high street was suffused with pale yellow light. It was slushy underfoot and Caz almost slipped as she stepped off the kerb to cross the road.

'Steady.' Jamie took her arm and they waited for an animal feed truck to pass. 'You know what,' he said once they were on the other side, 'I need a pint.' The Bay Horse was directly in front of them. 'Do you mind?'

It was lunchtime. A couple of grizzled men in boiler suits and flat caps stood at the bar. Otherwise, the pub was empty. Caz gravitated towards a table by the fire and sat down on a low stool, waiting for the warmth to envelop her.

'What are you drinking?' Jamie said.

'I'll have…' On the mirrored shelves behind the bar, the bottles were mainly whisky and rum. Their honeyed tones caught the light enticingly. As the mood in Geoffrey Walker's office darkened, Caz had begun to envy the lawyer the viscous amber liquid that sparkled in his crystal glass. If only it were possible to drink whisky on a freezing and miserable day and not suffer the consequences.

'I'll have a ginger ale, please,' she said. It was the right colour, at least.

When Jamie came back with the drinks, he slurped the top off his pint and sighed. She knew that feeling; it was always the first sip that made everything feel better. It wasn't the same with ginger ale.

'I honestly never gave their money a thought,' he said.

'Me neither.'

'I mean, it's not like I ever had plans for it or anything, although I suppose I must have assumed there'd *be* an inheritance.'

'But we didn't know they were going to die.' Caz pulled out a tissue. 'God, these bloody tears! Mum and Dad should have had years yet.'

'Exactly. I don't care about it, even now. But to have lost it all, without *saying* anything…'

'Yeah.'

'And what about Ruth, and Willie? There's nothing we can do for them. Bloody *hell!*'

'It's awful.' Caz blew her nose.

They sipped their drinks in silence.

'Poor Mum,' said Caz. 'I'm sure she didn't know.'

'Do you think he was sparing her, or too chicken to fess up?'

'Does it matter? I suppose at least she wouldn't have been worrying about it, at the, at the…' Her words tailed off in a kind of wail which came from somewhere inside her and was loud enough to make the two farm workers at the bar turn and stare in irritation. For them, she guessed, female emotion had no place in the pub. That probably extended to females, full stop.

Jamie was finishing his pint.

'Oh, Dad,' he said. 'You really weren't as perfect as you thought, were you?'

eighteen

Another Saturday and Jamie found himself standing in the courtyard of The Hall. Although he was more of a crazy golf man than an eighteen-holer, he'd felt obliged to accept Steve's invitation to play a round at the local course. Having lived in his brother-in-law's box room for weeks now, it would have been rude to refuse. And so here he was, hoping to find his father's clubs in what Bernie used to rather grandly called the sports store, which was actually a lean-to adjoining Ruth Cole's cottage.

Jamie closed his eyes and inhaled. The air was cool and fresh but with a note of slurry. His father always grumbled about living downwind of a pig farm, but to Jamie it smelled of home. It was the first thing he used to notice when he came back from school. In fact, if he looked only left, nothing much had changed since then. The cottage and the sports store, along with the other outbuildings, were still intact. But if you turned and looked right, well, that was different.

Surveying the yards of ebonised debris, he thought of finding a stick and poking around to see whether he could find something, anything, that hadn't been incinerated. But the ash was too dense; more likely he would come across some dreadful, half-burned reminder of what had been lost. Instead, he kicked at a charred brick and stared out towards the Cleveland Hills.

For the moment, there was nothing to be done about the house. A loss adjuster was being called in. No-one seemed to know how long the process would take. What Jamie did know was that this chilling, gaping hole in the middle of the village could not be left indefinitely. The house would have to be rebuilt. But when that would be was anyone's guess.

In the sports store Jamie found, amongst other things, cricket stumps, a croquet set and a vinyl golf bag in garish eighties colours. He rooted through it, inexpertly examining the clubs. The driver had a Sooty head-cover which he remembered giving his father one Christmas. Sooty, of all things. He laughed through his nose at the irony. Then he dragged the bag out of the store and slung it into the boot of the Fiesta.

'Jamie Fenton, were you leaving without saying hello?' Ruth Cole stood on the doorstep of her cottage, her arms folded across her chest.

''Course not. Just picking up Dad's clubs first. I'm playing golf with Steve. It's supposed to be something to look forward to after the funeral.'

'Hmm.' She narrowed her eyes at him. 'That's nice. Come in, then. The kettle's not long boiled.'

As he approached, she stayed in the doorway, blocking his path.

'Let me look at you.' She reached up and took him gently by the chin, peering into his eyes. 'Are you all right, pet lamb?'

Jamie wished people would stop asking him that. Sympathy was the absolute worst thing, guaranteed to drag you down even if you were feeling reasonably chipper and were hoping to stay that way. He swatted away her hand and forced a smile.

'I could murder a cup of tea.'

Inside, Jamie claimed an armchair in the sitting room while Ruth pottered in the kitchen. In just over a week he would be back in the village for the funeral. He and Caz had agreed that it was best to get it over with. To his slight surprise, she had shown no more enthusiasm for organising the service than he had. When the vicar and the Rotary Club chairman offered to take care of the details, they had both agreed without hesitation. Apart from questioning the choice of organist and politely declining to give a reading, Jamie had played no part in the decision-making. To his shame, he didn't even know which hymns they would be singing.

Ruth reappeared with a tea-tray and set it down on the coffee table.

'How are the arrangements coming along?'

'Oh, fine. It's all in hand.'

'I hope you're having *Jerusalem*.'

'Er, yes. Absolutely.' He made a mental note to check with Reverend Dalby. 'And how are you, Mrs C? It must be horrible, looking at *that* all the time.' Jamie nodded towards the window where the ruins lurked. 'I wish we could find you somewhere else…' Ruth didn't know about Bernie's financial implosion and he was unsure how much to tell her. '..but there isn't as much money as we thought. Dad, well... We'll have to wait till everything's sorted out. Hopefully the insurance will help. After the inquest.'

'It's all right, love, I've got my pension. It's just the house, having it right outside…' She took a long sip from her mug. 'I still haven't spoken to Caroline. I think she's avoiding me.'

'Really? I'm sure she isn't.'

'Is she drinking?'

Jamie had been about to ask if there were any biscuits but this made him look up.

'No. There's never any booze in the house apart from Steve's beer. Why are you asking me that?'

Ruth rubbed at a patch of dust on the coffee table exposed by a sudden shaft of sunlight from the window.

'Jamie.' She gave him her serious face, the one she always used when he was in trouble with his parents and looked for her to take his side, which she never did. 'I know you didn't look out for her, like I asked. As I said, it's bothering me. I'm worried she might go back to her… old ways.'

'She won't. She's a grown woman,' said Jamie. 'She's got kids and everything.'

'That's not the point.'

'I might as well tell you,' said Jamie, seeing the opportunity to drop in some news that he hadn't mentioned when he rang Ruth to tell her about the funeral, 'I'm living with Caz now. Zoe kicked me out.'

'What? How could she do such a thing? You've been orphaned.'

'I'm twenty-two,' he said, 'and it wasn't quite like that.'

'Silly girl,' said Ruth in a softer tone. Now that Jamie was the perceived injured party, he could do no wrong. 'It's her loss.'

'Not really,' said Jamie. 'It was probably fair enough. Oh, and the Pleyel's been delayed. Not that I'd be able to play it, anyway. The only place to put a piano at Caz's house would be the garden.'

Muttering to himself over Ruth Cole and the way she was fussing over them, Jamie got back into the car. Caz was OK. A little teary, which was awkward at times, and she had definitely slackened off on the fresh food obsession, although that annoying shoe basket was still by the front door.

No, Caz was fine. She had Steve. He, on the other hand, didn't have Zoe. She phoned him often enough, but only when he was in the office and she was at the surgery, which kept their conversations brief and business-like. There had been no more visits to Caz's house. When he suggested meeting in the pub, she told him it wasn't a good idea. They should wait until he was ready, she said. Maybe Jamie had missed the conversation where they'd agreed that he wasn't.

If ever he rang her at home, she didn't answer. An impartial observer might conclude that Zoe was moving on. But the fact that she hadn't cut ties with him completely must mean something. She had left the door open for them, after all.

And then there was the piano. It was nearly four months since he'd played. He looked at his fingers, again working imaginary phrases on the steering wheel. Flaccid and blundering from lack of proper practice, they felt to have the muscle and agility of ten sausages.

Jamie flicked on the indicator to turn into the new estate where Caz and Steve lived and waited for the sense of deflation to kick in as he drove past the half-finished houses. His home had stood for two centuries and been destroyed overnight. This was the reverse: an attempt to create a community from scratch in just a few months.

In work mode, Jamie would have described Caz's house as an executive home in a sought-after location and it was true that the street was just a few minutes' walk from the primary school. The house had a block-paved drive, a downstairs loo and fitted wardrobes. But the walls were thin; at night he could hear every cough and whisper from the other bedrooms. Jamie was grateful but not comfortable.

It would help if he could fit into their family routine, but it was so far removed from everything he knew. He was still learning about when he was allowed to play rambunctious games with Ruby and Pearl and when they had to be left alone to do their reading. Steve went to work early every morning, but by the time Jamie got back in the evening he would be sitting at the kitchen table, reading his newspaper, lager in hand. He liked fry-ups, Madness and golf. Steve's enthusiasm and positivity were inexhaustible. He had the look of a man who had achieved that rare thing in life: contentment.

Above it all floated Caz. The rebellious teenager was long gone. Since having Ruby so young, then marrying Steve and having Pearl, Caz had managed to mould herself into a completely different role. The angry, grungy older sister he remembered now wore clothes from Marks and Spencer and sensible shoes. They were a generation, not four years, apart. As he turned off the ignition and went into the house, Jamie wondered what she had done with her collection of Clash records.

nineteen

If there were a grimmer setting for a funeral, Jamie couldn't think of one. Despite the occasion, it should have been a reasonably uplifting scene; stone church, village green, cricket square, a smattering of Georgian cottages. A tableau of rural England. The sky was a confident spring blue. Wind blasted flat the banks of daffodils. But beyond it all, in clear sight, lay the black and abandoned ruins of The Hall.

From the back seat of the funeral director's limousine, Jamie and Caz watched the mourners arrive. Extended family, friends, colleagues; some smart, others more agriculturally dressed, all with their heads down, filing into church. Then, when there surely could have been no more room inside, what Bernie would have called the smart brigade appeared. A black city car pulled up and deposited the foreign secretary, who was also the local MP, by the lych-gate. The politician glanced briefly at the wreckage of The Hall and averted his eyes. It was the same instinct that Jamie had seen in others as they arrived; the one that makes you look away when you drive past a crash on the motorway but not before you've taken a quick peek and felt ashamed for doing so.

The time that had passed since the fire should have taken away some of the rawness, but that took no account of geography. There was no way of putting distance between the house and the church. All of these people, these respecters and well-wishers, would be sitting in their pews in the awful knowledge that they were just yards from where Bernie and Esther had perished.

From behind the glass screen, the driver gave a brief nod.

'Ready?' said Jamie. He wasn't ready for any of it. Caz was crying silently. She had a tissue in her hand and was pulling it to pieces. When they got out, the seat was covered in little flecks of white.

They waited on the muddy verge by the gate. Caz brushed at the long, black coat which she said had been a gift from their mother. Apart from the bits of tissue, it made her look dignified.

'Funny, really,' she told him before they left the house. 'I could never think when I was going to wear it.' It was the only thing she had said all morning.

With inappropriate ease, the pallbearers hoisted the two coffins out of the hearses and onto their shoulders. Jamie thought they might have *tried* to give the impression that there was anything of substance inside them. He glanced at Caz but she was staring straight ahead. Then, the pallbearers appeared to discover the sensitivity to walk slowly, as though they *were* carrying heavy weight, and set off towards the church. Jamie and Caz followed. Caz was like a sleepwalker; present and moving but utterly unengaged.

Inside it was jam-packed. As the funeral party entered, the congregational murmur fell silent, exposing the ineptitude of the organist. People were rammed into the pews and down the sides of the church, peering from behind pillars. The atmosphere was hot and chaotic, pregnant with unexpressed emotion. At the back, people stood five deep, fanning themselves with their hymn books even though there was no heating. The church was a seething mass of forbearance; everyone faced forwards in ostentatious rectitude. Zoe, wedged into the back row on his left, gave Jamie a sad little smile which was exactly the kind of thing that could scupper his composure. He ploughed on, clinging to Caz, matching her metronomic plodding. Ruth Cole was half-way down; Willie, the gardener, by her side. Jamie zoned in on the stained-glass window above the altar, trying to focus on the familiar image of St George slaying the dragon, not wanting anyone else to catch his eye.

As they trudged behind the coffins, the organ fired off one dissonant chord after another. Jamie ground his teeth and wished he had been more assertive. Jean, the village organist, the vicar had argued, had never missed a funeral in fifty years and would have been mortally offended were she not required at this one. He glared at Reverend Dalby, wondering whether his sombre expression was in response to the occasion itself or to the bastardisation of Elgar's Nimrod.

When they reached the front of the church, Jamie and Caz squeezed into the first pew where Steve and the girls were already seated. The coffins were placed next to each other on stands in front of the altar; Esther's with an ornate floral arrangement, Bernie's left plain. Ruby and Pearl stared at them. Caz stared too, but glassily and without focus. A sickly scent emanated from the flowers.

During *Abide with Me*, the distraction of the ham-fisted organ-playing began to fade. It was just a mess of notes to be endured. Jamie held up his hymn book; not for the words, he knew those, but to shield his face. The letters washed over the page. As the hymn ended, inwardly cursing, he tugged a crumpled handkerchief from his pocket and wiped his eyes. There was an expectant silence. From behind came the clack of leather-soled shoes on flags. Timothy Harding-Page, coiffed and patrician, strode up the aisle, stopped to bow his head and mounted the lectern.

'As chairman of the Rotary Club, I knew Bernie and Esther Fenton for many years,' he began. 'Bernie was a loving husband, a devoted father, and a fine businessman…' Jamie shot a look at Caz but she didn't appear to be listening. '..Esther was his tireless companion, both in life and in his charitable work…'

Steve put an arm around Ruby. Pearl burrowed into Caz. On her other side, Jamie felt the soft thickness of his sister's cashmere coat against the polyester of his sleeve. The high-street suit was a world away from the kind of tailoring his father considered a basic human right. He was almost glad his parents couldn't see him. He fidgeted on the shallow pew.

'And now I must move on,' Harding-Page was saying, 'to Bernie and Esther's first meeting. It was at the 1964 Christmas drinks reception for the National Farmers' Union, Lower Wensleydale division. Not, you might think, the most romantic of settings…' He paused for polite laughter.

'..but it was, nonetheless, the legendary occasion where Bernie Fenton won the affection of the Honourable Esther

Forrester. And how did he achieve this? By persuading her to eat a sausage roll.'

Proper laughter erupted. It was slightly too loud; the laughter of relief, a release valve for the contained emotion.

'I can't say whether she ever ate another one, but there we are.'

Harding-Page looked across the congregation with satisfaction, but the levity was short-lived. When Reverend Dalby took over for the prayers, Jamie tuned out again, staring at the coffins and the false neatness of their polished wood and gleaming handles; a parcelling up of the horrific, made to look acceptable. He wanted to wind forward in time, to be out of the church and at the burial, to not have to look at these boxes any more. But then they would be gone and his parents would forever exist only as a headstone in a windy churchyard. The vicar had stopped speaking. Again there was a pause.

'And now, Jamie, I believe you are going to read a poem?'

This was definitely *not* what they had agreed. He nudged Caz and she looked at him impassively. Other people were looking, too. He gripped the hymn book, his shoulders so tense that his neck was aching.

The vicar was nodding at him, throwing his eyes towards the lectern. The only part of Jamie's body that could move was his head and he was shaking it slowly in response. The moment stretched on; the nodding and shaking like a mime act in slow motion.

'Ah,' said the reverend, finally, 'perhaps I should…'

There was a shuffling from the other side of the church. The foreign secretary was sidling along his pew to get to the aisle. At the altar, he, too, bowed his head. He spoke briefly to the vicar and was handed a sheet of paper. Then he stepped up to the lectern.

'Do not stand at my grave and weep.

I am not there. I do not sleep…'

Jamie closed his eyes. The foreign secretary's voice was rich; fluent and practised. Jamie's shoulders dropped. The muscles unfurled. When the poem was finished, he looked up and gave the man a grateful smile.

For *Jerusalem,* Jean the organist really let rip; the introduction was so butchered as to be almost unrecognisable. But the congregation rallied, perhaps fired up by the intervention of the foreign secretary, perhaps bolstered by the knowledge that the service was coming to a close. Voices roared above the organ, beating it into submission. Jean, not to be vanquished, bided her time until the end of the second verse before delivering a final, dreadful flourish.

And then they were outside for the burial that wasn't really a burial of anything.

When it was done, Jamie stood at the graveside, accepting condolences, alternating stiff handshakes and brief, fierce embraces. He thanked the vicar while Caz stood, mute. Timothy Harding-Page gave his shoulder a manly pat. The foreign secretary came to stand alongside him as he gazed into the double plot into which, moments before, he and Caz had crumbled handfuls of soil. Behind the graves, two mounds of earth were piled up in readiness.

'I'm sorry for your loss, Jamie. You too, Caroline.'

'Thank you for saving me in there,' said Jamie.

'Something told me the vicar landed you right in it.'

'That's true,' said Jamie.

'Typical clergy. Never listen to a bloody word anyone says.'

He marched off to his waiting car. Jamie felt the wind whip through the inadequate fabric of his suit and turned back towards the village green.

The person he most wanted to speak to was Zoe. It had been weeks since he moved out. The act itself wasn't much of an event; Caz only lived on the other side of their tiny town and all he had was a bag of clothes. But regardless of what Zoe had said about the brittle nature of their relationship, she was the one who had been there in the immediate aftermath of the fire.

He *could* have spoken to her about it if he'd needed to. It would have been a conversation on his own terms; he would have had control over it and Zoe would have been fine with that, whereas Caz was always on the brink of tears; not just today but every day. If they began to discuss the fire, he felt that the floodgates would open and he would be fully exposed to her grief while he was trying so hard to contain his own. So far their conversations had stayed on a level but at some point, he was sure, she would want to make him her confidante. The thought of it made him want to lock himself in her box room and stay there.

Jamie spotted Zoe standing beneath a yew tree towards the back of the churchyard. She was wearing the dress from the party which she had managed to tone down with thick tights and a dark winter coat. Jamie had to duck under some low-hanging branches to reach her and she stepped forward to hug him.

'I couldn't go without saying hi,' she said. 'It must have been tough in there.'

'Yeah,' said Jamie. 'That organist should be reported for crimes against funerals.'

'That's not what I meant.' She pulled away but held onto his elbows, her arms outstretched. 'Although even *I* could tell she was useless.'

'And you're tone deaf.'

'Exactly.'

They allowed each other a small smile. The wind had dropped and Jamie felt the sun on his back through the filter of the tree.

'Come for a drink?' He looked over his shoulder towards the King's Head. There was to be no formal wake on the grounds of there being nowhere suitable to hold one. Instead, Jamie and Caz had put some money behind the bar for anyone who wanted to toast their parents' memory. When he turned again, Zoe was shaking her head.

'I've got to get back to work,' she said. 'Stay strong. I'll call you.'

He kissed her cheek and left her under the tree as he walked back across the churchyard, through the lych-gate and onto the village green. It had been agreed that they would all go for one drink, as Steve put it, 'to show their faces'. As Jamie crossed the road, he could see Steve and Caz ahead with Ruby and Pearl close behind them.

Not feeling the need to hurry, Jamie moved slowly along the little lane past the quoits pitch. When he reached Steve's van, which was parked just outside the King's Head, he lingered for a moment. He wished he had Zoe with him but he knew he had no right to expect that. On the painted wooden sign above the door, a poodle-haired Charles II smirked at him in encouragement.

'Right, you old roisterer,' Jamie said as he picked up his pace and went into the pub.

twenty

Ruby and Pearl, kneeling at the coffee table, were eating fish-finger sandwiches and watching a video of a St Bernard dog causing mayhem in a series of increasingly farcical episodes. Still in her black dress and tights, Caz watched without interest as the dog upended a lunch table and everything on it. Steve was on the phone.

'A few of the lads from five-a-side are going for a curry,' he said when he came in from the hall, 'but I've said I won't go.'

'Why not? You might as well. I won't be any company.'

He leaned over the back of the sofa so that his face was near to hers, clearly torn between doing what he imagined was the right thing and going out for some light relief. Caz had stopped short of saying that it barely mattered whether he was there or not. He wouldn't want to *talk* to her. The best she could hope for was a warm body next to hers on the sofa.

'Are you sure? I won't be late.'

When Steve had gone, she lay back on the cushions. The girls were engrossed in the film, laughing like drains at the dog's antics as if it were a day like any other.

The past few hours were mostly a blur. Some unidentifiable force had propelled her out of the house that morning, into church and out again, to the burial and then the King's Head and home, without really taking part in anything. She had smiled at people's kindness without letting it touch her. And now her parents were buried. There was no more waiting to say goodbye; the day of the funeral was no longer there to be dreaded. She had an urge that wasn't unlike wanting to celebrate. Perhaps it was relief that it was over. That was when she remembered the two bottles of wine hidden in the kitchen.

'*Beethoven*. My favourite.' Jamie had come in and was squatting on the floor next to the girls in his dark suit. There was redness around his eyes. 'Have you got to the bit with the evil vet yet?'

'Shush, Uncle Jamie,' said Ruby, 'you'll spoil it.'

Caz jumped up from the sofa. The heaviness in her limbs had gone. They were no longer leaden but almost weightless. A quick rummage at the back of the freezer produced a home-made chilli, long-since forgotten in favour of convenience food. She put it in the microwave on defrost. Then, she went to her bedroom and put on a shirt and jeans. When Jamie came into the kitchen she was standing at the stove, stirring the chilli and boiling rice.

'You did well to get home so quickly. I couldn't seem to get away. Everybody wanted to talk about Dad. The video's finished, by the way.' He sat down and began flipping through Steve's newspaper. The front page was all about the upcoming general election. Everybody seemed to think that Labour was going to win. Caz broke off from stirring to retrieve one of the bottles from the back of the drawer. Jamie looked up in surprise as she handed it to him.

'Can you open this while I put the girls to bed?'

'I'm not sure - '

'It's my house,' said Caz. 'I can do what I want.'

'But you don't drink.'

'Oh,' she said. 'I'm not worried about that any more. It was ages ago. I was practically a child. This is only wine, anyway. And after the day we've had…'

She set two glasses on the table and went upstairs. When Ruby and Pearl were ready for bed she tried again with *The Lion, the Witch and the Wardrobe.* By the end of the second chapter, Pearl was already asleep.

'Was it all right to laugh at *Beethoven*?' Ruby said as Caz turned off the lamp.

'Of course, sweetie. Why wouldn't it be?'

'We were supposed to be sad because of the funeral but Daddy got us a funny film.'

'He was trying to cheer everyone up.'

'You didn't laugh.'

'No, well, *Beethoven*'s not really my thing.'

'I'll tell Daddy.' Ruby wriggled down under the duvet. 'You get to choose next time.'

'That sounds like a deal. Night night, angel.'

Before the tears could start again, Caz smoothed Ruby's hair and left the bedroom. Back in the kitchen, she went to the hob to check on the chilli. 'Hurry up. I'm dying of thirst here.'

Jamie shrugged and poured the wine. 'Your life, I suppose.'

Of course it was her bloody life. What a stupid thing to say. After eight years of abstinence, surely she deserved a treat today, of all days. She held the glass up to the light; the chardonnay was a deep, unctuous yellow.

'I've been looking forward to this. Cheers.'

She closed her eyes and took a sip; it was unexpectedly sweet, not harsh like spirits but more like melted butter. It should probably have been chilled, but she didn't care. The taste was a vindication. There couldn't be anything wrong in what she was doing when it felt so good.

Over supper, Jamie told her about the people he had seen and spoken to in the pub. The cricket club, whose pavilion had been destroyed by the fire, was going to name the new one after their father, once it was rebuilt. They drank more wine. Caz ate the last mouthful of her chilli and put down her fork.

'How did you find today?'

'Difficult,' Jamie admitted. 'I'm angry with myself for crying in front of all those people. It was pathetic.'

'No, it wasn't,' said Caz. 'That's what you're supposed to do at funerals.' She waited for Jamie to respond, but instead he got up to help himself to seconds. 'Oh, come on, J, talk to me.'

'About what?'

'About the fire, obviously.' She picked up the wine bottle. There was nothing left. Jamie offered to go to the off-licence for another. He looked troubled; no doubt reluctant to encourage her drinking but at the same time desperate to end the conversation.

'No need.' Caz reached into the laundry cupboard and pulled out the second bottle from behind a box of detergent.

'Jesus,' said Jamie. 'When did you get so devious?'

'Don't say anything to Steve,' she said. 'He'll only worry.'

Caz leaned back in her chair as Jamie opened the bottle and poured. Her face was hot and probably flushed but she was more relaxed than she had been in ages. She felt bold, energised, alive. Jamie stacked the plates and took them to the sink.

'Why won't you talk to me?' she said.

'It's not just you. I haven't spoken to anyone. I don't want to.' He came back to the table and sat down again. 'I'm worried that if I start, you know, letting it all out, I might never stop. And I've got to stay functioning. I've got work.'

'Is that why you stopped taking my calls?'

'Yeah,' said Jamie. 'Sorry about that. It doesn't mean I don't miss them.'

'I can't bear it. They should still be here. My foundations have gone. There's a great big hole where they used to be. Sometimes I think I might be falling into it.' Jamie was watching her closely, his expression unreadable. 'Do you feel like that?'

'No, that's not it,' he said. 'I'm just sad. It's not complicated. There isn't anything else to say.' He spread his hands wide and shrugged. 'And anyway, it's not as if we were ever encouraged to talk about stuff. That wasn't their style. You just got on with it. Old school. Isn't that what drove you mad about them?'

'God, yes.' In her head her voice sounded loud. The vestiges of local accent she'd picked up from Steve were all but gone and now she sounded exactly like their mother. It must have been the wine. 'Heaven help us if we showed our feelings about anything.' Caz gave an unamused laugh and stared into her glass. 'They didn't exactly equip us to cope, did they?'

Jamie sat silent, watching.

'Oh, I'm lucky, I know I am,' she continued. 'I've got Steve, the girls, all of this.' She waved her hand around in the air. The gesture seemed rather grand given the size of the room.

'I guess you've had to put on a brave face,' said Jamie.

'Well, I've done a rubbish job with *that.*' Caz drained her glass. 'What I mean is, they're my life. Even before what happened, they're what kept me straight. I mustn't…'

'Maybe give the wine a rest, now.' Jamie reached over for her glass but she didn't want to give it up and snatched it in towards her chest.

'No. I need to let my hair down. I can polish my halo in the morning.' That struck her as funny and she started to laugh until she realised that Jamie was not laughing with her. What was she thinking? They had just buried their parents.

'I wish we hadn't rowed with them that day,' she said instead. Seeing Jamie sobbing at the funeral made her wonder whether part of what he was feeling was guilt. He had, after all, been the one to storm out.

Jamie said nothing for a long time and was looking down at the table.

'It wasn't your fault,' he said eventually in the quietest of voices. 'I'm such a hypocrite, crying in church like a little boy when the last thing I said to them was so offensive. I didn't think it mattered; I thought I'd just be able to apologise later. In fact that's not even true. All I cared about was how angry I was with Dad. And poor Mum, what had she done to deserve having her family lunch ruined like that? Now they're gone and I can't make it up to them.'

Caz knew she should say something to make Jamie feel better, but first she wanted more wine. She emptied the last of it into her glass and grasped it to her mouth, sipping while she tried to come up with a suitable response. The clear-sightedness she had felt when she had that first mouthful had deserted her. Her instinct was to agree that in the light of events, calling their father an arsehole wasn't Jamie's finest moment. She could be angry that their parents' final day had turned out so badly. But saying any of that wasn't going to help. She didn't really think she was angry anyway but it was hard to tell *what* she was. With a clumsy hand she patted Jamie's arm, harder than she intended so that it was more like a slap. When she tried to rest her elbow on the table, she missed.

'It's all right,' she said, finally. 'He lost all the money, didn't he? Without telling anyone. Maybe you were right.'

'Is that supposed to make me feel better?'

'No, no, well, yes. It's quite funny really, isn't it? He was always the big I Am, when all the while he'd bankrupted us...'

She started laughing again. Jamie looked appalled. The front door thudded closed.

'What's all this?' Steve's gaze was trained on the empty bottles.

'We were just catching up,' said Jamie.

Steve looked at his watch. 'We've got golf in the morning, mate. You might want to call it a night.'

'Oh,' said Jamie. 'Yes, you're right. I'll go up.'

Caz managed to stop laughing and then couldn't remember what had been amusing in the first place. They had been talking about their parents; surely there wasn't anything funny about that? She gave Steve a quick kiss on the cheek and scuttled up to bed. For the first time since the fire she had no recollection of him coming upstairs.

twenty-one

Somewhere between the first and the thirteenth, the fretting drizzle had graduated to full-on rain. Steve, head-to-toe in waterproofs, looked up at the sky, unwrapped another stick of Wrigley's spearmint and folded it into his mouth. Jamie shivered in his sweatshirt and chinos as wind flapped across the course. His brother-in-law selected a club and stood over the ball, shimmying his hips in the way that professionals did on television. He struck the ball cleanly and it traced a perfect arc through the air. Both men watched as it dropped, bounced three times on the fairway and stopped within easy reach of the green.

'Nice shot,' said Jamie.

He wiped water from the face of his watch with an index finger. They'd been out for three and a half hours and this was entirely because Jamie was incapable of hitting a ball in a straight line. He couldn't blame last night's wine; he was just useless. In any case, Caz had drunk most of it. Maybe Ruth Cole understood more than he thought. Caz's drinking was greedy, almost desperate. By the time

Steve came in, the conversation had taken a bizarre turn. Perhaps it was just as well that he arrived when he did.

Now down to the last two of his father's golf balls, Jamie planted a tee in the sodden turf. It wasn't that he minded being beaten; he was always suspicious of men who were bad losers, but he was bored, wet, and finding it hard to see the merits of the game. It was, after all, just a matter of hitting a small object with a bit of metal on the end of a long stick. Not that he would have said so to Steve but really, golf didn't measure up favourably to the piano. The comparison only reminded him how desperately he wanted to play. Might he have already forgotten how?

Rain dripped into his eyes and down the back of his neck as he stepped up to the tee. He shook water out of his hair, wriggled his grip into an approximation of the one Steve had shown him, and swung. The ball grubbed along the ground for twenty yards or so and dribbled off down a bank to the side of the fairway into the rough. Steve slapped an arm around his shoulders.

'Never mind, J,' he said, chewing. 'It's practice, that's all.'

They set off in search of the ball. Jamie jabbed the handle of his three-iron into the furze while Steve poked around half-heartedly with the toe of his golf shoe.

'Don't worry about it,' he said, when it became clear that the ball was lost to the undergrowth forever. 'I've got plenty.'

Steve strode back up the hill, reached into his pocket and dropped a ball onto the middle of the fairway.

'There you go,' he said. 'Take your time.'

Jamie hazarded another swing and shanked the ball, high and right, back towards the previous hole.

'That's it,' he said. 'I'm hopeless at this. You carry on. I'll just walk with you.'

They trudged along in silence until they reached Steve's ball. He dug around in his bag, inspected several clubs, then stopped and turned to Jamie. Fat splodges of rain splashed from the peak of Steve's baseball cap as he yanked it down further over his forehead.

'You know,' he began, 'sometimes I wake up in the morning and I think I'm the luckiest man alive. Things have been rough lately but when I look at your sister I still think to myself, wow, how did I ever manage that?' He shook his head in disbelief at his own good fortune, drew out a club and chipped the ball onto the green.

The fairway pooled with water. Jamie sploshed through the puddles in his work shoes. It was obvious from the little things that Steve did for Caz that he worshipped her: the cups of tea he took to her in bed, the unsolicited baths he ran for her, the way his first concern was always for her wellbeing, even before that of his daughters. Observing this at close quarters was an education; Jamie would never have done any of those things for Zoe, not because he wouldn't have wanted to, but because he would never have thought of them. He wondered how Steve knew. Was it something you were taught, did you pick it up by osmosis, or was it knowledge you possessed all along that just needed to be teased out and zapped into life?

Steve and Caz first met during the summer holidays when Jamie was fifteen. Bernie was raging because the electricity kept tripping off. In exasperation, Jamie's mother heaved the yellow pages out of the cupboard in the hall and called the electrician who was smart enough to name his company A1 Electrics.

When Steve arrived, Jamie was on the forecourt throwing a tennis ball for Juno and Caz was settling baby Ruby into the pushchair. Their father stuck his head out of a first-floor window.

'Stop that, Jamie, for Christ's sake. That dog's messing up my gravel.' He took in the elderly van with its hand-painted sign. 'Oh, Lord,' he said and disappeared back into the house. 'Esther!'

Caz was setting off with the buggy as Steve got out of the van. Strongly built, but not tall, he had a hairstyle that would now be called a mullet. He peered into the pushchair and said something that made Caz laugh. Bernie appeared at the front door.

'In you come, son. I'm paying you to fix the electrics, not flirt with my daughter.'

Six months later, the house had been completely rewired and Steve and Caz were married.

The ball had landed about three feet from the hole. Jamie propped Bernie's bag on its stand and went to pull out the flag.

'Thanks, mate.' Steve holed the ball with one hand, hooked it out with the end of his putter and marked the par on his scorecard with a stubby pencil. They turned right at an arrow pointing to the fourteenth.

'It's not good for her,' he said. 'Wine, that is. Or any alcohol, really.'

The rain began to ease as they walked to the next tee. Despite Ruth's suspicions, Jamie had never seen the adult Caz drinking, apart from that single brandy on the night of the fire. The previous evening could easily have been a one-off. OK, so the wine bottles, stashed in places where Steve would never look, were unexpected. Perhaps she had been storing them up, knowing that the day of the funeral would be difficult. On reflection, to an erstwhile student, the amount she drank, and the rapacity with which she went about it, were not all that remarkable.

'I know,' he said. 'You don't have to worry. I had most of it. Her tolerance must be pretty low.'

'That's what I was hoping,' said Steve. He pulled out his driver. 'Here we go again.'

One Christmas, Jamie came home from school and walked into a war zone. He'd thought it odd that Ruth Cole had been sent to collect him from the station by taxi; she didn't drive and normally one of his parents would make sure they were around to pick him up. When they got back to the house, the shouting could be heard from the courtyard. They tiptoed through the side door and into the kitchen.

'Maybe stay here for a bit, eh, love?' said Ruth.

But Jamie wanted to see what was going on. He crept through the hall to the drawing room. Caz, just home from her first term at university, was on the sofa nearest the fire, her knees drawn up to her chin, crying uncontrollably. She looked dishevelled and unwell. Bernie stood in front of the fire next to the fender, red-faced and flustered. His mother, who had been standing by the piano, took a couple of steps towards him.

'Hello, darling. We're just having a chat with your sister. Why don't you see if Mrs Cole will make you a sandwich?'

'Let him stay,' growled his father. 'He might learn something.'

The puppy, Juno, roused herself from the dog-basket. Jamie knelt on the floor and stroked her ears. His mother went to sit on the sofa opposite Caz.

'Leave the bloody dog,' said Bernie. 'Go and sit next to your mother.'

Jamie did as he was told.

'Right,' said Bernie. 'This is what's going to happen.' He moved nearer to Caz and stood over her, glowering. 'Look at me, for the love of God!'

She lifted her chin but stared past him into the fire.

'First, I'm going to have a word with your tutor, see if they'll let you make up all the coursework you've missed.' Caz was shaking her head. 'Second, you are going to sort yourself out. No more booze, no cigarettes, no more of... whatever else it is you've been taking. And third, you're going to get yourself back to Bristol in January and stay there until you've got that bloody degree. Look at me when I'm talking to you!'

But Caz had buried her face in her knees and was sobbing in great hoarse gulps. 'I can't,' she managed.

'Don't be ridiculous,' said Bernie. 'Of course you can.'

'I can't!'

'You can and you will.'

Finally, she raised her head and looked straight at him. 'I can't,' she said, more evenly. 'I can't because I'm pregnant.'

Jamie wondered how much Steve knew about Caz before Ruby was born. When they got together, she was already sober. The baby's father was never mentioned, or at least not in front of Jamie. No-one ever referred to Caz as an addict, but he could remember how she was changed by the pregnancy. With the baby growing inside her, Caz began her metamorphosis into a younger version of the woman she was now. When Steve stepped out of his van that day at The Hall, the transformation was already complete. The orange dye she'd put in her hair at Bristol had grown out to its natural brown, most of the piercings had been removed and her pasty skin had regained some colour. Before her pregnancy, Caz had the saggy, skinny frame of someone who took little fresh air or exercise. By the time she met Steve, she had been athleticised by long walks, pushing the buggy along country lanes. At the same time, she developed a gentle demeanour that neither Jamie nor his parents had seen before. This new persona had been honed and polished ever since, erasing every trace of her former self. Until last night.

'Do you think she's OK?' Jamie said now to Steve, who had hit a rare bad shot and was circling his ball which lay deep in the rough.

'How do you mean?' Steve's tone was sharp. He selected a pitching wedge and guided the ball back onto the fairway.

'Don't you think she's a bit, well, zoned out?'

'She's grand,' said Steve, striding forwards. 'She misses your mum and dad but she's managing. Don't rock the boat, mate, will you?'

twenty-two

The first thing that Caz did when she awoke was to drink the pint of water that someone, presumably Steve, had put on her bedside table. There was something familiar about the pulsating behind her left eye that she couldn't place. As was her habit, she tried to remember what she might have been thinking about whilst she was awake during the night, but couldn't come up with anything. She must have slept all the way through and yet she didn't feel refreshed. There was an alien, sour taste in her mouth.

Caz dug her nails into the scars on her left arm and scratched, hard. She had drunk nearly two bottles of wine, hardly leaving any for Jamie, and it had been delicious. It was also very wrong. Although she broke her promise to herself on New Year's Eve when she drank the brandy, that could be written off as an aberration. This, however, was not just one drink. Every time she was half-way down her glass she was already thinking about the next. The only reason she stopped was because there was none left. She was disgusting, weak, loathsome. Unfit.

Expecting to see Steve, she turned over in bed but it was Ruby lying there, wide awake but absolutely still, watching her. Steve and Jamie must have left for the golf course. She started up, suddenly panicked that she might have been snoring, or giving off wine fumes, but Ruby looked unperturbed.

'I'm hungry,' she said. 'Daddy didn't have time to make breakfast.'

'OK, sweetie,' she said. 'Why don't you go and get some cereal? I'll be there in a minute.'

'Can we have eggs?'

'Can we have eggs, *please*,' Caz auto-corrected. 'If we've got any.'

She managed to make the girls scrambled eggs on toast and got them to their dancing class only ten minutes late. Tap lessons were held at the community centre which was next to the primary school, just off the high street. Jamie, since his arrival, had taken charge of the Saturday morning logistics. Typical that he wouldn't be there on the day she really needed him. Unable to face the teacher or any of the other mothers, she sent Ruby and Pearl into class on their own. For a few minutes after they had gone, she sat in the car with the radio on, trying to assess her reacquaintance with alcohol and what impact it might have had.

The two bottles had been in the house for weeks and she hadn't touched them. Perhaps the funeral could excuse her behaviour; allowances could surely be made after a day like that? The hangover which, of course, was the cause of the pain behind her left eye, wasn't too bad. She'd definitely had worse. This was only wine, after all. The children were fine; she had given them a good breakfast and shepherded them to dancing lessons as normal. All that had happened was that she'd spent a Friday evening with her brother, having a few glasses over dinner. It had been fun and Christ knew there hadn't been much of that lately. And she had slept. Apart from a headache, the consequences were minimal. Nothing to be concerned about. Having intended to conclude that the episode was never to be repeated, she was, in fact, convincing herself of the opposite.

Before she had chance to think any more, Caz got out of the car and walked to the off-licence on the corner, where she bought another bottle of chardonnay. After that she drove home.

There was an hour and half before Ruby and Pearl would need to be collected. She wouldn't have to interact with anyone at the dance class; she could simply wait outside until the girls emerged. Steve and Jamie would be ages. As she unscrewed the bottle, she wondered whether Steve would mention her drinking when he got home, or choose to ignore it. He didn't normally try to tell her what to do or comment on her behaviour, although she had never given him reason to. She stood for a few minutes at the kitchen window, her hip resting against the worktop, watching bluetits flutter in and out of a holly bush. Then, she filled her glass and took a mouthful.

On the windowsill was a photograph of their wedding, a modest affair held not, to her mother's disappointment, at the village church but at the registry office in Ripon. Ruby, aged eighteen months, had stayed at home with Ruth Cole. In the photo, Caz, in a cream knee-length dress and holding a posy of paperwhites, smiled toothily at the camera, whereas Steve's face was in profile. If she ever needed to remind herself of Steve's affection (she rarely did), this picture told her what she needed to know. He was staring at her with an expression that could only be described as adoring.

Steve was an angel, really. Shortly after that day, they agreed never to tell Ruby that he wasn't her real father. Steve wanted to treat both girls exactly the same and argued that the only way he could do that was if Ruby believed that she was his. Unsure who Ruby's father actually was, Caz could hardly refuse. The truth was that it could have been one of several.

After escaping from both her convent school and her parents' unwavering scrutiny, Caz arrived at university like an unexploded bomb. Her history of art course was an irrelevance. The term was a haze of fuggy student rooms and unwashed bed linen, spirits, tobacco and weed, pubic hair and bodily secretions. It was vile but glorious and she careered towards Christmas at breakneck speed, utterly out of control. It was terrifying and thrilling and she loved it.

Caz replenished her glass, hardly tasting the wine now as she remembered how, before long, everything imploded. There was that agonising scene at The Hall where she confessed to the pregnancy, followed by the indignity of dropping out of university and becoming a teenage mother. All that whilst being denied the chaos and fun that she had loved so much. Other people partied as hard as she did without sabotaging every aspect of their lives. At the time, she didn't think to ask herself why. Perhaps she was too preoccupied by cleaning up her act in readiness for motherhood. Bernie and Esther had tentatively suggested adoption, or the 'other option', as they put it, but she was determined. She wanted to be a mother. Doing it at nineteen wasn't ideal, but a suspicion began to take hold in her mind that the baby had been sent to save her from herself.

She poured the last of the wine into her glass and put the empty bottle in her handbag to dispose of later. If Ruby *had* been sent to save her, then it followed that Steve, arriving at The Hall that day to fix the electrics, had been sent to rescue them both. She'd been brought up to believe that teenage mothers were the lowest of the low. According to Bernie they were the scourge of society, wilfully and inconveniently breeding for the prize of a council flat. But Steve was not put off by Ruby. He was kind, earnest and very keen. He was also good-looking, hard-working and, as it turned out, great in bed.

Caz yawned, noting with interest that for the past hour or so she had been thinking of things other than the fire. That must be the wine. Another plus. She sat down at the table and laid her head on her folded arms.

She was woken by the phone.

'Mrs Hopkins? This is Miss Janet. Ruby and Pearl are a bit concerned that you haven't come to pick them up.'

'Oh! I'm so sorry. I'll be there in a jiffy.'

'I'd appreciate that. The class finished twenty minutes ago.'

Caz dashed upstairs to brush her teeth. The space behind her right eye was now pounding in accompaniment to the left. Driving would be irresponsible; she would have to go on foot and that would take at least ten minutes. Drinking a bottle of wine mid-morning while your primary school-age children were at a dance lesson was also irresponsible. Not only that, but it was not what normal people did. Yet she felt reasonably lucid, apart from the headache. It had been pleasant to reminisce. If she hadn't fallen asleep, it would have been fine. In the kitchen drawer she found a packet of Steve's chewing gum and unwrapped it as she left the house.

'Mummy! Where were you?' said Pearl.

Miss Janet, unsmiling, held out their coats.

'Time ran away with me, sweetheart, that's all.' Caz tried to read the teacher's expression. Could toothpaste and chewing gum hide the smell of wine?

When they got home, Ruby asked if they could bake butterfly cakes and Pearl wanted to play hide and seek. Caz had the energy for neither. Instead, she suggested a game of snap, which seemed to mollify them. They sat in a little triangle on the floor to play.

'Snap!' Pearl shouted almost immediately.

'That's not a snap,' said Ruby.

'Yes it is.'

'No it's not. It's a six and a nine.'

'It's not snap this time, sweetie,' said Caz. 'Keep going.'

They began again.

'Snap!' This time it was a king and a jack.

'Stupid,' said Ruby.

'Ruby!' said Caz.

'She's too little,' said Ruby. 'She can't do it.'

'I can!'

'You can't!'

'Listen,' said Caz, 'we're going to start again and we're only going to call out if it's an exact match. OK, Pearly?'

She nodded.

'Right. Let's go.'

They took turns and went around and around. They were almost out of cards when Caz laid a queen, Pearl laid another, and Ruby shouted, 'Snap!' She swept up all of the cards from the floor. Pearl began to cry.

'It's not fair,' she said. 'I wasn't allowed to say snap and now Ruby's won.'

Caz was about to explain how Ruby's snap was the first legitimate one but the pain was like a dagger stabbing her eyes from behind. The central heating had come on and she was sweating beneath her jumper. She mumbled something about having a lie down and crawled onto the sofa. Ruby switched on the television. Minutes later, Jamie and Steve came back from golf. Jamie was soaked through and smelled of wet dogs.

'I've got a splitting headache,' Caz murmured, as Steve stooped to kiss her forehead.

'You stay there,' he said. 'I'll sort tea.'

That evening, when the girls were in bed and Jamie had gone to his room, Steve brought his beer to the sofa and Caz nestled against him while he described their game. It was difficult to concentrate on what he was saying; something about an eagle on the sixteenth, but she was content to let him talk, not having anything to contribute to the conversation and hoping he didn't ask about her day. Telling him that she had drunk a bottle of chardonnay alone would definitely spoil the mood.

'..and then we came home,' he was saying. 'And how are you, babe? How's that headache?'

He rubbed her temples; although the pain was elsewhere, the sensation was not disagreeable and she closed her eyes. His fingers traced the edges of her face, down to her jawline, then he leaned over and kissed her. If she still smelled of wine, Steve clearly wasn't aware. It struck her that they hadn't properly kissed, or been intimate with each other at all, since the fire. She hadn't noticed until now, hadn't missed it, but Steve must have. If he had found it difficult that she had become distant, he was hiding it well. With Jamie around, they had a lot less privacy, but he hadn't complained. As she began to kiss him back, he sat up sharply.

'I've been thinking. Maybe we could all do with a holiday. How about we go away somewhere at May half-term, just the four of us. What do you reckon?'

'Oh,' said Caz. 'I hadn't thought about it.'

'Yeah,' Steve said, 'we could go camping in the Lake District, or, or Filey. The girls would love that.'

'What about Jamie?' said Caz. 'We can't just leave him.'

'He's a big boy.' Steve put a hand on her waist and began to kiss her again. 'We might even get a bit of time on our own, you never know.'

In a tent? she wanted to say. *In a tent in the middle of a field with two children?* The idea was laughable but it seemed mean to dampen his enthusiasm, which had extended into the present moment, manifestly in the hand which was now stroking her ribs.

'Go on, what do you say?'

'I don't know.' She kissed him, wanting to show willing, but the idea of going away held no appeal. It was so much easier to stay at home. Her mouth felt dry and unresponsive. What she really wanted was a glass of wine, just one, to get her moving again.

'Oh, OK. Maybe you're not ready for that yet.' He ran the back of a finger down her side. 'Maybe we're fine here.' Caz listened for a note of disappointment in his voice but couldn't detect one. She knew he wouldn't push her but also that he was prepared to content himself with what he thought was about to happen. The trouble was, she didn't have the energy for that, either. She took hold of his hand.

'I'm sorry,' she said. 'I'm just really, really tired and my head still hurts.'

For a split-second Steve looked downcast, then he gave his head a little shake and blinked.

'You don't have to be sorry,' he said. 'There's no rush. Why don't you go on up, if you're knackered? I'll just watch the FA Cup highlights for a bit.' He reached for the remote control.

Upstairs, Caz lay in bed, listening to the roar of an unknown football crowd. It hadn't been a lie to say that she was tired, but that was different to being sleepy. Her limbs were no longer light; her head itself felt like an enlarged football that had been repeatedly kicked. She missed her parents viscerally; their absence was a darkness that squatted over her, pressing her down. Only the wine had allowed her to slip briefly free of the grief, to drift upwards again and focus on what was happening around her. She needed to function. It seemed she couldn't do it alone.

twenty-three

Chris returned from the bar with a pint for himself, a gin and tonic for Charlotte and a lemonade for Jamie. Between his teeth he held two packets of crisps. The packaging was the violent shade of pink that signalled prawn cocktail. Jamie was quite partial to crisps, but Chris was in a different league. It wasn't even half-time and this was their fourth packet. Charlotte had bailed out after the second.

They were in the Hornblower Inn, acknowledged in the office to be Ripon's worst pub but also the one most beloved by the Archer's staff. Its unique selling point, of which the landlord was movingly proud, was a connection to a Norwegian satellite channel. Being illegal, this didn't feature on the chalk board outside on the street which advertised cask ales and darts. But for those in the know, it allowed televised access to First Division football on Saturday afternoons.

Chris sat down and dropped the crisps into his lap without taking his eyes off the TV. He handed the gin to Charlotte before giving the lemonade and one of the bags to Jamie, who discreetly wiped it on his sleeve.

The pub wasn't full but was crowded in one corner, where a decrepit television sat on a shelf, sprouting wires. So far there had been no goals. Most of the drinkers who clustered on chairs beneath the screen were around Jamie's age, garrulous from lager and from frustration at the lack of a score. Jamie sat politely watching the action. As far as he could see, Charlotte was the only woman in the pub.

Although he wasn't interested in the football, Jamie had several reasons for being present.

Firstly, as all of his mates were now working in London, Chris and Charlotte from work were the nearest thing he had to friends. His relationship with Chris was more of a regular trading of insults interspersed with solid drinking, but still. Charlotte, he suspected, was only there because she had nowhere else to be. Her dislike for football was only slightly more vocal than her dislike of Chris. They made a strange triumvirate.

Secondly, he wanted to avoid another Saturday loitering at Caz's house. While he enjoyed playing with his nieces, there was something in the discrepancy between Steve's relentless jollity and Caz's trance-like state that made him uncomfortable.

Thirdly, with only a few hours before he at last had a date with Zoe, he needed a distraction. His usual recourse in such a situation would have been the piano. The Pleyel, he'd been told, was now back from France but there was still more work to do on the frame, and in any case he'd made no progress on finding a home for it. So desperate was Jamie to be occupied that he'd even agreed to drive Chris home once the match was over. At least he might be able to amuse Zoe later by recounting how he had volunteered to go to the Blower for a couple of hours of ritualised boredom.

'So,' Chris was saying, 'aren't you going to congratulate me?'

'I doubt it,' said Charlotte.

'For what?' Jamie said.

'Haven't you heard? I've had a sale.'

Chris lit a Silk Cut and sat back for the effect of his words to sink in, trying to cross an ankle over his opposite knee. There wasn't room and he kicked the back of the chair in front, spilling lager on his jeans. The chair's occupant turned round and swore. Chris put his feet back on the floor and took a defiant pull on what was left of his drink. Charlotte sniggered into her gin and tonic.

Jamie *hadn't* heard. 'Congratulations,' he said. 'Was it one of those wendy houses down at the nursery school?'

'No,' said Charlotte. 'He was playing Monopoly and got confused.'

'Tossers.' Chris puffed on the cigarette amicably, making no effort to blow the smoke away. 'Seriously, though. D'you want to know what I sold?'

'Not especially,' said Jamie.

'Nope,' said Charlotte.

'That three-bedder in the cul-de-sac near the rugby club. Couldn't have come at a better time.'

It was the house with subsidence, the one that Jamie had refused to sell to Mr and Mrs Sidgwick and considered trying to flog to Mrs Roe. Perhaps the survey would derail this sale, too. Chris was holding his cigarette in the air, about to make a point.

'You know your trouble, both of you?' he said. 'You're not pushy enough. These people don't know what they want. You have to tell them. If I were you I'd be careful. Archer's on the prowl. Last in, first out and all that.'

Before either Jamie or Charlotte could respond, Chris leapt up and started chanting, 'Leeds, Leeds, Leeds!' On the screen, a ball sailed into the net in a slow-motion replay.

'Bloody hell,' Charlotte sighed. 'Why, oh why, am I here?'

'You beauty!' Chris shook a clenched fist in the air and then jumped up and down until the television demanded his further attention.

'I'll get more drinks,' Jamie muttered and slid out of his seat.

'And crisps!'

'I'll give you a hand,' said Charlotte.

At the bar, Jamie ordered refills while Charlotte disappeared to the ladies'. That she had dressed up for the pub, in a navy blazer and white jeans, Jamie found rather endearing. More or less everyone else apart from Jamie himself was wearing a Leeds United shirt.

'Seriously,' she said when she came back with freshly applied lipstick, 'if he ever suggests this again, talk me out of it.'

'If you don't mind me asking, why *did* you come? I didn't think this would be your scene.' Jamie looked over to where Chris was sitting, absorbed by the action, sipping from an empty pint glass.

'Oh, I don't know. Desperation? Masochism? A flawed sense of humour?' She poured tonic from a small bottle into her gin, which was graced with neither lime nor ice. 'Chris described it as team-building. I should have known better.'

Jamie held out his hand to receive change. 'That'll teach you.'

'You're not kidding.' She put the empty bottle on the bar. 'I can't believe he's sold a house, the spawny bastard.'

'I don't think *you* need to worry,' said Jamie. 'Haven't you got some big deal lined up on Whitegates Grove?'

'I wish! That was just for Chris's benefit. I didn't think he'd buy it. I'm obviously a better actress than I thought.'

Another cheer went up from behind. The Leeds fans were on their feet, their arms spread in the air as though they deserved personal credit for the goal. Chris turned to the bar, arms still aloft, and gave Jamie a questioning look. Jamie held up the drinks in response.

'I'm not into football, either.' Jamie had to shout to make himself heard. 'This will make me sound like a complete dork but I'd rather be playing the piano.'

'So why aren't you?'

'Well, that requires an actual instrument, which I have, but it's in the workshop being repaired. And when it's ready, which will be soon, I still won't be able to play because I'm living at my sister's and there's no space for it.'

'YESSSS!' Another goal. Three nil to Leeds.

'OOH! AAH! CAN-TONA! OOH-AH-CAN-TONA!'

Chris had forgotten about the beer and was standing on his chair, chanting and pointing rhythmically at the television.

'Listen,' said Charlotte. 'Do you want to go somewhere else? I don't suppose he'll miss us as long as he gets his drink and his crisps.'

'I can't,' said Jamie. 'I promised Chris a lift home.'

'Fair enough.' Charlotte drank the gin in one and pulled a face. 'Then I'll leave you to it. Thanks for the drink. I'm off to watch some drying paint.'

twenty-four

When Jamie, freshly shaved and aftershaved, came downstairs, Ruby and Pearl were watching Noel's House Party. Caz, with wine in hand, was staring without focus at the screen, while Steve monitored her glass with a troubled expression.

'You look nice, Uncle Jamie,' said Ruby, 'doesn't he, Mummy?'

'Handsome,' said Caz absently.

'Babe magnet,' said Steve.

'What's a babe magnet?' Pearl said. 'Ooh! It's Mr Blobby!'

Jamie closed the door on the unrelenting hilarity at Crinkly Bottom and wandered out through Caz and Steve's front garden, noting for the first time the plantless terracotta pots, the empty bird-feeder and the straggling laurel hedge. Caz, who had been so proud of her gardening skills, acquired since motherhood, had clearly been letting things slide.

The housing estate formed the outer limits of the town and from farmland beyond, the reedy bleat of lambs carried on the early evening air. On Chestnut Drive, mothers gathered toy prams from newly-mown front lawns. Fathers tinkered under car bonnets. At one house, birthday cards were lined up on the sill of the front window, showing their white cardboard backs to the street. Jamie walked down the hill, past the more established bungalows and semis where tulips in borders enlivened concrete driveways and pebble-dashed walls.

Neither the news that Chris had sold a house, nor the unsettled feeling he had about Caz could detract from his optimism regarding his date with Zoe. Even the physical ache he now had for the Pleyel could be put aside for the next few hours. He was going to convince her that he had become fully house-broken. If he could call Caz and Steve as witnesses, they would testify that he now washed up after himself, did his own laundry and had even produced an edible supper once or twice. During weeks of phone calls, he had been assuring Zoe that he was functioning fully without her and that, yes, he was loving sharing a house with his sister and her family. Then, finally, she had agreed to meet him for dinner.

On the high street he turned left. Paolo's was right at the end, just before the park. It was unfortunate that it was next to the veterinary surgery; aside from it being Zoe's place of work, you could sometimes hear dogs barking while you were eating. The pizzas were good, however. On his way past the wool shop he caught his reflection in the window. The shirt and jacket were inoffensive; smart, if not exciting. He ran a hand through his hair and strode on, pleased by the purposeful clip of his boots as they struck the pavement.

Only as he opened the door to the restaurant did it strike him that he should have been more adventurous. They could have gone to Ripon, or even Harrogate. They could have taken a taxi! He briefly imagined Zoe in a cocktail dress sipping something with an umbrella sticking out of it. Paolo's was run by a septuagenarian couple from Brindisi who had not updated so much as a checked tablecloth since Jamie's childhood. They used the kind of wineglasses you got free at the garage with a tank of petrol. He screwed up his face at the own goal. It was not the choice of a sophisticated adult.

The eponymous Paolo shook Jamie's hand and led him to a corner table. He ordered a beer and tried to decide what Zoe might like to drink. Paolo stood while Jamie craned his neck to scan the rows of bottles behind the bar, looking to surprise her with something chic and unexpected. He discounted peach schnapps on the grounds of it being called Archer's and decided against Midori because it was bright green and he had no idea what was in it.

'Dry white wine, please,' he said.

While he waited, Jamie made a show of studying the menu even though he could have recited it in his sleep. Zoe arrived just before their drinks. She had left her hair down and it lay over her shoulders, looking soft and velvety under the restaurant's dim but unsexy lighting.

'Cheers.' She drank some wine. 'Inspired choice.'

'I'm sorry,' said Jamie, unsure whether she meant the pinot grigio or the venue. 'I wasn't really thinking...'

'I'm joking,' said Zoe. 'How've you been?'

'Fine,' said Jamie. 'Great.' It wasn't what he'd intended to say. His plan had been to think of something that would make him appear strong and in control, yet engagingly vulnerable. Also, not to speak in sentences of only one syllable.

'It's been good,' he continued, 'staying with Caz. We haven't spent this much time together since we were living at home. Plus I'm getting to know Steve better, and the girls. They're great kids.' *Bloody hell.* The only time anyone ever said that was in American sitcoms.

'I'm glad,' said Zoe.

'How are you?' Jamie said. 'How's Minty?'

'Oh, fine.'

From the other side of the wall, a faint but insistent yapping could be heard over the Gypsy Kings.

'Christ,' said Zoe. 'It's that Pekinese that came in earlier for a claw removal.'

'Sorry,' said Jamie again. 'Shall we go to the Gate of India instead?'

'He'll quieten down soon. Andrew's there. Let's order.'

Zoe picked up her menu and they spent several minutes discussing whether Jamie should have the Diavola or the Pepperoni and whether the chef would do Zoe a Fiorentina without the egg. The barking continued, adding a deranged strain to the music. Paolo took their order and shambled off to the kitchen. Jamie snapped a breadstick in two and gave half to Zoe in what he hoped she might see as a symbolic act.

'I've missed you,' he said.

'Me too.' Zoe bit into her half and chewed. Clearly the gesture had been lost on her. 'Listen. I think it's stopped.'

They both cocked their ears towards the wall.

'Thank God for that.' Jamie sipped his beer, his train of thought interrupted. Then he remembered that he was holding half a breadstick. 'Why wouldn't you meet me till now?'

'Honestly?'

Jamie nodded, swallowing.

'I don't know. I mean, I wanted to. The house is very… quiet,' said Zoe.

'But?'

'I wasn't sure what it would achieve.'

'Does it have to *achieve* anything?' Jamie said.

'No. Well, I didn't think so, but then I didn't think we'd be living together after such a short time. We'd only been seeing each other for a month. And I know that wasn't your fault. I felt terrible when you left.' She reached for his hand. 'It's selfish, but I just had this horrible thought that I couldn't shake off, that this was it, that I'd be tied down, even though I was never looking for a live-in boyfriend. If I was going to do it, I'd at least have wanted to choose *when*.'

'But I lost my parents. I lost my home.'

'I know. You could have stayed, but that didn't mean I could do the whole shebang.'

'I'm quite domesticated now, you know.'

She laughed, but in a half-hearted way. At the time she had told him it wasn't just about the washing up; she'd given him that whole spiel about grieving and now she was saying she hadn't wanted commitment, but perhaps there was even more to it than that. He'd asked her once, but that was in front of Caz. He needed to know for certain.

'Was it because of, you know, what happened at the stables?'

Zoe pulled her hand away.

'Of course not!' She lowered her voice. 'I told you, that had nothing to do with it. At first I thought that *sex*,' she mouthed the word in deference to their surroundings, 'might help. But then I decided to wait, take my lead from you.'

'After you suggested it in the café, you didn't mention it again. I thought you must have gone off the idea. I wasn't even sure I could do it anymore. I didn't get to find out.' He shifted in his chair and drank the rest of his beer.

'Oh, Jamie.' Zoe looked as though she was about to say something else but two large plates were thrust in front of them. A bottle of wine was opened and poured. Chilli oil was brought, followed by the inevitable three-foot pepper grinder. Jamie and Zoe sat back for them to be administered and waited until they were alone again.

'So you're saying you can't live with me?' Jamie said. Zoe cut a segment from her eggless Fiorentina. She took a bite, then put it down again.

'I'm not saying never. It was just too early - it wasn't our time. What happened was so dreadful, it put huge pressure on us. You needed chance to grieve without the complication of a relationship.'

'But I'm OK.'

Zoe shook her head, sadly.

'Jamie, you're not. Think of what you've been through, what you're still going through. You don't even know exactly what happened. I bet the inquest's dragging on, isn't it?'

'It's been adjourned until later in the year. Just a formality,' he mumbled.

'Somewhere in there,' she pointed at his chest, 'is a whole heap of who-knows-what that hasn't begun to come out yet. I wasn't ready for you to move in with me. But you weren't, either, not in the real sense of living together.'

Jamie ploughed on through his Diavola, not wanting to take in what she was saying. It was preferable to believe that he had been kicked out over a few fixable bad habits.

'What do we do now?' The last mouthful was particularly

spicy and he wiped his eyes with a paper napkin. Zoe put down her knife and fork. Two-thirds of her pizza lay untouched.

'That's the trouble. I don't know.' She was looking at him, her face utterly serious and it struck him that rather than this being a date, she had come to break up with him properly.

'Zo,' he began, but she was already speaking again.

'When you came into the surgery that day, I really fancied you, even though your dog bit me.' Despite the knowledge that a *but* was surely coming, Jamie allowed himself to luxuriate in the compliment for a moment. 'You seemed kind,' Zoe continued, 'a bit immature, but I thought, so what? I'd never been with anyone kind before. OK, so I didn't want to get hammered *every* Friday night, or play on the quiz machine in the pub for hours, or watch *Rugby Special*, but at least we were having fun.'

'And great sex,' Jamie murmured.

'That too,' said Zoe. 'If only everything could have stayed that way. But you wanted me to hold your hand in the supermarket, meet your work colleagues, have lunch with your family. You were already too much, Jamie, even before you lost your parents. I'm sorry.'

When she had finished speaking she winced, as though she had delivered a cruel but necessary blow, and was worried that she had been too harsh. But the sucker punch hadn't come and something told him that if he could get the next bit right, there could be a chance for them after all.

'I get it,' he said. 'I was too full-on. Too intense.' She nodded. 'But I know that now you've told me. I can do casual.'

Zoe gave him a dubious look. 'Can you?'

'I'm living with Caz now. I won't be pestering you to stay over or messing up your house.'

She laughed. 'You make me sound very anal.'

'No, I understand. You need time to yourself.' He poured more wine. 'Whatever I have to deal with, I'll deal with it. How about we have a few dates, see how it goes?'

'Just dates?'

'Yep. Like this. Well, not exactly like this. I'll be more imaginative next time.'

And then she smiled; it wasn't a humouring smile, or an exasperated smile, but a real, warm one, with teeth.

'Excellent,' said Jamie. 'Now, are you going to eat that, or not?'

After they had finished the wine, and Jamie had eaten nearly two pizzas, he asked for the bill. He swapped fifteen quid for a handful of mint imperials and they went out onto the street.

'Walk you home?' She smiled up at him and took a mint from his outstretched palm. When he put his arm around her, she didn't object and even tucked her hand into the back pocket of his trousers.

At Zoe's front door, Jamie bent to kiss her goodnight but she already had her key in the lock. As the door creaked open, she pulled him into the sitting room. They took off their coats and looked at each other for a moment, then Jamie put out a hand to smooth her hair. She tilted her face to kiss him and started on the buttons of his shirt, moving down from the top until she reached the buckle of his belt. The flicker he felt when she brushed against his fly gave him an actual jolt and she sprang away.

'Everything all right?' she said.

He reached for her again. They hadn't touched each

other like this in months. It was electrifying; no different to all the other times they had been together before the fire, when they were barely able to get through the door before they were undressing one another. Zoe flicked the shirt away from his shoulders, then crossed her arms and whipped her jumper over her head. Then they were on the sofa and everything was fine and it was going to happen, at last, and everything was fine and it was going to be amazing and he was back to normal and everything was fine and they were still kissing and then, inexplicably, the space around them was black and there was burning. He sat up.

'What's wrong?' said Zoe.

'I can't,' said Jamie. 'I'm sorry.'

He grabbed his shirt from the floor and shoved his arms into the sleeves, haphazardly doing up the buttons while Zoe stared at him, flushed and frowning.

'It doesn't matter,' she said. 'Come here. Shall we talk about it?'

'No!' said Jamie. 'God, no!'

He snatched up his jacket and tore out of the house, running at full pelt. When he reached the corner of the high street he stopped, hanging onto a lamp-post while he caught his breath. He took a step back and kicked it, hard, with his right foot. There was a dull pain as it connected to the metal and then a jarring as the shock went up through his leg and into his spine. Better. He kicked it again, this time with the left. His right leg buckled and he clung to the lamp-post like an exhausted pole-dancer. Zoe would never want to see him again after this and he couldn't blame her. He had humiliated them both. Jamie peeled himself off the lamp-post and lumbered home in shame and despair to Caz and Steve's box room.

twenty-five

Jamie could bear it no longer. He had spent a demoralising Monday afternoon showing Mrs Roe a series of houses, each apparently more offensive to her sensibilities and those of Norman *and* her absent son than the last. The suspicion that Mrs Roe's ideal house was yet to be built was starting to harden in his mind. His legs still ached from kicking the lamp-post but that was nothing compared to the enormity of the mess he had made of his date with Zoe. It was four-thirty and he was sitting in his car, watching through the rear-view mirror as Mrs Roe's BMW disappeared from view. Archer's office didn't overlook the carpark; as far as the boss knew, Jamie was still out on viewings. He turned on the engine.

Although the sign outside Robinson's Piano Sales and Repairs declared that it was still open, there was an abandoned air about the place that Jamie recognised from his own office on a slow day when everyone had found a reason to leave early. He jogged towards the door and tried the handle but it was locked.

There were still a couple of cars parked outside the building. Jamie knocked and a young woman appeared, her handbag hooked over her arm.

'Can you come back tomorrow?' she said. 'We're closed.'

'But it's only quarter-to,' said Jamie.

The woman sighed and dropped a hip. She extended her arm into the building in mock-welcome and Jamie went inside. In the showroom, a man was wandering between the pianos, lowering their fall-boards.

'Colin,' said Jamie. 'Thank goodness. You're still here.'

The receptionist glowered at him from the doorway.

'It's all right, Vicky,' said Colin. 'You can go.' She whirled around and a few seconds later, the front door banged. 'What can I do for you, Mr Fenton?'

'I need to see it. I don't care if you think I'm weird. It's been so long, I just need to see it.' Jamie didn't think he sounded particularly desperate, but Colin's face told him otherwise.

'Er, it's not finished yet. As I said, it's going to be a few more weeks. Restoring the veneer on the casing is an intricate and highly-skilled job. It can't be rushed.' Colin was standing by a Feurich baby grand, a finger resting lovingly on one corner.

'Colin, please.' Jamie needed to clear his throat. Something strange had happened to his voice.

'We're normally very strict about… Oh, never mind. Follow me.'

They traipsed through the showroom to the workshop. The Pleyel was standing more or less in the same place as before. The broken parts of the frame had been replaced but were unpolished, giving the piano the appearance of being cobbled together from random bits of wood. More piebald than thoroughbred. Better than before, but only just. Jamie realised that he was holding his hands to his head.

'It's more finished than it looks,' said Colin. 'The action is good as new. What those Parisians can do…' He tailed off in wonder.

Jamie took a step towards the piano. 'Can I try it?' Regardless of its appearance, it was the Pleyel and it was within his grasp.

'Absolutely not.' Colin darted between Jamie and the piano so that he was standing just inches from Jamie's outstretched hand. 'Look,' he said, softening, 'these were such delicate repairs. Everything needs to settle while we finish the outer work. We can't risk upsetting the piano's equilibrium. You're a pianist, Mr Fenton. Surely you must understand such things.'

Jamie lowered his arm in defeat. His shoulders dropped.

'You're right,' he said. 'That's the last thing I want.'

'We'll let you know the minute it's ready,' said Colin. 'I promise.'

twenty-six

There was a soft rap on Jamie's bedroom door. Steve poked his head inside. Hearing something about a broken-down van and a sixty-mile round trip, Jamie deduced that he was being asked to help out with his nieces again.

'So if you could just give them their breakfast - nothing fancy, just cereal or toast or something - and then take them to school, mate, that would be grand. Caz is having a little lie-in.'

There was still no news about the Pleyel. Although Jamie had seen it with his own eyes, the likelihood of him playing it again seemed as remote as ever. Since their disastrous date, he hadn't spoken to Zoe, either. With nothing to occupy his evenings and weekends, Jamie had ample opportunity to observe Caz's gradual withdrawal from family life. Most mornings, Steve would come to his room. Steve's requests were usually couched within an elaborate set of electrical-based circumstances and always ended with the news that Caz wouldn't be getting up. Each time, they were delivered with fresh wonder, as though his wife's unwillingness to leave her bed came as a complete surprise.

As it turned out, Jamie didn't mind. The girls became his warm-up for the day. By the time he had tussled with them over breakfast and the brushing of teeth he was ready for anything. The only problem was that it made him late for work. There was simply not enough time to drop Ruby and Pearl at school and be at the office by nine.

He didn't blame Caz for wanting some time out. What bothered him more was that Steve was pretending that everything was normal.

They could manage without her in the mornings. In the evenings, they ate freezer food for supper, which Caz picked at in silence before slinking away with her wine to the sofa and the television. She drank glass after glass every night but it didn't make her sociable; quite the reverse. Her conversation skills were in danger of drying up completely. Ruth Cole was more perceptive than he'd realised.

Breakfast passed swiftly and without incident, but just as they were about to leave the house, Pearl declared one of her shoes to be missing. After a good ten minutes of searching, it was found under Ruby's bed. When they got to school, Pearl tripped on a loose piece of paving, grazing her knee, and had to be pacified. Then, on the Ripon road, a tractor towing a trailerful of sheep pulled out in front of him. There were too many bends to even consider overtaking. By the time Jamie arrived at his viewing it was twenty-past nine. Mrs Roe tapped her wristwatch and shook her platinum perm at him. Norman eyed him with reproach.

'You're lucky I'm still here,' she said. 'This poor dog hasn't had his walk, yet.' Jamie ran through a range of adjectives that might apply to him at that moment and concluded that lucky wasn't one of them.

'I'm so sorry,' he said. 'Shall we?'

Mrs Roe was sizing up the house with a dubious air. They were on a quiet street near the river; a pretty enclave of Georgian terraced houses whose front gardens spilled rhododendrons and magnolia onto the pavement. The house they had come to see was approached through a wrought-iron archway with an antique lantern built into it and had a flagged path leading to the front door.

'This isn't a new-build,' she said.

'No,' said Jamie, 'you're quite correct. The house dates back to the early 1800s.'

'What are we doing here, then? I told you I wanted modern.'

'Yes,' said Jamie, 'but we know you're looking for something smart, and Mr Archer thought...'

'I don't care what *he* thought. I've told you what I want, and it's not some museum piece. If I'd known where you were bringing me, I'd have told you to sling your hook.'

She glared at him and stuck out her chin. There was a line where her make-up ended, exposing the white flesh of her neck.

'Please, Mrs Roe,' Jamie said. 'Now that you're here, why not have a quick squizz inside? What harm can it do? It really is a very nice house.' He produced the keys from his pocket and set off at a jaunty pace up the path. 'The owners are abroad, so we can wander undisturbed. And it's priced to sell. A bargain, you could say.'

The door opened onto a capacious entrance hall, where a richly-coloured runner sat on top of parquet flooring. To one side was a sitting room; to the other, a dining room.

Even to Jamie's undiscriminating eye, the house had been decorated by someone with elegant taste and attention to detail. There were multiple bookcases, armchairs scattered with oriental-patterned cushions and an arresting mix of paintings, both figurative and abstract. Appended to the kitchen, a conservatory filled with wicker furniture looked out over a small but well-stocked walled garden.

'There's no garage,' said Mrs Roe.

'Actually,' said Jamie, 'beyond that wall is an alleyway and beyond *that* is the garage.' He studied his notes. 'The current owner uses it as a studio but there's plenty of room for a couple of cars.'

'Hmm,' said Mrs Roe.

'Obviously, the books and paintings aren't included, but the vendor would be happy to discuss the rest of the contents with you.'

Mrs Roe fingered one of the curtains in the kitchen and let it drop. 'Someone else's old tat? I don't think so.'

She wheeled around and marched up the stairs, the creaking of floor-boards announcing her progress around the first floor. Norman took a more considered inspection of the kitchen, sniffing at cupboard doors and licking the tiles on the floor. Jamie considered letting him out into the garden before concluding that any decision he might take involving Norman would undoubtedly be the wrong one.

'Bugger me,' said Mrs Roe from the doorway as the dog trotted towards her. She bent to clasp his dripping jowls between her hands and planted a kiss on his muzzle. 'He likes the place.' She straightened and the two of them swept out of the house. She hadn't even stuck around long enough to inspect the all-important garage.

Jamie lingered in the kitchen, wondering whether it would be against company guidelines to make himself a coffee and drink it in the garden. On balance, he decided it probably was.

Back at the office, Chris was eating Cheesy Wotsits and reading a magazine with greater concentration than he ever applied to selling houses.

'All right?' he said without looking up. 'Your grandma and grandad have been on the phone.'

Jamie sighed. Mr and Mrs Sidgwick appeared to think that every house that came on the market could be their perfect home. He was fending off their enquiries on a daily basis. Despite the consensus in the office, Jamie was convinced that they *were* serious buyers, if a little under-occupied. On the other hand, as illustrated that very morning, nothing he showed Mrs Roe produced even a flicker of enthusiasm. If anyone was wasting his time, it was her.

Jacob Archer was expecting him to come up with a sale. His job was at risk if he didn't. That should have been enough to focus the mind. But despite his best efforts, the squirming embarrassment he was still suffering over Zoe relegated everything work-related to the bottom of his list of priorities.

It wasn't just the physical aspect of it; that was bad enough, but it was almost worse that during their date he had played a blinder. Zoe hadn't dumped him, as he'd expected. He'd done the difficult part. But when they got to her house he had, as his father would have said, snatched defeat from the jaws of victory. If he'd only stayed and talked to Zoe she would have understood, but he had left her standing there, sweaterless and bemused while he raced off down the street to attack a lamp-post. Excruciating though the prospect was, he really needed to speak to her and she hadn't returned any of his messages.

Confident that Chris was sufficiently distracted not to eavesdrop, Jamie picked up the phone. But as he punched in the first three numbers for the veterinary surgery, Chris slapped the magazine down onto the desk.

'This is bloody dynamite,' he said, shaking his head in disbelieving admiration.

Jamie stopped dialling.

'*Cosmopolitan?* I didn't think you'd be interested in that sort of thing.'

'I know. It's a birds' magazine. But look.'

He held up the front cover. *Hot Sex Tips: How to Keep Him Coming Back for More* was written in large red letters.

'Brilliant, eh? There's all sorts in here,' He flicked through the pages with lascivious haste. 'Listen…'

'No.' Jamie held up a palm. 'You're disgusting. Grow up, will you?'

'Hey!' Charlotte, just back from a viewing, strode up to the desk and snatched the magazine out of Chris's hands. 'That's mine.'

'Who'd have thought you women were so horny? All that hard-to-get bollocks is just a con.'

Charlotte swatted Chris around the head with the rolled up *Cosmo*. 'You. Are. Gross!'

'Stop her!' Chris yelled. 'She's assaulting me!'

'For goodness' sake, you lot.' Maggie was bearing down upon the desk, hands on hips. 'You're like bunch of schoolchildren. Jamie, you're wanted in the boss's office.'

Unsure whether to be relieved or worried, Jamie went to Archer's door and knocked.

'Come in, come in,' Archer said. 'How's it going with Mrs Roe?'

'She's quite particular,' said Jamie. 'I've just shown her College Lane.'

'And?'

'It's fabulous. But she didn't seem to think so. I can't find anything she *does* like.'

'That house is an absolute gem,' said Archer. 'Good value too. Why on earth can't you get her interested?'

'I don't know,' Jamie admitted. 'Maybe she's not really all that serious?'

'Nonsense!' Archer banged the desk. The Newton's cradle trembled. 'I know her type. You'll have to flatter her a bit. Flirt with her if you have to. You're a good-looking lad. Use it to your advantage.'

'Mr Archer,' said Jamie, 'she's old enough to be my mother. I can't flirt with her.'

'Well, you'd better come up with something. These interest rates are killing me. We need sales.'

'I was thinking,' said Jamie, 'of showing College Lane to the Sidgwicks. It could be exactly what they're looking for.'

'You will not,' said Archer. 'Don't waste any more time on them. No, Mrs Roe will buy that house in the end. You just need to make it happen.'

Jamie went back to his desk. Chris and Charlotte had gone out. He clenched a fist and rested his forehead on it. Flirting with Mrs Roe would require acting skills he didn't possess; the very thought of it made him queasy. The only person he could imagine flirting with was Zoe, and as things stood that might never happen again. He picked up the phone once more and held it to his ear until the dialling tone became a continuous wail and he put it back in its cradle. A phone call would be no good. They needed to see each other in person.

twenty-seven

At five-fifty on a sultry Friday in June, Jamie was alone in the office, doodling on a notepad, reassured that Archer had gone home and that he was therefore no longer obliged to look busy. It had been a cheerless day, largely spent trying to dampen the Sidgwicks' interest in the same properties that he was attempting to sell to Mrs Roe. Zoe, he'd managed to ascertain, had been away for a couple of weeks, helping her parents at the riding school. By his calculations she would have been back for two days.

Someone was knocking on the window behind him. It was Chris, wearing an England football shirt, doing a drinking mime and pointing towards the Hornblower Inn. Later that evening England were due to play Sweden in the European championships. Telling himself that some of the other agents were doubtless already in the pub, Jamie flashed both hands at the window, mouthing 'ten minutes', even though he had no intention of joining them. Chris, apparently satisfied, shambled across the road.

—

Half an hour later, Jamie gave a third, shrill ring on Zoe's doorbell and let the bunch of flowers he was holding fall to his side, debating whether to try once more or give up and go home. It had seemed important not to turn up empty-handed and he hadn't been inspired by anything else at the petrol station. The carnations, which appeared quite acceptable amongst the Pot Noodles and flagons of screen wash, now looked limp and unappealing. They even smelled vaguely stale, like the afterthought which, of course, they were.

The cellophane around the flowers crackled and sweated in his hand. Bees were buzzing around a lilac bush but the sky was dark and the air had turned cold, threatening rain. He checked the street again; the dusty pickup sat stolidly in front of the gate.

Jamie's bladder made the decision for him. He needed to pee. Either he tried the bell again, or he would have to do it in Zoe's front garden. He pressed the doorbell, holding down the button for a little longer as the first plump drops of rain chased the bees from the lilac.

A shadow moved on the other side of the frosted glass and the door inched open. Zoe was in her dressing gown. Whenever she'd had a shower she would wrap her hair in a towel like a turban. Now, she wore it loose; it was dry and unbrushed. And it was only just six.

'Hi, Zo.' Jamie presented the flowers in the manner of a conjuror.

'Oh,' she said. 'Hi.' There were dark smuts of make-up under her eyes. She darted a wary glance at the flowers.

'Did I get you out of the shower?'

Zoe put a palm to the back of her neck and looked down at the towelling robe.

'Can I come in?' Jamie said.

There was something defeated in the tilt of her head as she turned and wandered into the sitting room, the muscles of her bare calves flexing and contracting. When she reached the sofa she sat down and tucked her legs beneath her.

Jamie set the flowers on the coffee table.

'Sorry, I really need the loo. Do you mind?'

She mumbled something inaudible and waved her arm at the stairs. He dashed from the room and took them two at a time until he reached the landing. The door to Zoe's bedroom was ajar. Through the gap he could see that the bed was unmade. He pushed the door open, more powerfully than he intended, and it banged against the wall.

The room smelled familiar, not in a good way. On the bed, the pillows were misshapen; indented by recent heads. The duvet had been cast onto the floor. Next to it was a small pile of discarded clothes. It looked like Zoe's bedroom when they had been in there together. The trouble was, *he* hadn't been.

The impulse to pee became unbearable and he staggered to the bathroom. He sat on the loo seat, not trusting his legs or his aim. When he had finished he washed his hands slowly, loath to go back downstairs. A crack of lightning blanched the room. Rain hammered at the window, ruling it out as a viable escape route and leaving Jamie to begin the most dignified descent of the stairs that he could manage.

Zoe hadn't moved from the sofa and was examining her nails.

'Has someone been here?' Jamie said. As an attempt to sound casual it was not a success. She gave a heavy sigh.

'It was just Andrew.'

'From work? The clothes guy?' Australian Andrew, with his chunky watch and freckled forearms, the emergency wardrobe provider, who only ever spoke in questions.

'He's gone now,' said Zoe, as though that explained everything. 'He was on call.'

'Hold on.' Jamie laced his fingers together behind his head. 'He was upstairs? With you?'

Zoe tightened the belt on her fluffy dressing gown. She looked around the room with a resigned air. Jamie paced up and down on the small patch of carpet, swearing under his breath.

'I knew it!' he said. 'I bloody knew it. You said it didn't matter.'

'It didn't,' she said. 'It doesn't. Well, maybe just a bit. But not really. You mustn't think…'

He stopped pacing as her words petered out. The wilting flowers admonished him from the table. Zoe unfurled her legs and got up. As she came nearer, he smelled a ripeness on her skin that made him turn away from her.

'I didn't think we were finished,' he said quietly. He looked back to the sofa and thought of the hours he'd spent lying on it, watching TV, when she'd told him she was on a late shift, or dealing with a crisis, or riding that bloody horse, Minty, or Monty, or whatever its name was.

'We don't have to be.'

'It looks like we are if *that's* the only thing you care about. We both know it's me. It was the fire. It's done something to me. I can't…'

'It's all right, it's all right.'

'It's *not!* How can it be, otherwise you wouldn't have… Shit! This is a nightmare.'

By now she was standing right in from of him and he wished she didn't smell so… unclean; he knew the feel of that dressing gown and he wanted to bury himself in its white softness. She took hold of two of his fingers and looked up at him.

'It's not your fault. It'll come back. You've had a lot to deal with.'

'But you couldn't wait that long.'

'I don't know what I was thinking. Maybe that it wouldn't hurt anyone, as long as you didn't know.' Zoe dropped her chin and screwed up her eyes as if she were trying to blot an image from her mind.

'Oh well, that's fine, then!' Jamie shook off her grip.

'No,' said Zoe, 'it's not. It was wrong. I realised that tonight. I told him just now that it was the last time.'

It struck Jamie that when he failed to find Zoe at midnight at the party, Andrew was nowhere to be seen, either.

'The last time of how many?' he said. 'Was it just recently? Or before? What about New Year's Eve?'

She looked up sharply.

'What do you mean?'

'Was there something going on then?'

'No!' She grasped his hand again. 'I was plastered that night. There was a lot of random kissing. But nothing else.'

They looked at each other. Zoe seemed to want to keep his gaze.

'OK. OK.' He thought for a minute, unsure whether this made it better or worse. Better that she hadn't cheated on him before the fire. But that she'd needed to look elsewhere after just a few months without sex? So much worse.

'That *was* really why you kicked me out, wasn't it?' he said. 'All that stuff about me needing to grieve was just an excuse.'

Zoe closed her eyes for a moment, shaking her head slowly.

'We've been through this,' she said. 'Please. Don't get hung up on it.'

'*You* obviously did. Christ!' Jamie flung his arms out. 'What am I supposed to think?'

'We talked about it,' said Zoe, her voice slightly tremulous. 'It *was* too soon. I thought you understood. And we agreed we'd be casual, just dates.'

'I didn't mean it like that.'

'Neither did I. It wasn't that I wanted to go around sleeping with lots of people or anything. I don't even know why this happened. He was just there, and...'

'No, don't tell me. What I saw upstairs was more than enough.' Jamie threw back his head and took several deep breaths. 'I've really tried to give you space,' he said in a more measured tone. 'I've kept my distance, even when I've been dying to see you. I thought...' He took a couple of unsteady steps backwards, towards the door.

'I know.' Zoe was clearly trying not to cry; at this point he really didn't want the complication of her tears. 'I'm sorry about that. Don't go.'

He backed into the tiny hallway and stopped. Andrew's jacket was hanging on the back of the door. It still smelled of sheep.

'Doesn't he ever wash that bloody thing?'

Zoe said nothing. They stared at one another. Jamie snatched up the flowers from the table and strode out of the house into the storm, stopping in the front garden to ram them into the dustbin.

twenty-eight

The television in the Blower had football pundits on mute. The rows of plastic chairs which had been assembled in front of it were as yet unclaimed. Kick-off was clearly still some time away. At the only occupied table, a trio of men drinking Guinness bickered over a game of dominoes. By the wall, a group of teenage boys pounded the fruit machine. There was no sign of anyone from work. Having driven through torrential rain all the way back to Ripon, this was not good news.

An elderly lady with wild hair and a violent slash of lipstick was sitting at the bar, smoking. As Jamie approached, she raised what looked like a glass of port and winked. He swerved around her towards the landlord.

'If you're looking for your mate,' he said, 'you've missed him. Said something about boring bastards from work and went off to watch the match at home. Shame. He'd have been good for at least six pints.'

Jamie bought a beer, feeling a pang of sympathy for Chris which he instantly dismissed, and retreated to a table.

As he took the first sip, there was a shout from the other side of the pub. The fruit machine trilled, heralding a rhythmic expulsion of ten pence pieces which the assembled boys were stuffing into the pockets of their tracksuits. The woman raised her glass towards him again as if she had forgotten that she had done so once already.

Above him, a speaker on the wall began to hiss and crackle. Having disembowelled the fruit machine, the boys were feeding coins into the juke box. An electric guitar riff, unmistakably AC/DC, exploded into the pub.

'This is bullshit,' Jamie said under his breath. Being alone in a godforsaken bar on a stormy summer's evening after what he had just experienced was too depressing for words. For the first time he could recall, he left what was almost a full pint of beer and marched out, past the drunk woman at the bar, onto the sodden street.

The road home was a twisted switchback of hairpin bends and blind summits, strung between a series of underpopulated villages. Jamie gripped the steering wheel of the Fiesta and accelerated past dripping trees and hedgerows, grimly watching the speedometer as it notched up to sixty. The storm had now passed and the sky had turned silvery grey; the clouds, backlit by a labouring sun, were reflected in the puddles on the surface of the road.

He prodded the stereo, wanting his head to be filled with something soothing so that he wouldn't have to think. The first of Satie's Gymnopédies was playing on the radio, which did the trick until a long dip in the road reduced the reception to sibilance. In frustration he switched it off again.

It was incredible how, when you thought things were as bad as they could conceivably be, they could always deteriorate further. A few hours earlier, when he was agonising over the loss of his libido, it hadn't occurred to him that Zoe might replace it with someone else's. He had been right to regret not sticking around on the night of the date to discuss what had gone wrong. If he'd been mature enough to do that, he and Zoe would have moved on by now. Instead, she had. Without him.

He floored the accelerator, one hand on the wheel, one on his thigh, both bashing out what he dimly recognised as a mazurka that had come to him unbidden.

Rainwater glistened on the potholed tarmac as he slowed into a village and out of the other side, speeding up into a sequence of bends, leaning left and right, feeling the car judder as it clung to the road which was empty but slippery from the rain. Unquestionably he was driving too fast, on the cusp of being out of control and pushing the car beyond what was safe. Both hands should have been on the wheel but his left hand couldn't, or wouldn't, stop pounding chords on his thigh. He braked for a narrow stone bridge, snaked in and out of the next hamlet and then coasted down a steep bank to a straighter stretch of road below. Here, he gathered speed. The little engine of the Fiesta screamed as he reached eighty, racing towards a sloping bend that was always sharper than he remembered.

The car slew to the left as he yanked hard on the wheel and the back-end swung out across the road. Jamie braked again, finally using both hands, veering right in an attempt at correction and causing the car to bounce from side to side. Not breathing, he held on, knowing that if anything came round the next bend there would be a head-on collision. He closed his eyes. If he were about to plough into another car, to be responsible for someone else's injury or worse, he didn't want to see. He gripped harder, still braking and now trying to pull left. The car was fighting him, determined to go right. They struggled on, wrestling each other for mastery of the steering.

With his foot off the accelerator, they began to slow down. At last he was able to keep the car steady. He opened his eyes again; he was back on the correct side of the road. The car lurched forward and stalled, inches from some estate fencing. When he exhaled, he realised that his seat had slid forwards and his legs were jammed beneath the steering column. He reached underneath for the release lever, summoned the strength to push the seat back again and collapsed forwards over the wheel.

It started as a sort of whinny, the kind of noise someone would make if they were desperate not to cry but unable to stop it. Jamie raised his head to see where the sound had come from but the road was deserted; it could only have originated from him. He put his head down again as the sobbing overtook him. All he could think was *crescendo*, until he was roaring into the elliptical blue Ford badge on the steering wheel and beating it with his fists, sounding the horn in staccato blares. Then, the roaring gave way to a howling yawl and he let his hands fall, giving himself up to it. He could have been screaming for minutes, or just seconds. Afterwards, he would have no idea. When it began to subside he stayed, slumped against the wheel, his nose squashed into its hard blackness, inhaling its plasticity.

Sensing movement to his right. Jamie eased himself up and wound down the window. An elderly man in a battered trilby peered in. Behind him, in the middle of the road, stood an ancient tractor, the cab high on spindly tyres and caked in mud.

'You all right, lad?'

The man gripped the door with both hands and leaned so far into the car that Jamie could smell his breath, which had a slightly faecal kick to it. He drew away involuntarily before he saw to his shame that the man's expression was kind.

'Yes,' he said. 'Thank you. I was just a bit tired. Didn't get much sleep last night. I'm fine now.'

'Right you are.' The man stepped back, nodded once and returned to the tractor. Jamie watched it chug away, took a few slow, deep breaths, and restarted the engine. As he set off again he remembered the name of the song on the jukebox in the pub: *Thunderstruck*.

twenty-nine

Steve didn't demur when Caz poured herself a third glass of wine. The girls were still up, even though it was after seven, because Steve was reading the newspaper and Caz couldn't be bothered to move from the kitchen table. The phone had been ringing intermittently. When it rang again, Steve looked up and sighed.

'Babe, can you get that? It'll be Zoe again. She's called twice already and she sounded in a right state. I think you should speak to her.'

Caz dragged herself into the hall. Zoe's voice was so quiet that she couldn't catch what she was saying.

'Can you speak up?'

'I've made a mess of everything.' It was strange to hear someone else in tears. 'I need to speak to Jamie. Is he back yet?'

'No. Where's he gone?'

'I don't know. He was at my house and... oh, God. Never mind. Can you just ask him to call me?'

'What's happened?'

'I should have thought about what I was doing. I should never have...' Her words ended in a kind of whimper.

'Never have what?'

'I... I don't want to go into it over the phone. Jamie can tell you himself, if he wants to.'

Caz remembered her first instinct on meeting Zoe; that she should be angry with her for making Jamie move out, that being friendly to her was disloyal. But the sympathy that Zoe had offered her had been so rare, and Caz was still grateful for that. On the other hand, something else serious had now clearly taken place between them.

'I'll make sure he calls you when he gets home,' said Caz.

Zoe gave a great, heaving sniff. 'Thanks, Caz,' she said. 'I'm sorry to have bothered you.'

Ruby and Pearl, in their pyjamas, jumped up as Jamie came in. His face didn't look right; it had a new, wild look that Caz hadn't seen on him before but which she recognised from her own reflection when she looked in the mirror.

'Uncle Jamie,' Pearl said, 'come and do cat's cradle.'

He allowed himself to be led to the kitchen table. Something American played noisily on the television in the sitting room. Ruby wound wool around Jamie's hands and showed him how to slide his middle fingers underneath, but when he pulled, it snagged in a knot.

'You're not concentrating.' Ruby tutted and unravelled the yarn. 'He's rubbish at this,' she said to Pearl. 'Your go.'

Jamie stood up, looking relieved. In the brightness of the overhead light his neck was striped with red marks. His eyes were dull and puffy underneath. On his forehead was an oval-shaped indentation which looked as if he'd been stamped with something.

'Steve,' said Caz, 'could you take the girls up, please?'

'Pardon? Oh. Yeah. Sure.' He put down the newspaper and clapped his hands. 'Right, you two. The bedtime monster's coming.' Ruby and Pearl bolted upstairs, giggling, chased by Steve on all fours.

'What are those marks on your neck?' said Caz.

'Marks?' Jamie put an exploratory hand just above his collar. 'Nothing. It must have been the seat belt. I had a little… issue with the car but it's fine. No harm done.'

'That's not nothing. It's… what do you call it… whiplash. And what about your forehead?'

He traced the outline with a finger and shrugged. Caz stumbled slightly as she stood to take a closer look and had to put a hand on the table to steady herself. The room swam. She must have got up too quickly.

'The road was wet after the storm. I lost the steering on a bend and nearly ended up in a fence.'

'Oh my God, Jamie. You could have killed yourself.' For a second she envisioned him in a mangled car, alone and bleeding.

He waved her concern away. 'I'm fine. Or at least I am now. In fact I feel better than I have in ages.'

That didn't make any sense. It was harder to compute what he was saying than it should have been. There was only a finger of wine left in her glass and she topped it up nearly to the brim.

Steve came back into the kitchen and fished in one of the drawers for his wallet.

'Fancy a pint, J?'

'Thought you'd never ask.'

'Are you sure?' said Caz. 'You've bumped your head. It might not be a good idea.'

'Er...' Jamie eyed her refilled wineglass.

'Fine,' said Caz, offended. 'Do what you want.' It wasn't as if *she* had bumped her head.

'Don't fuss, Cazza,' said Steve. 'I'll watch out for him. He looks all right to me.'

'Fine,' said Caz. The shape her mouth made when she said the word felt familiar. Had she just said that? She turned back to her wine as Steve grabbed his house keys from the dresser. Jamie didn't want her concern. And if they went out, she could carry on drinking wine with impunity, which was what she wanted more than anything else.

After two more glasses, Caz was less clear about what Jamie had said. Had he crashed the car? She didn't think so, but he hadn't really explained the whiplash and that funny mark on his head. Judging by his eyes, he had been crying, but she didn't know why. Had she asked him? She couldn't remember. There was something else, too, that she'd forgotten, something that she was supposed to do. Now onto a second bottle, Caz nursed her glass, casting around for the answer that was just out of reach.

Her inclination was that it related to Zoe, but she couldn't think how. Jamie and Zoe weren't seeing each other anymore, as far as she knew. She was pretty sure that Jamie hadn't mentioned her when he came in. And she had only met Zoe once, that time she came to the house, just after Jamie moved in. When she was kind. She hadn't been back. It was maddening: why was Zoe on her mind when she clearly had nothing to do with Jamie injuring himself in the car?

No, she must be going mad. There was a much more obvious reason for Jamie to be upset: he was still grieving for their parents just as much as she was. Now that she was self-medicating with wine she was overcome by emotion less often, but the capacity to be taken by surprise was still there. Grief could creep up at any moment, reducing you to rubble in an instant. That must have been what happened to Jamie in the car. The only time she had seen him cry was at the funeral and that was ages ago. The built-up misery locked away inside him must be immense.

And then there was the argument when Jamie had stormed out on New Year's Eve. How must he feel, knowing that he would never be able to make things right with their father? It wasn't even his fault. He'd been defending her. Before that, she'd never known Jamie defend anyone, not even himself. She was to blame for all of this. Her stupid comments had started the whole thing. It wasn't as if she even really cared about pheasant shooting. Well, it was wrong, surely, but not worth falling out over. And now Jamie and their father could never bury their differences because of her.

That was the nub of it; she was a hateful drunk who had caused a family argument and then her parents died. Jamie was doing his best to keep going but was so upset that he had almost killed himself on the road. She was no use as a daughter, a sister, a mother or a wife. There was pain in her chest where her heart was.

The scars on her wrist itched and burned. She rubbed them with the fingers of her right hand but that only made it worse. Then, she dug her nails in, tearing at the skin, but they were bitten too short to be effective. In desperation she struggled up from the table, clinging on to the furniture, the doorframe, the bannister, trying to get to the bathroom without being heard. Somehow she got up the stairs without waking the girls.

The bathroom door clicked quietly shut behind her. She slicked the bolt across. Steve's spare razor blades were on the second shelf of the bathroom cabinet, near the back. The throbbing in her wrist was uncontrollable and there was only one way to stop it. She was like an animal out alone at night, all of her senses in a heightened state. Her motor skills suddenly sharp, she extracted a blade from the box, leaving the packaging undisturbed. She tore off a long length of loo roll and sat on the edge of the bath.

Her whole body was pulsating with anticipation. The moment was exquisite, thrilling. Caz rolled up her left sleeve and studied the pale skin, luminous under the bathroom lights. Her fingers caressed the scars, priming them, her arm poised over the basin. Then, when she couldn't wait any longer, she took the razor blade between her thumb and forefinger. Holding it near one corner, she angled it towards her bare skin, aiming for the biggest scar, away from the vein. She pushed the pointed edge, gently, gently, so that it grazed the skin, savouring the scratching, scraping sensation. Keeping it there, she stretched her head back and closed her eyes, breathing deeply. Excitement stirred deep inside her. There was roaring in her ears.

How she had missed that glorious split-second, the hiatus between the cutting and the bleeding. The thin, papery feeling, the body frozen in shock for the tiniest moment before the blood forced itself free in perfectly uniform droplets. Only afterwards would the pain assert itself; familiar but mystifying, reassuring but overwhelming.

She eased the point of the blade into her wrist, making the smallest of incisions. Thousands of little stars exploded behind her eyes. The excitement between her legs was unignorable. She moaned and shifted on the edge of the bath, watching the blood pulsing steadily into the white ceramic of the basin where it was diluted to a watery pink as it swirled down the drain. That blood was the most beautiful part of her; a reminder that there was still something left that was untarnished.

As the blood dripped faster, her arm began to ache. The ecstasy was over. What followed, and what she always forgot, was the dull, thumping pain it left behind. This, more than anything, was what she deserved. Her inadequacies should have consequences. If no-one else would punish her, she would do it herself.

She blotted the blood with loo roll and leaned against the wall with her arm in the air until the bleeding stopped. The cut, when she examined it, was tiny, just a few millimetres and easily covered by a plaster. Once she was patched up she went downstairs and had another glass of wine. It was only when she was in bed that she remembered Zoe's message for Jamie.

thirty

After only four hours' sleep, not even the verbal gymnastics required to get Ruby and Pearl to school could sharpen Jamie up enough to face the day. It wasn't anger that kept him awake for most of the night; it was more of a dismal recognition that he had brought Zoe's behaviour on himself. She had wanted him and he had been left lacking in the most mortifying manner, causing her to look elsewhere. It made him want to stay under the duvet for ever. In the end he got out of bed by forcing himself to think about something else.

He gave the girls breakfast but didn't pay much attention to their appearance. Only as he watched them disappear through the school gates did he notice the extent of their unkemptness. The other children had tidy hair and matching socks. Perhaps these things were more important than he realised, although a badly-buttoned cardigan hardly mattered compared to, say, total emasculation.

In the office, Chris was reading the back page of *The Sun*.

'*Swedes 2, Turnips 1*,' he said in a funereal tone. '*Taylor's men get a Viking good hiding.* Bollocks!' He tossed the paper onto the desk. 'It's a national disgrace.'

Jamie shook his head in sympathy.

'I know, mate,' he said. 'Shocking.'

'Not like *you* care,' said Chris. 'You'd have come to watch if you did.'

For most of June, a vast St George flag had hung across the front of the pub. Now, on the other side of the square, the landlord was up a ladder, wrenching it down with an air of frustration, either at the team's performance, or lost future takings, or both.

'Where did you slope off to, anyway? You missed a great night.' With a crack and hiss, Chris opened a can of Coke which was on the desk in front of him.

'I had to get home.' Jamie refrained from pointing out that he wasn't the only one not to have turned up at the pub.

'Lightweight.'

In the hope of closing down the conversation, Jamie began to leaf through the *Estates Gazette*. Next to the phone, a dozen or so post-it notes had been stuck to the desk in formation, like a game of patience. Most of them requested, in Maggie's cursive hand, that he call Colin at Robinson's. The piano was almost ready and the insurance company had settled the bill. Colin's calls, Jamie was sure, were to find out where the Pleyel was to be kept and to that question, he still had no answer. The remainder of the messages, added since yesterday, were for him to call Zoe.

'You still shagging that bird?' said Chris. 'Is that where you went?'

'None of your business.' His reply sounded more peevish than enigmatic.

'Oof. She's dumped you, hasn't she?'

Jamie rolled his eyes. His head hurt from lack of sleep

and there was Weetabix on his tie. It occurred to him that looking after his nieces could be the closest he might ever come to fatherhood. He slowly put down the magazine and glared at Chris.

'Don't be an idiot.'

'Was it her, then?' Chris threw a nod towards the window. Outside, Charlotte was in conversation with a short, rotund man, bald except for a few tufts of tussocky hair which clung around his ears. 'I reckon she fancies you.'

'Jesus.' Jamie ripped the little stickers off the desk, one by one, balled them up and threw them at the bin. He missed.

'Oh,' said Chris, still looking at the window but now grinning. 'Hello…' The man, who was a head shorter than Charlotte, had moved far closer to her than a client-professional relationship should allow. With one hand on Charlotte's waist, he attempted to draw her closer by putting the other on her buttock.

'Bloody hell.' Jamie stood up and was about to make for the door but his sudden movement caught Charlotte's eye and she shook her head at him before expertly removing the man's hand and extricating herself from his grasp.

'Shame,' said Chris. 'That was going to get interesting.'

'Moron,' said Jamie, as Charlotte came into the office, brushing at her skirt as if trying to remove all traces of the man's advances. 'Are you OK?'

'What were you planning to do, come out and deck him?'

'No, I just thought - '

'Honestly, Jamie, it's fine. He wasn't going to try anything out on the street. It's on viewings that he really likes to show me how irresistible he is.'

'It's not fine,' said Jamie. 'You shouldn't have to put up with that.'

'Oh, please. She's a grown-up, isn't she?' Chris sauntered off to the gents', taking the can of Coke with him. Charlotte sat down at her desk and busied herself with a floor-plan, impatiently pushing her unruly hair back from her face.

Until a few moments ago, Jamie's thoughts had been on a continuous loop around the latest disaster with Zoe and the intractable problem of the piano. He had dismissed Chris's comment about Charlotte as ridiculous. But she *had* suggested they went somewhere else on their own when they were in the pub. Chris was a cretin, incapable of analysing human behaviour beyond the basest level. But was the possibility that Charlotte might be interested in him displeasing? He was surprised to find that it wasn't.

At the back of the office, Chris was at the senior agents' desk, trying to engage them in conversation. He bowled the now scrunched-up coke can, overarm, towards Jamie's bin. It flew in straight in with a metallic rattle. Chris dropped to one knee in a thinker's pose.

thirty-one

Mrs Sidgwick stepped out through the French doors of the conservatory and spread her arms wide, twirling like a schoolgirl.

'It's a proper sun trap,' she said.

The sun was at its highest point, casting no shadows over the little garden. Beneath an apple tree were a wrought-iron table and chairs. Attached to one of the high brick walls, a stone lion water-feature dripped water from its mouth into a tiny pond dotted with lilies. For a moment, Jamie imagined himself and Zoe, sitting there on a day like this, with a bottle of rosé and the kind of lunch people ate in Provence. Then he reminded himself that they were barely speaking. When he had finally taken one of her calls, she had repeated that the thing (her word) with Andrew was over. Since then he had been trying to choose between his self-respect and his desperate, unwanted wish to see her.

'Jamie?' said Mrs Sidgwick.

They were at the house in College Lane for what Jamie described to himself as an off-diary viewing. He had insisted that the Sidgwicks came in their own car.

'Look,' Mrs Sidgwick said, balancing on tiptoes, 'you can even see the cathedral.'

He glanced up at its pointed façade and twin square towers, just visible through the vibrating leaves of a silver birch. Some minutes earlier, Mr Sidgwick had found the door in the back wall and had vanished into the alleyway behind it.

'An actual studio!' He came back into the garden, triumphant with his discovery. 'I can do my modelling in there.'

'Your modelling?' said Jamie, confused.

Mrs Sidgwick clasped his arm. 'Not *that* sort of modelling,' she said. 'John likes to build things from matchsticks.'

'That's right,' said Mr Sidgwick. 'I've just finished the Tyne Bridge. I'd have a go at *that,*' he pointed towards the cathedral, 'if we lived here.'

'Ha,' said Jamie. 'Um, good idea, yes. Plenty of room for a hobby, I should think.'

'It's the secret of a good marriage, you know,' said Mr Sidgwick.

'Making models?' He pictured himself, grey-haired and bespectacled, with Zoe leaning over him, putting the final touches to a match-built Sydney Opera House. Presumably you took the sulphur tips off first.

'No, silly,' said Mrs Sidgwick. 'Space. Any marriage needs space. That and forgiveness.' She gently elbowed her husband's sizeable waist.

'Oh, I see,' said Jamie. 'How long have you two been married?'

'Thirty-three-and-a-half years,' they said in unison.

Back inside the house, they circuited the ground floor for a second time and then trooped up the stairs, where each room was declared a great success. Mrs Sidgwick gushed over the self-contained shower cubicle while her husband tapped the walls with his knuckles, nodding at their solidity. Jamie felt an inexplicable rush of affection for them.

'How's that piano of yours coming along?' Mr Sidgwick said.

'Oh, you know,' said Jamie. 'Getting there.'

'You'll have to play for us some time,' said Mrs Sidgwick. 'We'd love that, wouldn't we, John?'

They all filed downstairs and Jamie watched them flutter out like a chatty pair of sparrows. As they climbed into their elderly hatchback, a white saloon hurtled into view, Norman the Great Dane strapped into the passenger side with a human seatbelt. The Sidgwicks' car disappeared around the corner and Mrs Roe's BMW slid into the space they had vacated in front of the house.

'They said you'd be here. I want to have another look.' Mrs Roe was out of her car and advancing on him, followed by the lolloping dog.

Jamie staggered backwards as Norman placed both paws on his chest and tried to lick his face. It was nearly a month since her first viewing and since then Jamie had made five fruitless follow-up calls. 'Mrs Roe. What a lovely surprise.'

Mrs Roe raised an eyebrow and pressed on into the house. She wore a velour tracksuit in a deep plum colour and dazzling white trainers but showed no obvious sign of recent exercise. Norman returned to all fours, leaving two dusty paw prints on the lapels of Jamie's jacket.

When Mrs Roe reached the kitchen she looked pointedly at the open French doors.

'Has someone else been here?'

'Yes, actually,' said Jamie. 'There's been quite a lot of interest.'

'I need to see the garage. My son's got a Porsche.'

The studio was a pebble-dashed box across the alleyway at the back of the house, part of a row of garages which stretched along the length of the terrace. While most of these now had up-and-over doors, this one still had the old wooden ones, partly glazed and thick with layers of paint. A shaft of sunlight sliced into the room as Jamie pushed the double doors fully open. At the far end, the window had been enlarged to reveal parkland and beyond that, the upper half of the cathedral. Under the window was a spattered workbench littered with tubes of paint in assorted colours; to its side, an empty easel. Propped against the wall were probably two dozen canvases of varying sizes, showing the abandoned outlines of portraits and landscapes.

What was most striking about the room was that it had been painted a vibrant yellow; the colour of rubber ducks. At that moment it seemed the most cheerful space that Jamie had ever been inside. He imagined Mrs Roe and her petrol-head son ripping out all of the artists' paraphernalia and filling it with engine oil and turtle wax. It suddenly became imperative that this should be the place where Mr Sidgwick recreated Ripon Cathedral from a shipload of Swan Vestas.

'Big enough for a car, I suppose,' said Mrs Roe. 'But we'd have to get rid of all this junk.'

thirty-two

As she drove, keeping to second gear, over the brow of the hill into the village, Caz took her eyes off the road to look at what was left of The Hall and gasped at its wasted black skeleton. The steering wheel drifted with the direction of her gaze and the little Fiat swerved into the path of an oncoming lorry. Jamie lunged across her to grab the wheel and guided the car back into the left-hand lane.

'Jesus, Caz!'

Still mesmerised by the house, she let go of the steering wheel, allowing him to take charge. She probably shouldn't have been driving in the first place; she didn't feel in control and her reactions were non-existent, but Jamie had insisted.

The car kangaroo-hopped to a halt in the middle of the road. She had forgotten that she still needed to use the pedals. A horn brayed from behind.

'Jesus,' Jamie said again and swung round to look over his shoulder. They were on the main route into Wensleydale and were no doubt holding up a line of traffic. Raising a hand in apology, he got out while she sat there, still staring at The Hall. Jamie wrenched open the driver's door and glowered at her. Once she had guessed that he wanted her to move across, she heaved herself over into the passenger seat. They were in the full glare of the sun and she was sweating, too embarrassed to admit that she couldn't remember how the fan worked in her own car. Jamie turned on the engine and eased the Fiat into the narrow lane that ran off the village green, in front of the pub.

'What the hell was that?' he said as they stopped. 'You could have killed us both.'

Could she? Her hands were trembling and she gripped her knees in an attempt to still them. She couldn't tell whether the cause of the shakes was the sight of The Hall or the near-miss with the lorry.

'I don't know what happened. I've gone all wobbly.' She fanned her face with her hand.

'It's OK.' Jamie's face softened and he flicked on the cool air vent. 'Maybe driving wasn't a good idea.'

'It's just that I haven't seen it,' she said. 'Not since the funeral, anyway. I'd forgotten it was so… destroyed. Why hasn't it been knocked down yet?'

'You know why,' said Jamie. 'They're still investigating. For the inquest. At least we don't have to look at it every day like poor old Ruth.'

He seemed distracted by a filthy old truck which was parked outside the driveway to Home Farm and looked vaguely familiar.

'Is that Zoe's car?'

'Yeah,' said Jamie. 'She's probably checking on Mrs Thorneycroft's foal. She… never mind.'

It struck Caz that she had still not given Jamie Zoe's message. She was so rubbish these days. It had sounded important.

'Zoe rang you that night, you know, when you nearly had the crash. Quite a few times. It…it slipped my mind. Did something happen?'

'What?' He wheeled around to face her.

'I'm sorry, J. I should have told you. She wanted you to call her. She sounded upset.'

Jamie sighed. 'It's OK. She's been phoning me at work as well. Let's just say relations are suspended for the moment.'

'But why?'

'It's too boring to explain. Really. Come on, let's go.'

Jamie started the car again and turned it round. They sat, facing the charcoal wreckage of The Hall, waiting for a tractor and its resultant queue of cars to pass.

It had been Jamie's suggestion that she came; a transparent attempt to gee her up, but she suspected it would take more than a visit to Ruth's to shake her out of the protracted stupor into which she had fallen. The girls had now noticed; she could see it in the puzzled expressions on their faces. Only Steve was refusing to acknowledge it. Either he would absent himself from the house completely or he would strap a smile to his face and act as though everything was as it should be. In a sense, Caz was grateful. It was easier that way.

There was a break in the traffic and Jamie pulled across the road, up the driveway to The Hall and into the courtyard while she slumped in the seat next to him. She again had the sensation that she was just an observer, an inert object, unable to participate in the events surrounding her even though she could see everything in minute detail, as if from the other side of an invisible barrier. Now, what she saw was a woman standing in the courtyard wearing a glittery, low-cut evening gown. It took a moment to work out that the woman was Ruth Cole.

'Is everything all right?' Ruth said, squinting through Caz's window. 'I wasn't expecting you.'

'That dress isn't for our benefit then?' Jamie got out of the car.

With a girlish giggle, Ruth swept a hand down over its sequinned folds.

'Oh, this?' she said. 'Willie's taking me out for a meal later. I was just trying it on.'

'The old bugger,' said Jamie. 'I hope his intentions are honourable.'

'Do you think it's a bit much?'

This was aimed at Caz. Under normal circumstances, hearing that Ruth had a date, and with Willie, of all people, would have been major gossip. Today, however, she couldn't bring herself to show any interest and concentrated instead on wrestling her way out of the passenger seat.

'Up to you,' she muttered. Of course it was a bit much.

They followed Ruth into the clutter of her sitting room and sat down; Caz on the small velveteen sofa, Jamie in the armchair. The contrast between the dowdy comfort of Ruth's cottage, unchanged since she was little, and the wreck of her childhood home just outside, was unbearable. It was Jamie's fault for demanding that she came when all she really wanted to do with her Saturday afternoon was lie on the sofa. More unbearable yet was the fact that Ruth was still there, carrying on with her life, when her parents weren't. A heavy weight was settling on her chest, forcing her to take convulsive little gulps of air.

'What is it, pet lamb?' Ruth handed her a tissue from a crochet-covered box on the sideboard.

'I'm fine.' She seemed to be dissolving into the ancient cushions.

Stiffly, as though trying not to split the dress, Ruth manoeuvred herself onto the sofa next to Caz, exposing a crepey amplitude of cleavage. As Ruth reached out to take Caz's hand, she snatched it away.

'She's a bit upset,' said Jamie.

'I can see that.' Ruth shuffled in her dress and nipped at it under the arms where it was clearly too tight, then wriggled up onto her feet. 'I'll make some tea.'

Caz should have refused to come; she had only agreed to the visit to please Jamie. How laughable that was; all she'd done so far was cause him trouble. She was in no mood to make conversation. Her presence was pleasing no-one. It would have been better if she had stayed at home, where there was a bottle of white wine in the fridge. She could already hear the tinkling of the liquid as she poured her first glass, full of promise for an afternoon of pleasant insensibility.

'How long do we have to stay?' she said when Ruth had gone into the kitchen.

'Ssh!' Jamie said. 'She'll hear you.'

They sat in silence; Caz was happy not to talk but Jamie, who always had to fill a gap in conversation, was fidgety, performing what looked like piano scales on his thighs until Ruth reappeared with the tea.

'Don't let me keep you, Caroline, if you've got better things to do.' She was holding out a mug, waiting for Caz to take it from her. 'I know things are difficult, but there's no need to be rude.' It was an admonishment reminiscent of ten years earlier.

'As I said, she's a bit upset,' said Jamie, accepting his tea.

'Yes,' said Ruth, now back on the sofa, 'but that's no excuse for bad manners.' She offered a plate of biscuits; Caz took one even though she'd intended to say no. It was a custard cream; she nibbled off the top layer and scraped off the yellow filling with her teeth as she used to do when she was a child. Jamie took two.

'So,' Ruth said to Jamie, 'what's the latest with you and that Zoe? Will you be getting back together?'

'They've fallen out,' said Caz.

'It's nothing,' Jamie said.

'It was enough to make you almost crash the car.'

He glared at her.

'Did you?' said Ruth. 'Are you hurt?'

'It was a misunderstanding,' said Jamie. 'Anyway,' he turned to Caz, '*you're* a fine one to talk after this morning.'

'What happened this morning?' said Ruth.

'Nothing!' Caz sank back onto the cushions. 'Let's just leave it.' She didn't know why she was being so argumentative.

'There's a lot of nothing going on here today.' Ruth sucked her lips together and spread out her hands on her sequinned lap. 'Look,' she said, 'I always love to see you both, but I'm getting the sense that Caroline wasn't too keen to come. Why *have* you, if you don't mind me asking? Not just to bicker with each other, I imagine.'

'Just a social call.' Jamie swallowed his first biscuit and was contemplating the second. 'But now that we're here, what about this date? Your love life sounds a lot more interesting than mine.'

Caz squirmed in her seat. This was last thing she wanted to hear about: that Ruth had not only outlived her mother but was actually happy.

'Oh, it's not *intimate* or anything,' said Ruth. Caz winced at the thought. Jamie coughed. 'It's companionship, mainly. There's no passion.' She clasped her hands together. 'No, that was your mum and dad's department.'

Please, Caz thought, leave Mum and Dad out of it, but Jamie was hurrying to finish his biscuit and nodding as though relieved to have stumbled across a less problematic topic of conversation.

'Yeah,' he said, 'I've been meaning to ask you. What was that story that old Harding-Page was telling at the funeral about a sausage roll? Is that how they met?'

'It was,' said Ruth. 'I was working for your grandparents, then. Your father seemed to turn up out of nowhere. He'd obviously made a lot of money. He was quite a rough diamond, mind.'

'He was proud that his family was poor,' said Jamie. 'He used to say he dragged himself up by the bootstraps.'

'Yes,' Ruth laughed. 'That sounds about right.'

'Mum's parents were a bit hard core, though,' said Jamie. 'We were terrified of them, weren't we, Caz? How on earth did they accept someone like Dad?'

'Well-bred they might have been, but they weren't snobs.' Ruth took a slow sip of her tea. 'The thing is, love, your mother was on the rebound. Goodness me, what a mess she was in.' She shook her head at the memory. 'Esther had been engaged but the young man called it off at the last minute. She was heartbroken. Her confidence was shot to bits. Your dad helped her get it back. I think he bought The Hall to impress her. It certainly impressed Sir and My Lady. They believed in hard work, and they were desperate for Esther to find her feet again.'

This was news.

'He proposed after less than a month. When you came along, Caroline, I went to work for them as your nanny.'

'What about their wedding?' Jamie asked. 'The photos are all gone now. Was it a big do?'

But Caz was still thinking about her mother. It was the first suggestion she'd ever heard that her mother was vulnerable. Did Esther have the same genetic glitch that had caused Caz to run wild in her teens and which was threatening to subsume her now? Caz couldn't decide whether that was comforting, or troubling. She had always entertained a rather idealistic image of her parents' courtship; like a Cathy and Heathcliff scenario, but with a better outcome. The reality was likely more prosaic; that her mother, jilted and stripped of her self-esteem, had looked to Bernie for stability and security. The fact that Bernie adored her must have been an added bonus. When Steve turned up in her own life, that was exactly what she had been looking for, too. Were she and her mother a pair of desperados who had settled for less than they really wanted, or pragmatists who recognised the chance of happiness when it presented itself?

Beneath her sleeve, one of the plasters had come away at the edge and she began to pick at it. Ruth broke off from saying something about the Rotary Club and gave her a sharp look.

'Aren't you hot in that jumper? It must be twenty degrees outside.'

'No.' She tugged at the cuff but Ruth reached across and took her arm in a firm grip. 'Let me see. Oh, Lord.'

'Bloody hell, Caz,' said Jamie, leaning forward in his chair. 'Why didn't you tell me? You said they were from ages ago.'

'They are.' Caz pulled back her arm. How stupid she was to have drawn attention to herself. 'It's no big deal. They're just little scratches.'

'Little scratches, my foot.' Ruth stood up. 'Right. I've seen enough. You and me are going to the doctors. And don't even *think* about saying I'm not your mother.'

'You're not my mother,' said Caz. 'And there's nothing wrong with me.' What qualified Ruth, with her ridiculous over-the-top dress and her sanctimonious manner, to order her around?

'No?' said Ruth, 'Well, I'm telling you, this is not normal. You need help, Caroline.'

Caz stood up too, her face inches from Ruth's.

'For God's sake!' she shouted. 'Why can't you just fuck off and leave me alone?'

'Caz!' said Jamie.

Ruth took a step backwards and turned her face away. The room was silent except for the low rumble of traffic on the road outside. Where had those words come from? She had gone too far; how was poor Ruth to know that her very presence was intolerable?

'Sorry,' Caz mumbled. 'I didn't mean it.'

'I think it's time you left,' Ruth said in a quiet voice.

'Come on,' said Jamie. 'Let's go.' Suddenly exhausted, Caz allowed him to propel her by the shoulders out of the sitting room and into the waiting car.

Jamie insisted on driving. Caz tussled with the seatbelt on the passenger side and collapsed back, her cheek resting against the window. Jamie wedged the gearstick into reverse. Caz's face bashed against the glass when the car jerked backwards, and then again when he shoved it into first.

Behind the wheel, Jamie grimaced at the road ahead. Caz doubted whether he would have noticed the plasters on his own; she was pretty sure that she had kept them hidden from Steve and the girls, but Ruth was more difficult to deceive. He slapped the steering wheel with both hands.

'Shit, Caz!'

'Don't be angry with me.' What was it to him if she needed to cut herself a little bit? It was a release valve. Not that he would recognise the need for that.

'You shouldn't have spoken to Ruth like that. She was only trying to help.'

'I said I was sorry. I'll call her tomorrow. I just wish she wouldn't go on at me.'

'I know, but she didn't deserve *that*. Look… I'm… This is out of my league. I don't know what to think.'

'It makes me feel better, J. Truly.'

Jamie was shaking his head. He looked completely at a loss.

'I *want* you to feel better, really I do. Why won't you go to the doctor?'

'I'm fine.'

'*That's* not fine.' He pointed to her wrist. 'Your family needs you. How can you be there for them when you're doing that?'

She could try explaining that puncturing new skin was like making the first footsteps in fresh snow, or writing on the first page of a new exercise book, only more thrilling, but Jamie wouldn't want to hear that. Neither would he understand that there was an essential purity to it. People tended to assume that cutting yourself was the first step on an unstoppable path to self-destruction. It didn't feel like that; it was an end rather than a means.

'God knows what's going through your mind,' Jamie was saying.

Caz stretched and yawned, already thinking of the wine awaiting her.

'Not much,' she said.

He sighed as they stopped at the kerb outside the house.

'No offence, but this is doing my head in,' he said. 'I'm going for a drive. I'll see you later.'

thirty-three

A couple of weeks later, Jamie got to the office to find Chris eating Hula Hoops off his fingers. A beefy tang hung in the air and Charlotte was making choking noises.

'My sale completes today,' he said. 'I had eight pints and a curry last night to celebrate. Mental, I tell you…' He circled an index finger around his ear.

'Delusional,' said Charlotte.

Jamie couldn't help himself. 'Does the buyer know about the subsidence?'

'They had a survey, didn't they? Anyway it's happening. They've already exchanged contracts. No backing out now.'

With nothing useful to add, Jamie dug out some polaroids of a new property that he hoped might appeal to Mrs Roe. His extension rang.

'Jamie?' Mr Sidgwick sounded as though he had just run up and downstairs several times.

'What's happened, Mr Sidgwick? Are you all right?'

'I'd like to make an offer on College Lane,' he panted. There was a gravid pause. 'Asking price.'

Across the desk, Chris was listening without any obvious embarrassment. He lined up an elastic band. Jamie ducked just in time.

'College Lane? Wow,' he said. 'That's amazing.'

Mr Sidgwick started to speak again but was interrupted by his wife in the background. 'John, tell Jamie we can move in at once,' she was saying. 'Next week!'

'Yes, yes, Pat, in a minute. Sorry about that, yes, it's exactly what we've been looking for. We don't want to leave anything to chance.'

'OK,' said Jamie. 'I'll let the vendor know. Congratulations.'

He put the phone down.

'Good effort, Jamie,' said Charlotte, looking at Chris. 'That's fantastic.'

Chris gave a low whistle and chugged the remnants of the bag of Hula-Hoops into his mouth, like a drink. 'This'll be interesting. Didn't Archer tell you not to show them that house?' He wiped his hands on his trousers.

'Ugh,' said Charlotte.

'Yeah,' said Jamie, 'but a sale's a sale. Isn't it?'

'I dunno about that,' said Chris, perfecting his aim again. 'He's desperate to flog it to Mrs Roe. Probably wants to give her one.'

'Is that all you can think about?' said Jamie. 'He's scared of her, more likely. Either way, it's too bad. I'll tell him this afternoon. And will you stop flicking those bloody things at me?'

Maggie appeared at the desk with another of her post-it notes. It was a message to ring Mrs Roe, complete with a giant tick in the urgent box. Mrs Roe had never tried to contact him before. Jamie waited until Chris had gone out for his cheese and onion pasty before calling her back.

'I want to buy College Lane,' she said.

'I'm so sorry,' said Jamie. 'An offer was made at the asking price this morning.'

'And was it accepted?'

He thought of Mrs Sidgwick in the garden, stretching up onto her tiptoes.

'Yes,' he said. 'It's been taken off the market.'

Mrs Roe gave a loud tut and then was quiet for a few seconds.

'Right,' she said. 'Tell them I'll pay another ten thousand pounds.'

'But Mrs Roe, the house is no longer for sale.'

'That's balls,' she said. 'Who in their right mind would turn down an extra ten grand? I want you to put it to the vendor.'

'I can't,' said Jamie, 'that would be unethical, um, against the professional code of conduct.'

'Sod that,' said Mrs Roe. 'I bet your Mr Archer couldn't give a toss about codes of conduct when there's money at stake.'

'He's a very principled man,' said Jamie, weakly.

'Well, we'll soon find out,' said Mrs Roe, 'because if you don't make that offer, I'll be telling him all about it.'

Jamie sighed. 'OK,' he said. 'Leave it with me.'

When the call ended, he sat for a moment, gazing blindly at the polaroids.

'I think I got the gist of that,' said Charlotte. 'What are you going to do?'

'No brainer,' said Jamie. He picked up the phone for the third time and called the owner of College Lane, who accepted Mr Sidgwick's offer without hesitation.

Jamie found Archer in his office, fixing a new string to his guitar. The instrument lay cradled in his lap and he was tending to it with an affection that Jamie had never seen him display for anyone or anything else. Archer tightened one of the pegs and strummed with a thumbnail that was unnaturally and grotesquely long.

'Do you have something to tell me?' Archer said, without looking up. Because he was pulling the string taut with his teeth as he spoke, it was impossible to tell whether this might be a leading question. It was unlikely that Mrs Roe would have followed through her threat already. Archer plucked a few more notes, gave the peg a final twist and released the string from his mouth.

'Make me a happy man and tell me Mrs Roe has bought College Lane.'

'Um, no,' Jamie began. 'Not exactly. The Sidgwicks have offered asking and the vendor has accepted.'

'Good Lord.' Archer played a chord which Jamie recognised as a decent G7, patted the body of the guitar a couple of times and set it reverently on the floor. 'Well, I never.'

'Yes,' said Jamie. 'It was rather a surprise.'

'You're not kidding,' said Archer. 'This is good news, Jamie. Very good news. Well done, lad.'

Back at his desk, Jamie was still basking in the afterglow of Archer's praise when the phone rang yet again. He reached out to answer it.

'How are you, Jamie?' Zoe said.

'Yeah, I'm fine. Great, actually.'

'That's good. I just wanted to make sure. I thought today might be a bit tough.'

'Um…' Jamie was staring out of the window, wondering why Zoe was so concerned about him. He glanced at his desk calendar. It was midsummer's day: his mother's birthday. 'How did you know?'

'You told me, remember? When it was *your* birthday. You said it was funny because you were born on the shortest day of the year and your mum was born on the longest.'

His last birthday. Less than two weeks before the fire. They had rounded off an evening in the Bay Horse with the best sex he could ever recall. For a moment, Jamie envied his own past virility and his ignorance of what was to come. It was touching that Zoe had remembered his mother's birthday, especially when, to his shame, he had forgotten. Perhaps she too thought fondly of the time when they had fun together, before everything went wrong. And they *did* have fun. If they could just recapture some of what brought them together in the first place… He asked himself whether this was the definition of madness. But she was adamant that whatever was going on with Andrew had ended, and he still suspected that the whole thing was his own fault in any case. As a fully-functioning boyfriend he hadn't been much use. Who could blame her for looking elsewhere?

'I've sold a house,' he said, before he could examine his thought process any further. 'At last. It's my first one. Will you come for a picnic after work? To celebrate?'

The cork gave a pleasing pop and shot out across the grassy bank, into the river.

'Litter lout,' said Zoe.

'Biodegradable,' said Jamie.

Zoe held out her glass at an angle so that the champagne didn't fizz over the top. It had been an impulse buy; the only bottle in the fridge at the Co-op. He'd also bought strawberries and a pair of plastic flutes.

They were sitting on a plaid woollen rug from Caz's understairs cupboard that must have come from their parents. It was scratchy and smelled of spaniels.

'So, this elderly couple,' he said, 'the ones who bought the house, are so sweet. I think I remind them of their son who's moved away.'

'That's nice.'

'They made me imagine what it might be like to be their age.'

Crickets stridulated, a dog barked distantly and Jamie stretched out in the late sun, admiring Zoe in her summer dress. It wasn't one he recognised. Perhaps she had actually been shopping.

'Old and married?'

'Happy and settled. Zo, this house is charming. You would love it.' He dismissed thoughts of matchstick sculptures and pictured instead the little table and chairs in the corner of the garden.

Zoe picked up a strawberry by the stalk and bit off the fruit beneath.

'Jamie.' She flicked the stalk away. 'I know you're celebrating, but can we talk about it? We can't pretend it didn't happen, even though I'd like to.'

Jamie had been lying on his side on the rug with his head propped on one arm, in a pose he hoped was both appealing and nonchalant. What he wanted most of all was to show her that he was mature and magnanimous enough not to be upset any longer. He pulled himself upright, aiming to look like a serious person with grown-up things to say.

'It wasn't a big deal,' he began, remembering how he'd booted Zoe's wheelie bin over after thrusting her flowers into it. 'Who you see is up to you.'

'Oh, come on,' said Zoe. 'I saw you. Through the window. There was rubbish all over the garden. It took me ages to clear it up.'

'Sorry about that,' he muttered.

'No.' A faint smile played at the corner of her mouth. 'I deserved it.'

In the distance, another couple wandered onto the field, hand in hand, with a little dog pogo-ing around in front of them, yapping. Appearing not to notice, the man and woman stopped and wound themselves together in a long, slow kiss. The dog became frenzied, throwing itself at their legs. Zoe stared fascinatedly at them for a moment before turning back to him.

'Listen,' she said. 'If I'd known you were going to rock up that night, I wouldn't have asked Andrew over.' She plucked a rotten strawberry from the punnet and lobbed it into the river.

'Are you blaming me, for not making an appointment?'

'No! I just didn't mean to rub your nose in it.'

'If you're saying it's my fault for not being able to… well, that's a fair cop - God, I wish that dog would shut up - but you can't take issue with my *timing*.'

Jamie looked away from her to the couple with the dog, willing them to take their happiness and their noise elsewhere, when a new thought struck him.

'You didn't tell him, did you? Andrew?'

'Of course not,' said Zoe, hotly. 'I would never do that.'

'So what was it? A frustration shag? A series of frustration shags?'

The other couple had turned and were walking away from them again, unentwined. Now quiet, the dog scampered ahead of them. Two ducks came to land on the surface of the river and glided away downstream, leaving a puttering wake behind them.

'I don't know what it was,' said Zoe. 'I'm not proud of myself. Quite the opposite.' She shifted slightly on the ground. 'I need to stretch my legs,' she said. 'They're going numb.'

She got up and walked to the edge of the bank where she stood sipping the champagne, her back towards him. The radiance of her hair in the warm light of the sun and the paleness of her cotton dress gave her an angelic quality. Jamie was glad of a moment to recover himself, to be reminded of what he wanted to prove to her; that he had got over the Andrew episode and was ready to move forward. His plan hadn't gone overly well so far and he needed to regroup. Zoe came to sit down again, placing her glass on the rug beside her.

'It doesn't matter,' said Jamie, his hands held up in a capitulating gesture. 'I forgive you.'

This made her look up, as though genuinely startled.

'What? Why would you forgive me for doing that to you? In those circumstances? I'm not sure I'll ever forgive myself and it makes you look like a masochist.'

'I - '

'Actually, no, it's worse than that. Aren't you angry? Don't you respect yourself at all?'

She glared at him, eyes wide and challenging, as though he had said the worst possible thing, as though she were the offended party. He had imagined that Zoe would be grateful for his forgiveness, that it would remove the barrier that had formed between them. There was an issue of trust, sure, but they could build that up again over time, couldn't they? He was the one making concessions here; all she had to do was accept them.

'Are you trying to confuse me?' In his helplessness, Jamie flung his arms outwards and knocked over Zoe's champagne. The bubbles pulsed on to the rug and sank into its woolly depths. 'Oh, bloody hell!' He snatched up the glass and righted it. 'First you say I'm needy and suffocating, then I try to be more laid back and you don't like that, either. What am I supposed to think?'

'I don't know.'

She looked away towards the languid churn of the river. Jamie touched the smoothness of her arm, tanned up to the short sleeve of her dress from working outdoors. Above that, it would be white and soft. Against the dimming sky, the outline of Zoe's face was still clear. But the evening, hushed and perfect as it was, had been ruined. He jerked his hand away.

'I've had enough of this,' he said, shaking his head. 'I'm out. I haven't a clue what you want. Everything I try is wrong. Maybe you're right. Maybe we don't know each other well enough. Maybe you should go.'

Zoe absently rubbed her upper arm where Jamie's fingers had been, then retrieved her cardigan from the rug and put it on. Jamie collapsed onto his back and lay there without moving. He stared at the wisps of clouds drifting and reforming in the inkiness above, not blinking until his eyes watered. Only when he was sure that she had gone did he allow himself to get up. In the fading light he gathered up the picnic things. Zoe hadn't wanted him enough. His body had decided not to want her. He had no idea which came first. If he had made the right decision, he wondered why it felt so terrible.

thirty-four

Caz had reached the point in the evening where she needed to open another bottle of wine before the headache really kicked in. Steve was putting Ruby and Pearl to bed. She had been drinking since four, just after Steve brought the girls home from school.

'Mummy,' Ruby called from upstairs, 'please can you read to us?'

'Inaminute,' she replied.

The cork broke in half as she tried to pull it out. She pushed it down inside the bottle with her finger and refilled her glass.

The walk from the kitchen was surprisingly troublesome, as if the doorway had been made narrower and the hall wider. She lurched from side to side, grabbing at the walls. When she reached the bottom of the stairs, Ruby and Pearl were on the landing, peering down at her over the bannister. She tripped on the first step, falling forwards. Unable to put out her free arm in time to save herself, she landed on her face, her nose colliding with the edge of one of the stairs. The impact made her lose her grip on the glass, which rolled back down and smashed, spraying wine up the wall.

'Mummy!' Pearl shrieked.

Powerless to move, Caz lay spreadeagled, a dull ache in her nose. Then Steve was there, hoisting her up and piloting her back to the sitting room. As always, his touch was gentle, but when he deposited her on the sofa his expression was unlike anything she had seen before.

'Stay there,' he hissed. 'I'll deal with them.'

He was gone a long time. She wanted more wine but didn't dare go back to the kitchen. In the hall, she could hear Steve brushing broken glass into a dustpan. She sat motionless, bracing herself for a telling-off, but when he came into the room he was stuffing his wallet into the back pocket of his jeans.

'I'm going out,' he said. 'The girls are asleep. You crack on with whatever it is you want to do.'

'Steve,' she said, but after that she stalled. What was it that she wanted to say to him? She wished he could bring her a nice glass of wine and that they could snuggle up together on the sofa, but she couldn't say that. Her nose throbbed. Normally, if she injured herself in even the tiniest way, he would be hovering nearby, asking if it hurt, offering painkillers, plasters, or hugs. Now, she could have broken her nose and he wasn't interested.

'What?' said Steve.

'Nothing,' she said in a quiet voice.

'Right. Then I'll see you later.'

She waited until the front door closed and then went to the fridge. It was obvious that Steve didn't care what she did so she might as well please herself. After three more glasses, the pain was subsiding. Jamie came home just as she was contemplating a fourth.

'Jesus, Caz, what's happened to you?'

She tried and failed to form a sentence. 'Fell.'

Jamie sat on the arm of the chair and rubbed a hand across his face. 'Where's Steve?'

'Pub.'

'Oh, for God's sake. I'm going to bed. I suggest you do the same.'

When she awoke she was still fully dressed and the sun was projecting shadows from the window panes onto the curtains. Downstairs, she could hear Jamie trying to persuade Ruby and Pearl to eat breakfast. She must have been asleep for twelve hours. Steve had been to bed, got up and left for work without her noticing. She put a finger to the bridge of her nose; it felt doughy and swollen with a lump that wasn't there before.

Once she was sure that everyone had gone out, she slid out of bed and shuffled to the bathroom. Her reflection was horrifying. On the top of her enormous nose and beneath her eyes, the skin was black with bruising. She splashed cold water onto her face which woke her up slightly but made no visible difference. One of her front teeth was aching; when she probed at it with a finger it wobbled, making her nauseous.

Caz sank onto the edge of the bath. She couldn't remember if anything specific had happened to make her drink so much that she fell. The look exchanged between Ruby and Pearl when she opened the first bottle flashed before her. If they had said anything, would she have put the wine back in the fridge and switched on the kettle instead? She doubted it.

Rather than seeing that look as a sign that she was distressing her daughters, she had treated it as a challenge. So what if she was being judged? They had no idea what it was like to be her. All they had to think about were the trifling concerns of primary school children; they knew nothing of the things she needed to forget about, every day.

Someone had poured away the dregs of the wine and left the empty bottle on the window-sill. Her glass had been washed up. She checked the fridge, the cupboards and her emergency hiding places; all the wine had gone.

Caz put on some shoes, grabbed her purse and keys, and left the house.

By the time she got to the Co-op, she wanted a drink. The headache was starting early. It was a warm day and the air-conditioning in the shop was a relief after the short walk, which had left her sweating and breathless. She idled by the chillers where it was coolest before moving on towards the wine shelves, where she stopped in front of the chardonnay and put her basket on the floor.

Maybe the wine wasn't agreeing with her; maybe that was why she tripped. It might be a good idea to try something else, just to see.

Shuffling the basket along with her foot, she found herself in the spirits section. Vodka had been her drink of choice as a teenager because no-one could smell it on her breath. The clear bottle of Smirnoff with its red label was like an old acquaintance. Steve was angry with her; she needed to be careful. But she could hide the vodka and he would never know that she was drinking it as long as she didn't fall over again. Caz picked up the basket, reached over and put two bottles into it.

At the corner of the aisle, she stopped. A couple of women were standing in front of the checkout, chatting, one of them facing her. They were mothers from Ruby and Pearl's school, people with whom she'd had coffee in the time she now referred to in her head as BF: before fire. They had been to her house and sat gossiping in the kitchen while their daughters played in the garden.

Caz took a step backwards. The name of the woman opposite her was Deborah, or Donna, or Diana. How could she not remember? She stood, torn between fleeing empty-handed and brazening it out, but she had already seen the dart of the woman's eyes towards the vodka in her basket. She approached the checkout.

'Caz,' said Deborah, or whatever her name was, 'are you all right? What's happened to your face?'

It was hotter by the tills, which were near the door. She swung the basket onto the rack next to the conveyor belt. The cashier, too, was staring at her nose.

'Nothing,' she said. Deborah tutted and shook her head, swapping glances with the other woman. Caz handed over some banknotes. As soon as she had been given the change, she bolted from the shop, aware that the women were muttering behind her. Passing through the open doors she was sure she heard Steve's name.

With a carrier bag in each hand, Caz laboured up the hill past the nursery school and the doctor's surgery. If she had seen a friend with a face like hers, she would have assumed that the husband was to blame, too. That she hadn't offered any explanation must have made Steve look even more guilty. She should have gone back and told them that her injuries were self-inflicted, but that would have meant admitting to those women, who weren't really her friends, that she was a falling-down drunk, and what good would that have done?

At home, the red light of the answering machine was flashing again. Caz went into the kitchen and stashed one of the bottles of vodka in the freezer drawer, under the chicken nuggets. Without bothering to check for ice or even considering a mixer, she took the other bottle and a tumbler back to the hall, where she poured herself three fingers. Sitting on the bottom stair, from where she could reach the machine, she sniffed the glass. It smelled more like lighter fuel than something you could drink and left her nostrils burning, but she took a sip nonetheless.

'Hello love,' said Ruth's voice when she pressed 'play'. 'I'm just ringing to say I accept your apology. You weren't yourself the other day but it's all right, pet, I understand. I still think a trip to see the doctor would be a good idea, though. Maybe...'

Caz jabbed the 'stop' button and drank the vodka down in one. Bloody Ruth wouldn't leave her alone. Why couldn't she get the message? It wasn't a doctor she needed, it was peace and quiet. She poured another vodka, and another. As she finished the fifth glass, she realised that she hadn't eaten anything all day, not that she was hungry. It was after three; Steve would be home soon with the girls. After a struggle to stand she managed to clamber up to her bedroom, where she hid the bottle and the glass at the back of the wardrobe and collapsed into bed. When she awoke it was almost dark. With the curtains still open she turned over in bed and didn't wake up again until morning, when she noted with bleary satisfaction that she had slept twice through the night for the first time since BF.

thirty-five

Jamie hugged the girls goodbye at the school gate. Pearl's hair hadn't been brushed and he tried to smooth it down with an incompetent hand before he released her, aware that they were being scrutinised by a cluster of mothers by the fence. This happened every day. His practised response was to wish them all a good morning with exaggerated politeness, but today their attention shifted to a woman walking past Ruby and Pearl in the opposite direction, through the playground towards him. She was probably forty-ish, with laced-up shoes and an apologetic smile.

'Can I speak to you for a moment?' she said. 'I'm Miss Wood.'

'Jamie Fenton. The girls' uncle. Are you Ruby's teacher, or Pearl's?' Jamie gave her his estate agent's grin; the one he used when he wanted to look confident. In no way was he equipped for a teacher-parent conversation.

'I'm the head. It's a small school. We get to know all of our children pretty well.' She fiddled with a long string of beads around her neck. 'Is everything all right? At home, I mean. After what happened to your parents. Their grandparents.'

'We're managing,' said Jamie. 'The girls are OK. Apart from having to put up with me, that is.' He checked her face. The smile had gone. Although he had turned away from the other women, he could sense their eyes on his back.

'Ruby keeps asking why her mummy doesn't like getting up any more. She seems quite worried about it.'

There was a simple answer to that question: wine and, more recently, vodka. Caz said it helped her sleep. Whether that were true or not, it *didn't* help her to get out of in bed in the mornings.

'I'd speak to Mrs Hopkins myself except that we haven't seen her here for a while,' Miss Wood continued, 'and Mr Hopkins always stays in his van at pickup time so I can never catch him, either.'

'He's rushing to drop the girls at home so he can get back to work,' said Jamie.

'I see,' Miss Wood said, frowning.

Jamie consulted his watch.

'Um, I really need to be getting to the office. If that's everything?'

Miss Wood was looking at the Fiesta, which was parked on the zigzagged lines in front of the school gate with the engine running.

'And who looks after them when they're at home?'

'We all do,' said Jamie. 'Is there a problem?'

'Academically they're doing well, but we've had a behavioural issue that I can't discuss with you. I'd be grateful if you could ask one of their parents to come in.'

'Sure,' said Jamie. 'No worries.' He stepped off the kerb.

'And Mr Fenton?' said Miss Wood. 'Where *is* their mummy?'

'She's at home,' said Jamie. 'She's fine. She'll be in touch.'

He got back into the car, questioning for the first time whether he should have stopped on those zigzagged lines. Other parents didn't; they parked at a respectful distance down the road. But then, he wasn't a parent. He was just a clueless uncle.

Poor Ruby and Pearl. Even without Ruby letting slip that Caz was never out of bed before they went to school, it was impossible that their ragged appearance would have gone unnoticed. They could see their mother's withdrawal even though Steve was ignoring it. Caz still made an evening meal some of the time, or rather heated things up out of tins or the freezer. In every other way she was unavailable to her daughters. When Jamie came home from work they would be on the sofa, still in their school uniforms, knees drawn up to their chins, engrossed in the television. Caz was always in her room. Was it any wonder if they were misbehaving at school?

He turned off the high street and slipped the Fiesta into a long line of cars behind a combine harvester, assessing the likelihood of either Caz or Steve going in to see Ruby and Pearl's head-teacher. From what he could tell, Steve didn't set much store by education and tended to avoid any interaction with school. Caz could only just drag herself to the Co-op.

As the situation deteriorated at Chestnut Drive, Jamie had become correspondingly less enthusiastic about being there. The trouble was that he had nowhere else to go. The previous evening, he had sat at the kitchen table, practising the fingering to Elgar's *Salut d'Amour* while Steve watched television. Caz had slunk away upstairs and Steve was so distracted that he forgot about the girls. It was well past ten before he shooed them off to bed. Only now, after his encounter with Miss Wood, did Jamie wonder whether he should have intervened.

At almost nine-thirty, Jamie took off his jacket and flopped into his chair. It was, thankfully, almost the end of the school year, which would mean six weeks before he would need to be late for work again. This should have been good news, but it was hard to imagine how Caz was going to cope with the girls every day on her own. Somehow he would have to find a way to get her out of bed before he left for the office.

From the opposite side of the desk, Chris drew a finger across his throat.

'What?'

'You're for it, mate.'

'What do you mean? I'm not *that* late.'

'Archer's doing his nut. He's been storming in here every five minutes asking where you are.'

'Shit.'

Later that day, the Sidgwicks were due to exchange contracts on College Lane. On his desk was a Tupperware box of fairy cakes that Mrs Sidgwick had brought in as a thank you.

'JAMIE FENTON! IN HERE! NOW!'

Everyone in the office looked up. Chris rubbed his hands together. 'This,' he said, 'is going to be good.'

As he stood up, Jamie swiped a hand over his sweating top lip and gave Chris what he hoped was an unconcerned smile.

'If I'm not back in ten minutes,' he said, 'send a search party.'

'If you're not back in ten minutes,' said Chris, 'I'm having those cakes.'

Archer's door was open. Jamie went inside and shut it carefully behind him. He needn't have bothered. The office had a floor-length glass window that would afford the entire staff an uninterrupted view of whatever was about to happen and there was no way that the walls were thick enough to be sound-proof.

On Archer's desk, the Newton's cradle quivered from recent use. Jacob Archer clasped his hands together and stretched them out to the front, eyes closed, breathing deeply. After three or four loud exhalations he lowered his arms and opened his eyes.

'What did I tell you,' he said quietly, 'about wasting time on those witless old fools?'

'They're not witless old fools,' said Jamie. 'They're decent people and they're buying one of our houses, at full price.'

'Yes,' said Archer, 'but it's not full price, is it? Not when another party, who you'd been ESPECIALLY told to look after, offers TEN THOUSAND POUNDS MORE!' He thumped the desk with an upturned fist. The chrome balls of the Newton's cradle clacked together several times before Archer clutched at them in wild irritation and held them still. Jamie ground his teeth and wondered whether it would be best to speak or stay silent.

'I suppose you should tell me what you were thinking,' said Archer, in a more moderate tone.

'Estate agents get such a bad name,' Jamie began, 'and the Sidgwicks really love that house, I mean *really* love it.

It didn't seem fair to let someone steal it from under their noses.'

'It's called gazumping,' said Archer, 'and it happens all the time. That house was far too cheap. Jeepers, we can't afford to turn down extra commission at the moment.'

'But it's not right,' Jamie protested.

'It's BUSINESS! Did you think I wouldn't find out?'

'I don't know.'

'Idiot! What would your father have said? Have you considered that?'

Jamie *had* considered it. He hoped that Bernie would have agreed with him even though, as it turned out, his father was the last person from whom to take business advice. He decided to say nothing. Bernie's approval would be no use to him now. Outside, the whole office had stopped work to watch.

'Well,' said Archer, 'you'll be pleased to know that the deal's still going through. I've taken a right ear-bashing from Marian Roe over the phone. She's taking her custom elsewhere.'

'Oh,' said Jamie. Mari*an,* not Mari*lyn.* 'Sorry about that.'

'You will be,' said Archer. 'Your services are no longer required.'

Even after all the warnings, Jamie hadn't really believed that Archer would sack him. Maybe on a subconscious level he'd assumed that because his boss and his father had known each other, and his father was now dead, he would somehow be protected. In the battle for his headspace, any work issues were consistently less important than his problems with Zoe, Caz's burgeoning addiction and the absence of the piano. Wasn't it always the things you hadn't considered that hit you hardest? It was called a blindside for a reason.

'But Mr Archer,' Jamie said, 'I need this job. I haven't got anything else to live on.'

'You should have thought about that.'

'But aren't there… laws about this or something? Don't I at least have to work my notice?'

'Nope,' said Archer. 'This is Ripon, sunshine, not London. It's my business and I'll do whatever I like. Now, hop it.'

In the office, Chris was already half-way through the box of fairy cakes. 'Told you,' he said between mouthfuls, as Jamie stuffed his belongings into a plastic bag. They consisted of an industrial tape measure, half a packet of cup-a-soups and a framed photo of Zoe which he had recently relegated from desk top to top drawer. Not much to show for eight months' work. On the way out, Jamie stopped at reception to hand over his car keys.

'I'm sorry, love,' said Maggie. 'I hope you find something else soon.'

The switchboard buzzed and flashed. Maggie held up a finger while she answered the call and he stood, tapping the edge of the desk in his impatience to get away.

'Yes, he's just here,' said Maggie. 'I'll put him on.' She handed him the phone.

'Mr Fenton? This is Colin from Robinson's.' The man could barely keep the excitement from his voice. 'I've got some good news. The piano's ready.'

'Um, wow.' Jamie didn't know what else to say. The curse of pernicious timing had bitten him again.

'I know! There's just one thing, though; there's not enough space to keep it in our workshop. My boss says we'll need to deliver it within fourteen days.'

—

A few minutes later, Jamie was crammed inside a phone box that was like a shrunken greenhouse. With the toe of his shoe, he nudged the door open a few inches for some air and wedged the carrier bag into the gap. He had a piano that he couldn't play, no job and no income. Caz and Steve's house was twenty miles away and he had no means of transport.

He shoved a ten-pence piece into the slot and dialled. The number rang and rang. The little beige phone was under the bay window in the hall, no more than a few seconds away from any part of the house. He held on. The line clicked.

'Hello.' Caz's voice was breathy and incurious.

'It's me,' said Jamie. 'I've been fired.'

'Jamie?'

'I've been fired. Sacked.'

'S-a-ck-e-d?' She enunciated it as though she were trying out the sound of a word she'd never used before.

'Yes. Sacked. Can you come and pick me up?'

'I'm not well.' This time, the words came out in a slurry jumble.

'Please, Caz? I can't get home.'

There was a pause on the line.

'I need to go back to bed.'

The phone clunked down. Jamie banged his own receiver back onto the wall and leaned sideways against the glass. Steve would be too busy. Ruth Cole didn't drive. Going back into the office and begging for a lift was unthinkable. In desperation, he dialled the surgery. The receptionist answered but it took three more coins before Zoe came to the phone.

'What's so urgent, Jamie?' she said. 'I'm in the middle of a consultation with a parrot and the bloody thing won't stop nipping me.'

'I've lost my job.'

Zoe sighed heavily. 'I'm sorry to hear that,' she said, 'but I'm not sure what I - '

'Can you give me a lift home? Please? I had to give the car back.'

In the several seconds it took for her to respond, Jamie dared to hope that she was actually going to help him.

'I don't think I can,' she said eventually. 'I'm booked up all afternoon, er... Hang on a minute.' Jamie heard muffled voices, one female, one male and possibly Antipodean. Zoe must have put her hand over the microphone. He fed another coin into the slot. 'Someone here's suggesting the X10. Apparently it goes every half an hour.'

'Oh,' said Jamie. 'Thanks. I hadn't thought of that.'

'You're welcome. Bye, Jamie. And good luck.'

Eyes stinging, he put down the phone and blundered out into the market square, unable to see clearly, furious with himself for even thinking of calling Zoe. It was only a few weeks since their picnic when he told her to leave. There was no reason for her to bail him out now. It wasn't her job any more, even though she appeared to have given it brief consideration. As a partner in the practice, Andrew could easily have forbidden Zoe to leave the surgery to help her ex-boyfriend. In fact, if Zoe had ended whatever was between them, it probably wasn't her finest ever career move to ask. She was probably right not to argue.

It wasn't as though helping people won you any plaudits. For trying to do the right thing by Mr and Mrs Sidgwick he had been fired in the most public and humiliating manner.

He had known, when he refused Mrs Roe's inflated offer, that he was taking an enormous risk and yet he had gone ahead anyway. But despite that, it was impossible to regret what he had done. The Sidgwicks would have the house that they had set their hearts on. They would never know what it cost him, and he was fine with that. The trouble was, it had been hard enough to find a job in the first place and this one had only come about because of his father's intervention.

Still clutching the plastic bag, he sank onto a bench, blinking up at the fierce blue sky until his eyes were drier. Mercifully, the bench was on the far side of the obelisk which meant that no-one at Archer's would be able to see him. Across the square, the X10 pulled into the bus station. Jamie reached a weary hand into his trouser pocket and found only one more ten-pence piece. His cashcard had been swallowed by the machine a couple of weeks ago when he forgot his ATM number and he hadn't got round to contacting the bank. There were no notes in his wallet and he doubted the bus would accept credit cards. Defeated, he lay down on the bench and closed his eyes against the sun's accusatory glare.

'Jacob Archer is a bastard.'

Jamie blinked his eyes open. Charlotte was bent over him, her hands on her knees, blocking out the sun.

'I've just heard,' she said, straightening. 'I was out with the octopus client. Come on, up you get. I'm going to buy you a cup of tea and then I'll take you home.'

thirty-six

Tea was an elaborate affair involving china and a strainer. Across the room, an elderly man in tails was playing *The Entertainer*, not making a bad fist of it considering that the piano was offensively out of tune.

'This is so good of you,' he said to Charlotte. 'Was Archer OK about it?'

A lethargic fan whirred overhead. At surrounding tables, ladies in cardigans complained about the heat and wafted themselves with their menus.

'As far as he's concerned I'm out taking photos of Whitegates Grove. And no, I haven't sold a house there yet, although I'm still letting Chris think that I have.' Charlotte waited while a vanilla slice was loaded onto Jamie's plate and a chocolate eclair onto hers. 'So, have I got this right: you screwed over Great Dane woman in favour of the clients Archer told you to ignore and he fired you for it?'

'Pretty much,' said Jamie.

'It sounds as though you did a good thing.'

'Archer said I was an idiot.'

'Naïve, maybe, but not an idiot.'

'Is that what you think? That I'm naïve?' Jamie said, surprised that Charlotte would have taken the time to form an opinion of his character. Blunt as she was, she'd never seemed like the analytical type. He gave her a challenging look across the table.

'I always find these things so awkward.' Charlotte picked up the dainty cup and took a sip. 'I get my fingers stuck in the handles.'

Jamie cut a chunk of vanilla slice with a cake-fork.

'This place was Mum's favourite,' he said. 'She used to say they knew how to do things properly. Dad said it was a licence to print money.'

'He wasn't wrong,' said Charlotte. 'I'll be on beans on toast for a week after this.'

'Join the club.'

'Really?' said Charlotte. 'I'd have thought you were used to something a bit more sophisticated.'

'As if,' Jamie said. 'My sister Caz has us on a strict diet of freezer food and takeaways.'

'Is she OK? The fire must have been hard on all of you.'

Jamie put down his fork and looked at Charlotte, who carefully placed her cup back in its saucer.

'Jamie,' she said, 'I'm here as a friend. My comment about you being naïve was supposed to be a complement. Too many men I meet are either cynical or arrogant or both. You're not like that. You seem like one of the good guys. I don't know you very well, but I'm guessing that if you were stuck for a lift, you're not blessed with many people to talk to.'

'I did have a girlfriend,' said Jamie, 'but that's… never mind.'

Charlotte stirred her tea for a long time.

'No job and no friends,' said Jamie. 'What a loser.'

'Don't talk like that. Self-pity's not attractive.' She reddened slightly. 'Only joking.'

He finished the cake and dabbed his mouth with a napkin. As he sat back in his chair, he caught one of Charlotte's ankles with an outstretched leg and hurriedly apologised. She was looking at him in anticipation, as if she knew before he did that he was about to confide in her.

'Remember I said I was a pianist and that my piano was being repaired?' he said. Charlotte nodded. 'Well, it's not just any old piano; it was Mum's and it's the most beautiful thing ever. It was taken away on the day the house burned down. It was the only thing that survived.'

'Some people might call that fate,' Charlotte said. 'At the very least it's something to remember her by.'

'The repair people rang me today, wanting to bring it back, but I've still got nowhere to put it.' He dug the heel of his hand into his forehead. 'I've got two weeks and then, well, I don't know. I might have to sell it.' In saying the words, Jamie was articulating a thought that had been percolating in his mind for the last couple of hours. It made him feel sick enough to regret the vanilla slice.

'It's hard to explain but I feel as though if I could just sit down and play, everything would be… not fine, obviously… but better.'

After a smattering of applause, the pianist moved onto an old show-tune, the kind of thing his grandmother used to play on her ancient gramophone, a Sobranie smouldering in her hand. The tune was in F major but he couldn't place it.

'Anyway,' he said, 'that's the least of my worries. Losing

my job isn't even the worst of it. Caz is falling apart. She hasn't been coping since the fire.'

'Poor her,' said Charlotte. 'That must be tough.'

'Yeah,' said Jamie. 'When she was younger she was a real rebel, always getting into trouble, arguing with Mum and Dad, drinking, smoking, God knows what else. She sorted herself out when she had Ruby, but now she's relapsing and I don't know how to stop it. The girls can't understand what's going on and Steve's in denial.' He paused for a second, distracted. 'What *is* that music? It's bugging me.'

'Oh, that's easy,' said Charlotte. '*Bewitched, Bothered and Bewildered*. It was my grandma's favourite.'

'Fitting,' said Jamie. He'd been about to tell Charlotte about Miss Wood and her concerns for the children, but on reflection that seemed a step too far. 'The thing is,' he said instead, 'I want to help Caz, but I'm clueless. I'm not up to it.'

'Of course you are.' Her tone was brisk. 'You're a grown man.'

The thought made him laugh.

'It's not funny. You *are*. Plenty of people have families at your age. Our age.'

'But what can I do? I don't know where to start.'

'You have to be there for them and try and give them what they need. You've got the time now, at least.'

'Easy as that,' said Jamie.

Charlotte signalled for the bill. She slapped a ten-pound note on the table and Jamie tried not to show his relief.

'No arguments,' she said. 'You're unemployed, remember.'

Without needing direction, Charlotte took the route home that Jamie used every day, the one where he had almost crashed the car. Driving at a leisurely pace with the windows down, she changed gears smoothly into the bends and was gentle on the brakes, allowing him to take in the passing farmland that he was normally too rushed to notice. Some of the fields were bright with dry, yellow wheat; others, where the combines had denuded them, were browner and stubbly. Even the grass was parched and faded.

'This must be horribly out of your way.'

'It isn't,' said Charlotte. 'I live just behind the dentist's.'

'You've been round the corner from me all this time?' said Jamie. 'Why didn't you say?'

'It didn't come up. And it's not like we would have bumped into each other in the pub. All my mates live in Newcastle, so I don't really go out.'

They drove on in silence as Jamie digested the news that Charlotte was virtually his neighbour. He'd never thought about where she might live, but if he'd had to guess he would have gone for somewhere a bit more happening than his stolid, unfashionable home town.

'What are you doing?' Charlotte was saying.

Jamie looked down at his hands. 'Oh. I'm practising. Most of the time I don't realise. I know it looks weird.'

'I didn't think it was weird. Although I'd rather have some proper music.'

She turned on Radio One and began to sing along, loudly and without inhibition, to the tune that was playing. Her voice was toneless and arrhythmic, making Jamie set his teeth.

'Don't you love Take That?' she said.

'I used to,' said Jamie, 'before somebody murdered one of their songs.'

She laughed. 'I'm not having that,' she said. 'I was in the school choir. Well, in infant school I was.'

'Actually, I lied,' he said. 'I've never liked Take That. Especially not that cocky one with the dark hair. Zoe, my… ex, was into them. Give me Beethoven, any day.'

They turned into Chestnut Drive and stopped outside Caz's house.

'I've been thinking,' Charlotte said. 'Why don't you store the piano at mine?'

'What? Oh, no. I couldn't.'

'Why not? Where else are you going to put it?'

'I don't know,' Jamie admitted.

'Well, then. You can come round to practise whenever you like. Give your thighs a break.'

She looked sideways at him through her eyelashes, then turned her gaze away.

'Only if you want to,' she said. 'It's up to you.'

It was a mad idea. He and Charlotte hardly knew each other. But the thought of being able to escape from Chestnut Drive, especially now that there was no office to go to, was irresistible. During the day, Charlotte would be at work. He could play for hours at a time. She didn't seem to want paying. It was too good to refuse.

'What's the matter with me?' he said. 'You must think I'm so ungrateful. Thank you. That would be fantastic.'

Jamie almost skipped into Caz's front garden. He had somewhere to keep the Pleyel; at last he would be able to play. But he had lost his job, his car and his income. And now he had to tell Caz that he had been collared by Miss Wood. The chances of either Caz or Steve going into school before the end of term were probably zero. It was only a few metres to the front door but by the time he reached it, he was dragging his feet.

thirty-seven

Jamie hacked off the tops of two boiled eggs and peered inside.

'Oh, dear,' he said. 'You can't eat those.'

'Yuck,' said Pearl. She stuck a finger into the watery albumen, stirring. 'It's like bird poo.'

'I'm afraid you're right,' said Jamie. 'How about some Coco Pops?'

He glanced up at the ceiling, willing his sister to get out of bed. Not three weeks into the summer holidays, he could barely remember what it was like to have a job, having been transformed overnight from estate agent to unpaid childminder. He was trapped in the role; he had no money to move out, Steve was at work and Caz stayed in her room all day. Short of leaving Ruby and Pearl to fend for themselves, he had no choice but to entertain them. The only bright spot on the horizon was that later that day, the piano was being delivered to Charlotte's house. Despite Colin's insistence that it needed to be moved out of the workshop, there had been an annoying delay, something to do with removal staff being on holiday. Resisting the urge to turn up again at Robinson's, demanding to be allowed to play, had taken all of Jamie's powers of restraint. Instead he'd made a mental list of the pieces he would reacquaint himself with first, and in which order.

'What are we doing today? Can we go to Whitby again?' said Pearl.

'*I* know!' said Ruby. 'We could go and see Uncle Jamie's girlfriend.'

'Hang on, what?'

'Zoe. You said she was a vet. She could show us some animals. There might be some lambs.'

'I love lambs,' said Pearl.

'Wow,' said Jamie. 'You two have good memories of someone you've never met.' He shook chocolatey cereal into two bowls and poured milk. 'Zoe's busy. And anyway, you only get lambs in the spring.'

'Awww,' said Pearl.

'Isn't she your girlfriend anymore?' Ruby said. 'Did she *chuck* you?'

Pearl chortled into her hand. Jamie looked despairingly between them.

'Something like that,' he said, pulling an upside-down smile. He set the bowls in front of them and handed out spoons.

'Don't worry.' Ruby patted his arm. 'You'll find another girlfriend soon.'

'No doubt,' said Jamie. 'Hey, I've got a treat for you today. You're going to Mrs Cole's for a sleepover.'

'No!' said Pearl, the spoon in her hand halfway to her mouth. 'I don't want to see where Granny and Grandpa died.'

'You won't have to, Pearly. It's been covered up.'

'But it's still *there*,' said Pearl. 'The place where they got burned.' She mashed brown pulp into the bottom of her bowl.

'Listen,' said Jamie. 'Granny and Grandpa loved living at The Hall. They wouldn't want you to be sad.'

'Mummy is,' said Ruby. 'She must be, or she wouldn't stay in bed all the time.'

Jamie sighed into his coffee. 'She's just a bit tired. She'll be better soon.'

'How soon?' Pearl said. 'Today?'

'It might take longer than that.'

'But she's getting lots of sleep,' said Ruby.

'I know,' said Jamie. 'I also know that Mrs Cole is really looking forward to seeing you both. And I'm pretty certain she's made a cake.'

'What kind?' said Pearl. 'Does she know I don't like lemons?'

'I'm sure she does,' said Jamie. 'Have you finished? Off you go and get dressed. And fold your pyjamas.' He wondered at the phrases he was beginning to use; the cajoling words of parenthood that he had adopted without thinking. It was terrifying.

'Look,' said Ruby. 'Daddy's forgotten his newspaper. What's that man doing to that lady?'

Jamie picked it up and studied the photograph on the front page. Some bloke was sucking the Duchess of York's toes.

'Ugh,' said Pearl. 'What if she's got sweaty feet?'

'Exactly.' Jamie folded it in half, with the photo hidden in the middle. 'Now. Clothes!'

—

Seagulls circled above Willie's little tractor as it heaved its mowing equipment around the village green. Irritation flashed across his face when a dog darted in front of the machine, chasing a tennis ball that its owner had thrown. On the cricket square, a couple of men grappled with an old-fashioned roller. There was still no new pavilion. Behind them, the ruins of The Hall were now hidden by a length of hoarding, bound around with police tape and plastered with signs declaring that the site was alarmed. The hoardings were the one concession the insurance company had allowed in advance of the inquest, which was not listed for another month.

'There you are,' said Jamie. 'I told you.'

'Has it really gone?' whispered Pearl from the back of Caz's car.

'No,' said Jamie, 'but we thought it would be better if people couldn't see it any more. Especially Mrs Cole.'

They pulled into the courtyard and parked outside his father's old sports store. In Ruth's kitchen, the table was covered with newspaper and painting things.

'Hello my lambs,' she said, hugging the girls. 'I thought you might like to make your mummy a picture.'

They scrambled up to the table and began a half-hearted squabble over who had the biggest paintbrush. Ruth led Jamie into the sitting room and shut the kitchen door behind her.

'How is Caroline?' she said.

'Not good,' said Jamie. 'She stays in bed all day.'

'I know I've asked you this before, but is she drinking?'

'It started with wine but now she's moved onto vodka.

She fell and bashed her face a few weeks ago. I don't know what to do about it.'

'What does Steve say?'

'He's acting like nothing's wrong. He goes out at the crack of dawn every morning and she sometimes puts on a show of being around at tea-time when he comes home. It doesn't look convincing to me, but maybe he doesn't want to see it. I'm taking care of the girls and looking after the house, but she's letting him think she's doing it and I don't want to rat on her. I can't believe he hasn't noticed anything.'

'What about the cutting?' Ruth stroked the inside of her wrist. 'I honestly thought she was over that years ago.'

'Steve must be aware of *that*. She's always picking at the bandages.'

Ruth sighed and shook her head. 'Those poor little girls. They're like ragamuffins.'

'Even *I* can see that their trousers are too short and their shoes have got no soles left on them. But I don't know how much to get involved.'

'And in the meantime you're keeping the ship afloat.'

'Not really,' said Jamie. 'I'm a hopeless cook; can't even boil an egg. Literally.'

'Oh, Jamie, love, what a state of affairs.' She stretched up and patted his chin in the way he had found comforting when he was a child.

'What do you think, Mrs C? Should I talk to Steve?'

'I don't know that it would do much good. He doesn't want to see Caroline as anything but perfect and you'll get the blame for interfering. What she needs is professional help. The trouble is, we can't force her. Losing her parents has knocked her sideways. She's a tough one, though; she'll bounce back. And she knows we're here if she wants us.'

Ruth opened the kitchen door. Both girls were now painting quietly. Jamie picked up the car keys.

'Bye girls,' he said. 'I'll see you tomorrow.' He kissed them both on the forehead. 'Thanks for having them. I'm sure they've had enough of me.'

'It's my pleasure,' said Ruth. 'Now, off you go and play that piano till your fingers hurt.'

thirty-eight

Charlotte's street was not, as Jamie expected, a replica of Chestnut Drive, but a collection of 1960s bungalows built of greyish brick and with enormous plate-glass windows. He identified her house by the turquoise Fiesta on the drive. In the front garden was an ornamental pond, beside which a bearded ceramic gnome sat cross-legged, fishing. Charlotte was standing on the doorstep, apparently waiting for him.

'Don't say it,' she called before disappearing into the house, leaving the door open for Jamie to follow.

She led him into a sizeable room, empty except for an upright chair and a swirly pink carpet. A bluebottle ricocheted around the top of the casement window, monotonic against the silence of the outside street.

'What shouldn't I say?'

'This house,' said Charlotte. 'It's for old people.'

'I wasn't going to - '

'It belonged to my grandparents. The furniture's hideous and the carpets are doggo but it's rent-free. I'm saving up for a place of my own. And as you can see, there's lots of space.' She did a little balancing mime with her hands before checking her watch. 'I'd better go. Tell them they can put it in here.'

'Brilliant. Thanks.'

They were standing quite close together, close enough for Jamie to notice that she was wearing perfume. It was a heavy, floral scent which made him think again of what Chris had said in the office. Above them, the bluebottle gave a final, demented buzz and dropped, dead, onto the window-sill.

Charlotte produced a set of keys from her pocket. 'Here you go.' The keyring was an acid-house smiley face. 'No excuse for not practising now.'

After she'd gone, Jamie was standing at the window, watching for the arrival of the piano when a black Mercedes reversed onto the driveway opposite and a middle-aged couple got out. Both tall and straight-backed, they set off at a sedate pace up the narrow path towards the house. They didn't look especially like Jamie's parents, but there was something in their deportment and the way they were dressed that made him grasp the window-sill where the dead bluebottle lay prone. How was it fair that there were people like this, casually returning home on a hot Wednesday morning in August? He felt a stab of hatred for the benign-looking couple, staring at them fiercely until they reached their front door. Then, as the moment passed, he felt instead a swell of affection for them and hoped that somewhere they had children who loved them and treated them kindly.

It was another hour before the Robinson's van drew up outside. A team of men in brown overalls loaded the piano onto a trolley and wheeled it up the driveway into the house. Jamie watched from the corner of the room as it was unwrapped from its tarpaulin and reassembled.

'There you are, sir,' said one of the men. 'We'll leave you to enjoy it.'

The Pleyel was like a mirage, a relic from a different time; apart from Jamie himself the sole survivor from The Hall, teleported into Charlotte's grandparents' dining room. For a moment he was immobilised, afraid that if he touched it the piano might crumble before him, or vanish along with the rest of his life from before the fire.

The draw of the Pleyel was too great to keep him away for long. Something released him and he leapt across the room, circling it, stroking the fall-board, the music desk, the generous, sweeping curves of the casework which had been completely restored and polished with no sign of any patching up beneath the deep black gloss of the veneer. He lifted the lid and propped it, catching his breath at the workings beneath. This was the most beautiful part; the harp-shaped structure which contained the strings, thick and coarse for the lower notes and fine like tiny threads for the higher ones, all wound around a series of regularly-spaced pegs. Beneath them, the hammers and dampers that had been so badly damaged, now lined up in readiness like little soldiers.

Jamie made another circle, inspecting every feature. How he had missed the *belle époch* lettering above the keyboard, the solid brass feet and pedals, the eighty-eight silken keys. To have it standing there, good as new, was a miracle.

He positioned the chair at the piano and sat down. It was an inch too high and he had to wedge his legs under the keyboard, making it creak in protest. He reached for the first chord of the Beethoven, the piece that he'd been wanting to play since New Year's Eve. The eighth sonata, the *Pathétique*, number one on his list.

It wouldn't come; or rather, something sounded off. One of the right hand notes in the first bar was incorrect but he couldn't work out which. He pressed on regardless, but he was fluffing it, unsure where his fingers ought to be. Playing on his thighs was clearly no substitute for the real thing. Trying to remember the piece only seemed to chase the notes further from his mind.

Jamie lowered the fall-board and rested his forehead on the empty music stand. It was one of many pieces he knew by heart, or thought he did. When he was younger and still dreamed of performing, he would think nothing of playing from memory for hours at a stretch. His mother always said that sheet music had no place on a stage. She had never performed, although she probably should have. Even before Jamie learned to play, he loved to watch her at the piano. From her feet working the pedals to the euphoric expression on her face, her whole body would become liquid, dissolving into whatever she was playing. He lifted the fall-board again.

This time, his fingers sought the notes with more confidence. The duff note in the first bar had been a B flat instead of a B, a basic error given that the piece was in C minor. He found that he was able to propel the music forward through the introduction, upward into the wave of each crescendo and over it, until he reached the long descending chromatic that set up the allegro section. After that, he was hardly aware that he was playing. His fingers were fused to the keys. Flickering over the split octaves, his left hand grounded the right which, despite lack of proper practice, was still nimble enough to capture the acciaccaturas and mordents. The piano filled the room. His hands ranged over the keyboard. And then, he was at the frenzied end of the movement with its five emphatic fortissimo chords, suddenly conscious of what he must have already played to get there. He placed the final chord with great care, not wanting to ruin the thing that he had just created.

With his hands still on the keys, he paused for a moment, picturing the turn of the page into the second movement, the Adagio Cantabile. Then he began, both hands in the lower part of the keyboard, sliding into A flat major, reaching into the notes, conjuring the enveloping comfort of the melody. It was like a warm bath. The piano was singing to him; its voice was layers deep and effortless. The extreme dynamics of the first movement had given way to something so subtle and constrained that he almost ached with it. For a moment, the notes turned to sharps and the register was higher but then he was back to flats, the semiquavers now triplets, carrying him towards the final movement, the Rondo.

The pace picked up and he was in C minor again, but the dramatic chords of the first movement had been replaced by broken chords and arpeggios. The tone was mournful but rapid, switching between couplets and triplets but with no slackening in the tempo, the dynamics building and falling away. Then, the notes were so soft as to be barely audible before the last flourish, the magnificent descending scale, the fortississimo crash of the final chord and the extended rest that marked the end.

'That's better,' he murmured.

The room seemed to be vibrating. Jamie lifted his fingers, breaking the force-field that was connecting him to the keyboard, severing his synthesis with the music. He stretched out his shoulders, the muscles stiffening from playing for nearly twenty minutes after months of inactivity, and went to the window.

Across the road, the neighbours had come out of their house again and were standing in their front garden, facing him. The man put his arm to his wife's lower back in just the same way that Jamie's father used to do with his mother, both tender and chivvying. They raised their hands to applaud him, waited as he gave a self-conscious half-bow, then went back inside.

He played the Beethoven again and again, not yet ready to move onto anything else, each time remembering something new in the phrasing or the dynamics. It was hours before he gave in to the niggling sense that he ought to go home to check on Caz. As he drove, the sonata was still playing in his head and he had the feeling of being in two places at once. There was the Jamie now changing from second gear to third and there was another Jamie, seated at the piano at Charlotte's house. He could see the curls on the back of his own head. The tilt of his body, the angle of his foot on the sustain pedal, the way his arms almost levitated over the keyboard, were exactly like his mother.

Playing the piano was a physical necessity; that was now obvious. In the aftermath of New Year's Eve, he had longed for a place where he could forget about what had happened. Only the piano could have given him that. It wasn't about pleasure; that was something you chose. For him, music wasn't optional, it was indispensable.

Before the fire, sex with Zoe was an imperative, but it was also pure enjoyment. Was that his proof that guilt was partly to blame for the failure of their relationship? He had long suspected that on an unconscious level he felt disloyal to the memory of his parents; that abandoning himself to the act was a betrayal in some way. In binary terms, music was acceptable; sex was not. Now, however, months later, the two things - music and sex - were beginning to merge in his mind. Both were forms of physical gratification, regardless of the motivation behind them. Logically, if he could do one, then shouldn't he be able to do the other? What if, all along, the piano had been the key to his recovery? With no instrument to hand, he had worried that he might have forgotten how to play, or that his talent (he would admit only to himself that he *had* a talent) had disappeared. But having nailed the Beethoven after waiting for so long, who knew what else might be possible?

thirty-nine

When Caz came back from the shops, there was no-one at home. She took a child's beaker from the cupboard in the kitchen and carried it out to the garden along with the shopping bag. A plastic table and chairs sat on the small, paved area behind the house. A parasol, nipped shut, rested in a hole in the table. She put the bag and the beaker down and tried to open the parasol for some shade, but there was no strength in her arms and she didn't want to get her head trapped inside it, so she gave up.

Instead, she sat down and unscrewed the vodka bottle, turning her face to the sun. Apart from the tinny strain of pop music from a neighbour's radio and the sporadic drilling of a woodpecker on a nearby tree, the estate was quiet. Steve was at work, but she couldn't remember where Jamie had said he was taking the girls.

Against all of her expectations he was proving to be brilliant with them. Perhaps it was a blessing that he had lost his job; that there was someone around during the day to be responsible for her daughters while she sorted herself out. This was the phrase she was using in her mind to describe her situation. It was part of the grieving process: a phase; she just needed to *sort herself out*. It came in handy when she wanted to justify buying vodka, or drinking it, or cutting herself. Everything was allowable because it was only temporary. At some point she would have to feel better. Then, there would be no need to do any of these things that even *she* could tell were not a good idea.

In the meantime, the girls seemed OK. A little dishevelled, perhaps, but once she sorted herself out (there it was again) she would soon have them back to normal. For the moment she just needed a little vodka to smooth off the edges. The problem was that it was taking more and more; the edges were growing rougher, not smoother. She filled the beaker again and again. The heat was making her drowsy; she closed her eyes and shuffled down in the chair, her head lolling to one side.

When she awoke, her face burned and her neck itched. Her skin was dotted with little bumps which she scratched at distractedly. She couldn't remember removing the bandage from her wrist but it lay coiled on the table, exposing the scars to the sun. She poured more vodka and drank it in one, her eyelids flicking open and shut.

'Caz!'

She startled. Jamie was standing over her. Because he was so tall she had to crane her neck to see his face; his expression was impossible to see in the glare from the sun.

'For God's sake.' He snatched the beaker from the table and she flapped her arm at him in a useless attempt to get it back. She was getting sick of him nagging her. She wasn't doing anyone any harm and it was none of his business.

'I was having a nice time out here,' she said. 'It's not against the law.'

'What if the girls come back and see you like this?'

She slapped a reflexive hand over the scars. But then she remembered: Jamie had taken Ruby and Pearl to Ruth's for a sleepover so that he could play the piano. She drew the hand away and wagged a finger at him.

'You can't fool me. I'm not stu-pid.' For some reason she elongated the first syllable of the word so that it sounded weird.

Jamie sat down hard on one of the plastic chairs. Its flimsy legs wobbled and it almost toppled over, making her laugh.

'There's nothing funny,' Jamie said. 'And what about Steve? What about what he thinks?'

It wasn't clear what Steve had to do with anything. He went out almost every night and when he *was* in the house, he only spoke to her about practicalities. Instead, he was putting his energy into being Fun Dad, which was all very well for twenty minutes a day after work but they both knew that it was Jamie who was really looking after Ruby and Pearl.

'Steve doesn't care!' She banged the table. 'He only sees what he wants to see…' A surge of bile in her mouth forced her to stop speaking.

'What's going on, Caz?' Jamie said. 'Until the fire you didn't drink.'

'I know,' she said. 'Not since Ruby. But I did before… remember?'

'Of course I do,' said Jamie. 'I remember you getting expelled from school for being pissed at your confirmation, I remember you throwing up on the dog that Christmas…'

This made her laugh through her nose. 'I remember you getting caught smoking weed in the garden, I remember all the rows with Mum and Dad…'

'Was…fun…though.' She was having trouble with words.

'But you changed. Like you said, once you had Ruby, you were different.'

Caz shrugged. 'Leopard…spots.' Speech was becoming impossible. Worse, something was gripping her stomach and twisting it. 'Oh, God…' She put a hand over her mouth and retched, her whole body convulsing forwards.

'Are you going to be sick?' Jamie said. 'Christ!'

He leaped up and dragged her off her chair, propelling her towards the kitchen. They reached the sink just in time but it was full of dishes; they'd have been better staying outside. Whether Jamie was having the same thought was unclear because by now he was holding her hair with one hand and out of the corner of her eye she could see him put his face into the crook of his elbow as she vomited all over the breakfast dishes. When she had finished, he released her hair and she stood upright, eyes and nose running, gasping for breath, her hands braced against the sink.

'Sorry,' she managed. Her mouth tasted vile.

Jamie, casting around, tore off some kitchen roll and handed it to her. She swabbed at her eyes and nose, still breathless. He was disgusted with her. She was disgusting.

'I don't know what's wrong with me.' It didn't make sense. She didn't think she'd drunk *that* much vodka, not enough to make her sick, surely. But maybe she had.

'You beat this once,' Jamie said, misunderstanding her. 'You could lose everything if you don't do it again.'

'I know,' she said. 'It's just better when I can't feel anything.'

'It's not,' said Jamie. He drew her towards him; she was hot and clammy and she could smell the vomit on herself but he hugged her, resting his chin on top of her head. 'It's really not,' he said.

Her little brother had never been more heroic. Caz doubted whether *she* would have hugged someone who had just thrown up. Despite how revolting she was he was still there. At least someone cared about her.

'Steve's cross with me,' she mumbled.

'He's worried. You can hardly blame him.'

Her head snapped up. 'What, because I'm not being a good little wife?'

'No, because he loves you.'

'I know. But I can't be what he wants me to be. As soon as I wake up, I think about Mum and Dad and the fire and I can't stop. It's…it's…whelmingover me.'

Jamie sighed. 'You can't choose whether or not to feel sad about something.' He let her go. 'I'd better tidy up.'

'No, no.' That wasn't fair, but when she looked at the mess in the sink, she began to retch again.

'It's all right. You should go to bed.'

'Please, don't tell Steve.' She sounded pathetic, but despite everything she didn't want to give Steve any more reason to be repulsed by her.

Jamie had moved away from the sink and was staring at the open bread-bin, where bright blue mould flowered on a white sliced loaf.

'Please, J.'

'All right,' he said eventually. 'But you know this can't go on, don't you?'

She nodded and turned towards the stairs, stopping to hang onto the newel post.

'I love you, Jamie,' she said.

He waved her away. 'Get some rest.'

After a few hours of unconsciousness she would be awake again. Then there would be the whole night during which she would lie in bed, either sweating or shivering, still obsessing about the fire, alone even with Steve there beside her. Drinking was great until you stopped. That was the rubbish part. Nothing was ever as good as the first glass. Even as she hauled herself upstairs, she wanted to capture that taste again.

forty

As Caz tottered away, Jamie tied a tea-towel around his head, like a blindfold but for his mouth and nose, and opened all of the downstairs windows as well as the back door. The sweet smell of someone else's mown lawn floated in, partly dissipating the fug of vomit. In this way, he managed to clear the sink without chundering, even though he couldn't find any marigolds and had to plunge his hands into the fetid mess. Once that was done he dropped decomposing bread into the bin and wiped down all the surfaces until he was satisfied that the kitchen was presentable.

Caz was behaving like her teenage self. The difference was that she was not rebelling against their parents. In their absence, she was rejecting not just this life, the one that she had chosen for herself, but the people who relied on her. Jamie wondered if she had noticed how he had turned his face away when she was throwing up. A better person would have disguised their revulsion. Suddenly guilty, he jogged up the stairs. Caz was in bed with the duvet pulled up to her chin, sleeping like an innocent.

Jamie went back to the garden, where the vodka bottle was still on the table. It occurred to him that he and Caz were not all that different; both of them unable to control how they responded to the fire and the death of their parents. Her reaction was to return to the crutch she had used before. His body had chosen to fail him in a way that, for want of a better phrase, hit him where it hurt the most. Whatever Zoe said, his inability to have sex with her couldn't have helped. After all, what was a relationship based on sex and laughter without the sex, especially when the laughter had dried up too? And yet he couldn't be sure, but he thought he'd felt something that morning, coming from Charlotte. It was like a tiny electric charge, or a single iron filing attaching itself to a magnet. When he tried to properly identify it, he couldn't. It disappeared. Maybe it hadn't been there at all. Maybe there was a fault with his radar.

He took a tiny sip of the vodka and laughed out loud, which turned into a cough as the neat alcohol hit the back of his throat. In what kind of messed up world would he be attracted to Charlotte and not to Zoe, who had been his actual girlfriend? The farcicality of it, and possibly the vodka, made him snort with amusement. He was still laughing to himself when Steve appeared at the back door.

'All right, J?' Steve's eyes went to the bottle on the table.

'Yeah, fine, I was - '

'Where's Caz?' His tone seemed to suggest that Jamie might have hidden her or was responsible in some other way for her absence.

'Oh,' said Jamie, 'she wasn't feeling great so she went to bed. I just checked on her and she's sleeping. I was just on my way out.'

'Right,' said Steve. 'Well, I'm off to the driving range. No need for me to sit here all night if she's asleep.'

Charlotte didn't seem surprised to see Jamie back on her doorstep.

'Come for more piano?' she said, looking amused. 'I'm making risotto. There's plenty.'

Compared to the cavernous dining room, Charlotte's kitchen was unexpectedly small. There wasn't enough space for two people to pass one another between the rows of cabinets which lined the opposing walls. Jamie installed himself at the far end, leaning against the fridge. Charlotte was working a wooden spoon around a pan on the hob. Madonna played faintly from the sitting room.

'Thanks again for today,' said Jamie. 'The guys had no problem getting the piano in. It was wonderful to play again.'

'You're welcome,' said Charlotte. 'That's the beauty of a bungalow. Not a stair in sight.' She pointed to a wooden wine rack which sat on the floor in the hall. 'I need to keep the risotto moving,' she said, 'but as I'm stuck here, why don't you open one of those?'

To get out of the kitchen, Jamie had to sidle along the units, raising his arms and swivelling his hips to manoeuvre around Charlotte. She stood at the cooker, unperturbed, tasting the risotto from the tip of a teaspoon. Jamie selected a bottle of red, shimmied back into the kitchen, uncorked it and poured them both a glass.

The absence of a dining table meant that they had to balance their plates on their laps, side-by-side on a bobbly brown sofa in the sitting room.

'God, that's good,' Jamie said. After months of frozen food, the risotto tasted divine. His plate had three times as much on it as Charlotte's did.

'It's nice to cook for someone other than myself.'

'I can't imagine living on my own,' said Jamie. 'I wouldn't be very good at it. I'd starve, for one thing.' He shovelled the last of the risotto into his mouth and wondered whether there was any left in the pan.

Charlotte put down her fork and skewered him with a stare.

'Why do you do that?' she said. 'You're always suggesting that you can't look after yourself, or anyone else, when it's clearly not true. From what you've told me you're doing a great job with your nieces.'

'Hardly.'

'What does that mean?' Charlotte looked cross.

'No offence, but why do you care?'

She put her half-empty plate on the floor, hauled herself off the sunken sofa, and put Madonna on 'pause'.

'Come on,' she said. 'I want to show you something.'

Jamie followed her into the dining room. By now, most of the daylight had leached from the sky and the room was lit only by a street-lamp outside. She sat down at the piano and began to play.

It took Jamie a few bars to recognise the lugubrious opening to Chopin's third waltz. Stumbles Charlotte made over the quavers in the left hand caused her to stop repeatedly. She carried on in mechanical perseverance, into the sostenuto section, ignoring any changes in the dynamics. Each note was given the same plodding weight; there was no phrasing, the trills were fumbled. Her right hand missed the accidentals; her left kept up a metronomic three crotchets, littered with wrong notes. Jamie listened in pained politeness, fingers twitching, right foot working an imaginary pedal, until she came to a halt just before the final third. Pleyel had been Chopin's piano brand of choice.

'There,' she said. 'That's quite enough.'

Jamie laughed, for the large part in relief.

'Wow,' he said. 'Where did that come from?'

'I was one of those forced children.' Charlotte pivoted on the chair to face him. 'Even though I was dire, my mum wouldn't let me give up. I sometimes think I only went to university to get away from piano lessons. My poor teacher must have wondered what she did to deserve me.'

'It wasn't that bad,' Jamie lied.

'Yes, it was,' said Charlotte. 'You have a talent. I don't.'

'How do you know? You've never heard me play.'

'I just do. It was obvious from the way your face lit up when you said the piano had survived the fire.'

'Maybe,' said Jamie, 'but so what?'

'So if you can believe that, then you have to believe you can do other things. Much more straightforward things, actually. You're not useless. I can see that. Why can't you?'

The room was too quiet. Jamie, discomfited that Charlotte was quoting his own unspoken theory back at him, only with a different application, went back to the sitting room. Charlotte followed. The stereo was one of those new CD players; sleek and silver with a neat stack of boxed discs by its side.

'Do you mind?' he said, his finger hovering over the 'play' button.

'Be my guest.'

Madonna started up again, halfway through *Like A Prayer.* Jamie returned to the sofa and his wine. Charlotte perched at the other end, sipping hers. She kicked off her ankle boots.

'I'm sorry,' she said. 'I've always been a bit nosy. And I'm on my own most evenings. I think about you a lot.'

As she looked at him a hank of hair fell across her face. She shoved it away with an impatient gesture, but when he didn't respond straightaway he saw the slight slump in her shoulders, even though she smiled at him.

'Things are more complicated than you think,' said Jamie.

'So tell me.'

It should have been easy to open up. Even if he chose to keep the details to himself of what happened with Zoe, he could talk to Charlotte about the reality of living with Caz and Steve and how much worse things were since they had spoken at the café just weeks ago, after he was fired. She seemed to want to know. But there was nothing that Charlotte could do to help. It was a mess he couldn't see the way out of. He drank some more wine.

'I should probably go.'

'You've been drinking, Jamie. Stay. I've got room.'

'I'm not driving. I walked here.'

'As I said…'

Jamie paused. He had a sense that he was being drawn into something. But all he could think about was creeping back into his sister's house, not knowing how the evening might have played out. Ruby and Pearl were at Ruth's. He could still pick them up the next morning, as arranged.

'..actually, you'd be doing me a favour.' Charlotte was refilling his glass. 'It would be good to know that my spare bed's not going to fall to bits. It's about a hundred years old.'

He accepted the wine, sinking back into the sofa, resigned to having been talked into staying now that the spare bed had been specifically mentioned.

'The Sidgwicks came in today,' Charlotte said.

'Let me guess: more fairy cakes?'

'In one. I had to stop Chris from troughing the lot.'

'No change there, then.'

'They wanted to know where you were. I didn't have the heart to tell them you were sacked because of them so I said you were on holiday.'

'Thanks. I'm hoping they won't find out.'

'They're so lovely, it would have been mean to upset them. They're moving in on Monday and they're super-excited.'

She smiled at him again. Jamie held her gaze slightly longer than he intended.

'Right,' he said. 'We're always talking about me, or work. Tell me about you.'

Over the next couple of hours he learned that Charlotte was from Whitley Bay, where she had lived with her parents through school and Newcastle Poly (her father did indeed own a string of car dealerships), after which she moved to Ripon to work at Archer's. She had an older brother whom she loved and a younger sister who annoyed her, liked pop music, cooking, and, of course, cars, except for turquoise Fiestas.

'So that's me,' she said. 'You know everything now, apart from my plans to have my own chain of estate agents one day. I'll have a policy of nice clients only: no Great Dane Women, no Mr Octopuses.' She fiddled with a button on her jumper and pushed back her hair again. Jamie finished his wine and yawned theatrically.

'Bedtime for me,' he said. 'Can you point me in the right direction?'

The single bed in the spare room was unmade. Charlotte brought him sheets and a blanket and wished him goodnight.

'Monday, did you say? For the Sidgwicks?' he said before he closed the bedroom door. 'I think I'll go and give them a hand. I can be back from my 'holiday' by then.'

He lay in the dark, listening to her tidying the kitchen, playing Luther Vandross. After a while, the music stopped and the lights went off in the hall. He heard the opening and closing of drawers on the other side of the wall and tried not to imagine her undressing and getting into bed.

forty-one

When Jamie arrived at College Lane late on Monday morning with Ruby and Pearl trailing behind him, Mr Sidgwick was rifling around in the back of a transit van. In the front garden, his wife was bending over a shrub, examining its leaves.

'It's a skimmia, John,' she was saying as Jamie and the girls passed under the iron archway. 'There are little buds already forming. Jamie! Oh, my goodness! I thought you were away.'

She rushed forward and threw her arms around him. 'And who are these beauties?'

'My nieces, Ruby and Pearl. We've come to help.' Jamie gestured towards the van. 'Is that all you've brought?'

Mr Sidgwick stepped down from the transit, grasping a cardboard box to his chest. He gave Jamie a questioning look.

'Didn't you know? We bought the furniture along with the house. It was nicer than the old junk we had at home. We just brought the essentials.' He held out the box to

Ruby. 'Can you manage that, love? There's some orange barley and a packet of chocolate digestives in there. Why don't you girls take it through to the kitchen?'

Ruby and Pearl disappeared inside. Jamie grabbed the last box from the van, a big one marked 'matchsticks', and followed. The house looked exactly as it had during the viewings except for the absence of books and paintings. Mr and Mrs Sidgwick were walking into an entirely new life.

Holding the box level in case there was a work-in-progress inside, Jamie carried it to the studio. The yellow walls were still as bright as daffodils but the painting paraphernalia had gone. He set the box on the bench by the window. Even stripped bare, the room had an uplifting, suffusive light that made it hard to leave.

Back in the kitchen, Ruby and Pearl had unpacked the contents of the box onto the worktop and were standing demurely alongside.

'Did you go somewhere nice on holiday, Jamie?' Mrs Sidgwick opened the biscuits and gave one each to Ruby and Pearl. 'We're hoping to go to Spain next month to see Jake. He's in… where is it, John?'

'Madrid, or Barcelona. I forget which. He's always on the move.' Mr Sidgwick diluted two glasses of orange squash and laughed. 'I suppose we ought to check.'

Once the kettle had been located and coffee made, they spilled out into the garden, where the wrought-iron furniture sat waiting and the apple tree was heavy with unripe fruit. The girls played with the water feature, darting their hands in and out of the lion's mouth and giggling. The day was warm but with a serotinal air that always reminded Jamie of the end of school holidays. It was almost three months since he'd last stood in this garden, wishing he could share it with Zoe. They hadn't spoken since the disastrous picnic by the river.

'So, Jamie,' Mrs Sidgwick persisted, 'where did you say you went?'

'I didn't. It was more of an… extended break. I'm glad I could help you find a house, but I've decided I'm not cut out to be an estate agent.'

'Fair enough,' said Mr Sidgwick.

'But you were so good at it,' said his wife. 'We wouldn't be here if it wasn't for you.' She thought for a moment and inhaled sharply. 'Will you be all right? Isn't it really hard to find jobs these days? What are you going to do?'

'I'm not sure,' Jamie admitted. 'At the moment I've got my hands full looking after those two.' Ruby and Pearl were splashing each other and running in and out of the door which led to the alleyway.

'And how are things?' Mrs Sidgwick leaned forward and patted his arm, just as Ruby had when they were talking about Zoe.

'You've had a tough time of it, lad,' said Mr Sidgwick.

'Yes, well, I've got Ruby and Pearl, and my sis, and my piano…'

'Is it back?' said Mrs Sidgwick. 'How lovely.'

'A friend's keeping it at her house for me.'

'Oh,' said Mrs Sidgwick. 'A lady-friend?'

'Just a friend. Who happens to be a lady… er, a woman.' Jamie's fingers were beginning to twitch and he wondered whether Charlotte would mind if he took the girls there for an hour. He wanted to pin down the haunting, hypnotic first movement of Schubert's twentieth sonata before tackling the violence and chaos of the second. 'Anyway,' he said, standing up, 'I should probably get out of your hair.'

'Keep in touch,' said Mr Sidgwick. 'We don't see enough of our own son. If there's anything you need, you will tell us, won't you?'

forty-two

Ruby clamped her arms to her sides as Jamie held out the cardigan for her to put on.

'I'm not going,' she said. 'I hate school.'

'Come on,' said Jamie, 'that's not true. It'll be fun to see your friends again.' He threw a desperate look up the stairs to where Pearl, the end of a toothbrush sticking out of her mouth, was banging on her mother's bedroom door.

'Mummy! Get up! Get up, Mummy!'

'Pearly,' he called. 'Finish your teeth and come down here, sweetheart. It's time to go.'

'I don't want to,' she said. 'I want Mummy.'

Ruby bent to undo her shoes then kicked them away across the hall. Bits of dried mud flew off as they somersaulted in the air and landed on the carpet. As she stood up again, Jamie saw that the front of her school dress was encrusted with tomato ketchup. How could it be so dirty when they hadn't been at school since July? He dashed to the kitchen for the dishcloth and rubbed at it.

'Ow,' said Ruby. 'You're making me all wet.'

'I'm not hurting,' said Jamie. 'You can't go to school looking like that.'

'I'm not going. I'm staying here.'

'Is something the matter, Ruby?' Her head was down, watching her toes wriggling through the holes in her greying white socks.

'Rubes?'

The latch on Caz's bedroom door clicked open and she emerged, blinking, onto the landing. Swamped by a shabby yellow dressing gown, she reminded Jamie of Yoda but without the big ears. Caz took an unsteady step towards Pearl and put her hand on the door frame for support.

'Mummy!' Pearl lunged at Caz and wrapped her arms around her mother's waist, knocking her backwards.

'Ssh,' said Caz, stroking Pearl's hair. 'What's going on?' Her voice was so quiet that from the bottom of the stairs, Jamie could barely hear her.

'We're not going to school,' Ruby declared.

'Where's Daddy?' said Caz.

'Work,' said Jamie. 'He left ages ago. Look, now that you're up... they seem really unhappy. Maybe they should stay at home. It's only the first day; I can't imagine they'll be missing anything much.'

'No.' Caz replied so quickly that she almost interrupted him. She ran a hand across her face. 'They need to go to school. It's important.'

'But Mummy!' Ruby ran up the stairs leaving Jamie kneeling on the floor. 'We don't want to.'

With effort, Caz lowered herself down to face her children, still clinging to the door jamb.

'Listen, girls,' she said, 'if you're good and go to school now with Uncle Jamie, I'll make you something special for tea. I'm sure I'll be better later.'

'Spaghetti bolognese!' said Pearl.

'Sausages!' said Ruby.

'We'll see,' said Caz. 'Now, off you go. Uncle Jamie's waiting.'

The two girls traipsed down the stairs; Ruby put her shoes on again and shoved her arms into the sleeves of the cardigan. Jamie looked up to receive his thanks but Caz had already disappeared back into the bedroom.

As they crossed the high street, Jamie tried again.

'Is there something you're not saying, Ruby? About school?'

She stopped and scuffed her shoes against the pavement. 'No.'

'Please, Uncle Jamie,' said Pearl. 'Can we go home?'

'Everyone has to go to school,' said Jamie. 'It's the law.'

In the playground, clusters of children were already forming, shoving each other and shouting. Jamie said goodbye to the girls at the gate and watched as they trudged along the path. Rather than joining any of the others, they stood on their own at the edge of the playground. In his experience, it was the playground where trouble always lurked, away from the restraining presence of teachers. He waited until the bell sounded. The girls separated to line up for their respective classes and he wandered off to Charlotte's house.

The supposed benefit of the new school term was that Jamie would be free to play the piano. During the holidays, unable to get away during the day, he had spent as many evenings at Charlotte's as he could, although they would invariably end up chatting and this would eat into his playing time. Now, alone at the keyboard, he struggled to shake off the sense that something wasn't right at school. It took a good twenty minutes of scales to dispel his unease.

Several hours of practice later and Jamie was reacquainted with Mozart's Sonata number Twelve in F Major. He had also partly convinced himself that he was being paranoid and that it was quite normal that the girls hadn't wanted to go to school. After six weeks of holidays, who would? As a child, he'd never been in any rush to go back. Their reticence with the other children was harder to explain. It struck him that there'd been no mention of them seeing friends over the summer. Caz would have needed to facilitate any social activities, which would probably explain why they hadn't happened. No wonder Ruby and Pearl were a little shy. A whole summer was a long time when you were seven and five. They would need some time to bed in again.

Arriving at school at pickup time, any confidence he had in these new theories evaporated when he saw Miss Wood approaching amidst the oncoming rush of small children.

'Hello, Mr Fenton,' she said. 'Ruby and Pearl will be along in a minute but I just wanted a quick word. Neither of their parents were in touch at the end of last term and I still really need to speak to them.'

Jamie was about to say that he had passed on the message but reconsidered on the grounds that it mightn't be wise to drop them in it.

'Really?' he said. 'Is there anything I can help with?'

Miss Wood pulled at her beads. 'It has to be a parent, I'm afraid. But I wouldn't be speaking out of turn to suggest that someone might wash their uniforms. There've been a few comments.'

'Right. Yes. Absolutely. Consider it done.'

Ruby and Pearl appeared and they set off home, Jamie hoping without expectation that Caz had remembered their special tea.

forty-three

One Thursday, later in September, Caz lay propped up on the sofa in her cashmere coat, clutching a glass and blinking at the six o'clock news. In front of her on the coffee table, partially obscuring her view, was a bottle of white wine. The sun had dropped behind the house across the road giving the room a dingy feel, but it was too much effort to get up and turn on a lamp. In any case, she preferred it like this. She had begun to find bright light intolerable.

Earlier, at the inquest, the coroner had recorded an open verdict. The post mortem had confirmed what they already knew: that the difficulties in identifying Bernie and Esther made it impossible to establish an exact cause of death.

The hearing seemed to take forever. She knew the details were important; she tried her best to listen but as the coroner began his pronouncement, her head had hit Jamie's shoulder. It was so much easier to sleep during the day than at night. When he tried to push her upright again, she collapsed back into him and missed the conclusion. She only learned what the verdict was as they were leaving the building.

On the way home, she slouched in the passenger seat of Steve's van, her head aching. Lately she had been drinking only in secret, fed up of being watched and judged. Today, however, she couldn't wait until she was alone; she needed it sooner. Not daring to suggest vodka, she begged Steve to buy her some wine and he relented, stopping at an off-licence on the outskirts of town. It was all she could do not to crack it open then and there in the van.

Now, after several glasses, she was wide awake. The wine was honeyed and soothing; not harsh on her throat, like vodka. But it was no match for the pain in her head. Although she was staring at the television, she couldn't concentrate. The economics correspondent was talking about the exchange rate mechanism, whatever that was. It didn't matter. The background noise was enough to keep her from her thoughts. That and the chardonnay.

She didn't know where Steve was, or even if he was in the house. His silence in the van had made it clear what he thought about the wine. He'd probably gone to the pub. She wondered briefly whether he would see the irony in that, or whether he might consider himself a hypocrite. Not that she really cared. All she wanted was to be left to sit like this, drinking wine with a blank mind, undisturbed.

The front door rattled open. Ruby and Pearl burst into the sitting room, followed by Jamie. Caz winced as she realised that she was dreading the sight of her own children.

'Mummy!' Pearl launched herself onto the back of the sofa. 'We went to Paolo's for a pizza!'

'Why have you still got your coat on?' said Ruby, hesitating near Jamie by the door.

'Mummy!' said Pearl again, prodding her. 'I had a capri-something. It had mushrooms on it.'

Pearl's voice was loud in her ear, her finger jabbing too hard into Caz's arm. And why was Ruby bugging her about wearing her coat? She hadn't got round to taking it off, that was all.

'Mummy!' said Pearl for the third time.

'Jesus Christ!' she said. 'I'm trying to watch this. Go upstairs and give me a bit of bloody peace, will you?'

Pearl sprang off the sofa. Ruby backed into the wall. Both girls looked as though they had been slapped. Caz squashed an urge to apologise. She was too soft; they needed to be told. They couldn't just expect her to drop everything as soon as they appeared, especially after the day she'd had.

'Maybe do as Mummy asks,' said Jamie. 'Just for a bit.'

Ruby and Pearl stared at him, not moving.

'You've got three seconds,' said Caz. 'One… two…'

'Go on up,' said Jamie. 'We'll have a game of cards in a while.' Still, neither of them moved.

'Right!' Caz swung her legs off the sofa and tried to stand but she was too unsteady.

'Caz, for God's sake!' Jamie said.

She tried again to get up but collapsed. Then, out of nowhere, a small dog rushed in, scampering in circles around the sitting room. Steve was standing in the doorway, grinning.

Suddenly the room was in chaos. The puppy leapt onto Caz's lap, causing the wine to spill; then, when she shooed it off, it peed on the carpet. It wasn't clear which wet patch was pee and which was wine. Ruby and Pearl were literally bouncing; both calling for the puppy repeatedly so that it didn't know what to do with itself. Jamie was asking Steve how old the puppy was and where he'd got it from and Steve was saying something about a breeder in a nearby village.

Caz poured the last of the wine into her glass. Her wrist was throbbing. She tried to concentrate on the television to blot out the noise but she couldn't hear what was being said. The wine had gone. It probably wasn't reasonable to be this angry but she couldn't help it; she was consumed by fury. Was it too much to ask for a quiet evening on the day of her parents' inquest? They had spent hours raking over the grimmest of details. Nine months after the fire, none of it was any less difficult to hear. At one point during the hearing she had actually looked around for her mother, wanting her reassurance. And Steve thought the answer was to get a *puppy*! How was she supposed to care for a dog when she could no longer look after her own children?

Actually, it was worse than that; not only could she not care for them, she could barely stand to be in the same room as them. All their presence did was remind her what a terrible mother she had become. Steve didn't want to see her drinking, but really, they were the reason she needed to be so secretive about it. The disapproval she was most afraid of was theirs; they surely knew that her behaviour wasn't normal. None of their friends' mothers were like this. It was irksome to know that she would be compared, unfavourably, to people she barely knew, the Donnas of this world, who didn't have the same things to deal with as she did. Ruby and Pearl, when she thought about it, were the human impediments to her happiness. She could only do what she wanted with impunity when they weren't around.

From what she could see, they were managing perfectly well without her. Didn't people always say that children were innately self-sufficient? If she wasn't there at all, they would probably be better off. She loved them, of course she did; they were her children and on an instinctive level she needed them to be near. It was just the noise, the demands, the way they made her feel so inadequate, that she couldn't cope with. If drinking herself to sleep every day and cutting her wrists on an ad hoc basis could be counted as style, then her children were cramping it.

The four of them; Steve, Jamie, Ruby and Pearl, were on the floor with the puppy. It was a tiny thing, liver and white with a snubby little nose and enormous paws for its size. Now that it had calmed a little, Caz could see that it was a springer spaniel, the same breed that her parents had always kept. Its markings were similar to Juno's. That poor dog, burned to death because a silly old man dropped his bloody *cigarillo* and started a fire.

Jamie left the room and came back with kitchen roll to blot the mess on the floor. Steve picked up the puppy and put it into Ruby's arms where it snuggled against her, its eyes closed.

'He's a boy,' Steve said. 'What shall we call him?'

'Nigel,' said Ruby immediately.

'Nigel?' Jamie laughed. 'Is that a dog's name?'

'Why not?' said Steve. 'It's as good as anything.'

Typical Steve; never voicing an opinion. Fun Dad avoided any confrontation whatsoever with the girls; parenting to Steve was simply a matter of rough-housing and going with the flow. Although she had always slightly resented being the sole provider of discipline, at least she had given Ruby and Pearl an idea of how to behave. Steve had no rules for bedtime or table manners. He and Jamie were the blind leading the blind.

From where she lay on the sofa, it seemed that Jamie had taken her place in the family. There was no longer space for her. She had left a vacancy and Jamie was filling it. The most awful part was that she wasn't upset: she was relieved.

'J,' said Steve, 'are you all right to take *Nigel…*' he stopped as the girls giggled at the name, '..to the vet to get his jabs?'

'Um,' said Jamie, 'to Zoe's vets?'

'Well, yeah,' said Steve. 'It's the only one in town. That's not a problem, is it?'

'No, no, of course not. I'll get onto it tomorrow.'

'Thanks, mate. There's a vaccination card thingy on top of the dresser.'

Caz inched up from the sofa and wobbled towards the stairs. Pearl was rolling a tennis ball around for the puppy to chase. He was hopelessly unco-ordinated and the ball was too big for his miniature mouth. They were all laughing; nobody noticed her leave.

Inside a knee-length boot in her wardrobe was a bottle of vodka; in the other boot was a tumbler. Caz undressed and got into bed with the curtains drawn and no lights, cradling the drink. Her parents' story had ended in a soporific courtroom in Harrogate. It didn't matter whether they died of asphyxiation, or burning, or anything else. The point was that they were gone. There was nothing else to be said. Now that it was over, she supposed she would be expected to move on, but she couldn't see how. It was impossible to think of her parents without being drawn into a vortex of their imagined suffering. It didn't help to tell herself that there were people who needed her. That wasn't enough; they wanted what she couldn't give. Deep within her, a battle was raging between the Caz who knew her responsibilities as a mother and the Caz who only wanted to get drunk so that she could sleep at night. The second Caz was winning.

forty-four

The dresser, which divided the sitting room from the kitchen, had the insubstantial feel of self-assembly. With the puppy snuffling around at his feet, Jamie sifted through the mess of paperwork on top of it but there was no vaccination card. Trust Steve to give him duff information. Nigel's vet's appointment wasn't for another two days but it would be better to find it now if he could. It would be one less thing to think about at the point when he needed to psyche himself up for a potential encounter with Zoe. And once it was found he could disappear to Charlotte's until pickup time.

An experimental pull on a cupboard handle revealed Mousetrap, Monopoly and Buckaroo. How long was it, he wondered, since Caz had played board games with her children? There was also a wedding album, a *Home Alone* video and a putting machine.

Jamie closed the cupboard door. A floorboard creaked upstairs. This did not necessarily mean that Caz was awake; the construction of the house was so flimsy that she only had to turn over in bed to make the floor groan. Nonetheless, in the hush of mid-morning on a school day, it felt grubby to be ferreting among the appurtenances of his sister's family life, even though he was only acting on Steve's instructions.

The first drawer contained blu-tac, a bag of balloons and a clothes brush, a dymo and a set of silver napkin rings. He slammed it shut and the dresser quivered in reproach. Jamie tugged open the second drawer.

Resting on yet more paperwork was a small photograph of his parents. Until recently it had been in a frame on the mantelpiece; for some reason Caz must have taken it down. The picture was in black and white. His father, with short hair and a chevron moustache, was only faintly recognisable.

Jamie had always found it difficult to imagine his parents before he was born. That they lived, worked and had thoughts prior to his existence was hard to grasp. In his mind, they were suspended in monochrome, awaiting his arrival. He lifted the photo from the drawer and slotted it into the chest pocket of his shirt. As he did so, his eye was caught by the top of a letter which was folded into three, as though it had been pulled from an envelope but never read. The letterhead was that of Ruby and Pearl's school.

'Leave that.'

Jamie whipped the letter out of the drawer. He turned. Caz was stooped over the sofa, blanched and unkempt, gripping the back of the cushion. Nigel was jumping up at her but she paid him no attention. As well as the bandage on her wrist, there was a large plaster covering her left thumb. Wondering how she had made it down the stairs so quietly, Jamie took in her bare feet. Her toenails were unpainted and yellowed. Beneath her matted dressing gown she wore a thin t-shirt that could have belonged to Ruby and which clung, shockingly to her protruding ribcage. He hadn't realised that she was so thin. She must have weighed barely more than her seven-year-old daughter.

'What is it? This letter?' He held it up to her, still folded.

'Give it to me.' Caz reached out, making grabby movements with her fingers, holding onto the sofa with the other hand.

'I *could* do that,' said Jamie, 'but how about we just read it instead?'

With an exaggerated shrug, Caz sank onto the arm of the sofa and covered her face with her hands. Jamie scanned the letter.

'It's from Ruby and Pearl's head-teacher,' he began. 'She's writing because you haven't been into school like they asked to discuss this behavioural issue, whatever it is.' He paused and lowered the letter to look at Caz, who was nodding into her hands. 'It says that if you don't engage with them, they'll be forced to escalate the matter. What does *that* mean? Jesus, Caz, I told you she wanted to speak to you. Why the hell didn't you or Steve go in?'

She shook her head.

'Does Steve even know about this?'

'He never looks in that drawer.'

'Oh well,' said Jamie, with a mirthless laugh. 'That's all right, then.'

Caz sat up. She took her hands away from her face and hugged her arms around herself, widening her eyes at him.

'Can you speak to them?' she said. 'Can you tell them everything's OK?'

'No, I bloody well can't. You're their mother, not me!' Casting around, he kicked at a stack of *Hello!* magazines on the floor, sending them slithering across the carpet. As he put his foot down again he stood on one as it was still moving and almost did the splits.

'Shit!'

The puppy clamped his teeth around one of the magazines and ran off with it. Jamie pulled himself up straight and re-read the letter.

'How could you ignore this? You told me the girls were your life, what kept you straight. Don't you remember?' He thought of Ruby and Pearl on New Year's Eve, brushed and scrubbed, complaining about their velvet party dresses. 'And what's this?' He indicated her thumb, then took Caz by the wrist, taking care not to touch the bandage wound thickly around it. 'And this? You didn't ever give me an answer about *this*.'

She shrank away from him, holding her arm like a wounded wing.

'You need help. You know that, don't you?'

The doorbell rang. Nigel began to bark.

'Ignore it,' said Jamie.

The bell shrilled again. As Jamie and Caz stood, frozen, a shape passed in front of the small, faux-leaded panes of the sitting room window and stopped. Ruth Cole pressed her hands up to the frame and peered in.

'Caroline?' Her voice was muffled through the glass. 'Jamie?'

'Nice timing,' Jamie muttered, and strode to the front door, almost tripping over Nigel.

Ruth untied a plastic rain bonnet, took it off and shook it.

'Hello, love. Oh, and who's this?' She bent down to pet the puppy, who pawed at her leg and laddered her tights. 'Little bugger. When did he arrive?'

'Steve brought him home yesterday. It was a surprise.'

Ruth inspected the ladder and stood up.

'What on earth was he thinking? As if you all haven't got enough to deal with.' Nigel rolled onto his back, his paws bicycling in the air. 'He's a looker, though. Just like poor Juno.'

She followed Jamie into the sitting room. 'Anyway, I just thought I'd pop in. After the inquest and everything. So I jumped on the bus and oh, goodness me…'

Ruth had put down her handbag and was looking around, dismay etched into the corners of her mouth as she took in the cloak of neglect and that had settled over the room. Having had the energy sucked from their argument by the interruption, Jamie and Caz watched as she darted about, dodging the puppy underfoot, straightening ornaments, scooping up stray socks and shoes and dusting surfaces with a series of tissues she pulled from her pockets.

Caz, still immobilised on the arm of the sofa, tried to tuck her thumb out of sight but it was too late.

'Caroline, what *have* you been doing to yourself?'

Caz muttered something about chopping onions but Ruth took hold of her arm, more tenderly than Jamie had done, pulling it towards her. Slowly, she peeled away the bandage on Caz's thumb. The gauze kept catching, which made Caz flinch, but at length the wound was exposed; a bright red, yawning gash, notched into the skin.

'Oh, pet lamb,' said Ruth. 'Let me see the rest.'

Ruth's arrival seemed to have taken all of the fight out of Caz. She meekly held out her arm, but the bandage on her wrist was dirty and had stuck to itself. Ruth went to the kitchen for the scissors and cut through it gently until the dressing fell away. It left bare the same rusty scars that

Jamie had seen on that hot day in the garden, except that now they were bigger and more encrusted, seeping yellow at the edges. Ruth let out a small gasp but Caz glared at her, defiant again, challenging her to react further.

As Ruth looked away, Caz said, 'I'm fine.'

'Don't be ridiculous,' said Ruth. 'You need to see a doctor.'

'That's what I've been saying,' said Jamie.

'No,' said Caz. 'I told you.'

'I can't listen to any more of this,' said Jamie. 'She won't help herself.'

Ruth picked up the magazines which were still splayed across the carpet and arranged them into a pile on the table, then took Caz lightly by the elbow.

'We're going upstairs,' she said. 'I'm going to get Caroline cleaned up, we'll have some lunch and then we'll both go and collect the girls from school. Why don't you make yourself scarce, love? I can manage here.'

Unashamedly relieved, Jamie seized Caz's car keys from the hall table. Once he was inside the Fiat he turned Radio Three up loud, not wanting to imagine any more of what might be going on between Ruth and his sister, and began to drive without any idea where he was going. On the high street, he stopped outside the post office and turned off the ignition with a shaky hand. Rain was sheeting down from a sky the colour of pencil lead, cascading over the windscreen and thundering on the roof of the car.

Despite what he said when the doorbell rang, Ruth's arrival *had* been nicely timed. Grabbing Caz by the wrist had been pure reaction; the discovery of the letter had taken the abandonment of her role as a mother outside the house and erased any residue of sympathy he had for her. Jamie didn't know how he would have dealt with the situation if Ruth hadn't turned up. What he really wanted was to sit Caz down, talk to her properly, get her to see what she was doing, but she didn't want to engage, she only wanted him to clear up her mess.

For now, Ruth would make Caz look respectable for the trip to school and with any luck her attendance would both pacify Miss Wood and clarify what had happened last term. Hopefully, Ruth would hang around long enough to prepare Ruby and Pearl a decent meal. But something would need to change. They couldn't carry on like this.

Jamie's own efforts to help the girls had been woefully inept. He should have confronted Steve, told him that bringing home a puppy in the circumstances was ludicrous: they had just come back from the inquest, Caz was on the verge of a breakdown and the girls were being neglected. Instead, he had played with Nigel as though everything was normal. Jamie was sickened by his own uselessness. But Caz was now beyond the point of reason and Jamie was bewilderingly and terrifyingly out of his depth. He wished he could remember how his parents had helped her as a teenager, but all he could recall was her pregnancy. If that was what saved her before, it wouldn't save her now. Where once the idea of motherhood was enough to bring her round, the opposite now seemed to be true.

Jamie slid the photo out of the pocket of his shirt. In it, his parents were standing in front of a twin-prop aeroplane, holding champagne saucers. His father wore a dark suit; his mother's coat was pale with a fur collar and huge buttons. While Bernie held up his drink to the camera with an expression of undiluted pride, his mother nursed hers towards her and was smiling rather shyly. As he studied the picture, it struck him that he had never asked them anything about their younger selves. He turned the photo over. On the reverse, Esther had written, *Honeymoon, Jersey, March 1964*, the ink now faded to a washed-out sepia. It was the year before Caz was born.

'Why the hell aren't you here?' he said to his newlywed parents. Something in the very existence of the photograph, of his mother and father, with nearly thirty years of marriage and parenthood ahead of them; the hopes, plans, and fears which would end in a brutal inferno at the dawn of a new year, was too much to bear.

He threw the picture onto the passenger seat and flung open the door into the teeming rain. Cursing, he crossed his arms and ducked his face down. The pavement had cleared of people; shop windows were fogged up, their wares invisible. Jamie splashed through the puddles. A loose paving stone threw a sluice of water up the back of his calves. He walked on, past the butcher's and the wool shop. Two elderly ladies in macs loitered mutely in the doorway of Paolo's. At the vet's, Jamie noted that Zoe's pickup was parked outside and then carried on towards the end of the high street.

When he reached the entrance to the park, he stopped. By now, the rain had found its way through the dense plaid of his shirt, weighing it down so that it stuck to his shoulders and chest, sagging at the hem. A tractor pulling a slurry tank crawled through the flooded street and he had to jump back from the kerb to avoid the spray. For no reason other than to keep moving, he went in through the park gates.

Apart from a few school-kids, smoking in the bandstand, Jamie was alone. He set off around the pond, its glossy blackness absorbing the deluge. When he was small, his mother used to bring him here to feed the ducks. He paused for a moment, remembering how they would cluster around him, treading water, waiting for him to fling the scraps of crust at them. As soon as the bread was gone they would swim away, leaving him standing at the concrete rim of the pond with an empty paper bag. It was never worth the sense of abandonment once they realised he had nothing left for them and moved on.

Rain was soaking through the front of his jeans and he moved off again. Dog turds, now made liquid, metastasised across the tarmac path. Jamie glanced over to the children's playground. It looked as though someone had left a cuddly toy on top of the slide, but on closer inspection it was a squirrel, hunched against the rain.

At the far end of the pond he turned back towards the town. A couple of ancient paddleboats, strung together at the concrete edge, were filling up with water and only just afloat. Beneath the dense bushes, a group of ducks huddled together, their little beaks opening and closing in silent protest.

As Jamie reached the park gate again the rain was so hard that he couldn't see the high street. He pressed on in an approximation of where it was, almost enjoying the sensation; stumbling blindly through torrential rain blocked out all other thoughts. The two women in Paolo's porch stared as he passed them and he nodded in acknowledgement of how bedraggled he must have looked. Someone called his name from behind.

Zoe was wearing a floor-length stockman's coat and a wide-brimmed hat. Water trickled from the hand clutching her vet's bag. She spread her arms in a question.

'Don't ask,' Jamie shouted over the noise of the rain. 'I've no idea.'

She nodded towards the truck and got in. He hesitated for a moment, then followed.

'What's wrong?' she said once he was in the passenger seat. 'Why are you outside getting drenched like that?'

'You don't want to know,' said Jamie.

'Was it the inquest?'

'Not really.'

'What, then?'

All of the windows had steamed up. Jamie stared ahead, enveloped by the car's familiar horsiness, biting his lip. If he started talking, he might never stop, and he wasn't sure that Zoe would really want to listen. It wasn't her responsibility anymore; hadn't been for a long time. They sat for a few minutes in silence. Water dripped from his jeans onto the floor. Zoe wiped the inside of the windscreen with a cloth.

'If I'd been going up the dale you could have come with me,' she said. 'But I'm only going to your parents' village. Mrs Thorneycroft's got greasy pig disease.' Her mouth twitched at the side, the way it did when she was trying not to smile.

'Hope she doesn't give it to the animals.'

They turned to face one another at the same time. Jamie caught the amusement in Zoe's eye. He had forgotten the way she had of being entertained by little things, and how infectious it was.

'Do you want to tell me about it?' she said.

'I'd rather not,' he said. 'You should go. It's probably good that I can't come. Don't worry. I'm fine. Really.'

'Sure?'

Jamie opened the door and got out. The rain had eased to a steady downpour.

'It's good to see you.'

'You too, ' she said. 'Take care, Jamie.'

He pushed the heavy door shut and watched as she turned on the ignition and the windscreen wipers. She gave him a little wave and mouthed, 'Bye,' as she reversed out into the road. When he got back to the car, he sat, turning Charlotte's smiley face keyring over and over in his hands, wondering why he was hesitating and unable to come up with an answer.

'Sod it,' he said to himself, and set off towards her bungalow.

forty-five

Jamie went straight to Charlotte's bathroom, unlaced his boots and emptied them of water. Then he stripped off his clothes and towelled himself down. Next to the washing machine was a primordial tumble dryer. He shoved the clothes inside and turned it on. Wrapping the towel around his waist, he calculated that everything should be dry before Charlotte came home from work.

His hands were too cold to play the piano. He filled the basin with warm water and submerged them, tensing and relaxing his fingers. As the water began to cool, the movement returned, first to his fingers, then to his hands and up into his wrists.

Jamie wandered into the dining room, barefoot, and settled himself at the piano, hoping that Charlotte's neighbours weren't around to see him half-naked. His fingers probed the keys, trying to unlock the opening to the Rachmaninov he had been longing to play, the Prelude in C sharp minor. Learning the piece as a teenager he had been daunted by its shameless theatre; the sudden extremes in the dynamics and tempo, the emotion in the chords. It was like an uncontrolled outburst of passion, alien and dreadful. But once he had control of the fingering, he found that he loved the challenge of jumping from one end of the keyboard to another without missing a note, ripping through the agitato section to the presto, the percussive chorded thirds at fortissississimo and the majestic, inexorable approach to the pianississimo conclusion.

Unsure at first, Jamie began a few notches down from fortissimo while he felt his way into the slow introduction, almost groaning as his fingers found the keys, remembering where the accidentals lay, feeling the delicious combinations of notes and the drama of the phrasing. Now and again he forgot part of a chord, or a finger would slip, but on the whole the music was there, its power and grandeur somehow preserved inside his brain. He went over the frantic, chromatic sequential phrases of agitato several times, making sure he had them correctly. Then he was back to the processional chords of the second lento section, by which point he no longer cared how loud the last fortississimo passage was. And, just as he had completely lost himself, he was at the final cadence, ending on a whisper.

After that, it was as though a chemical had been released in his brain. He moved onto Schumann, Liszt and then Bach's Goldberg, which he had never fully mastered. He was still tinkering with the aria when he heard Charlotte in the hallway, shaking a wet umbrella.

'Well,' she said as she walked into the room, 'this is the first time I've come home to find a man in a loincloth. That's not my face towel, is it?'

'I got soaked,' said Jamie. 'I hope you don't mind - my jeans are in your tumble dryer.'

'I'm kidding,' she said. 'Don't stop. It sounded amazing.'

Jamie looked down at the keyboard. But the spell had been broken by Charlotte's arrival and the fact that he was wearing only a towel. The scene felt overly intimate; Zoe had never heard him play or seen the effect it had on him, and here he was with Charlotte, undressed in more senses than one.

'I think I need trousers.' He scurried to the bathroom to retrieve them.

'Stay for dinner?' said Charlotte when he returned. 'It's still chucking it down outside.'

Jamie offered to go out for take-away but Charlotte insisted on cooking. They drank pinot grigio while she sautéed chicken and potatoes and threw together a ratatouille. The wine was bland but drinkable; it was gone before the food was ready. By the time they had finished eating, they were a good portion through a bottle of merlot.

To be polite, Jamie chose to sit at the springless end of the sofa. As a result his bottom was more or less on the floor while his knees were up by his chin. Charlotte, at the other end, had her legs tucked beneath her. Every so often she grabbed a handful of her exuberant hair and arranged it behind her neck, away from her face. The attractiveness of the gesture reminded Jamie of Zoe, and how he'd have liked to have stayed in the car with her. The wine was making him morose. In this mood he was no company. He should be at home, but what was going on *there* was the reason he was *here*.

'I'm so angry with Caz,' he said.

'I can tell,' said Charlotte. 'You haven't said much all evening. What's she done?'

He drank some more wine and put down his glass.

'It doesn't matter. All I know is that the way I feel right now I wouldn't care if I never saw her again.'

'You don't mean that.'

Charlotte reached across and gave his forearm a little rub.

'She's not looking after the girls,' he said. 'They've been in trouble at school and the head-teacher's got involved. I'm doing my best with them, but I'm crap at it. Someone needs to step in and sort things out. It should be me but I can't seem to do it. I'm pathetic.'

Charlotte began to speak but he carried on, talking over her, wanting to tell her everything before his instincts kicked in and made him stop.

'I hated Caz this morning, Charlotte, properly hated her. Steve's been a spineless bastard but I should be doing more. I'm weak and I'm useless.'

'You're not, Jamie, you're not.'

'I am! My nieces are living in virtual squalor right under my nose with a mother who's addicted to booze and a father who pretends he can't see it.'

The curtains were still open and the blackness outside seemed an extension of the gloom in which they were sitting. The only light came from a standard lamp behind the sofa which acted as a kind of mini-spotlight over them.

'Where are they now?' said Charlotte.

'At home. Ruth Cole's there. Our old nanny.'

'So they're safe,' said Charlotte. 'Don't be too hard on yourself. You'll work out how to manage until Caz can get some treatment.'

'Thanks, Charlotte.'

She got up to put her wine glass on the table; when she sat down again she was closer to him. Their legs were touching. Charlotte leaned over and stroked Jamie's face with the tips of her fingers, so lightly that they didn't snag on his evening stubble. She pushed back her hair again and kissed his cheek.

Jamie slid a hand to the back of her neck, losing it in her chaotic hair, and kissed her mouth, tasting merlot. She twisted towards him, allowing him to pull her nearer. As Jamie shifted his position there was a loud twang from the insubstantial springs beneath him and they drew away from each other as they laughed. It was enough of a pause to allow an iota of uncertainty into his mind and he looked at her, not moving. A police siren wailed faintly from the direction of the high street. Charlotte stood and took hold of both of his hands. Later, Jamie would swear that she had pulled him up and led him into the bedroom, when really that wasn't possible. The only one of them with the strength to move all six-foot three and fifteen stones of him off that sofa was Jamie himself.

forty-six

Jamie woke to a sea of little red hearts. He was alone in Charlotte's bed with his head beneath her patterned duvet. Lying still, he listened for movement inside the house. From beyond the insistent ticking of a clock came the distant bleat of a pneumatic drill from somewhere outside, but nothing else.

Concluding that Charlotte must have gone to work, Jamie wriggled his head out of the duvet. The curtains were made from the same heart-motif fabric as the bed linen. On the dressing table, hair products, paperbacks and cosmetics wrestled for space. One of Charlotte's work suits wilted on a hanger on the back of the door. A couple of sensible bras (unlike the one she was wearing last night) dangled from the radiator.

Jamie stretched, smiling at the memory. Then he caught himself, swore and drew his knees in to his chest. He'd had sex with Charlotte. He had followed her here, into her bedroom and they had calmly disrobed each other, as though it were the only logical conclusion to the evening. In one sense he had known exactly what he was doing; in another, he'd allowed his mind to go blank and let his body take over. And it felt great. He stretched again, lengthening his limbs. Something elusive had clicked back into place; not just the capacity for the act itself, but the real, undeniable desire for it. As Charlotte pulled him close, it didn't occur to him to doubt himself. They were gentle with each other, tender and respectful. Afterwards, she rested her head on his shoulder and stayed there, the two of them sandwiched together in the middle of her slightly rickety double bed.

Charlotte had offered him kindness and understanding. Might her compassion have unlocked the part of him that had been paralysed by the fire? If so, she would have no idea of the enormous service she had done him; he was sure he had given her no reason to suspect. Then, he remembered the moment before he fell asleep when he had whispered *thank you,* over and over again, into her hair.

Jamie cringed at the recollection. He had no idea what she might think of his gratitude, but he could guess how she might feel about being the instrument of his sexual liberation. Put in those terms, he had taken advantage of her in the most indefensible way.

It wasn't as though Zoe had lacked compassion. If he could have responded to her as he had to Charlotte, there was no way that he would be here now. Perhaps it was the piano that had allowed him to access what had become unavailable. He hadn't thought of the fire at any point during the evening. Was that what healing felt like? How would he know? And, of course, it was Charlotte who had offered to house the piano for him. Without that he would still be wondering whether he could remember how to play.

He glanced at the clock on the bedside table. Next to it was a framed photo of Charlotte, clutching a mortar board to her head, standing between her parents. Her mother wore what he believed was called a fascinator; her father, besuited and puff-chested, gripped Charlotte's shoulder as if he were worried that she was about to run away. She probably was, in a manner of speaking. As a scene it was too intimate; it made Jamie feel like an intruder. He rolled from the bed, dressed and closed the door behind him.

In the safer terrain of the kitchen, Jamie made coffee and slathered marmite onto a slice of toast. He should probably leave. What could he do in Charlotte's kitchen except think about Charlotte? Yes, he had regained a visceral, necessary, much-missed ability, but at what price? What, in God's name, had he been thinking?

He and Charlotte would have to speak to each other. Maybe they could laugh it off as a bit of over-excitement after too much wine. But he had seen the way she looked at him and felt the care with which she touched him. And then there was the lacy underwear: was she wearing it specially, on the off-chance that they might spend the night together?

Ruby and Pearl would be at school by now. For once, he had abandoned his post and left Steve to do the school run. No doubt he would be in Steve's bad books for that. But as he was here, it would be a wasted opportunity not to play the piano. If he had ruined things with Charlotte, he might not get another chance until he had found somewhere else to keep it. Nobody needed him at Chestnut Drive until later and he was in no hurry to be alone with Caz.

In the dining room, Jamie swept some dust from the top of the piano with his sleeve. After a moment's pause he spread his hands wide to the ends of the keyboard for the opening of Debussy's impressionist masterpiece, *La Cathédrale Engloutie.* His fingers caressed the notes, listening for the ringing of the bells beneath the sea. Both his hands moved into the treble clef, anticipating the key change at the end of the first section where the mythical cathedral rises from the water and slowly emerges from the fog. What followed came easily: the fortissimo section, where the organ, clear and sonorous, rings out across the sea; but he struggled with the next part, the gradual descent of the cathedral back below the water. The accidentals were tricky to remember; the notes jarred whenever he missed one and he almost gave up. But then, he was at the beautiful, rumbling, final section, both hands in the bass clef, where the organ is still being played, under the surface, hidden again from view. Just then, the legend of the sunken cathedral, allowed to rise above the sea for only the briefest of moments, seemed overwhelming and hopeless. Jamie sat back and forced his fingers into some scales and arpeggios, wanting something mechanical to play that didn't require any emotional investment.

The phone rang. He let it trill a few times before concluding that it was probably Charlotte and that it would be rude not to answer, given that he was in her house.

'Hi,' she said in a bright tone. 'How are you this morning?'

'Good,' said Jamie. 'Playing a few pieces before I go home.'

'Don't let me stop you. I was just wondering if you'd be around later. We could have some pasta, or a curry. Whatever you fancy.'

'I can't tonight,' said Jamie. He had nothing planned. 'Sorry.'

'Oh, OK.' Her voice was flat. 'Not to worry. I'd better get on.'

'Look, Charlotte,' Jamie began, but she cut him off.

'Really. I have to go. Bye, Jamie.'

The disappointment in her voice was horrible. He had messed things up by having sex with her just as he had messed things up with Zoe by *not* having sex with *her.* It was all the wrong way round. Even though he hadn't consciously identified it, he must have known what was going to happen with Charlotte. By not articulating the thought he had allowed himself to ignore the potential consequences. And now, having upset her, there was also the imminent prospect of facing Zoe at the vets'. He closed the fall-board of the piano and stood up. When he reached the front door, he went back and stroked its ebony top before he left.

'Is Charlotte your new girlfriend?' Pearl said later as they idled on the kerb beneath the canopy of a horse chestnut tree. At their feet lay dozens of green, spiny shells, denuded of their fruits. Conkers, russet and glossy, studded the carpet of leaves on the pavement.

The lollipop lady waited for a succession of cars to pass before stepping out into the road, her arms spread wide. Jamie grabbed both girls' hands and strode across, Ruby and Pearl trotting either side of him.

'Is she?' said Ruby when they reached the other side. 'Your girlfriend?'

'No,' said Jamie. 'Why?'

'You had a sleepover at her house,' said Pearl.

Jamie laughed. 'She's my friend. She's looking after Granny's piano and I went there to practise. You know. We went there on the day Mr and Mrs Sidgwick moved in.'

They turned the corner onto the high street.

'But she promised you something,' said Pearl.

'Sorry?'

'When you didn't come home, Daddy said you must be on a promise.'

'Did he now?' said Jamie. The cheeky bastard.

Pearl wriggled free of his hand. She flipped around and began to skip backwards in front of Jamie and Ruby.

'Shall we tell Uncle Jamie who came round last night?' she said, dodging a lamp-post.

'Careful,' said Jamie. 'Hang on, what?'

'He won't care,' said Ruby. 'He likes Charlotte now.'

'This is getting ridiculous.' He stopped in the middle of the pavement. 'What are you talking about?'

'It was Zoe,' said Pearl. 'I saw her from our bedroom window. She came up the path and knocked on the door.'

'Yeah,' said Ruby. 'We were supposed to be asleep but I was reading to Pearl under the covers with my torch. Mummy won't read to us anymore and we wanted to find out what happened to Aslan.'

'But you've never met Zoe. How did you know it was her?'

'We asked Daddy this morning,' said Pearl. 'She's really pretty.'

'Right…So what did she want?'

'No idea!' Pearl had stopped skipping and was twirling on the spot. 'Is she going to be your girlfriend again?'

'What about Charlotte?' said Ruby.

They had stopped outside Maynews.

'If I buy you a bag of wine gums,' said Jamie, 'will you please stop quizzing me?'

—

Caz was sitting on the bottom stair when they came in. Any effort by Ruth to clean up her appearance had been swiftly undone. She was in the yellow dressing gown again and her skin was a pasty off-white.

'There she is,' Caz said, pointing at Ruby, 'my little prize-fighter.'

Ruby took a step backwards.

'What?' said Jamie.

'Scrapping in the playground.' Caz's voice was flat and cold and loud. 'Didn't I bring you up to know better? I'm ashamed of you.'

'Hey.' Jamie put himself between Caz and Ruby and put his hands out, face down, in a calming gesture. 'Take it easy. What's all this?'

'I hit someone,' said Ruby in a small voice. 'It was last term.'

'Yeah,' Caz sneered. 'You kept that quiet, didn't you?' It wasn't the tone of a loving mother; a note of borderline hatred had crept in which Jamie didn't like at all.

'They deserved it,' Pearl said.

'Why?' said Jamie. 'What did they do?'

Both girls were silent. Miss Wood would have spoken to Caz when she went to school with Ruth, so why leave it until now to berate Ruby? The answer was clear enough: Ruth had been around the previous evening to act as a buffer zone and Caz wouldn't have been out of bed when they left for school with Steve that morning. Caz took a long swig from a glass of clear liquid.

'Get out of my sight, both of you.' The two girls bolted past her. 'You're ruining my life,' she shouted.

'I'll deal with you in a minute,' Jamie hissed as he dashed after them, leaving Caz muttering to herself on the stair.

Ruby was standing in her room, sobbing. Pearl, next to her, was cuddling her precious stuffed dog.

'What happened, Rubes?' Jamie knelt down in front of them and Ruby launched herself at him, her thin arms clinging around his neck. 'Shh, shh. It's OK.' He scooped her up and sat her on the bed, hugging her while she took the agonising little gasps of a child trying to stop crying.

'I thought she was my friend,' Ruby said.

'Who, darling? Who did you think was your friend?'

'Lydia Green,' said Pearl. 'But she's a liar.'

'Why?' said Jamie, suspecting that he knew the answer.

Pearl was holding the stuffed dog under her chin. 'She said Mummy was drunk in the supermarket and Daddy was a wife-beater.'

'*What?*' However unsurprised Jamie was by the first allegation, the second was straight out of left-field. He thought back to the end of the summer term, when Miss Wood first approached him. Might that have been around the time that Caz fell and hit her nose? It hadn't occurred to him at the time but it probably did look as though someone had beaten her up.

Jamie pulled both girls onto his lap.

'Listen,' he said. 'Your daddy would never hurt your mummy. When she bashed her nose, it was because she tripped on the stairs. You were there, remember.' He watched, helpless, as Ruby tried to frame the inevitable next question.

'Was… was Mummy drunk?'

Jamie sighed. 'Your mummy loves you very much. She didn't mean what she said just now; she's not very well at the moment. I know it's hard, but we all have to believe that she'll be better soon. It might not be tomorrow, or next week, or even next month, but she'll get there, OK?' He needed to believe his words as much as the girls did. 'And for the record, Rubes, I'm proud of you. I probably shouldn't say this but I would have done exactly the same.'

Caz was still at the bottom of the stairs, slumped against the bannister, clutching the glass which was now empty. She reached out to him as he passed but he brushed her off.

'What can I say, Caz? That was so out of order, I... They're *children*. Your children. How could you speak to them like that? What's wrong with you?'

'I don't know.' She began to cry silently, shrinking into herself. 'I'm a... I'm a... witch. I'm a... I'm a monster.' Jamie tried to find a reason to argue but couldn't come up with one. 'Will you tell them I'm sorry?' Her head nodded forward as though despite the tears she was struggling to stay awake.

'Tell them yourself. On second thoughts, don't. Wait till tomorrow.'

Jamie paused. Having cut off his own escape valve, he couldn't go to Charlotte's. Instead he went to the kitchen in search of something for the children's tea. Afterwards he played with them until bedtime. Neither Caz nor Steve were anywhere to be seen.

forty-six

Nigel's appointment was straight after school drop-off the following morning. Jamie suggested to Caz, through her bedroom door, that she might like to come. He didn't really think that she could help control the puppy in the car, but he hoped she might be sufficiently ashamed of her behaviour towards Ruby to engage in a proper conversation. There was no response; she was either asleep or ignoring him. He put Nigel on the passenger seat of Caz's Fiat and arrived at the surgery only mildly flustered by the prospect of seeing Zoe again. The receptionist directed him to the waiting room.

Ten months earlier, Jamie had sat in the very same place, trying to quiet a yowling dog. Juno was clearly in dreadful pain and could be calmed by neither shushing nor stroking. The waiting room was busy; other owners were glaring at him and the receptionist was having to shout to make herself heard on the telephone. Jamie sat, helpless, ingesting the disinfected air and rubbing Juno's side as she pressed her weight against his leg. The dog was leaning against him so hard that if he moved she would have fallen over.

As he studied a poster warning of the dangers of rabies, he became aware that someone was yelling at him. Juno chose that moment to take a break from howling and as a result the vet was now bellowing the dog's name into a silent room. Amused, Jamie looked up. The vet was unglamorously dressed, in a navy polo shirt and leggings, but her brown hair, which was tied back in a ponytail, was thick and lustrous. Her eyes, also brown, were intense and lively and her mouth had a playful twitch. She was, in short, the most attractive person he had ever seen.

'Er, Mr Fenton?' she said at normal volume. 'I'm Zoe, one of the vets. Come this way, please.'

He followed the swinging ponytail into the consulting room and wrestled Juno onto the examination table where she began to yowl again. Jamie hugged her close and clamped his hand over her muzzle as he explained that she had come back from her morning walk scratching her ear and that the scratching had quickly mutated into the high-pitched wail that they were now witnessing.

'It's probably a grass seed,' said Zoe. 'They can drive dogs crazy.'

She lifted the flap of Juno's ear and peered inside.

'Yep,' she said. 'It's quite far in. The good news for Juno is I'm quite good at these.' Zoe flashed Jamie a smile that almost made him ask her out for a drink there and then. 'If you could just keep her still for a minute.'

He steadied Juno's head while Zoe tried to tweeze the offending seed from the dog's ear. They were close enough for him to smell citrus shampoo on her hair. This would, he thought, be a great story to share years later, when anyone asked them how they'd met.

'Almost there,' said Zoe, just as Juno wrenched her head out of Jamie's grasp and sank her teeth into the pad of Zoe's thumb.

'Ow,' she said. Fat drops of blood were already pulsing from the break in her flesh. Jamie let go of the dog and she jumped from the table.

'I'm so sorry,' he said. 'Let me see.'

'It's nothing. I…' Holding her thumb aloft, Zoe fled the room. Juno was now making even more noise than before, if that were possible. After a few minutes another vet, this time male and Antipodean, came in and said tersely that Juno would need to be sedated for safety reasons and that Zoe was on her way to A and E where she would likely need stitches.

The day after the thumb-biting incident, Jamie went to the florist and bought the biggest bunch of flowers he could afford, in a tasteful mix of pinks and whites. When he arrived at the surgery, forearmed with a little speech to convince Zoe that he was not an irresponsible dog owner but in fact a pretty good guy, he learned that it was her day off. Having decided to buy himself a consolatory pork pie, he almost bumped into her as he was coming out of the butcher's. She was wearing jodhpurs.

'Oh,' she said. 'Hi again.'

'How's the thumb? I went to the surgery to apologise. It's really not like Juno to bite anyone. She's normally a total softie.'

'It wasn't your fault. She was probably in agony.' She wiggled her bandaged thumb at him. 'This didn't make tacking up any easier this morning though. Is that for me? You shouldn't have.'

Jamie held out the bouquet, slightly thrown by her forthrightness, but she was looking at the pork pie. She gave him the same smile from the day before and lifted the pie out of his hand. 'And yes, I will have a drink with you. That *was* what you were going to ask me, wasn't it?'

Perhaps the unwanted flowers were a giveaway. But she *had* been bitten by his dog, and what kind of person wouldn't try to make amends for that?

'Are you some kind of mind-reader as well as a hotshot veterinary surgeon?'

She grinned. 'I took a punt. Don't humiliate me by saying I was wrong.'

He put out his hand to mime taking the pie back and she laughed.

'Where do you work, Jamie?'

'I'm starting a new job on Monday, at Archer's in Ripon.'

'An estate agent, eh? I don't normally go out with yuppies but I'll make an exception in your case.'

When the arrangements had been made and Zoe had wandered away along the high street, Jamie went back into the shop to buy another pie. The thought of them both in different places, eating the same lunch, was so pleasing that he bought an extra one for Juno as a reward for causing them to meet. The flowers he gave to his mother.

'Jamie?' Today the waiting room was deserted and this spaniel was quiet. He followed Zoe into the consulting room and closed the door.

'Did she get rid of it?' Jamie said. 'The greasy pig disease?'

'Ha! Sadly not. It's pretty ugly up there, I can tell you.'

He lifted Nigel onto the table.

'Oh, wow,' said Zoe. 'He's a stunner.' She lifted up one ear, as she had with Juno. Inside it was bright pink and perfectly clean. 'Beautiful.'

'I know,' said Jamie. 'Shame Steve picked the worst possible moment to bring him home. Honestly, Zo, I can't think what possessed him.'

'I came to see you.'

'I heard.' Nigel performed a kind of figure-of-eight manoeuvre with Jamie's hand still inside his collar. 'Ouch! Bloody hell. He almost broke my fingers.'

'I always said you were a drama queen. Seriously, is everything OK? I was worried after I saw you on the high street the other day. And Steve looked terrible when he answered the door.'

'Things could be better,' Jamie conceded.

'Is there anything I can do?'

That phrase; the one people use when they don't know what else to say, knowing that the likelihood of them needing to actually *do* anything is vanishingly small. Zoe's face, however, was sincere, and he was grateful for it.

'I was at a friend's when you came round,' he said, nonetheless wanting her to know that he had other people to do things with.

'Right. Yes.'

'She's letting me keep Mum's piano at her house. It escaped the fire, remember?'

He thought her head jerked slightly when he said *she*, but he could have imagined it.

'I'd forgotten. Great that it survived. I know how much you love it.'

He waited for her to make a joke about him not having to do that weird practising on his legs any more, but she didn't. Instead she went to fetch a syringe.

'Can you hold him steady? This won't take a second.'

Jamie bear-hugged the puppy, as a result of which Zoe's face was within inches of his as she eased the needle into the back of Nigel's neck.

'There you go, little one,' she crooned, stroking his head. 'You're a brave soldier. Have you got his vaccination card?'

'Um, no,' said Jamie. 'We seem to have lost it.'

'Brilliant. Great admin.' She stood for a moment with a hand on her hip and then ducked out of the room. Jamie put Nigel on the floor where he immediately peed.

Zoe came back in holding a folded card. 'Luckily, he was registered here when he was born, so we've made you a new one.' She handed it over. 'Mind you don't lose it.'

Jamie put the card in his back pocket. 'Why *did* you come round the other night?'

She crossed her arms and leaned back against the counter. 'As I said, I was worried. And then I found out you had an appointment. I wanted to see you properly before you came in here, so that I could decide whether to give your appointment to someone else. I was trying to avoid any awkwardness but then, when you weren't at home, I told myself I was being silly and that of course I could do Nigel's jabs.'

'And *is* it awkward? I mean, *I* don't think it is.'

She laughed and stepped towards him, so that they were facing each other across the consulting table.

'We're never awkward, and God knows we've given each other enough reason to be.'

'You've got that right.'

Zoe looked down. 'I think I might be standing in puppy wee.'

'Sorry about that.'

She reached over for a roll of blue paper and bent down to soak it up.

'You know,' she said, fighting off Nigel, who was trying to eat the paper, 'whenever I think of you I picture you doing that fingering thing on your leg. Do you still do it?'

'All the time,' said Jamie. 'Mostly I don't even notice.'

'And do you realise,' she stood up and dropped the paper into a surgical bin, 'that I've never actually heard you play?'

'There are reasons for that,' Jamie muttered.

'I know,' Zoe persisted, 'but you did come to the stables that time.'

'Don't remind me.'

'Yeah, but I owe you. Will you play for me one day? Show me the magic?' That little smile twitched at the corners of her mouth.

'I'd love to,' said Jamie. 'I've just got a few things to sort out first.'

forty-eight

Jamie put down the phone in the hall at Chestnut Drive and stood for a moment, deliberating.

The meeting with Charlotte that he'd just proposed might turn out to be difficult or even embarrassing, but he needed to talk to her about that night, to let her know that what happened wasn't as casual for him as she obviously thought it was. He was yet to work out how this was to be achieved without revealing why it was so momentous that they'd had sex, but surely he could come up with something.

In Charlotte's prolonged avoidance of him, he sensed that she was trying to make things easier for them both, which he would normally have found admirable. It *would* have been more straightforward to simply move on without having any kind of conversation about the night they had spent together. They were no longer colleagues and running into each other in the town was no more likely than it had ever been, but it didn't seem right to duck the issue completely.

There was also the matter of the Pleyel. Although he *did* want to do the grown-up thing and speak to Charlotte properly, to say that the piano wasn't a factor would have been a lie. In offering to look after it, she had provided him with the perfect arrangement - permission to play whenever he wanted - and he had blown it by sleeping with her. To have it sitting there, in her house, without being able to touch it was almost worse than when it was being repaired (although, of course, that had been his fault as well).

The situation needed resolving. It was time to call in a favour. He picked up the phone again.

Later that evening, Jamie and Charlotte were in her dining room, standing on either side of the piano. Charlotte was drinking a glass of white wine. Jamie had just finished explaining that the Sidgwicks had agreed to have the Pleyel in their bright yellow studio-cum-garage.

'You didn't have to do that.' Charlotte flapped her hand in the air. 'It could have stayed for as long as you wanted. I wouldn't have minded.'

'It needs to be out of your way,' said Jamie. 'And so do I.'

He was desperate to play something, even just a few scales to keep his hand in, but the removal was booked for the end of the week. Until then, he would have to be patient.

'We should probably talk about that night,' he said.

'Why?' said Charlotte.

She was about six feet away from him, in her work clothes, her hair tied sensibly back. He wanted to tell her how much he had enjoyed their night together, but perhaps that was not what you said to someone when you had no intention of repeating it.

'I understand more than you think,' she said. 'You like me but you've got too much going on, it's not the right time, you need to work out what you want, blah blah blah.' It was exactly what he had been about to say. 'But also,' she continued, 'you're just not that into me. You're still in love with the girl you were seeing before. Zoe. And that's fine.'

The way she spoke was matter-of-fact; she could have been talking about a dish she was planning for supper, or the weather forecast for the weekend. She gave him a small smile and shrugged.

'Do one thing for me,' she said. 'Start thinking about *your* life, not Caz's, or Steve's, or even your nieces'. You're twenty-two, Jamie. Get living.'

He drove away thinking about what Charlotte had said. It was all very well in theory but he was directly involved in whatever happened at Caz and Steve's house. Even if he'd had the money to move out, he couldn't just leave. Getting another job was unthinkable for the time being; the situation with Caz was worsening by the day and he couldn't ditch Ruby and Pearl. Miss Wood kept cornering him at school, asking how things were, wanting Caz and Steve to go in for a proper meeting. There was no disputing the woman's commitment.

Soon, someone would have to do something about Caz. That person, he was sure, wouldn't be Steve. Jamie wanted to help Caz for her sake, and for his nieces', but Charlotte was right; he needed to move forward, too.

Back at Chestnut Drive, Steve and the girls were watching television with the volume up loud, the puppy slumbering on the sofa next to them, his paws twitching as he dreamed.

'Have you seen this, J?' Steve shouted over the action. '*Die Hard*. Brilliant film. First time it's been on TV.'

Bruce Willis was shooting someone. He said the F-word twice in one sentence.

'Are you sure they should be watching this?' Jamie said. 'Isn't it a bit violent?'

'Nah, they're loving it,' said Steve. 'Look at them.'

Ruby and Pearl were literally on the edge of their seats, their eyes fixed on the screen. What could he do? Steve was their father and this was his house. Jamie sighed and went through to the kitchen.

Caz was at the table with a bottle of vodka. It was two-thirds empty. So she was no longer going through the charade of hiding it. The girls had a mother mainlining Smirnoff in one room and a father watching unsuitable films in another. He sounded like Mary Whitehouse. Not caring, he went back to the sitting room and squatted on the floor in front of Ruby and Pearl, blocking their view of the television.

'Would you like me to read to you?' he said.

'Yes, please,' said Pearl. 'I'm tired.'

'I like this film but I can't tell who are the goodies and who are the baddies,' said Ruby. 'And Aslan's just been rescued from the big stone by the mice.'

When Jamie had finished reading, Steve was still watching the film and Caz hadn't moved except to pour and drink more vodka. He took her hand. It was flaccid and sweating.

'Cazza,' he said. 'Are you OK?'

She shrugged her emaciated shoulders. 'Dunno.'

There was some kind of explosion on the tv, followed by sub-machine gun shots and lots of shouting.

'If you don't get it together, you could lose the girls. School are on my case. I'm doing what I can but it's you they need.' She looked up at him. 'You know that, don't you?' There were tears in her eyes. She had another drink.

'I don't know what to do, J,' she said. 'I can't sleep without the vodka.'

'OK,' he said. 'Look. If I make you an appointment at the doctor's, will you go?'

Caz gave a slight nod. When she raised the glass to her lips again, her hand was shaking.

forty-nine

Dr Jennings couldn't have been much older than Caz was. He had thin fair hair and a milky complexion. There was a patch of something white on the shoulder of his dark suit jacket that Caz recognised as baby sick. The man looked almost as tired as she felt. Perhaps he was one of those fathers who got up in the middle of the night to give feeds and still managed to go to work. Steve had never done that. It would never have occurred to him to offer and it didn't occur to her to ask. It struck her now that if she had, he would probably have obliged.

Walking into the doctor's room she had that funny, detached feeling, as if she were somewhere else, watching herself. Perhaps that was because she hadn't slept. Despite what she'd said to Jamie, these days even the vodka wasn't working. A couple of months before, wine had become purely recreational and now vodka was going the same way. She had lain awake all night, perspiring and shaking, her head pounding, desperate for oblivion.

'Hello, Caroline,' said Dr Jennings. 'Have a seat. And is this your mother you've brought with you?'

The only appointment Jamie could get was after school. With Steve pleading work, Jamie was looking after the girls, leaving Ruth to be the designated chaperone.

'This is Ruth, a family friend,' said Caz. 'My mother was Esther Fenton. She died in a fire at our family home. My father died too. You might have heard about it.'

The doctor's pale face blanched further. 'Oh,' he said. 'Right. Can you just give me a minute to read your notes? I've had a busy day.'

On his desk was an open-ended brown envelope, stuffed with papers. He pulled them out to examine them.

'That's why we're here,' said Ruth from the back of the room. 'Because of what happened.'

'Of course,' said Dr Jennings, still reading. 'What can I do to help?'

'I think she's depressed,' said Ruth.

'Thank you, Ruth,' said the doctor. 'Perhaps Caroline might like to answer the question herself.'

As far as Caz knew, being sad wasn't the same as being depressed. Grief would pass, that's what everyone said. It didn't mean you needed antidepressants or counselling.

'I'm not mentally ill,' said Caz.

'No-one's suggesting you are,' said the doctor. 'Why would you say that?'

'You're looking at my notes. You tell me.'

'Caroline,' Ruth said. 'That's not helpful.'

'Well,' said Caz. 'It'll all be in there, if he goes back far enough.'

'Show the doctor your wrists,' said Ruth.

Her most recent cut was five days old. The others were mostly healed and didn't look too bad, although the evidence was plainly there.

'No,' she said. 'That's not relevant.'

It wasn't. The cutting was just something she did when she was at her most desperate. There was nothing this doctor could do about that.

'Caroline,' he said. 'I can't force you, but it would help me to see the full picture.'

'Caroline!' said Ruth.

'Oh, for goodness' sake.' It was maddening; they were ganging up on her. What she chose to do to her own arm was her business. It didn't affect anything or anyone else. She flashed the doctor a quick view of her wrist.

'I see,' said Dr Jennings. 'How long have you been doing this?'

'A while. But I'm feeling better now. I don't imagine I'll do it again.'

The doctor consulted the notes again. 'And are you drinking?'

'A bit,' said Caz.

Ruth gave an exaggerated cough.

'It helps me sleep,' said Caz. 'Or it was helping me.'

Dr Jennings made a note then sat back, waiting for her to continue.

'I'm tired,' Caz said. 'That's all. I'm so tired. If I could just sleep properly I know I would feel much better. When I go to bed is when I think about the fire and it keeps me awake.' She looked the doctor in the eye for the first time. 'My daughters are seven and five. They need me, but I'm useless without my sleep.'

The doctor pulled out a prescription pad and held a pen ready.

'I've got two-month old twins,' he said. 'We know a bit about sleep deprivation in our house.'

'Congratulations,' said Caz. 'That must be lovely. Hard work, though.'

Dr Jennings looked as though he was about to say something but appeared to change his mind.

'Anyway,' he said instead. 'We're not here to talk about me. I'm going to give you something to help you sleep.'

'Give her what?' said Ruth from behind, her voice laced with suspicion.

'Sedatives. And they're quite strong, so no alcohol, OK?' He wrote something on the pad that Caz couldn't read upside down. 'I'll need you to come back in a month's time. Then we'll assess how you are when you're sleeping. I want to see those wrists completely healed.' He tore off the prescription and handed it to her. 'These should keep you going until then. You can make your next appointment on the way out.'

fifty

Just back from the school run and with Nigel under his feet like a mobile trip-hazard, Jamie surveyed the state of the house. Having persuaded Miss Wood that the only way she was going to get a meeting with Caz was to come to Chestnut Drive, he was beginning to regret the effectiveness of his argument. Steve had already absented himself. Caz couldn't be trusted to handle the visit on her own. The place was a pigsty. Jamie had until two o'clock.

First, he needed to drag Caz out of bed. Although he was grateful to Ruth for taking her to the doctor, the only thing that had changed as a result of it was Ruth's level of concern. The vodka intake was as high as ever. She was refusing to take the pills. In the intervening week, Ruth had taken to dropping round and trying to coax Caz into getting up, or dressed, or doing some food shopping. Caz was not to be chivvied. Just the previous day, Ruth had badgered her so relentlessly to wash her hair that she had called her an interfering old bag, causing Ruth to retort that Caz was a spoilt madam and flounce away home.

Jamie knocked on Caz's bedroom door, convinced that she would have forgotten about the meeting, but she was awake and sitting up in bed.

'Whoa,' she said. 'This is so weird.' She pointed to a bottle of pills on her bedside table. 'I took one last night instead of vodka. I didn't think it would work but I slept right through.' As Jamie came closer she clutched his arm. 'I wanted to be on form for today. I'm nervous, J. Why does she need to come?'

'I'm not sure,' he admitted. 'Just for a chat, I think. She's had a bee in her bonnet for ages about sitting down with you so I guess we need to give her what she wants.'

Encouraged, he sent Caz into the shower and burrowed amongst her clothes for something suitable. The mumsiest things he could find were a polo-necked jumper and a pair of cords, which he laid out on the bed before he went downstairs to set about the house.

By lunchtime he had cleaned and tidied everything from the bathroom cabinet to the back of the television. Surfaces were decluttered, floors hoovered, every stray item put away. Jamie found and disposed of empty vodka bottles from the laundry basket, the freezer, the airing cupboard and, remarkably, the bottom of his own wardrobe. Caz hovered behind him but didn't offer to help.

'I need a drink,' she announced.

'You do not,' said Jamie. 'I'll make you a cup of tea.'

Miss Wood arrived at the appointed hour to find Caz sitting in an armchair looking composed, one leg crossed over the other, leaning forward, completely focused. Somehow she had got a grip of the situation and seemed ready to give the performance of her life. By the side of the chair was a splodge of Shake 'n' Vac that Jamie had missed while hoovering.

With her hair washed and dried and wearing a bit of make-up, Caz looked just like she had twelve months earlier, only thinner. He hoped that she would remember to keep the sleeve of the jumper pulled down over the bandage on her wrist.

Miss Wood scrutinised the sofa before sitting on it, as if checking for crumbs, or dog hair. Nigel did his best to attract her attention by jumping in circles at her feet but she showed him no interest. That marked her down in Jamie's eyes; he could never understand people who didn't like dogs. But then he thought, more charitably, that she was probably just trying to concentrate on her work. Having to visit people because you were suspicious of their parenting skills was a responsibility he didn't envy.

'Mrs Hopkins,' Miss Wood began. 'How have things been recently?'

'Fine,' said Caz. 'Well, as you know, I had some bad news earlier this year and that's been pretty tough. But I'm coping much better now.'

'Yes,' said the head-teacher. 'You lost your parents. I'm sorry about that.'

Caz sat with her hands between her crossed knees, her head bowed. It was a convincing impression of someone who had been hit hard by grief and was coming to terms with it.

'And how do you think your daughters have dealt with their loss?'

Caz looked as if this was a question she wasn't expecting. Jamie realised that he had never seen Caz talking to either Ruby or Pearl about the death of their grandparents.

'Oh,' she said. 'They're OK.' She allowed herself a smile which came across as an acknowledgement of their bravery. 'Great, actually.'

The head-teacher waited. Her dark, tightly-permed hair hung in a fringe and around her ears, reminding Jamie of a more anxious version of Nigel. When it was clear that Caz wasn't going to answer in any more detail, Miss Wood tried again.

'I've been trying to arrange a meeting for quite some time. We briefly discussed an incident in the playground.'

'We've dealt with that,' said Caz. 'It was ages ago, now.'

'Yes. However…' Miss Wood gave a little cough. '..this is a bit delicate… I only found out recently what was behind it, and I'm afraid it's something I'm duty-bound to look into.'

It was obvious what was coming. Since her outburst on the stairs, Caz hadn't said anything else to Ruby or Pearl about the fight. She certainly hadn't shown any curiosity as to why Ruby might have attacked another child and Jamie hadn't wanted to betray their confidence by telling her.

Caz was frowning. 'You've lost me.'

Miss Wood fidgeted on the sofa. 'Certain things were said about your home life. I have to ask, is everything all right between you and your husband?'

'Yes, of course,' Caz said. 'Why wouldn't it be?'

This was excruciating. If Miss Wood wasn't going to speak plainly, Caz was going to need some help.

'Someone saw you after you fell,' Jamie said. 'They thought Steve did it.'

'Oh!' Caz put a hand to her mouth. 'Lord, no. He would never do anything like that. It was me. I can see how it must have looked. Donna Green…'

'Deborah Green,' corrected Miss Wood. 'There was something else. I'm concerned it might be related.'

Caz nodded slowly. She lowered her eyes in contrition. 'It's been difficult,' she said. 'I can't deny it. For a while

I… let things get on top of me. It was such a shock, what happened to Mum and Dad.'

'Of course. Grief can be very debilitating. But I'm worried by what I've heard.'

'Please, don't be.'

'I need to be sure we don't need to get anyone else involved. Social services, for example.'

'No!' Caz pulled the sleeves of her jumper further over her hands. Her eyes were huge and imploring. 'No, honestly. I'm fine, now. My girls are everything to me.'

Miss Wood looked sympathetic. 'No-one doubts that, but why did neither you nor your husband come into school like we asked?'

'That was a misunderstanding,' said Caz without hesitation. 'We didn't know you wanted us to. My brother didn't realise it was important.'

'Is that right?' Miss Wood addressed Jamie in a sharper tone.

'Yes,' said Jamie, discombobulated. 'A stupid mistake.'

'What about the letters?' Miss Wood turned again to Caz.

'Letters?' Caz looked genuinely mystified. 'We didn't receive any letters. If we had, of course we would have responded.'

Miss Wood sighed. 'And how does your brother get on with the children?'

'Fantastically well,' said Caz.

'Does he spend a lot of time with them?'

Jamie looked from the head-teacher to his sister, sensing the beginnings of a conspiracy between them.

'He did his best while I was…incapacitated. He still likes to do the school run in the mornings.' Caz, now animated, gave Miss Wood a sisterly smile. 'But he *is* a man. He can't be expected to get everything right.' She laughed. Jamie wanted to dissociate himself from the whole charade. The deceit was unbearable, but he couldn't see how exposing the real truth of the situation would help.

'I ought to be getting back,' said Miss Wood, standing. 'Thank you for your time.'

Caz ushered Miss Wood towards the door, her childhood manners kicking in, telling her how lovely it was to have met her properly and that she hoped they had put the matter to rest. Miss Wood lingered a little, taking in the neatness of the hallway and bending to the side for a view into the kitchen. The phone rang. Jamie sprang to answer it, thinking he would rather talk to anyone, *anyone,* than witness another second of Caz's play-acting.

'Hello?' he said.

'Jamie? It's Pat Sidgwick.' The front door clicked shut. Through the window he watched the head-teacher walk to her car.

'Are you there?'

'Yes, I'm here,' said Jamie. 'Sorry. I was a bit distracted.'

'I thought you'd like to know that the piano's just arrived. We got the men to put it in the studio. John said it would be fine in there because there are no radiators. Central heating isn't very good for pianos, he says. Anyway, there's still plenty of room for his matchsticks. He can't wait to get cracking on Ripon Cathedral.'

'That's wonderful. Thanks so much.'

'Well, I'll leave you to it. See you soon, Jamie. Come whenever you want.'

Jamie leaned his forehead into the window as the puppy tried to chew his shoes, wondering whether they would mind if he was there within the hour.

fifty-one

It was a Saturday in late October. Steve was out. Caz was in bed. Later that afternoon, Zoe would be arriving at the Sidgwicks' for her private piano recital. Jamie had agreed, as usual, to be on uncle duties for the morning, but only after extracting a promise from Steve that he would take Ruby and Pearl swimming after his round of golf. Jamie needed some time to prepare for his big moment.

'There you go.' He put two plates on the table. 'Amazingly, these don't look too bad. You'll be awesome dancers with bacon sarnies on board.'

Nigel cruised around under the table, looking for crumbs.

'Uncle Jamie,' said Pearl with her mouth full, 'you're getting good at this.'

Ruby finished her sandwich but didn't move when Jamie asked her to fetch her dancing shoes.

'Lydia Green's starting tap,' she said glumly. 'I don't want to go if *she's* there.'

'Oh, sweetheart,' said Jamie. 'Is she still bothering you?'

'She doesn't say anything,' said Ruby.

'She just *looks*,' said Pearl.

'Ignore her,' said Jamie. 'Don't let her think she can upset you. And remember, you've been going to tap for ages. You'll be way better than she is.'

After dropping the girls at their lesson, Jamie wandered up to the park with Nigel on the lead. There was something about walking with a dog, even a badly-behaved one, that made it so much more pleasurable than walking alone. It also gave him reason to be out of the house for longer. He went in through the gates, past some boys playing football and along to the boating lake. It was the kind of day you got most often in North Yorkshire: grey and windy; not warm. There was no false promise of a blue sky or bright sunshine. Perfect conditions for seeing Zoe again: unremarkable, ready to be moulded into something. What that would be was anyone's guess.

Jamie turned away from the water and back towards the high street not, as he'd intended, mulling over what he might play for her, but thinking about Ruby and Pearl. Since Miss Wood's visit, he had procured them new school uniforms, home clothes and shoes. He had taken them for haircuts, got them dental appointments and signed them up for a range of after-school activities from Brownies and Rainbows to recorder lessons. All of this, Steve was happily bankrolling, no doubt grateful that someone was assuming responsibility. Jamie still couldn't believe that the person taking charge was him.

Despite what Caz seemed to think, this gear change was not in direct response to Miss Wood's veiled threat about social services. At the meeting, Caz had shown, briefly and tantalisingly, that she was still capable of engaging with the world. Afterwards, she had celebrated with vodka. Jamie was ashamed of his collusion in her performance, but the answer was not to risk any further intervention from outside. He couldn't see how that would help. The girls needed not only to look cared for, but more importantly, to *be* cared for. They needed family, not strangers. If their parents weren't available, he was the next best thing. He had no idea whether the advice he'd given to Ruby that morning was any good, but it was the best he could come up with.

Steve's approach to Caz had become outright avoidance. He was trying with the girls, Jamie could see that, but while he was good at games and banter, he would always scuttle back to work before long. The majority of the attention they received at home now came from Jamie.

Really, he thought as he passed the doctor's surgery, it was a wonder that the household was still functioning at all. He remembered reading somewhere that broken societies could last for a long time, longer than anyone would think possible, before they finally collapsed. Something to do with complexity of structure. At Chestnut Drive they had been limping on for months, edging nearer to the point where a crisis with Caz would come. But none of them knew how close to it they were, nor what form it would take. If there was a way to stop it, to break the cycle, Jamie couldn't think of it. He was less convinced than ever by Ruth's argument that Caz just needed time, particularly as Ruth herself seemed to have changed her mind. But after being bawled out again by Caz, she was keeping her distance.

'She knows where I am,' she told Jamie on the phone, 'but I won't be spoken to like that.'

Whether Caz was addicted or depressed, or both, was hardly his area of expertise. She had been clear-headed enough to convince Miss Wood that everything at home was fine, but that had been a single spike of lucidity in a quagmire of oblivion. If Steve had been present to witness it, perhaps he might have taken the opportunity to reason with her. As it was, he seemed to have thrown in the towel.

By now, they were back at the house. Jamie unlocked the door and stepped inside, feeling something underfoot. Nigel planted a perfect paw-print on a single white envelope which lay on the doormat. Jamie stooped to pick it up; it was addressed to Mr J Fenton and bore the frank of his parents' insurers. He tore through the seal with his finger. The house was silent; the door to Caz's bedroom was still closed. Following inquest's conclusion, the letter said, their claim had been accepted and would be settled in full within the month.

'Yesss,' he said into the somnolence, dropping to one knee with a fist pump, exactly in the manner of his former colleague, Chris.

Despite the swirling autumnal gloom, the Sidgwicks' yellow studio was relentlessly cheery. The Pleyel sat square in the middle; underneath its body were several boxes which Jamie was prepared to bet were full of matches. The thought made him shudder; having survived one fire, the piano now had a literal tinderbox beneath it. As he contemplated the likelihood of the matches spontaneously combusting, Mr Sidgwick staggered through the door carrying a piano stool, Mrs Sidgwick close behind him.

'Oh, wow,' said Jamie.

'We found it in the charity shop on the market square,' he said, setting it down in front of the Pleyel.

'You'll probably want to adjust it,' said Mrs Sidgwick, 'what with your long legs. I said to the lady in the shop that it would be just the ticket and she let us have it for a fiver. Wasn't that nice of her? I think I might re-upholster it. I've got a piece of brocade left over from the waistcoat I made for John for our nephew's wedding. He got married down in Hastings last year. Lovely do…'

'Yes, yes, Pat,' said Mr Sidgwick. 'Let's leave the poor boy alone. He needs to frame himself before his girl gets here.'

The room felt very quiet once they'd gone. Jamie sat on the piano stool, twiddling the knob until it was low enough, wondering if what was about to happen could be classed as a date, almost a year to the day after their first one.

He still needed to decide what Zoe might like to hear him play. Ideally a melody that would draw her in, not leave her cold. Nothing too saccharine. And, of course, something that he could remember.

Before long, he would be able to afford some actual sheet music. The settlement of his parents' life insurance, plus the building and contents policy for The Hall, would mean that other things were possible, too. Possible, but not practicable. Much as he would love his own space, he didn't dare think of moving out of Chestnut Drive.

Footling with a Chopin nocturne, he tried to summon the score to mind. He played his way gently into the piece, savouring the richness of the E flat key and leaning into the pedal, but his fingers got stuck on the troublesome, delicate right-hand trill near the end. The soothing hush of the final chords were perfect, but it was no good if the trill, the climax of the piece, was going to elude him. He would have to think of something else.

Looking to the tips of the cathedral's towers for inspiration he sat back, flipping through the musical rolodex in his brain, rejecting everything from Haydn to Khachaturian, thumbing through imaginary sheet music for something dramatic, impassioned and yes, he had to confess, impressive.

And then he had it: Brahms' Rhapsody No 2 in G minor. A big romantic piece if ever there was one; full of ripe harmonies, grand gestures, bursting with emotional impact. If that didn't blow Zoe away, nothing would.

Jamie laid his fingers on the keyboard and closed his eyes. The music rest was empty, but he could see his old, yellowing copy of the score, limp from years of use and covered with his teacher's scrawling annotations; the circling of an accidental or a change in dynamic, fingering suggestions in the more difficult passages, the crossing out of a tied note so that he wouldn't repeat it. Everything was there, like a photograph. All he had to do was play it.

The piece opened with an instruction: *molto passionato ma non troppo allegro.* Typical Brahms; always open to interpretation. Very passionate, quick but not too quick. No metronome value given. To Jamie, the joy was in the melody and the expression, not the speed, which probably meant that he had always played it too slowly. No matter. He began.

Who could fail to be seduced by the orchestral first theme; a statement of intent, a sweeping challenge of a thing, and the delight of the *main gauche*; the left hand leaping over the right to punctuate the melody? No sooner had it begun than it hit a *fermata*, an exaggerated pause; a moment of theatre to set up the next section which was almost military in nature, with multiple fanfares in the right hand. Another *fermata*, and then the pleading, beguiling second theme which had Jamie undulating at the keyboard. Then, the introduction of the mysterious, ominous repeated triplets in the right hand beneath which, in the left, octaves moved stealthily up and down.

Pattern established, Jamie let his fingers run. They flew between key changes, the volume constantly swelling and receding, back and forth across arching triplets, broken octaves, a slow trill in the left hand and a zigzag descent in a *ritenuto lunga.* A brief respite in the return to the main theme; a false lull before the huge build-up to the shattering climax, ratcheting up the tension and suspense. And then, quiet. The coda, where the triplets became a trill-like alternation, slowing, slowing, slowing and fading into pianissimo before the two final, dominant chords, so satisfying to put down; the perfect end to the drama. Long after the last chord should have ended, he left his fingers lingering on the notes, unwilling to break the connection, the walls of the studio resounding with the sonic power of the piece.

He had no idea how long Zoe had been there. Leaning back against the door with her hair loose, tucked into her chunky scarf, she was looking at him as though he were a total stranger.

'Oh my God,' she said. 'I had no idea.'

'You were supposed to hear it from the start,' he said. 'I got carried away.'

'You were on a different planet. It was… I don't know. To say amazing would be an insult. I've never seen you like that. All these months I've known you, and you can do *that?*'

Zoe unwound her scarf and came to the piano. Its lid was propped open.

'Can I?'

He nodded and she reached inside, running a finger along one of the strings, stroking the felt of the hammers.

'I've never seen one close up before. It's so beautiful.'

'As beautiful as Minty?'

She laughed. 'Not the same. You can't compare riding to this. All I do is jump onto a horse and try to control it. This is… this is *art*.'

Now, Jamie laughed. Zoe seemed so far out of her sphere of knowledge, as far as he had been when he and Minty had trotted around the manège. But she wasn't bored; she looked entranced. She went to the window and sat on an old paint-splattered chair in the corner.

'Please can you play some more?'

He gave her the Chopin nocturne, managing the trill tolerably well, followed by a Scarlatti sonata, by way of a contrast, and finished with the *Pathétique*, because it was his favourite. Afterwards, Mrs Sidgwick brought them tea and they drank it sitting at the wrought-iron table in the garden where it was mostly sheltered from the wind.

'I feel as though I'm in the presence of greatness,' said Zoe.

'Don't be ridiculous. The piano's just my thing, like horses are yours.'

'And I mocked you for practising on your thighs.'

A sudden gust rearranged the biscuits on a plate on the table.

'Have you any idea what you might do next?' Zoe said. 'For a job, I mean? Because I've had a thought.'

'Not estate agency,' said Jamie. 'Apart from that, no.'

'What about the piano? That's obviously what you really love.'

'I wanted to be a concert pianist when I was little, but my father put a stop to that. He said it was arty farty nonsense. Not that I was good enough,' he added. 'I'm sure I wasn't.'

'I'll ignore that last bit,' said Zoe. 'But that's not what I meant. You could teach. You're good with people. Isn't it obvious?'

'Bloody hell,' said Jamie. 'I'd never thought of that.' It was true. Other than entertaining the distant prospect of teaching Ruby and Pearl, he hadn't. He saw himself now, in the sunny studio, welcoming in a succession of children. Some of them would practise, some of them wouldn't, and then there would be the ones like Charlotte. Their parents would be the pushy, vicarious livers who insisted on sitting in on every lesson, wanting to be told that their child could be the next Glenn Gould or, horrors, Richard Clayderman.

'No,' he said. 'I'd be rubbish. And anyway, it looks like I'll have a while to decide. The insurance is finally coming through.'

'That's great,' said Zoe, 'isn't it?'

'Yeah,' said Jamie. 'But I can't move out yet. Caz is drinking, Steve can't cope with her and the girls need me.'

'So that's what it is,' said Zoe. 'No wonder you didn't want to talk about it. That must be hideous.'

When Jamie didn't answer, she took a biscuit and nibbled on it.

'Listen,' she said. 'It's my birthday in a couple of weeks. I'd like to cook you dinner.'

If Jamie ever paid any attention to dates, he would have known this. On her last birthday, he had told her that he was taking her out for a special supper and she had been the most overdressed person in the pub. God, he had been clueless. It was embarrassing. But the thought of another evening in Zoe's company, at her house, was too good to refuse.

'Thank you,' he said. 'I would love that.'

fifty-two

On Zoe's birthday, Jamie was already awake when the front door clicked shut. It was still dark. There had been no footsteps on the stairs; Steve must have slept on the sofa again. Jamie shuffled in the single bed. His toes were cold where they poked out over the end and he pulled them in under the duvet.

Stretching his arms, he allowed himself to speculate as to why Zoe might have invited him. He hardly dared articulate the thought, but the most obvious answer was a potential *rapprochement.* As far as he knew, she hadn't been seeing anyone else since her fling with Andrew and that had been over for months. Jamie himself was better equipped for a relationship, and not just because of the sex. He cringed to think of how he was when they were first together: lazy, self-centred, over-dependent on his parents. And now, well, he wasn't perfect, but definitely an improvement on the old Jamie.

It was tempting to venture that his piano playing might have helped win her over. She had certainly seen him in a different light. How pleasing to think that she might be a music lover after all, that he might have opened up a world that had never previously existed for her.

Before his imagination went completely wild, he dressed and went downstairs, where he folded away Steve's bedclothes and started on breakfast.

The upside of Caz's abdication from nutritional responsibilities was that Jamie could give the Ruby and Pearl Nutella on toast every day on the condition that they went to school without complaint. This morning, however, the girls were sleepy and sullen, playing with their food and complaining as they set off. Jamie asked if anyone had been horrible to them in the playground but they were adamant that no-one had. A thick fog hunkered over the town; it was promising to be one of those fag-end autumn days where it didn't ever really get light.

At the school gates, when Jamie crouched down in the murk to hug the girls goodbye, Nigel straining on the lead, Pearl pulled up her sleeve to reveal a red mark like a chinese-burn.

'Jesus, Pearly!' he whispered, gently lowering the fabric back over her arm.

'Where were you, Uncle Jamie?' Pearl looked as though she might cry.

'At Mr and Mrs Sidgwicks'. I was playing the piano until very late. I'm so sorry.'

'Mummy got cross when we wouldn't go to bed,' said Ruby.

'Was Daddy there?' There was no sign of Steve when, just before eleven, he came home to a silent house.

'He went out. Mummy fell asleep. Then she woke up and shouted at us.'

'Mummy doesn't like us any more,' said Pearl.

'Oh, God, this is...' Half-way up the path, Miss Wood was standing, watching them. All of the other children had gone inside. It struck him that by helping to fob off the girls' head-teacher he might have done more harm than good. 'Listen.' Jamie pulled them both close. 'I've got a surprise for you. Mrs Cole has invited you for a sleepover.'

'I thought we weren't allowed on a school night,' said Ruby.

'You are today,' said Jamie, hoping that Ruth had no other plans, and that her current avoidance of Caz didn't extend to the girls. 'Now, off you go. Miss Wood's waiting.'

He ran back to the house and straight up the stairs, flinging open the bedroom door, the puppy on his heels.

'Caz!'

The air in the room was thick and stale and smelled of decay. In the grey dimness there was little he could make out except for the shape of the bed. As he moved to the window, discarded pieces of clothing hooked themselves around his feet, impeding his progress. Nigel sniffed around approvingly. Jamie wrenched back the curtains, swearing at the locked window. He found the key on the floor and thrust it open. A cold draught rushed in, blowing the door shut with a bang.

Caz didn't stir. He stepped over a dressing gown and a pair of knickers to peel back the edge of the lumpen duvet. She was lying on her front, her cottery hair over her face, her arms stretched out to the sides. There was a clean bandage on her wrist. The whiteness of the gauze stood out against the sclerotic grubbiness of the bedclothes and of Caz herself.

Jamie jabbed a finger into her lifeless shoulder.

'Wake up!' he shouted, close to her ear. 'Wake up, you selfish bastard.'

He prodded her again, this time in the top of her arm, but she was unresponsive. Suddenly panicked, he reached for her wrist, searching for a pulse. Under the covers, her legs jerked. She groaned, moved her head to the side, and farted loudly. Jamie stepped back, repulsed. Taking Nigel with him he left the room, closing the door behind him.

The kitchen was a wreck of food debris and unwashed dishes. Jamie rinsed out a cup and made coffee, sipping it slowly. He needed to be calm enough to call Ruth with a reason why she should have the girls to stay without causing her to worry. Caz wasn't Ruth's problem; she was his, and Steve's. They needed to do something, but he didn't know what.

He began to clear away some of the rubbish into the bin, all thoughts of Zoe forgotten, unable to think beyond what he was going to say to Caz when she surfaced. In the corner, the laundry cupboard hung open. Remembering the wine that Caz had stashed there, he fished around at the back and pulled out a bottle of Smirnoff Red, almost empty. Jamie remembered the night when he and Caz got drunk together; or rather, Caz had got drunk and he had watched her. He could have tried harder to stop it, before things got out of hand. Having seen her then, should he have known what would follow? Was that when it all started, or could it be traced back further, to when she drank brandy on the night of the fire?

At that point, she was still fully functioning. It was surely the loss of their parents that had taken away her strength to resist. The repressed, neurotic, unambitious Caz of recent years had been frustrating, but at least she had cared for her children, put them above everything else.

As he dried the dishes, he began to suspect that Steve no longer considered himself the luckiest man alive. More likely, he was baffled by what was happening. Steve had believed he had the perfect life. The only way that he could cope with the loss of it was denial. But denial wasn't working, whether Steve could see it or not. Squeezing Jif into the sink, Jamie mentally rounded on his brother-in-law. Steve had a responsibility to his children not to allow their home to degenerate into a flop-house where they were neglected to the point of harm. Instead, had chosen to absent himself from giving them any emotional support at all.

By late morning, Caz was still in her room. Jamie phoned Ruth, saying only that Caz needed a break. Ruth said that she would be delighted to have Ruby and Pearl. He then rang Steve's office. As he spoke to the receptionist, asking Steve to call back urgently, Jamie sensed movement behind him. Caz was grappling with the zip of the hoody she was wearing over saggy tracksuit bottoms. She threw him a malevolent glare.

'It's freezing up there. Who opened the window?'

'I did.'

'You've got no right, coming into my room when I'm sleeping.'

Caz lurched towards the front door. Nigel was jumping around at her feet, trying to bite her shoelaces and she tripped, turning her ankle.

'Ow! Shit!'

'What are you doing?'

'I need to go out.'

'Well *I* need to speak to you about Ruby and Pearl. Your daughters. Remember them? Remember what you did to Pearl last night?'

Caz rubbed her ankle. It was hard to tell whether she was conflicted or confused. Possibly both. She reached for the catch.

'I need to go out,' she said again.

'Wait.'

Jamie rushed towards the door, intending to bar her way, but short of pinning her against the wall, there was nothing he could do. As she blundered out into the street, he put his hands to his head and turned away, furious with his own weakness. He couldn't see how to get through to her. Did Caz even remember what she had done? Would she feel remorse if she did? Perhaps she had lost the capacity. It was months since she had been properly around for the girls. Whatever path she had chosen, voluntarily or otherwise, she was determined to follow it and he had failed, yet again, to stop her.

The phone began to ring, making him jump.

'J? It's Steve. What's the problem?'

'My sister,' said Jamie. 'But I think you know that.'

Steve sighed heavily but didn't say anything.

'I've asked Ruth to collect the girls from school and have them overnight. They need to be somewhere that's not home,' said Jamie. 'Caz hurt Pearl. Not badly, but she actually hurt her.'

'Right.'

'Right? Is that all you can say? She's out of control. There was a mark on Pearl's skin this morning. It's only a few weeks since I helped convince their head-teacher that everything was fine. You weren't even there. What does that say about us, Steve? If we don't do anything, we're no better than she is.'

'Hang on a sec.' There was a pause followed by a door closing. 'I'll talk to her.'

'And say what?'

'I don't know, J, to be honest. I'll have to think of something. She's not herself but she loves those girls. Look, I know I've been crap. This shouldn't be your job. It's mine. Leave it with me. Honestly.'

'I'm supposed to be going to Zoe's later but I can cancel if you need me to.'

'No. This is for me to sort out.'

Jamie put down the phone, unsure whether to be relieved or worried. Just because Steve was, at last, offering to do something didn't mean that he was capable of persuading Caz to seek proper help. In the meantime, Zoe was expecting him. And he needed to buy her a birthday present. Caz's car keys had disappeared from the table in the hall. Not having the stomach to poke around amongst the detritus in her bedroom, he decided to take the bus to Ripon.

Even though it was only November, the Christmas lights were already switched on, strung between the lamp-posts and throbbing like lodestars through the mist. As Jamie walked, shops revealed themselves, rising out of the fog like Debussy's cathedral. He went to a little jewellery place he knew Zoe liked and chose a silver necklace with a pendant in the shape of a horse which he slated to his Access card and decided to worry about later. Then he went to the Sidgwicks' and lost the rest of the afternoon playing the piano.

fifty-three

The last thing Jamie did after he froze Caz out of her bedroom, forcing her to go in search of more vodka, was to ask if she remembered what she had done to Pearl. That was ridiculous; she hadn't done anything to Pearl. As if she would.

On the street, everything was fuzzy and dark. She couldn't work out whether it was actually foggy, or whether the mist was just another malfunction in her brain. There was certainly no sun. Not even any proper light. It was difficult to see where she was going. All the way from the house to the shop, she fumed with righteous anger. How dare Jamie come into her bedroom when she was sleeping - God knew she needed to sleep - and then accuse her of... what? He didn't say. She remembered Steve going out to the pub but she didn't remember going to bed. The next thing she knew, there was an arctic gale blowing through her room. Everything in between was blank.

She bought two bottles of Smirnoff at the cut-price off-licence behind the Co-op. The cashier gave her a questioning look but took the money without comment. Caz's tracksuit bottoms were a bit dirty, but whose business was that apart from her own? Not everyone was obsessed with their appearance. People were always badgering her about how she looked. So what if she wanted to wear the same t-shirt for days? It wasn't a crime.

At the corner of the street, she stopped. Her ankle ached from tripping over the puppy. The handle of her carrier bag had slid down onto her wrist and was digging into where she cut herself. As she adjusted it, Caz felt a flash of pain, but not her own. She saw Pearl's shocked, recoiling face. She had twisted the skin on her own child's arm, just because she wouldn't go to bed. The memory almost made her drop the vodka.

When she got home, Nigel rushed to the door and she crouched down to pet him. Her vision was clearer indoors; the fog must have been real. Jamie wasn't around, thank goodness. He was being a nuisance. There was a little dog turd on the floor in the kitchen near the fridge but she wasn't going to deal with that. It hadn't been her idea to get a puppy.

She put the bottles on the table while she ate some cereal and made herself a coffee. Just because she had bought them didn't mean she had to drink them. What would happen if she didn't? There were always the pills if she needed them; still a couple of weeks' worth in her pocket. She was supposed to take one every night but often didn't because of the vodka. Drinking was more fun than staying sober all evening and she was still smart enough not to mix the two. But if the evenings were fun, the nights definitely weren't. They were the worst. Only the Restoril could guarantee sleep now; in her more sober moments she could admit that the vodka was no longer any good for that. The wine she had given up on.

Caz tried to piece together why she had become so angry with Pearl. It couldn't only have been because she was refusing to go to bed. Or perhaps it could. She didn't know. Whatever it was, no level of provocation could excuse her behaviour. Only a monster would do that to their daughter.

It was too quiet in the house and too dark. The fog outside was sucking the oxygen from the atmosphere. She got up and turned on a couple of lamps, then fiddled with the dial on the radio. The first station she came to was Radio Three. Classical music was not her preference; it was Jamie's, and their mother's. She recognised the opening of *The Marriage of Figaro*, which Esther used to play on vinyl at home on Sunday mornings, loudly enough to be heard in the garden through the windows of the drawing room while she pottered in the rose beds. Caz went back to the table. Nigel jumped onto her knee and she stroked the softness of his little body, enjoying the warmth of him. The puppy, at least, was incapable of judgement.

The movement came to an end. In its place came Vaughan Williams' *Thomas Tallis* and then something she couldn't identify, but the music and the sleeping dog on her lap were calming; her brain began to clear.

What she needed to do was collect the girls from school. She could apologise to them, bring them home and play with them, cook for them, read to them, make amends. Jamie, if not exactly pleased to see her, would be glad that she was making an effort.

As she was sober, she could drive. It would save walking any more in that horrible fog with her painful ankle. The keys were on her dressing table upstairs. Fed up with Jamie using her car without asking, she had claimed that they were lost. She didn't know if he was planning to collect Ruby and Pearl. It didn't matter. They were her children and she would pick them up from school if she wanted to, like a normal mother. The other parents, the teachers and whoever else would see that she was perfectly capable. She could get everyone off her case. It was a good plan.

Now that her path to redemption was clear, she could perhaps have a little nip of the vodka. A finger or two, just as a sharpener. No-one would know. She went to the cupboard and got out a glass, then put it back again. No, she had come this far; she would resist. Once she opened the bottle, she wouldn't be able to stop. She shut the cupboard door and leaned back against it. Then, she put the two bottles of vodka in the pan drawer.

It was almost time for pickup. She fetched the car keys from her room, put Nigel into his basket and set out again into the fog.

The first thing she noticed when she got out of the car was that she was the only person there without a coat. There was something wrong with the zip of her hoody; she couldn't get it to engage and it flapped open, exposing the thin t-shirt beneath. Earlier, she hadn't registered the cold but now it bit into her. Hovering behind some parked cars, Caz scanned the assembled cluster of people for Jamie but couldn't see him. Instead, there was Ruth, in a headscarf and her woollen coat, chatting easily to a group of mothers beneath the bare branches of a horse chestnut tree.

She waited until Ruby and Pearl emerged onto the path and then crossed the road towards where Ruth and the others were standing, already lifting her face into a smile. Her ankle was so sore that she was dragging her foot.

Then, several things happened at once. On seeing Caz, Ruth stopped speaking. A couple of people actually backed away. Another asked if she was OK, but not in a friendly way. As she spread her arms for her daughters, they halted on the path and looked around as if they weren't sure whom she had come to greet. They stayed there, rooted, while the other pupils swerved around them and were escorted away by their parents. Then, they were alone on the path, still inside the school gates, with herself and Ruth standing on the outside.

'Caroline,' Ruth said, 'what are you doing here? Jamie asked me to pick the girls up and take them home.' Her gaze took in the dirty trousers, the broken hoody, the lack of coat. Caz put her hand up to her hair. She didn't remember having brushed it; in fact, she couldn't even remember the last time she looked in a mirror. The ends felt dry and brittle and her scalp was oily. Hair-washing was the reason she and Ruth had fallen out. Except it wasn't, not really.

'I'm sorry I shouted at you,' she said.

'That doesn't matter right now.' Ruth's eyes kept darting towards the girls and back again. 'I need to take them back to the cottage.'

'No,' said Caz. 'Let's all go to ours. We can have tea together.'

Ruth turned away from the Ruby and Pearl and leaned in towards Caz.

'Have you seen the state of yourself? You shouldn't be out, dressed like that. Look at the girls. They don't want to go anywhere with you at the moment. They're safer with me tonight. We can talk tomorrow.'

'But I haven't been drinking!' Caz cried. 'You have to believe me. I did something bad yesterday and I need to make up for it. Girls! Come here!' She spread her arms again but still they didn't move. Pearl started to cry.

'Caroline, love,' said Ruth. 'I'm not saying this to be nasty. I'm trying to help you. Go home. Go home now. Get a grip of yourself. As I said, we can talk tomorrow.' She stepped through the school gates and the girls ran to her. Ruth murmured something to them and they turned to look at Caz, Pearl crying hard, Ruby with an expression of pity.

'No!' Caz said. 'Please.' She stepped back towards the kerb as Ruth shepherded the girls past her.

'Get yourself home,' said Ruth. 'Don't upset them anymore. Leave them be for now.'

The three of them crossed the road and continued walking until they turned onto the high street towards the bus stop. When Caz looked back towards the school, the lone figure of Miss Wood, who must have seen the whole episode from the entrance porch, turned and went back inside.

Caz inched the Fiat home, stinging with injustice. The fog was dense and stifling. Although she had the heaters turned up high she was so, so cold. Something inside her was screaming for vodka, so loudly that it drowned out the traffic and even the car radio. All she could hear was the crackle of the bottle's plastic seal being broken, over and over again. Her children didn't want her. They would rather be with Ruth than with their own mother.

The mindless enthusiasm of Nigel's greeting as she opened the front door was no comfort. She could probably kick him and he would still love her, and where was the value in that?

In the drawer, the bottles of vodka lay waiting. She pulled them out and cradled them to her like old friends. With a quick twist, the first one was open. Quivering with anticipation, she filled the tumbler way, way fuller than normal and drank the lot in one. More. The radio was still playing classical music; nothing she recognised, but it made her want her mother. None of this would be happening if her parents hadn't died. She wouldn't be this unhappy. More. She wouldn't have made her children so unhappy. They would be better off with Ruth. They would be happier if she wasn't there. More. She was the only person making them miserable.

And then there was Steve. How he hated her for what she was doing to their family. Jamie, too. All she did was upset her brother and make him worry and ask him to clear up after her mistakes. More.

At the back of the cutlery drawer she found an old razor blade that she'd hidden there when Steve started locking the bathroom cabinet. It was so blunt that she had to slice hard into her arm, which hurt enough to make her give up. Nigel was looking up at her from the floor with questioning eyes, probably wanting food. He would have to wait.

The first bottle of vodka was gone. She broke the seal on the second and poured. Everything was too painful. She needed her mother. She wanted to be a little girl again. Slouched on the kitchen chair, her legs stretched out under the table, time began to rewind in her head until she was playing in the attic with Jamie, both hooting with laughter when one of them tripped over in the dark because they hadn't switched the lights on. That was when things were easy, when nobody shouted at her, before she was trouble.

The tears began again as she remembered how that little girl became a teenager who didn't want to play with her brother, or obey her parents. Instead, she went looking for other people to befriend; as long as her mother and father disapproved of them, she wasn't fussy.

One of these was the son of the village cricket captain. She couldn't remember his name but he hated cricket. Together they formed a brief alliance of misbehaviour until she was sent to boarding school and he was banned from The Hall. They had fun while it lasted. Once, they stole the line-marking machine from the cricket pavilion and drew a giant penis in the middle of the pitch, set at a jaunty angle and stretching from mid-off to fine leg. On another occasion, they pilfered a bottle of brandy from her father's drinks trolley and hot-wired Mr Thorneycroft's tractor. God, she'd been in trouble for that. They'd almost hit a horse and rider in the lane. She remembered the woman, astride her horse on the forecourt of The Hall, berating Bernie in tones the whole village could hear.

Was that when it started, when she went haywire, always looking for the next thrill? There was no reason she could think of for her to go off the rails, as her father put it. Jamie hadn't. Their parents loved them, they didn't get divorced, they always had plenty of money. What was wrong with her? Why couldn't she cope?

On paper she was the responsible one; married with children, whereas Jamie was the overgrown child who'd never done anything for himself. And yet, here they were, him looking after her, as if he were the big brother. The way she had gone wrong as a teenager was nothing compared to how she'd gone wrong now. Her children had shrunk away from her. Her husband couldn't stand her.

By now she was crying volubly but it didn't matter; no-one could hear her except the puppy, who was pawing at her leg, distressed by the noise she was making. She blew her nose and fondled his velvety ears.

'It's all right, little one,' she said. 'I'm going out now.'

It was dark outside, nothing visible through the windows except the choking fog, but anything would be preferable to staying where she was. Everything about the house, from the encrusted dog poo on the floor to the bottles on the table seemed to be reproaching her. She grabbed her keys and went upstairs for a few other things. Then, for the second time that day, she closed the front door on the bewildered puppy.

fifty-four

The cottage had the warm, moist feel of cooking on a cold evening. Zoe unwrapped the necklace and Jamie put it on for her so that she could see it in the mirror.

'I love it,' she said. 'Thank you.'

Jamie's attention was caught by something on the television in the sitting room. As they went through to investigate, they saw the round turret of Windsor Castle, black against the night sky, surrounded by cavorting flames.

Jamie gasped. He could almost hear the beating roar of the blaze and taste the acrid smoke on the air. Fire-fighters leaned out of aerial ladder platforms, siphoning water into the buildings as a breathless reporter described how quickly the fire had spread. With a more reassuring tone she confirmed that the Queen was not, repeat not, in residence.

'Poor Liz,' said Jamie, 'she's had a rotten year.'

Zoe blinked at him. 'Yours hasn't been a barrel of laughs, either.'

'I suppose,' he said, but he couldn't drag himself away from the pictures, the awful reminder of what fire could do.

If even the Queen was not immune from such catastrophes, what hope was there for everyone else?

'Come on.' Zoe pulled gently at his arm and turned the television off.

Back in the kitchen she gave him a beer and he held it up, toasting her a happy birthday. Two steaks lay seasoned on a plate beside the cooker. On the hob was a simmering pan of vegetables.

'It's good to see you,' said Zoe. 'Properly, I mean.' She looked sidelong at him. If there was one thing he did not want from her after all this time, it was coquettishness. He put down his beer.

'Why am I here?'

But Zoe had her head in the fridge and was rifling around for something. She closed the fridge, then opened the oven door and prodded a couple of baked potatoes with the point of a knife.

'This is almost ready. Shall we eat first?'

Despite himself, Jamie was already imagining the long-forgotten sensation of chewing steak. There was a juicy slap as Zoe dropped them into the pan and then a hiss. He hadn't eaten since breakfast. He wasn't even sure he could wait for them to cook.

'God, Jamie,' said Zoe. 'You're practically salivating…' She turned abruptly. 'What on earth is that?'

Someone was hammering on the back door, just feet away from them, making it rattle in its frame. They looked at each other.

'I'm not on call,' said Zoe. 'Even vets are allowed their birthdays off.'

Jamie opened the door a few inches.

'I don't know where she is.' Steve was panting, wild-eyed and puce, with Nigel under one arm. As Jamie pulled the door fully open, Steve put the puppy down, hunching forward over his knees. He wiped his mouth with the back of his hand, emanating sweat into the cold air. Steve was a fit guy; to be so out of breath he must have sprinted from home.

'It's OK.' Zoe stepped in front of Jamie and put a hand on Steve's shoulder. 'Breathe. Take a minute.'

But he wasn't just out of breath; he was struggling to take in air at all. He straightened and put a hand to his throat as if there were something stuck there, looking from Zoe to Jamie in terror.

'You're hyperventilating. Focus on me. On my face.'

Taking hold of both his shoulders, Zoe forced him to be still. He looked at her, their faces level with each other, taking tiny hiccups, just managing to ingest enough air to keep breathing.

'Try and slow down,' said Zoe. 'You're all right. Concentrate on what I'm doing.'

Steve kept his eyes on hers; she was taking deep breaths for him, exaggerated ones. Jamie found himself doing it too. Imperceptibly at first, Steve's breaths started to lengthen until he was no longer gasping for air, but his pale and clammy face was no less terrorised. The three of them stood there together, in front of Zoe's cooker, breathing in and out as if they were in some kind of group yoga session.

'Shit.' Zoe reached over and pulled the pan off the heat. The steaks were charred and smoking. Something told Jamie that they wouldn't be eating them anyway.

'What's happened?' he said.

'I came home from work,' Steve paused, still short of breath, 'and she wasn't there.' A breath. 'I thought she was in bed.' Breath. 'But she wasn't…Her car was gone…She's not well…I was going to talk to her…I should have done something earlier…She could be anywhere.' The next breath became a huge, gasping sob. 'Oh, Christ,' he cried. 'What have I done?'

His eyes and nose oozed tears and snot. He looked like a child who had suddenly grasped the concept of consequences.

'Have you searched for her?' Jamie's tone was sharp.

Steve looked around the kitchen, as if he might find Caz hiding in a corner. Then, he shook his head violently, as though he couldn't be expected to have any idea where his wife might have gone.

'I called Ruth,' he said. 'She said Caz turned up at school this afternoon. She wanted to take the girls but Ruth wouldn't let her. There was a bit of a scene. Ruth thought she might have been drunk.' Steve was still shaking his head, now more in sadness and confusion.

'Oh, Jesus,' said Zoe. 'Poor Ruby and Pearl.'

'I've failed them,' said Steve. 'I've failed them all.' Zoe had hold of his hand and was chafing it gently, but Jamie could find no sympathy for him. He grabbed his coat from the sofa in the sitting room.

'I'm going to find her.'

fifty-five

Jamie shoved past Steve and out into the fog. It was beginning to freeze. There was a street lamp outside Zoe's house but once he moved out of its radius, the evening was disorientating; blank and inscrutable. He had no clue how he was going to find Caz when he couldn't see six feet in front of him. Wherever she was, it was unlikely that she would be adequately dressed for this. The best outcome would be that she had parked up somewhere and fallen asleep. Her driving was erratic at the best of times; the idea that she might be behind the wheel of a moving car, drunk, was terrifying.

The street, as far as he could see it, was deserted. As a starting point, he inspected every parked car, having to get up close to distinguish one model from another. The fog seemed to be closing in around him. It was smothering. He took hold of his jaw with one hand and wiggled it; all of his joints felt to be seizing up, or freezing. There was no sensation in his toes. Jamie moved off again, sticking to the pavements, trying to pick out individual houses as waymarkers, but having to rely on the gradient of the road to lead him to the high street.

The first pub he came to was the Bay Horse. In this little town, neither fog nor recession would get in the way of a Friday night and it was packed. Just to step inside its noisy warmth was a relief. Jamie stood by the door and scanned the room. At the bar, people stood three-deep, the women chatting as they waited, the men waving notes to attract the attention of the staff. Groups of girls jabbed cigarettes into the air and drank blastaways. Everyone was young, dressed up, and working their way to the kind of pleasurable insensibility that Caz had gone beyond, months ago.

Jamie dragged himself back onto the street and checked out the Bolton Arms, the Co-op and Goldfinch Wines. Unhopeful glances through the windows of the Gate of India and the New Hong Kong takeaway were fruitless. She wasn't in the Green Dragon, the White Bear or the Wensleydale Ox. He even stuck his head through the door at Paolo's but quickly ducked out again before he could be recognised. By now he was at the end of the high street. There were no white Fiats parked in any of the cobbled spaces. He stood for a minute, blowing on his hands. Then, as an idea struck him, he set off at a jog, past the park and the church and out of the town, heading for his parents' village.

It was not a journey he had ever made on foot. The town had always been a five-minute drive from home; a quick blast through a series of bends that Jamie knew by heart. There was no pavement; the only way he could keep from running into hedges or ditches was by following the cats' eyes which winked dimly at the edge of the road. It felt a bit like a game he used to play with Caz. They would go up to the attic, where there were no windows, and stagger around in the dark trying to find each other. But, of course, Caz was missing and this was much, much colder.

He was underneath the sign for the sports club before he saw it, weakly washed over by a single orange light. Somewhere behind that sign were a football pitch and some tennis courts. Even the clubhouse, which butted up to the road, was invisible. He pressed on. There was, blessedly, no traffic. In his black coat and with no street lights it would have been difficult enough for a driver to see him even in normal conditions. Not far beyond the sports club Jamie recognised the entrance to a farm which meant that he was half-way to the village. He picked up his pace as much as he dared. With his head down to keep the stinging, freezing fog from his eyes, he ran, focusing only on the cats' eyes and trusting that there would be nothing to bump into. Somewhere close by, an owl screeched. As he reached the crest of a little bridge where the road crossed the disused railway line, a pair of headlights appeared out of nowhere, piercing the blackout. He threw himself flat to the wall, out of the path of the car. The oblivious driver laboured past him and disappeared.

As Jamie ran, his theory as to where Caz might have gone coalesced into certainty. There was nowhere else she *could* be. He patted his way along the brick wall of the bridge until he reached the gate that led down to the railway line.

The steps were steep and irregular. There was no handrail. Having to take them one at a time slowed him down but once he got to the bottom, progress was easier. The track stretched in a straight line, its edges slippery but identifiable by their icy, metallic glint. He began to move more quickly, only stumbling now and then on the frozen grass where it poked through the gravel between the sleepers.

To cut off the corner between the road and the village, he would need to find the footpath which crossed the railway line. It was probably a few minutes' jog from the bridge. He ran on his toes, keeping to the edge of the track, past the dense mass of fir trees which he knew to be there but couldn't see, trying to work out where the wood ended and the path began. As it was, he almost missed it because he was concentrating on the smooth lines of the track which were his only firm point of reference. By chance, he glanced left and saw what looked like something pale in a break in the trees. He edged towards it, reluctant to leave the reassurance of the railway line, taking tiny steps, walking into the clouds of his breath as they merged into the fog. It was a metal gate, painted white, presumably once put there as a safety precaution against passing trains, now unused and left ajar. Jamie slid through the gap between the gate and the post, onto the narrow path.

The ghostly haze of the railway line now gave way to utter darkness. The bushes which crowded in on either side of him formed a barrier to the fog. This was a different kind of darkness; suffocating, claustrophobic and total. It made Jamie want to claw out at it, to rip it away to reveal something, anything, that could light his way. It was still bitingly cold. The only way to move forward was with both arms out in front, zombie fashion, feeling out to the sides to make sure there was a clear way through. His fingers were frozen stiff.

From memory, he knew that this section through the wood was not long. Beyond it lay a maize field which led into the back of The Hall. Jamie ploughed on through the grasping trees, trying to be rational, telling himself that he would soon get to where he needed to be. But that, in itself, brought a new sensation of dread. If he was right about where Caz had gone, he hardly dared think what he might find when he got there.

He tripped forwards over a low-hanging branch, just managing not to fall. For a moment he stopped to gather his balance, still unable to tell where the woods might end. The only option was to press on. Frozen peaks of mud dug into the soles of his boots. If he closed his eyes it made little difference. And then, without warning, he emerged from the oppression of the woods into what must have been the maize field. It was a relief to be back in the fog, which at least had an opaque brightness from the particles of ice which had formed within it. Even though it was November, and there was no crop, it was impossible to see more than a few feet ahead. He guessed at where his parents' hedge would be, and set off towards it over the hard, uneven soil.

As he drew closer, he caught the smoky tang of fire. When he reached the hedge he paused, sniffing the air, thinking that it was a trick of his memory, but no, it was definitely there and coming from the other side. With some difficulty Jamie found a gap in the foliage and forced his way through, chasing the smell of the bonfire across the orchard, past the compost heap and up the lawn, somehow seeing the frozen pond in time not to stand on it. At the top of the steps to the back terrace was a faint orange glow. Taking them two at a time, he raced into the smoke which drifted towards him.

He was on the terrace, just outside where the French doors to the orangery used to be. Jamie moved closer. The only sound he could hear was his own rasping breath. To his left, on what looked like a pile of sleeping bags, was Caz. Between them was the remains of a fire which was giving out more smoke than heat.

Caz was lying on her side, slightly curled up, with an arm stretched out above her head, her hair spilling out over the shoulders of her hoody. In the dim light from the fire, Jamie could see that her features were perfectly relaxed. He put a hand to her cheek; it was barely warm, but he could feel the shallow rise and fall of her body.

'Caz!' He shook her gently but she didn't stir.

'Shit.' An empty bottle lay discarded amongst the wet, grubby quilts.

Caz hadn't moved. Jamie knelt beside her, rubbing her hands in his, trying to generate some warmth, but they were lifeless. She lay like a discarded puppet. The bandage on her wrist was sodden, dull and coppery but showed, at least, no sign of fresh blood. He bent to her ear, whispering her name at first, before repeating it, more urgently. Then he slid one hand beneath her shoulders and the other under her legs to scoop her up. She was almost weightless. Although her hair was soft against the underside of his chin, the rest of her was skeletal; he could almost feel her bones shifting and he worried that something would snap inside her.

Jamie stood for a second, not wanting to take Caz into Ruth's house. It would be unforgivable if he allowed the children to see their mother like this. Still, she needed to be warm. He managed to wrap the two front edges of his coat around her. As he came around the corner into the courtyard, Ruth flew out of the house towards them.

'Ohh!' Ruth put her hand to Caz's forehead. 'I smelled smoke. What happened to you, pet lamb?'

'You need to call an ambulance,' he said. 'Quickly. Without waking the girls.' He gestured towards Bernie's sports store. 'We'll be in there.'

The old lean-to was dry, with a residual warmth from Ruth's fire which was on the other side of the wall. Still cradling Caz, he sat down on a wooden crate amongst the croquet mallets and cricket bats, continuing to call her name, begging her to wake up. Her rapid, shallow breathing made him think of Steve and his panic attack. He wondered whether he was still at home with Zoe, or whether they were both out somewhere, searching. As he bent to breathe warm air onto her hands, her eyelids fluttered and for a moment he saw just the whites of her eyes; half-open, unseeing. He checked her pulse and then, unsure what a healthy pulse was supposed to feel like, checked his own. Compared to hers it was pounding against his fingers. Balancing her against his chest, he wriggled free of his coat and swaddled her tightly in it, tucking it in at the sides. It was a relief to no longer be able to feel her bones. They stayed like this, Jamie rocking her gently, willing her to stay with him but without confidence that she could, until he saw the blue lights outside the door.

By the time the paramedics arrived, Caz's pulse was so faint that Jamie thought she was probably lost to them. Exhausted and numb, he laid her on their trolley, still wrapped in his coat, and stepped back while they fitted an oxygen mask over her face. As they fired questions at him, Ruth cried quietly. The girls, thankfully, were still asleep in the house.

He was about to climb into the ambulance when Zoe and Steve pulled into the courtyard in her pickup. Steve jumped out and rushed towards them.

'That's my wife,' he cried. 'Let me see her.'

But Zoe, with Nigel on the lead, was at his shoulder, gently tugging him back.

'Let Jamie go with her,' she said. 'Your girls might need you.'

Steve allowed himself to be led away, still straining for a sight of Caz, repeating, 'Oh God, oh my God.'

At the hospital, the doctor told Jamie that Caz wouldn't have been able to survive much longer. Apparently he had done all the right things. It was, the doctor said, impossible to tell exactly what she had taken but an empty bottle of sleeping pills had been found in her pocket. There was also the vodka bottle at The Hall, plus whatever she'd had during the day. All that, on top of months of heavy drinking, had left her with an acute kidney injury. Her mental state was yet to be ascertained.

fifty-six

The next day, Jamie and Steve collected Ruby and Pearl from Ruth's. They found Caz's car, miraculously undamaged, outside the village church. Once they were home, they told the girls that their mummy was in hospital and would need to stay there for a little while.

'Is that why she wasn't nice to us?' said Ruby. 'Because she's not very well?'

'Yes, angel,' Steve said. 'But she's going to get better now.'

'Will she be back to normal?' said Pearl.

'I hope so.' Steve, who was standing at the kitchen sink, turned his face to the window.

'Yes,' said Jamie. 'I'm sure she will.'

While Steve went to visit Caz, Jamie took the girls to school and went on an extended walk with Nigel. Then he went shopping for food and tidied the house. After lunch, when he could think of no more chores to do, he went to the hospital. It wasn't that he didn't want to see Caz; more that he was unsure whether she would welcome his intervention or resent it. In the end, he and Steve played hospital tag for three more days until she woke up.

When he arrived on the fourth day, she was propped up in bed, attached to a drip. She was wearing a regulation gown and a knitted lavender cardigan which made her look a great deal older than her twenty-six years. Although her hair was clean and brushed, her skin was waxy and she was very, very thin. She was watching an afternoon news bulletin; not staring vacantly at it, but properly focused. The Queen, in a green dress and huge spectacles, was giving a speech to some kind of lunch reception.

'Steve said you were awake,' said Jamie. 'How are you?'

Caz half-smiled and patted the mattress for him to perch beside her.

'Shall we see what Queenie's got to say?' Jamie said, understanding that she wasn't ready to speak.

'1992,' said the Queen, 'is not a year on which I shall look back with undiluted pleasure. In the words of one of my more sympathetic correspondents, it has turned out to be an *annus horribilis*. I suspect I am not alone in thinking so. Indeed, I suspect that there are very few people or institutions unaffected by these last few months of turmoil and uncertainty.'

The camera cut away from the Queen and back to the reporter.

'Wow,' said Jamie.

'She got that right.' Caz's voice was fainter than usual but her words were clear and not slurred. They watched for a little longer, then Jamie picked up the remote and turned it off.

'I thought we'd lost you,' he said. They regarded each other steadily. 'Not just the other night. Before then. You've been gone for ages.'

'I know,' said Caz. 'I couldn't stop. I didn't want to. I'm not even sure I do now, even though this is as painful as hell.' She pointed to where her kidneys would be, under the bedclothes.

'You have to.'

Caz nodded and shuffled herself further upright, wincing.

'You were there,' she said.

Jamie tried to get up, but her grip on his arm was surprisingly strong.

'Someone had to be,' he muttered.

'But you worked out where I was.'

'Don't be melodramatic. I'm your brother, for goodness' sake. Where else would you have been?'

A nurse came in with a couple of pills on a metal tray and a beaker of water. She waited while Caz swallowed them and left the room.

'Thank God for her,' said Caz. 'I was about to get all mushy on you.'

'Can't have that,' said Jamie. 'You're a Fenton, remember. We don't do that kind of thing.'

She gave him a little smile and shook her head.

'Steve said you were amazing.'

'He's been worried sick.'

'I know you blame him, at least partially,' said Caz. 'I've seen the way you look at him. It was me, though. I did this to myself.'

'He's your husband.'

'Yes,' said Caz, 'but he didn't ever sign up to this. He thought if he could pretend everything was fine, then in the end it would be.'

Jamie thought of Steve, on Zoe's doorstep, unable to

breathe, paralysed by panic and fear, finally forced, too late, to face up to what was happening.

'I should have done more,' he said. 'I was scared for the girls. I hated myself for going along with that charade with the head-teacher.'

Caz was shaking her head again, squeezing her eyes closed as though she were trying to shut out the memory. Her wasted arms lay on top of the blanket. On her wrist, the criss-crosses of little white scars were beginning to heal. Jamie wondered whether she had any recollection of hurting Pearl.

She opened her eyes, releasing runnels of tears.

'She was watching, that day when I turned up at the school. Miss Wood.'

'I know. Steve's going in to speak to her. Try not to worry.'

'I'm so ashamed.'

Jamie handed her a tissue and waited, not wanting to interrupt her. She cried as though she were grieving. Perhaps she was. Or perhaps she was afraid that the harm she had caused was irreparable.

'It's difficult to explain,' she said eventually. Her face was blotchy from the crying. 'I knew I was choosing the bad stuff over my family but I couldn't help myself. Losing Mum and Dad sent me a bit crazy. It was devastating for you too, I know, but in a funny way I think it's been the making of you, whereas I couldn't function any more. Everything that used to be easy was too hard.'

'Just answer me one question. Did you mean it?' It was the only thing he really wanted to know; whether she had actually intended to leave them all behind.

'I'm not sure,' she admitted. 'It was like being controlled by another force, from the inside. Like I was possessed.

When I saw the girls at the school gate, it seemed that all I was doing was hurting them. I hadn't even been drinking at that point but it was too late, I'd already done too much damage.' Caz gave another great sob and clutched at her ribs, her face contorted.

'Ruby and Pearl love you,' said Jamie. 'All they want is for you to be well.'

Caz blew her nose noisily and thrust the tissue up her sleeve. The effort seemed to tire her and she flopped back against the pillow, swamped in lavender wool.

'Nice cardi,' said Jamie.

'Ruth left it for me, apparently. She was always paranoid about us catching cold.'

Jamie laughed. 'I should have guessed.'

'Poor Ruth. I've put her through such a lot.' Caz fiddled with one of the purple plastic buttons, twisting it round and round until it came off in her hand.

'Damn it,' she said, looking tearful again.

'It's just a button,' said Jamie. 'Don't worry about it.'

'They've told me I'll be off to rehab when I'm better. I'm going to be in there for a month. I'll miss Christmas.'

'That's tough,' said Jamie. 'But there'll be others. And we'll visit, once we're allowed.'

'But the girls,' Caz persisted.

'We'll manage,' said Jamie. 'Just get better.'

fifty-seven

'So far so good.' Jamie dropped two sirloins into a frying pan.

'Should I check outside for uninvited visitors?'

'Nope, I'm confident.'

It was Jamie's birthday and he was again at Zoe's for dinner although on this occasion, he was doing the cooking. They were having steak in honour of the ones that were ruined on the night that Caz went missing. By some miracle he managed not to overcook them, although oven chips perhaps weren't quite the look he was going for. On the other hand, he'd managed vegetables and a sauce. Progress showed itself in unexpected ways.

They sat down to eat.

'How's Caz?' said Zoe.

'Getting there,' said Jamie. 'The rehab's going well but there's a long way to go. Everyone's sad that she won't be home for Christmas.'

'The poor girls,' said Zoe. 'It's been a huge amount for them to deal with.'

'Yeah, but they're desperate for Caz to get better.' He reached for the pepper; his sauce was slightly bland. 'I want to make Christmas as special as I can for them. Having some cash will help.'

Bernie and Esther's insurance company had settled in full. Behind the hoardings at The Hall, a team of bulldozers were busy demolishing its remains. There was enough money to rebuild the house with a chunk left over. Jamie would be able to buy somewhere to live and a car; Caz would have a lump sum; Ruth and Willie would receive lifetime pensions.

'Have you decided what to do with The Hall once it's rebuilt?'

'We're going to sell it. Caz and I have agreed we'll give the proceeds to charity. It seems like the right thing. We'll both have plenty.'

'Nice touch.'

'But the best news is, you know that house I told you about, in the village next to Mum and Dad's? They've accepted my offer. It's got the most perfect room for teaching.'

Zoe skewered a green bean but only took her fork part-way to her mouth. 'Hang on, what?'

'You were right. I've decided. I'm going to teach the piano. The more I think about it, the surer I am.'

'Jamie, that's brilliant. A new start.'

They finished their steaks and Zoe got up from the table. When she came back she was holding a large, flat parcel, gift-wrapped in paper covered with musical notes.

'Happy birthday.' She held it out to him.

Inside was the sheet music for all thirty-two of Beethoven's sonatas, in two volumes, hard-bound in blue with gold lettering.

'Just in case you ever forget an accidental, or whatever.'

'Great knowledge. I'm impressed.' She was smiling broadly as he bent to kiss her cheek. 'Thank you.'

Zoe put on a tape of Christmas carols and they went to the sitting room to decorate the tree that they had chosen together that afternoon; Zoe taking the baubles, Jamie the lights.

'You did an amazing thing,' said Zoe, hooking a plastic snowman over an upper branch. 'With Caz.'

'Not really.' Jamie plugged in the lights and unravelled them into a long string. 'Anyone would have done the same.'

'Steve didn't.'

'He couldn't cope,' said Jamie. 'That's all.' He began to wind the lights around the branches, starting at the top. 'At least he's more on top of things now. He's taking some time off until Caz gets back on her feet. Ruth's going to help, too.'

'He loves her,' said Zoe. 'That's obvious. He loves her so much that he was too paralysed to help. Without you she wouldn't be here.' She reached up to wedge an angel onto the top of the tree. 'And this is the guy who was barely house-trained this time last year.'

The tree lights suddenly went dead and Jamie began a process of unscrewing and re-screwing, looking for the offending bulb, aware that Zoe was studying him.

'I'm trying to work out whether we're thinking the same thing,' she said.

'That these lights are bloody annoying?'

'No.'

'OK, then,' said Jamie. 'You first.'

'We-ell,' she said, 'I was going to ask if you'd like to stay tonight. Not… you know, just stay.'

The lights sprang back to life and Jamie stood back, satisfied.

'You read my mind,' he said and flicked them off again.

Upstairs, Jamie stripped to his boxers and Zoe put on her pyjamas. They climbed into her bed and lay on their backs, side by side.

'Should we start again?' said Zoe.

'Didn't we try that?'

'Not really.' She turned onto her side to face him in the dark, her head propped on one elbow. 'I was a cow. You needed kindness and I was too worried about being tied down.'

'I had to work things out on my own,' said Jamie. 'I was a big child and I needed to grow up.'

'Evens, then.' Zoe nestled into him and they stayed that way until they fell asleep.

acknowledgements

Firstly, if you're here, then I guess you've read the book. Thank you. It means such a lot.

I'd also like to thank my family and friends (you know who you are) for all the help and support you've given me during Crescendo's birthing process. To say it's been a struggle would be a lie. It's been a joy and I've loved every minute.

about the author

Joanna Howat trained as a journalist and worked as a producer for BBC Radio 5 Live. *Crescendo* is her first novel. She lives in North Yorkshire with her husband, son, daughter and two spaniels.

Printed in Great Britain
by Amazon

57286592R00239